MeaSLe
aND THe
SLitherghoul

G.F.S. LIBRARY

Also by Ian Ogilvy

MEASLE AND THE WRATHMONK
MEASLE AND THE DRAGODON
MEASLE AND THE MALLOCKEE

Praise for *Measle and the Slitherghoul*:

'Measle's fourth outing is a characteristically, disgustingly addictive adventure told with pace and panache by Ian Ogilvy. As ever a more perfect choice of illustrator than Chris Mould could not be found for this series, his sublimely subversive illustrations breathe life, atmosphere and infinite expression to the array of situations and character studies.

'The return of old adversaries and accomplices make this a tour-de-force for those infected by Measle!'

Achuka.co.uk

Praise for other *Measle* titles:

'Ogilvy is a good inventive storyteller who writes with infectious enthusiasm... Genuinely creepy at times, *Measle and the Dragodon* is illuminated with flashes of surreal humour'
Jan Mark, *TES*

'The further adventures of Measle Stubbs for readers aged eight and up, with badder baddies, more dastardly plots, wicked spells—and what's more, our hero has his first bath in years!'
Sunday Express

'Brilliant. It's a work that's comparable to Roald Dahl'
Evening Express **(Aberdeen)**

MEASLE
AND THE
SLITHERGHOUL

Ian Ogilvy

Illustrated by Chris Mould

OXFORD
UNIVERSITY PRESS

FOR BARNABY AND MATILDA—AS ALWAYS

OXFORD
UNIVERSITY PRESS

Great Clarendon Street, Oxford OX2 6DP

Oxford University Press is a department of the University of Oxford.
It furthers the University's objective of excellence in research, scholarship,
and education by publishing worldwide in

Oxford   New York

Auckland   Cape Town   Dar es Salaam   Hong Kong   Karachi
Kuala Lumpur   Madrid   Melbourne   Mexico City   Nairobi
New Delhi   Shanghai   Taipei   Toronto

With offices in

Argentina   Austria   Brazil   Chile   Czech Republic   France   Greece
Guatemala   Hungary   Italy   Japan   Poland   Portugal   Singapore
South Korea   Switzerland   Thailand   Turkey   Ukraine   Vietnam

Oxford is a registered trade mark of Oxford University Press
in the UK and in certain other countries

Database right Oxford University Press (maker)

First published 2006
First published in paperback 2007

British Library Cataloguing in Publication Data

JF
OGI

Data available

ISBN 978-0-19-272616-2

1 3 5 7 9 10 8 6 4 2

Typeset by Palimpsest Book Production Limited,
Polmont, Stirlingshire

Printed and bound in Great Britain by
Cox & Wyman Ltd, Reading, Berkshire

CONTENTS

SHEEPSHANK

It all started with a sneeze.

A very, very long time ago—eight hundred years, to be precise—there lived a young wizard called Sheepshank. He only had the one name—'Sheepshank'—because at this time of history, that was the way wizards did things. Think of the most famous wizard that ever lived. Merlin. He wasn't *Duane* Merlin, or Merlin *Higginbottom*—he was just plain Merlin.

And so was young Sheepshank. Just plain Sheepshank.

Sheepshank was an apprentice wizard, which means he was still learning to be a real one. He was small and skinny and pale, with long stringy black hair, pale watery eyes, and a chin that was so small it didn't look as if he had one at all. Sheepshank's face made up for a lack of chin by having a really *enormous* nose. Sheepshank's nose looked like the big triangular sail that billows out at the front of a racing yacht. Sheepshank was teased about his nose a lot. But, apart from the teasing, the other apprentices pretty much ignored him, because Sheepshank wasn't a very likeable person.

One of the reasons for Sheepshank's unpopularity was his bitterness. He could never say anything nice about anything or anybody and all his remarks were tinged with sour sarcasm. There was not a trace of sweetness in Sheepshank—he was nothing but bitterness, through and through.

Another reason why his fellow students avoided him was because Sheepshank was brilliant—and he knew it. There's nothing worse than somebody who knows they're cleverer than everybody else, which was exactly what Sheepshank knew about himself. He was at the top of every class he attended. He was so brilliant that his teachers had started to say that there was nothing more they could teach him and—if ever Sheepshank wanted to start a class of his own—then they'd love to come and be his pupils. (Well, perhaps not *love*—the teachers didn't care for Sheepshank any more than the other apprentices did, but they couldn't help admiring his brilliant brain.)

The only trouble was, Sheepshank was just a little *too* brilliant. And a little too ambitious as well—with the extraordinary result that Sheepshank, at a very young age, had become a warlock. Nobody knew this. The idea of an apprentice wizard being a warlock was ridiculous —it could take years of expert wizardry before that happened. But Sheepshank was a phenomenon and had managed—through hard work, a lively imagination, and an obsessive yearning for power—to reach the rank of warlock while still a lowly student. He was careful to keep this a secret, of course. He grew his hair long to cover the telltale Gloomstains on his ears, and he kept himself to himself during classes and behaved like a hermit, staying in his cell, the rest of the time. So, for the moment, his secret was safe.

In those days, apprentice wizards lived in a series of deep, underground cells, beneath the building that would, eventually, become the headquarters of the Wizards' Guild. At this time, however, there was no large and imposing office-like structure above ground to mark the spot—just a plain stone house in a quiet corner of what was then a very small town.

The stone house just happened to be sitting directly above the greatest accumulation of natural mana the world had ever seen, which was why it was there in the first place. As everybody knows, mana fuels magic spells, so when a rich source is discovered, wizards are inclined to gather at that spot. The house itself was only there in order to hide the opening in the ground that led to the warren of corridors and rooms and cells deep beneath it—and it was here that young apprentice wizards like Sheepshank lived and studied and worked.

Sheepshank liked his cell. It was small and dark and quiet, and far away from most of the other apprentice cells.

Sheepshank didn't want anybody to know what he was doing, because he'd started experimenting with *combining* spells. Combining different spells was so *absolutely* against every rule in the apprentice wizard handbook, that nobody ever thought of doing it—except for Sheepshank.

Combining spells was dangerous, which was why it was forbidden. The only spells wizards were allowed to perform were 'clean' spells— spells that were pure and had only one function. Like the fire-lighting enchantment, '*Calorimus Nuncibut Carborflam!*'—which produced a small ball of intense heat, hot enough to light even the dampest of logs—or the rejecting spell, '*Regrasso Fulmina Expedita!*'—which sent objects flying away from you at high speed.

What Sheepshank was doing—secretly, of course—was seeing what happens when you put spells like that together. Sheepshank discovered a way of putting the fire-lighting enchantment together with the rejecting enchantment, with the result that he found he could shoot a ball of white-hot flame several hundred metres—a devastating weapon in the wrong hands. And Sheepshank's hands were definitely the wrong ones, because (though brilliant) he simply wasn't grown-up enough to handle such power.

There came a day when young Sheepshank decided to work on something really special. It involved trying out various word combinations in an attempt to create a brand-new enchantment. One of the spells he was working with was a very dangerous one indeed. It was reserved for the most senior wizards and Sheepshank had no business even *knowing* it, let alone playing with it. The spell was the Death Hex, and could be used only when a great wizard was in imminent danger of losing his life and needed it for self-defence.

Sheepshank was trying to see if the Death Hex could be *reversed*.

He was trying to see if it was possible to bring something dead back to life.

He'd killed a spider that morning and placed its small, curled-up body on a tin dish on the surface of his desk. Then he'd tried various combinations of words from the Death Hex, mixing them up with words from a number of fairly harmless spells all designed to make the recipients of the magic feel better—but Sheepshank was saying them all, first *forwards*, then *backwards*.

Sheepshank had been doing this for most of the morning and the spider hadn't even twitched.

Sheepshank sighed—then, feeling an itching sensation deep in his nostrils, he sniffed loudly. He wiped his enormous nose on the back of his sleeve.

Staring hard at the body of the dead spider, Sheepshank tried again.

'*Morticlo olcitrom! Pivaculus sulucavip! Dropsihop pohispord! Zorgasfat tafsagroz—*'

Suddenly, Sheepshank felt a sneeze coming—but he couldn't stop now! Not in the middle of such a complicated combination of magical words! He sniffed again and the tremendous need to sneeze subsided a little—

'*Baffabis sibaffab! Oominoligos sogilonimoo! Kromkrumquoo—*'

Oh, no! Here came the sneeze again! Sheepshank sniffed but the need to sneeze began to grow . . . and grow . . . and grow . . .

'Ah—ah—ah—' said Sheepshank, without at all meaning to. And now he was *furious*.

The spell was ruined and he'd have to start all over again—once this wretched sneeze finally arrived, that is.

And then, at last, it did.

'Ah—ah—ah—*SCSCSCHHHHHCABLA-MOOOOO!*'

The sneeze was a huge, explosive one. Sheepshank didn't own a handkerchief—and didn't think to use his sleeve, either. So, when the enormous sneeze blasted from his nose, a nasty little glob of greenish-yellowish-brownish snot shot out of one nostril and landed with a plop on top of his desk, only a few centimetres away from the dish with the dead spider in it.

Sheepshank's eyes were running, which sometimes happens when you do a really big sneeze. He wiped his eyes with the backs of his hands and, in that moment of blindness, he missed seeing something very extraordinary indeed.

What Sheepshank missed was this: the slimy little lump of snot . . . *moved*.

It seemed to slither a couple of centimetres closer to the body of the spider. Then, in the blink of an eye, it extended a little section of itself, forming what looked like a tiny tentacle of slime.

The tentacle reached out and touched the body of the spider—

Sheepshank blinked several times, trying to make the tears go away. Slowly, the mist cleared from his eyes and he turned back to the spider, determined to start the laborious process of spell-making all over again.

The spider wasn't there.

Sheepshank frowned irritably. Obviously, the force of his sneeze had blown the little body clean off his desk. Sheepshank knelt down on the hard stone floor and peered around but he couldn't see anything.

'Botherissimus!' muttered Sheepshank. 'Now must I seek out a second subject for my work! 'Tis a vexation, to be sure!' (*That's* how long ago this happened—when people talked like that.)

His knees were hurting a little, so Sheepshank reached up and put his hand on his desk, in order to pull himself upright again.

Sheepshank's thumb squelched against the glob of snot.

'Ugh!' He stood up and was about to wipe his thumb against his dirty robe, when something extremely horrible started to happen to him.

Sheepshank's cell was at the end of a short passage and the nearest room to his was a corridor and a half away—so his screams of terror weren't heard at first. But then they grew louder and more shrill and a fellow apprentice wizard, called Barstook, looked up from the manuscript that he and his friend Gantry were studying and listened intently.

'Hark,' said Barstook, putting one hand behind his ear and tapping the shoulder of Gantry with the other. 'Methinks I hear some commotion!'

''Tis that dolt Sheepshank,' said Gantry. 'Leave him be, Barstook—'tis an offence to be near him.'

'Nay, Gantry—he suffers! Hear his cries! Come, we must to his side!'

Barstook and Gantry ran from Barstook's cell and, together, the two young apprentices raced down the dark corridor towards the awful sounds of terror. When they reached the open door to Sheepshank's cell, both skidded to a stop and stared into the small room.

Their mouths gaped in horror.

Something seemed to be eating Sheepshank— eating him alive!

Already his whole right arm was engulfed in some sort of yellowish-greenish-brownish slimy jelly and now the jelly was moving steadily across his shoulder towards his open, screaming mouth—

Some instinct for self-preservation told Barstook and Gantry that there was nothing they could do. Neither apprentice had any intention of trying to get the revolting stuff off Sheepshank, because there was something about it that made them think that, perhaps, it was in some way *alive* and, if they touched it or even got too close, there was every likelihood that what was happening to Sheepshank would happen to them.

They watched with disgust and terror as the slime spread steadily over Sheepshank's skinny body. The stuff stank and both young wizards put their fingers to their noses. What was particularly ghastly was the fact that, once the foul-smelling slime had taken over any particular part of Sheepshank, then that part seemed to become the same shapeless substance as the slime itself.

And now the goo had reached Sheepshank's chin and, the moment it slid across his gaping mouth, the screaming stopped. Quickly the stuff spread over Sheepshank's head, and then it didn't look like a head at all, just a formless mass of moving jelly, which now moved downwards towards Sheepshank's legs and feet ...

Sheepshank's knees buckled suddenly and the whole mass of slime—and what was left of his body—crumpled to the stone floor.

The sudden collapse of what, only a minute before, had been Apprentice Wizard Sheepshank, shook Barstook and Gantry from their paralysis. They both had the same sensible thought at precisely the same instant—

Together, they grabbed the heavy ironwood door and slammed it shut. Then Gantry, who was a little bigger and heavier than his friend, volunteered to stay and make sure that the door remained firmly shut. He leaned all his weight against it—and Barstook ran for help.

Inside the dark cell, the slime slid over Sheepshank's legs, then his ankles, and finally over his feet. Then it simply lay there, a shapeless mass of slimy jelly, not doing anything in particular. And that's what the crowd of senior wizards saw when they arrived in a breathless collection of billowing robes a few minutes later.

The most senior of the wizards, an old wizened fellow called Crabgrass, carefully eased the ironwood door open. He put his eye to the crack and peered into the room but it was too dark to see anything.

But there was a horrible smell filtering through the shadows.

'*Luminensis temporando volantulum*,' muttered Crabgrass, and a little ball of pale blue light appeared in the cell and hovered in the dark air. It showed Crabgrass what he needed to see—and obviously it showed the mound of slimy jelly something too, because the stuff quivered suddenly and then began to flow over the floor, moving steadily towards the open door ...

Crabgrass slammed the door shut. From the voluminous folds of his purple robe he produced a large iron key. Crabgrass slotted the key into the keyhole and turned it. There was a grating sound as the lock slid home. Only then did Crabgrass take his shoulder away from the door. He turned and glared at Barstook.

'You say that our poor friend Sheepshank is now utterly within that foul entity?' he growled.

Barstook gulped and nodded.

'You and Gantry here witnessed the horrid occurrence?'

'Aye, sir.'

'And can you inform us in what manner this monstrosity came into being?'

'N-nay, sir. We cannot.'

Crabgrass turned and raised his bushy white eyebrows at the rest of the crowd of wizards.

'Can any person here enlighten us?' he rasped.

Almost as one, the collected wizards slowly shook their heads.

'Seal that door,' said Crabgrass. 'Post a guard. Let none come near. We shall study this manifestation at our leisure—and we shall, in time, understand it.'

They never did understand it.

They studied it—at a safe distance—for many, many years. They shot a thousand spells at it, to absolutely no effect. They shouted questions, they showed it pictures. They tried to burn it, then to freeze it. Nothing whatever happened. It ignored them, unless they got too close—then it would start to move towards them, which was why nobody ever opened the door of the cell by so much as a crack, unless they had a strong man by their side, ready at a moment's notice to slam the door shut again.

Nobody wanted to live anywhere near the

ghastly thing in Sheepshank's cell, so the apprentice wizards' rooms were vacated and the young scholars were moved to other quarters. Over time, the little rooms were turned into jail cells and the entire complex became known as the Detention Centre, where captured wrathmonks and other undesirables were held imprisoned.

They came and went, these other prisoners. Only the creature remained, forever locked in its sealed cell—and nobody ever discovered how, exactly, it had come into being. The fact was that the only person who understood even a fraction of what had happened was Sheepshank, and he was in no position to explain it to anybody.

The spell had worked, of course, but in a very peculiar way. Instead of bringing a dead spider back to life, it had actually created a very basic form of life and given it to the lump of snot that had shot from Sheepshank's nose. And the reason it had done this lay entirely in the sound that Sheepshank had made when he sneezed.

It was a sound that nobody else could make.

Everybody sneezes in a different way and nobody's sneeze sounds the same as another.

Which was why only *one* of these horrible creatures was ever produced.

Even if they had heard Sheepshank's sneeze in the first place (and nobody did) not even the greatest wizards in the world would ever be able to recreate *exactly* the sound that Sheepshank's enormous nose had made. And that meant that of all the wizards that had ever lived—and ever *would* live—only Sheepshank could have performed that extraordinary and dreadful spell.

Which, when you think about it, was a Very Good Thing.

Sam
Has an
Announcement

It was early evening at Merlin Manor.

Sam Stubbs had just gone to his study to answer a telephone call. Measle and his mother Lee were sitting in the living room, watching television. Tinker, Measle's little black and white terrier, lay on the carpet between them, his head on his paws, fast asleep. Measle's sister Matilda was fast asleep, too, but being only ten months old, she was fast asleep in her cot upstairs.

Nanny Flannel was sitting in the living room as well, but she wasn't really watching the TV—for two reasons. First, she was busy knitting another woolly hat for Iggy Niggle. This one was purple and it was the tenth woolly hat that Nanny Flannel had knitted for the little wrathmonk. Because of the constant drizzle that fell on Iggy's head, woolly hats were inclined to fall apart after a while.

Iggy himself was outside the living room, staring in through one of the windows—and that was the other reason Nanny Flannel wasn't paying any attention to the television. She was keeping half an eye on Iggy, just in case he tried to sneak into the house when nobody was looking. It was one of the conditions that Nanny Flannel had made when Iggy had first come to live at Merlin Manor: 'No wet things in the house, thank you very much. I'm not going to be mopping up after you all the time.' So, Iggy stayed outside or, when he wanted to sleep, he crawled inside his little house. Iggy's house was really Tinker's dog kennel but Tinker had always refused to use it. In return for the small wrathmonk agreeing to stay outside, Nanny Flannel, who had become secretly quite fond of the pathetic creature, knitted him a succession of woolly hats and, every morning, cooked up a batch of two hundred homemade, strawberry-flavoured, non-magical red jelly beans, which were the only things that Iggy Niggle would eat.

So, when Sam Stubbs walked into the living room and announced, 'We're going to the South Pole,' only Lee and Measle really heard him. The words meant nothing to Tinker, and Nanny Flannel wasn't paying any attention. Standing outside, Iggy Niggle couldn't even hear the *television*, let alone something that Sam had said from the doorway of the living room. (Iggy didn't mind not hearing the television. He wasn't bright enough to understand what was going on and he really only liked watching the moving pictures anyway.)

'We're going *where*?' said Lee.

'South Pole,' said Sam. 'Day after tomorrow.'

'It seems rather an odd place to go for a holiday, Sam,' said Lee, mildly. 'Not very sunny at this time of the year, is it?'

'Not going on holiday,' said Sam.

'Oh. Then why are we going?'

'Conference,' said Sam.

Measle was listening to all this with interest. First of all, he'd never heard his dad speak in such short sentences. He stared hard at Sam and noticed that he was looking a little nervous. The other matter that was catching Measle's attention was the prospect of going to the South Pole.

'What sort of conference, Sam?' said Lee. She too had noticed Sam's nervousness and her tone of voice was gentle and unhurried.

'Wizards' Guild Conference,' muttered Sam, staring at his feet. 'International thing. Wizards from all over the world are going. And I've got to go too—I'm the Prime Magus.'

'Well, of course you have to go, Sam,' said Lee. 'But why do we?'

There was a short silence, then Sam sighed heavily and said, 'Can't do it without you. You know that, darling. I need you by my side.'

There was another short silence, while Lee thought about this. Measle thought about it, too, and it made sense to him. Of *course* Sam would need his wife with him—for such an important event as this, it would be vital that the Prime Magus of the Wizards' Guild was accompanied by his wife, the celebrated Manafount. There could easily be circumstances where her ability to replenish his mana would be more than just useful.

Measle's thoughts were interrupted by Lee. She frowned and said, 'When you say "we", Sam, do you mean just you and me—or the whole family?'

Sam shook his head. 'Just you—and Tilly, of course. There's a lot of interest in Tilly.'

'I'm not surprised,' said Lee.

Sam shrugged. 'Besides, we can't leave her behind—she's still too young to be separated from us for so long.'

'And Measle?'

'No,' said Sam, sadly. 'Afraid not. Only magicals allowed.'

Measle's heart sank—but only a little way. The idea of going to the South Pole had sounded really cool—but then again, it sounded really *cold* as well.

By this time, Nanny Flannel was paying attention. Her knitting needles were still and she was looking up at Sam with one eyebrow cocked.

'And exactly how *long* will you be gallivanting about in the Arctic, Sam Stubbs?' she said.

Sam looked even more uncomfortable than before.

'Not the Arctic, Nanny,' he said. 'The *Ant*arctic. About ten days. And we won't be gallivanting. I wish we were! No, we'll be attending endless boring lectures, sitting around discussing lots of boring things—and I'll probably have to make lots of boring speeches. It'll be really, really boring, I'm afraid.'

Lee laughed. 'You make it sound such fun, Sam. Tilly and I can hardly wait.' Then she smiled down at Measle. 'I think you're the lucky one, Measle darling. As far as I know, there's not a lot to do at the South Pole.' She turned to Sam and said, 'In fact, *why* the South Pole, Sam? Why not just have the conference at the Wizards' Guild building?'

Sam shrugged. 'It's got to be somewhere really remote,' he said. 'Somewhere there aren't any people at all. There's always a lot of magical stuff going on at these things and we don't want to draw attention.'

Lee nodded and then turned back to Measle. 'You'll be much better off staying here with Nanny and Iggy and Tinker, darling. And it's only for ten days. You don't mind, do you?'

'No,' said Measle. 'I don't mind.'

The truth was that he *did* mind a bit but, on the other hand, the conference did sound extremely boring and Lee was probably right—there might not be anything interesting to do at the South Pole. And there was *plenty* to do here at Merlin Manor. He and Iggy had a plan to dig a swimming pool in the back lawn, which was something that Sam would probably tell them not to do; but if Sam wasn't *there* . . .

Nanny Flannel sniffed loudly and then barked out a single word:

'Security?'

'Security, Nanny?' said Sam, looking a little blank.

'You know what I'm talking about, Sam Stubbs,' said Nanny Flannel, sternly. 'Things always seem to happen to Measle when you and Lee aren't around. Bad things, too. If you are both going to be gallivanting round the Arctic—'

Sam nodded and smiled and said, 'Yes, you're quite right, Nanny. Not about the Arctic—but you're right that we should get some protection for you all. I'll organize that.'

Measle opened his mouth to say that he didn't think they really needed protection, but Sam was already out of the door. A few minutes later, he came back. He looked, thought Measle, even more uncomfortable than before.

'Well . . . er . . .' he said, 'I rang Lord Octavo and he's setting something up. There'll be a couple of people from the Wizards' Guild here day and night.'

'Who are they sending, Sam?' asked Lee.

Sam threw a guilty look in Measle's direction and muttered, 'Er . . . Needle and Bland.'

For the second time that evening, Measle's heart sank like a stone. Mr Needle and Mr Bland! Those two horrible officials from the Wizards' Guild, who were so cold and business-like and who had never given any indication that they held the Stubbs family in anything other than deep contempt— those two horrible men, in their matching dark suits and their matching dark sunglasses, were going to come and live at Merlin Manor?

'But, Dad,' said Measle, raising his voice almost to a shriek, 'they're *awful*! And they hate us! Why do we have to have *them*?'

Sam shook his head. 'They *used* to be awful, Measle,' he said. 'But they're not awful any more. They don't hate us, either. You see, they're just intensely loyal to whoever is the Prime Magus— which, right now, is *me*. So at the moment they're our best friends—and, since they're both warlocks *and* fully trained security people as well, we really couldn't ask for better protection. I wouldn't have them here if I thought they meant us any harm.'

Measle looked across the room at Nanny Flannel, to see what sort of reaction she was having to this news. Nanny Flannel seemed more preoccupied with the dangers she imagined Sam and Lee and Matilda might have to face. She said, 'You're sure to be eaten by polar bears.'

'There aren't any polar bears at the South Pole, Nanny,' said Measle. 'They live at the North Pole.'

'Is that so?' said Nanny, in a haughty tone of voice. 'But the creatures can swim, can they not?'

'Yes, Nanny.'

'Well, then,' said Nanny Flannel, in a triumphant

tone, 'who's to say that a polar bear couldn't swim from the North Pole to the South Pole? Eh? Answer me that, Mister Clever-Clogs!'

Measle started a long explanation as to why a polar bear really couldn't swim all the way from the top of the world down to the bottom—and that the only creatures his parents were likely to meet at the South Pole were penguins. But Nanny clucked her tongue and announced that, as far as she was concerned, penguins were the most dangerous birds known to man and had often been observed pecking explorers to death. So Measle gave up and went outside to tell Iggy the news.

'You know what this means, Iggy?' said Measle. 'It means we can make a start on the swimming pool.'

'Coo—dat will be nice,' said Iggy, a little uncertainly. He wasn't sure what making a start on a swimming pool entailed—but if his best friend Mumps Stubbs wanted to do it, then that was just fine by him. He pulled a handful of red jelly beans out of his pocket and threw the whole lot into his mouth. He didn't offer Measle any. He never had, and he never would. He was, after all, still a wrathmonk.

The Thing in the Dungeon Cell

The thing in the dungeon cell, deep below the Wizards' Guild building, was eight hundred years old.

It had seven mismatched eyes. The eyes belonged to four other creatures—a wizard, two rats, and a one-eyed mouse. The wizard had once been an apprentice called Sheepshank. The rats and the mouse had—unfortunately for them—been tossed into the thing's dungeon cell without anybody asking them if they wanted to be there. The creature's captors wanted to see precisely what became of living creatures when the thing in the cell got hold of them. The lesson had been useful for the Wizards' Guild, but unfortunately, the lesson had been learned so long ago that it had become lost in the mists of time. Now, nobody knew what, exactly, made the creature so horribly dangerous. It was simply assumed that mere contact with it was fatal.

This wasn't entirely true.

There were several strange facts about the thing in the dungeon cell and one of the strangest was its ability to keep *alive* any creature it had absorbed within its body. It was a strange sensation for its victims, being trapped inside that body of slimy jelly. It wasn't uncomfortable. They simply floated there, not getting ill or hungry or thirsty—and not getting a day older, either. For them, it was as if Time was standing still.

Since the creature had no eyes, nor ears, nor nose with which to experience the outside world, it used the senses of its victims to do so. It looked through their eyes and it made as much use of their brains as it could—which wasn't very much, since three of the creatures it had absorbed were a pair of rats and a one-eyed mouse.

Sheepshank was another matter, of course. Sheepshank had once had a brain—a brilliant brain. Unfortunately, Sheepshank's brain was also highly unstable and, within seconds of being absorbed, he had lost his mind—but not in the sense of going insane. What had happened to his brain was a bit like the difference between a busy office building during the day, with lots of workers bustling about and phones ringing and computers beeping and everything bright and on the go, and the same office at four o'clock in the morning, when everybody had gone home hours ago, and all the lights and computers are switched off. The whole space appears to be asleep. But there's always the possibility that somebody might come by and . . . turn on the lights again.

So, Sheepshank's brain had simply switched off. And that meant that he was useless as far as the creature was concerned.

The thing had a name. The name had been given to it by Crabgrass.

Slitherghoul.

The Slitherghoul had been content there in the darkness of its cell, because there was no particular reason why it shouldn't be. It was warm and comfortable. It didn't need food or water. It just lay there in one corner, a slimy mass of jelly, not doing anything at all.

But, recently, something had happened that had changed its attitude.

A month ago, the Slitherghoul's peaceful existence had been shattered. There had been noises outside the door of its cell—the sounds of humans being happy. (The humans were Sam, Lee, and Matilda, who were naturally overjoyed at being rescued by Measle at the end of the Mallockee adventure).

These were sounds that the thing had never heard before, so it stirred itself and began to take a little bit of notice.

There was something else outside the cell door, as well as the sounds of happiness, and it was this something else that woke a tiny spark deep inside the closed-down brain of Sheepshank. The spark was nothing more than the simplest form of instinct. This little spark of instinct felt the presence of something—and it was something Sheepshank had always wanted more than anything else in the entire world.

Power. Magical power.

The sudden flicker of activity inside Sheepshank's mind caught the attention of the Slitherghoul and, for a moment, it considered the world through what was left of the little wizard's brain. And because the spark of instinct it detected *wanted* something, then so did the Slitherghoul.

Whatever was beyond the door also possessed the ability to store and regenerate its power at will.

And now the Slitherghoul—because of Sheepshank's spark of instinct—wanted that power within itself. And it would do anything to possess it.

For the first time in centuries, the Slitherghoul started to move. It flowed across the stone floor of its cell, leaving behind a wide trail of sticky slime. When it got to the door, it pressed itself against it, using its whole body in search of an opening—any opening—through which it could pass. But the door was sealed, without even a hairline crack round its edges.

And now the sounds of the happy people were

fading as they moved away—and so was the power that the thing had sensed.

Sheepshank's spark was no use to it—*wanting* something was pointless if there was no way to *obtain* it. So, the Slitherghoul pushed aside the fierce feeling of longing and returned to the minds of the rats and the mouse.

Rats and mice have teeth that are designed for gnawing. They can scrape away at a flat surface for hours on end, and their teeth never stop growing, which allows them to chew their way through very hard materials.

The Slitherghoul's cell door was six inches thick and made of ironwood. Ironwood is very hard.

A rat's tooth is harder—and the Slitherghoul had plenty of rats' teeth at its disposal.

It took the Slitherghoul a month to gnaw a hole in the door.

Since nobody ever opened the door to its cell, the Slitherghoul could work in perfect safety, scraping away steadily, day and night, until it had removed all but a thin layer of ironwood on the outer surface. Then, one morning, it had finally broken through.

The Slitherghoul began to squeeze itself through the aperture. Being made entirely of jelly, this was easy for it. The rats and the mouse had bones—but the hole their teeth had gnawed was more than big enough to let them through. When it came time for Sheepshank's head to pass through the opening, it was a tight squeeze but, luckily for the Slitherghoul, not *too* tight. Within moments, the Slitherghoul was flowing stickily across the stone floor of the outer corridor.

At the end of the short passage, there was a heavy iron door. It was ajar. There was a yellow light spilling out through the narrow gap and the Slitherghoul moved towards it.

A junior apprentice wizard was in the office of the High Security Wing. He had replaced Officer Offal as the Detention Centre guard. Officer Offal had been convicted of his crimes against Measle and was now serving a very long sentence in the very same cell block where once he'd been in charge. The junior wizard was sitting in his swivel chair, his feet up on the steel desk, studying a manual on the various uses of powdered emeralds. His name was Corky Pretzel. Corky was twenty-two years old and he'd been given the job because, though he wasn't very bright, he did have enormous muscles in his arms and chest. Most of Corky's prisoners were wrathmonks—and it was felt by the authorities of the Wizards' Guild that if a wrathmonk should ever get out of his cell and try to escape, muscles rather than magic might be the best way to subdue him. All wrathmonk prisoners wore the iron wrathrings round their necks which stopped them doing any of their insanely dangerous magical spells. However, the wrathrings were no use against the effects of a wrathmonk's *breathing* spell, so muscles might, for once, prove more useful than magic.

At the moment, in the High Security Wing, there were only three prisoners and, unlike the wrathmonks, they were very quiet. One of them never made any sound at all. This suited Corky, because he needed absolute quiet when he wanted to read. Corky was trying to pass his elementary wizard exam. He'd been trying to pass it for the last three years.

The first thing that made Corky think that he might be in some sort of danger was the smell. It was a dreadful, disgusting, revolting stink that seemed to be coming from beyond the office door. It was so strong that it made him choke. The smell was appalling, because it was a *mixture* of some of the nastiest stenches imaginable. Part was the sharp smell when somebody is sick on the carpet; part was the foul odour of Brussels sprouts that have been boiled for six hours; part was the stink that comes from a mouse that's been dead for a week; part was the sort of smell you get from the breath of a person who hasn't brushed their teeth in a year; and parts were the sorts of horrible smells you can't really write about in a book. There was something else mixed in with it too, a strong smell of something chemical, like ammonia mixed with bleach mixed with chlorine—and it was this last ingredient that was making Corky choke and cough.

Corky put his hand over his nose and got up from the swivel chair. Cautiously, he went over to the office door and peered round the edge.

There, in the corridor, between the two pairs of identical cells, was something that hadn't been there before and, as far as Corky was concerned, had no business being there now. It was a mass of shiny, brownish-yellowish-greenish substance, about the size of a coffee table. It was quivering slightly, like jelly on a plate—and it was moving slowly towards him.

The stink of the thing was even stronger out here and Corky coughed—

And, instantly, the brown mass moved.

A section of it extended, like a long brown finger—*no, more like a tentacle*, thought Corky. The next thing Corky thought was: *perhaps I ought to move back a bit?* But it was already too late. The tip of the tentacle touched Corky's leg—

Immediately—and so fast that Corky never really saw it happen—the tentacle wrapped itself round Corky's ankle. Then it gave a powerful jerk that yanked him off his feet. Corky fell heavily to the floor, banging the back of his head on the stone. Half conscious, he felt himself being dragged across the rough surface. Then something damp and slimy and horribly smelly wrapped itself over his face—and, a moment later, Corky stopped being Corky and became just part of the Slitherghoul instead.

Corky Pretzel had been a big fellow—and the Slitherghoul swelled. Now, it was the size of a small dining table.

And now, it had Corky Pretzel's brain. For the first time, it had access to a mind that could think a lot further than where its next meal was going to come from. As human brains went, Corky's wasn't all that impressive, but compared to the thinking capacities of a comatose wizard, two rats, and a one-eyed mouse, it was close to genius level. It opened up a whole world to the Slitherghoul. There was so much information in there that the Slitherghoul was forced to push away anything that didn't deal directly with its immediate surroundings.

So. First things first—

It learned where it was.

It discovered what was nearby.

It decided what to do next.

Toby Jugg was dozing in his cell, when he was woken by the electronic *clonk!* of his door unlocking. Half awake, Toby sat up on his bunk and peered blearily out into the passage. He heard shuffling footsteps.

Officer Offal poked his jowly red face round the cell door. He was wearing a set of clothes identical to Toby's—a plain white jumpsuit and a pair of white canvas shoes. The only difference in their prison uniforms was the dull silver wrathring that encircled Toby Jugg's neck. Officer Offal had no need of a wrathring, he had no more magical abilities than a stone, but Toby Jugg was a very powerful warlock indeed and the Wizards' Guild took no chances with such a dangerous prisoner. They had slapped a wrathring round his neck the moment he'd been convicted of his crimes, which meant Toby Jugg now had no more magical ability than Officer Offal.

'Mr Jugg, sir?' whispered Officer Offal, a puzzled frown creasing his pink forehead. 'Any idea what's going on, sir? My cell door just opened and so did yours—'

'So it would appear, Offal,' said Toby. He got up and joined the beefy ex-guard out in the passage. Together, they strained their eyes in the gloom, looking towards the door that led out to the office beyond.

'I—I think that's open too, sir,' muttered Officer Offal into Toby's ear.

'Hmm. Let's take a look. Quietly now.'

Toby and Officer Offal tiptoed down the short passage towards the door. A little yellow light spilled out through the crack—and so did a disgusting, dreadful smell. Both men put their hands over their noses.

'What's that stink, sir?' whispered Offal.

Toby didn't answer. Instead, he slowed his pace a fraction, allowing Offal to take the lead. When the big man seemed to hesitate, Toby put a reassuring hand against the small of Offal's back.

'I'm right behind you,' he muttered.

Cautiously, Offal crept to the door and peered round it.

The room was empty.

'Corky's not here, sir,' hissed Offal over his shoulder. He felt Toby's hand pushing him gently, so he stepped into the office. Toby was right behind him.

Then, without warning, the Slitherghoul flowed out from under the steel desk, rearing its whole shapeless mass high in the air. Before either of them could do anything—other than Officer Offal letting out a short, high-pitched squeal of terror—the Slitherghoul was upon them.

Now the Slitherghoul was even bigger. It had six working human eyes—and human eyes are much better than rodent eyes. It also had three functioning human brains, and, while two of them were limited, one of those brains was in superb condition. The Slitherghoul shoved the two inferior minds to one side. If needs be, it could use them later, but right now it concentrated its efforts on making full use of the brain of Toby Jugg.

The sound of all the cell doors opening in the Wrathmonk Block of the Detention Centre took its occupants by surprise. Measle's old enemy, Griswold Gristle, was the first to pop his round, white head out of his cell and look up and down the corridor. Gradually, other wrathmonks also thrust their heads out into the passage, their fishy eyes swivelling suspiciously. All of them wore wrathrings round their necks.

'A little early for our exercise hour, is it not?' said Griswold, in his oily voice, to nobody in particular.

Buford Cudgel's giant form emerged from his cell. 'Not due for another forty minutes,' he rumbled, clenching and unclenching his banana-sized fingers.

'A bit peculiar, if you asssk me,' said Frognell Flabbit, scratching irritably at his red and lumpy face. The boil spell that had been breathed on him by Judge Cedric Hardscrabble was still operating, although its effects were slowly diminishing. The only comfort that Flabbit could take from this was the fact that *his* breathing spell he'd performed on Judge Cedric was also still working, because here was Judge Cedric tottering out of his cell and both the old wrathmonk's hands were—as always—pressed to his aching teeth.

'Are we to be released, Griswold?' asked Judge Cedric, in his quavery voice. 'Are we to be released at long lassst, dear friend?'

'I would hardly think ssso, Cedric,' snapped Griswold. He glared irritably at the small mob of wrathmonks, who were now milling aimlessly about in the corridor. He gestured at them with a contemptuous flick of his wrist.

'Look at them, Cedric! Do you ssseriously imagine that the authorities would release all of usss? At once?'

'Perhapsss we have been given time off for good behaviour, Griswold?'

Griswold snorted scornfully through his little snub nose. He started to say something—but he stopped when he saw the heavy iron door at the far end of the corridor click open. It didn't open very far but it was enough to tell Griswold that something very odd was happening, because this door led out to the guard's office and it was never, *ever* open at the same time that the doors to the wrathmonks' cells were open.

Griswold, who always assumed that he would be listened to, hissed, 'Sssshhhhh!' as loudly as he could. Frognell Flabbit, Buford Cudgel, and Judge Cedric all turned towards him respectfully, because he had always led them and probably always would; but the rest of the wrathmonks took no notice of him and went on with their milling and chatting.

Then, slowly, one by one they fell silent because, centimetre by centimetre, the office door was opening wider and wider.

Those closest to the door obviously saw something unpleasant emerging from the office, because they started to retreat, edging their way backwards up the corridor to where Gristle, Cudgel, Flabbit, and Judge Cedric were huddled together. Their mass of bodies hid whatever was coming through the door from Griswold—he was very small—so he tapped Buford Cudgel on the arm and squeaked, 'What do you sssee, Missster Cudgel?'

'I dunno,' said Buford, uncertainly. 'It's sssome sssort of brown blob.'

'Brown blob?' said Griswold, standing on tiptoes and trying to peer over the mob. 'What sssort of—'

And that was as far as he got, because the

wrathmonks at the front of the crowd started to scream—and then the wrathmonks in the middle of the mob started to scream—and then the wrathmonks at the back of the mob (the ones closest to Griswold and Flabbit and Cudgel and Judge Cedric) started to scream as well—and there was a general stumbling retreat by the crowd back down the passage, which forced the four wrathmonks to press themselves against the rear wall of the corridor.

And Griswold saw, for the first time, what Buford Cudgel had described as a brown blob. The mass of jelly had reared itself up, its quivering top almost touching the ceiling—

It looks like a huge wave, thought Griswold, *a huge wave that's going to come crashing down on us all*—

And then the Slitherghoul did exactly that—it crashed down on the collected wrathmonks and, quite suddenly, there was no more screaming.

Just a soft, squelching sound as the Slitherghoul—now a *lot* bigger than before—slimed its way back down the corridor towards the open office door.

The Dig

Mr Needle and Mr Bland arrived at Merlin Manor about an hour before Sam and Lee and Matilda left for the South Pole.

Measle let them in—and he was instantly struck by a marked difference in their behaviour. In the past, the two officials from the Wizards' Guild had been cold to the point of rudeness. Neither man had made any attempt to hide his disdain for the Stubbs family and, when Measle had needed their help, they had been thoroughly *un*helpful as well. So, when Measle opened the heavy front door of Merlin Manor and thin, dark Mr Needle smiled and bowed and said, 'Good morning, Master Measle, I hope you're quite well?' and stout blond Mr Bland had followed by smiling and bowing and saying,

'And may I add what a pleasure it is to see you again, Master Measle,'—Measle himself was about as surprised as it's possible to be.

He stepped aside and motioned for the two men to come in and Mr Needle and Mr Bland, both carrying small, identical suitcases, walked briskly into the house.

'Ah, there you are,' said Sam, coming out of his study. 'Welcome to Merlin Manor, gentlemen.'

Mr Needle and Mr Bland bowed and said, in unison, 'A pleasure to be here, Prime Magus. And, indeed, an honour, sir.'

Lee came and took the two men off to show them their bedrooms. As they walked away up the stairs, Sam turned and winked broadly at Measle.

'See what I mean, Measle?' he whispered. 'A pair of little baa-lambs now, aren't they?'

Measle wasn't sure that Mr Needle and Mr Bland quite qualified for that description, but he was certainly relieved that the two officials seemed to be a lot friendlier—and a lot more respectful—than they had ever been before.

An hour later, it was time for the departure. A big black car—the official vehicle for the exclusive use of the Prime Magus—purred up to the front door, its tyres crunching on the gravel. A smartly-dressed chauffeur jumped out and started to load the suitcases into the boot.

'Goodbye, darling,' said Lee, giving Measle a big hug. 'Look after everything, especially yourself.'

'Goodbye, Measle,' said Sam. Then he bent down and wrapped his strong arms around Measle and whispered in his ear, 'And, if you and Iggy are really determined to dig that swimming pool, just make sure it's a nice *big* one, OK?'

Measle grinned up at his dad. *I should've known that I couldn't get away with that!* he thought. *But, all the same, I wonder how he knew?*

The next moment, that question was answered. Iggy Niggle was standing by the black car, peering into one of the side mirrors and admiring his appearance. He was wearing his latest woollen hat. This one had orange and green stripes and a pink bobble on the top and Iggy thought he looked tremendously handsome in it. He looked away from the mirror, saw Measle and Sam together, and waved excitedly.

'I told Missster Ssstubbs dat we was goin' to dig de ssswimmin' pool *after* dey was gone, Mumps!' he yelled, happily. 'Dat way, dey won't know anyfing about it, will dey? And it will be all finished when dey come back, won't it?'

'I shall expect one at least twenty metres long,' said Sam, drily.

Lee was bringing Matilda down the steps. There was a delay while Matilda gave Measle lots of hugs and kisses, then another delay while she did the same to Iggy. Then Sam and Lee and Tilly all climbed into the back of the car and the chauffeur closed their door. He went round to the driver's side, climbed in and started the engine.

The car turned bright pink. Inside *and* out.

'Now, Tilly, stop it,' said Lee from the back seat, trying not to laugh.

'Sorry about that, Percy,' Sam called to the chauffeur. 'Don't worry—it'll wear off soon.'

Everybody shouted together, 'Goodbye!— Goodbye!—Be good!—Don't catch cold!—Keep warm!—Have a nice time!—See you in ten days!' and then the big pink car moved off down the driveway. Measle and Nanny Flannel and Iggy all waved until the car turned through the front gates and disappeared from sight.

Measle turned back to the house and saw, to his surprise, that Mr Needle and Mr Bland were standing, like a pair of sentries, on either side of the front door. Tinker was standing in front of them, eyeing the two men suspiciously and growling softly at the back of his throat. Tinker didn't care for Mr Needle or Mr Bland and being a dog, he hadn't noticed any change in their behaviour. They still smelt the same, and that to Tinker was all that mattered.

Measle went up the steps and approached the two men. 'Um . . . are you going to stand there the whole time?' he asked, politely.

'Oh no, Master Measle,' said Mr Bland.

'We were just seeing off the Prime Magus, Master Measle,' said Mr Needle. 'There's a way of doing these things, you see.'

Mr Bland nodded seriously and said, 'I expect you'd like to know our routine, Master Measle? Well, there'll always be one of us on duty, you see. Patrolling the grounds, keeping our eyes peeled, ready for anything.'

'Don't you worry, Master Measle,' said Mr Needle. 'Nothing bad is going to happen. Not with us around.'

Measle smiled politely and said, 'Thank you very much.' He wondered whether he ought to ask them to stop calling him 'Master' Measle—then he decided he quite liked it.

'Come on, Tink,' he said, bending down and patting the little dog on his fuzzy head. 'And leave Mr Needle and Mr Bland alone. They're our friends now.'

But, even as he walked away in search of Iggy,

Measle realized he didn't really believe that any more than Tinker did.

For the rest of that day, Measle and Iggy worked very hard.

First of all, Measle marked out a large rectangle on the back lawn, using a whole roll of silver duct tape.

'See, Iggy?' he said. 'That's how big the pool has got to be. Now all we have to do is dig it out.'

Iggy's fishy eyes grew even rounder than before. 'We is goin' to dig?' he whispered, in a tone of disbelief. 'But . . . but dat will make all de green ssstuff go away!'

It always amazed Measle how few words Iggy knew. 'You mean the grass, Iggy?' he said.

Iggy nodded. 'Dat's de ssstuff! De grass. Dere won't be any dere any more—jussst de brown ssstuff!'

'You mean the earth?'

'Dat's de ssstuff—de earf.'

'But there'll be water there instead, Iggy. And that'll look nice, won't it?'

Iggy—without really understanding what exactly they were doing—agreed that water would look very nice. So, without any further delay, he and Measle started to dig up the lawn.

It was a lot harder work than Measle had thought it would be. After half an hour they had managed to scrape away a patch of grass about three metres by three metres—and they were both hot and sweaty. For the first time, Measle felt a little envious of Iggy's tiny rain cloud, which scattered a fine mist of water down on Iggy's head, keeping the little wrathmonk just a bit cooler than Measle.

Tinker had joined in the digging when they first started, because he thought they might perhaps be burrowing for rabbits. But when no rabbits—nor even the *scent* of any rabbits—appeared, he'd quickly got bored with scratching away at the hard earth and had trotted off to a sunny corner of the lawn and gone to sleep.

'I don't like doin' dis,' announced Iggy, stopping his digging and leaning on his spade.

'Come on, Iggy,' said Measle, encouragingly. 'We can't stop now.'

'*I* can ssstop,' said Iggy, stubbornly. '*I* can ssstop whenever I want to.' He dropped his spade and began to wander off in the direction of the house.

Measle thought quickly. 'I'll give you some more jelly beans, Iggy!' he shouted and Iggy stopped in his tracks and turned round slowly.

'How many?' said Iggy, his eyes narrowing.

'If we finish clearing all the grass away today, I'll give you ten.'

'Wot colour?' said Iggy, slowly.

'Orange.'

Iggy thought about this for a moment and then nodded in satisfaction. He came back, picked up his spade and attacked the grass with renewed energy.

Measle joined him. He'd known all along that Iggy would do anything for more jelly beans. The two hundred red ones (which Nanny Flannel made fresh for Iggy each morning) were all that Iggy ate and, being a wrathmonk, he thrived on the dreadful diet. But Iggy craved even more sugar and was always on the lookout for ways to wangle an extra ration out of Nanny Flannel. Ever since he'd come to live at Merlin Manor, he'd had his eyes on the big jar of magical multicoloured jelly beans that stood on the sideboard in the dining room and, every now and then, Measle would slip him a handful of them. But never a green one. The green ones were Iggy's least favourite flavour and, if he ever bit down on a green jelly bean, Iggy would become invisible for thirty seconds, just as Measle would disappear from sight for half a minute if ever he swallowed a yellow one. It was lucky that Iggy never wanted to eat a green one, and it was equally lucky that Iggy's small brain had never made the connection between green jelly beans and half a minute of invisibility—because the last thing anybody needed was a small, damp, *undetectable* wrathmonk wandering about the place.

Just before Nanny Flannel came out to call Measle in for supper, they were finished with the first part of the project. It was growing dark now, but he and Iggy had finally managed to scrape away every last centimetre of grass from the marked-out area, exposing the earth beneath.

Iggy and Measle were exhausted, but Iggy had a big grin on his muddy face and he was dancing happily about on the bare earth, hopping from foot to foot like an excited stork. The pink bobble on his hat jiggled wildly, sending drops of water flying in all directions.

'I done it! I done it!' he shouted. 'I finished all de diggin'! All by myssself, I finished it!'

Measle couldn't help smiling to himself. Iggy always took the credit for something which had usually been done by somebody else. This time, Measle didn't mind—Iggy was a lot stronger than Measle and had, in fact, done at least half the work.

'Well done, Iggy!' he yelled.

'Can we put de water in now?' said Iggy.

I should have known he'd say that, thought Measle. Iggy was neither very bright, nor very patient.

'Not yet, Iggy. We've got to dig out all the earth, too.'

Iggy turned and stared beadily at Measle.

'We got to do *wot*?' said Iggy.

'Dig out all the earth. It's got to be deep, you see.'

'Why has it got to be deep, Mumps?'

'Because we can't swim in only a couple of centimetres of water, Iggy.'

Iggy wasn't entirely sure what 'swimming' entailed, but he began to get the feeling that—

whatever it meant—he wasn't going to like it very much. With water involved—and *deep* water at that—it sounded as if it meant getting wet and, if there's one thing wrathmonks hate, it's getting wet. What with their rain clouds hovering permanently overhead, they have quite enough wetness in their lives already.

'I don't want to dig no more, Mumps,' said Iggy, in a sulky voice.

'*Twenty* more jelly beans, Iggy?' said Measle, in a wheedling voice.

Iggy's hands were sore, and so was his back, and somehow he'd got a lot of mud on his nice new hat. The mud was mixing with the fine drops from his rain cloud and trickling in a little brown stream down his face. He felt tired and achy and rather cross, too.

'No,' he said, firmly.

'Forty?'

'No.'

'Will you do it for a hundred?'

'*No*. Not even for a *sssquillion*.' And, for the second time that day, Iggy threw down his spade and scuttled off towards the house.

Now what? thought Measle, staring gloomily down at the rectangle of bare earth. *I can't leave it like this—Dad'll murder me!*

And then Nanny Flannel's voice floated across the darkening lawn.

'Measle! Measle, dear! Time for supper!'

BREAKOUT!

The Wizards' Guild was in a state of panic.

Nobody discovered the disappearance of the prisoners from the Detention Centre for two days. Corky Pretzel hadn't reported anything to the authorities. He was highly trusted and there was no reason for anybody to check up on him, so nobody did. It was only when Corky's mother telephoned the Wizards' Guild to ask if anybody had seen her son recently that somebody thought to go down to the bowels of the Wizards' Guild building and see if anything was wrong.

When they did, pandemonium broke out.

Every single prisoner had escaped! All the wrathmonks in the wrathmonk block had disappeared into thin air, and so had both the special prisoners from the High Security Section! But how? The cell doors were wide open and the guard was missing, but the last door, which led out to the long staircase (which, in turn, led to various corridors and passages and, finally, to a set of lifts that arrived at street level and freedom), *that* door was still locked—and it had taken a powerful spell from one of the senior wizards to open it.

At first, nobody thought to look in the Slitherghoul's cell.

The door of the cell was still shut tight, so it was assumed that the Slitherghoul was inside. But a young apprentice wizard, who was a member of the search party, noticed a faint and disgusting smell that lingered in the air of the wrathmonks' cell block.

'What's that smell?' he asked, and one of the older wizards replied, 'That's the Slitherghoul, sonny. Smells horrible, doesn't it?'

'But . . . why can I smell it in *here*? This section only housed the wrathmonk prisoners, didn't it?'

'Merlin's Ghost! You're right!'

The search party returned to the High Security Wing—and it was the same young wizard who noticed the hole in the shadows at the bottom of the ironwood door.

So—not only had the entire prison population of the Detention Centre escaped, but the most mysterious and possibly the most dangerous creature the Wizards' Guild had ever had to handle had gone as well. The panic deepened. Nobody seemed to know what to do—

Then the sharp-eyed young wizard with the sensitive nose noticed something set in the floor of one of the toilets that adjoined the offices.

It was a manhole cover.

When they lifted the cover, they found dried slime round the edges of the hole.

The slime smelt bad. Very bad.

Only then did somebody think of calling Lord Octavo.

When the Slitherghoul's sticky mass had enveloped the entire mob of panic-stricken wrathmonks, its jelly body instantly enlarged to the size of a small lorry. Satisfied that it had caught every one of them, it squeezed its way out of the wrathmonks' corridor and into the office beyond. Once inside the room, it stopped and took stock of its situation. One by one, it discarded the minds of the wrathmonks it had liberated; they were all unstable and therefore almost useless to the creature, so the Slitherghoul examined the three that were still reasonably sane. One by one, it tested the minds of Toby Jugg, Officer Offal, and Corky Pretzel.

The Slitherghoul ended up using Toby Jugg's mind most of the time. It was Toby's brain which suggested that moving *upwards*, through the endless passages of the Guild building, was a bad idea. It was Toby's brain that made the Slitherghoul leave the final door of the Detention Centre firmly locked. It was Toby's brain that proposed that there might be *another* way out. But, while looking for an alternative route, it used the mind of Corky Pretzel. Corky knew every inch of those underground quarters. He knew about the manhole cover. He knew that under the manhole cover was a well and, at the bottom of this well, was a branch of the main sewer that lay beneath the Wizards' Guild building.

But, once Corky had told the Slitherghoul about the manhole cover, it was Toby's brain that put forward the idea of where to go next.

The huge thing slithered stickily out of the office and into the adjoining toilet. There, in the middle of the dirty tiled floor, was the heavy iron manhole cover. The Slitherghoul extended a section of itself, wrapped the jelly tentacle round the cover's handle and yanked it free. Then, without another thought from any of the minds inside it, the thing had slid over the lip of the gaping hole and, with a slopping, slurping sound, disappeared into the blackness beneath.

SOME UNEXPECTED HELP

Measle was fed up.

He'd been digging for three days and, for all his efforts, the projected swimming pool looked as if he'd hardly started it. All he'd managed to do was increase the depth of the dig by about ten centimetres, which was hardly scratching the surface of the job. At this rate, it would be at least a year before he could dive in! Already his hands were sore and his spine was so stiff he was having trouble straightening up.

Iggy hadn't come back to help. He hadn't even bothered to watch Measle at work. Instead he'd hung about at the kitchen door, hoping that Nanny Flannel might give him some more jelly beans. He was careful not to step over the threshold of the kitchen. He'd done that once and Nanny Flannel had whacked him over the head with a wet mop. Iggy was a little afraid of Nanny Flannel—but not so afraid that he wouldn't try a small lie on her.

'I been workin' ever ssso hard, Miss Fwannel,' he whined. 'For free whole days I been workin'! And I'm ever ssso 'ungry—'

Nanny Flannel was having none of it.

'You haven't been working at all, you lazy wet thing,' she said, peering crossly at Iggy through her glasses. 'You did a little on the first day and since then you've done nothing but clutter up my doorway. Now go away. If you're not going to help Measle, at least make yourself useful—go and breathe on the roses.'

Breathing on the roses in the gardens of Merlin Manor was Iggy's job. His wrathmonk breathing magic was a very weak spell—all it did was kill bugs. But that was useful on the Merlin Manor roses, particularly in the spring, when the aphids started sucking the sap from the stems.

'Go on now, Iggy!' said Nanny sharply. 'I won't tell you again!'

Iggy sighed mournfully and, muttering darkly about how cruel and sad his life was, he drifted off in the direction of the rose gardens. Nanny Flannel took his place in the doorway of the kitchen. She peered out across the expanse of lawn and watched the small figure of Measle in the distance, struggling with his heavy spade.

Poor little chap, she thought. *Well, good for him for trying. I wonder when he'll give it up?*

Measle was, in fact, at the point of giving up. The whole thing was obviously beyond him. Perhaps Iggy had been right to stop when he did—at least *he* didn't have sore hands, an aching back, and muddy feet.

'Hard at work I see, Master Measle.'

Measle turned round. Mr Needle and Mr Bland were standing there, at the edge of the rectangle of bare earth. Measle noticed that they were careful to keep their shiny black shoes away from the pile of mud that Measle had dumped by the side. Using the back of his hand, Measle wiped the sweat from his forehead. His hand was muddy and it left a brown streak across his face. He nodded politely.

'A major undertaking, Needle,' said Mr Bland, smiling faintly down at Measle.

'A *monumental* undertaking, Bland,' said Mr Needle. 'Perhaps a little *too* monumental, don't you think? For one so young, I mean.'

Mr Bland nodded. 'I'm rather inclined to agree with you, Needle. Master Measle could use some help.'

'Well, Tinker helped a little, when he thought we were digging for rabbits,' said Measle, leaning on his spade. 'And Iggy helped the whole of the first day but then he got bored and stopped.'

'Typical wrathmonk behaviour,' said Mr Needle.

'Typical,' said Mr Bland. 'What else could one expect?'

There was a short silence while Mr Bland and Mr Needle stood there, smiling faintly down at Measle.

It's no good, thought Measle, *I just don't like these two. So it won't matter if I tease them a bit—*

'*You* could help, if you like,' he said, smiling innocently up at the two men.

'Us?' said Mr Bland, slowly taking off his sunglasses.

'We?' said Mr Needle, doing the same thing. '*We* . . . help *you*?'

'Oh, thank you very much,' said Measle, opening his eyes very wide and grinning with pretend gratitude at the men. 'One of you could use Iggy's spade and there's a pickaxe in the potting shed.'

Mr Bland smiled uncertainly and then turned slowly and looked at Mr Needle. Almost as if he was a mirror image of Mr Bland, Mr Needle did exactly the same thing. For a couple of moments they stared at one another.

Mr Needle broke the silence. 'What if we—?' he said.

Mr Bland interrupted with, 'Possibly we could.'

'There's no particular reason why we couldn't.'

'None that I can think of.'

'I doubt it would do any harm.'

'It might even enhance our—'

'Our reputations, yes.'

'Which would be no bad—'

'Thing.'

Then both men fell silent for a couple of seconds before turning in unison to Measle.

'We would be delighted to help, Master Measle,' said Mr Bland.

'Delighted,' said Mr Needle. 'So—if you would kindly stand to one side, Master Measle?'

Measle stepped up from the bare earth and onto the grass next to the two men. He expected one of them to step down and pick up Iggy's spade, which was lying where Iggy had dropped it two days earlier, but neither man moved from his spot. Instead, Mr Bland said, 'A Restricted Excavatory Enchantment, I assume, Needle? Number three, do you think?'

Mr Needle inclined his head and said, 'The logical choice, Bland. It will be interesting to see how far we get with it. Shall I attempt it first?'

'Be my guest, Needle,' said Mr Bland.

Mr Needle narrowed his eyes and stared hard at the bare rectangle of earth in front of him. Then he said, in a loud, ringing voice, '*Humfuss quadrickle effodium limitudinus!*'

Measle had forgotten that the two men from the Wizards' Guild were minor warlocks. Two pale green beams of light shot from Mr Needle's eyes and sizzled through the air, striking a spot in the dead centre of the rectangle of bare earth. What happened next was very interesting.

A pair of gigantic, ghostly canine paws appeared

and started to dig in the centre of the rectangle. They were almost exactly like Tinker's white furry paws—only much, much bigger—and with no dog attached to them, either. They simply ended in a sort of wispy smoke, about where a dog's elbows are placed but they dug with all the enthusiasm that any dog shows when it thinks there's a rabbit down a hole. The earth started to shower upwards, landing neatly on top of the pile of soil that Measle had already dug out.

Tinker, asleep a few metres away, opened one eye at the sounds of frantic, doglike digging. When he saw what was happening, he pricked up both ears then he got up and trotted over to see what was going on. When he saw the disembodied paws, he flattened his ears and started to bark furiously at them.

'Shut up, Tink!' shouted Measle. 'It's all right!'

Tinker was used to strange things happening round the smelly kid but a pair of paws, smelling distinctly doggy and suddenly appearing out of nowhere, was a bit much to ignore. However, the tone of the smelly kid's voice was firm and reasonably reassuring, so Tinker turned and slunk back to his patch of warm grass, throwing suspicious looks over his shoulder.

Measle settled down to watch the process with growing delight. The magical paws dug very fast—far faster than he and Iggy could possibly manage, even with all the enthusiasm in the world—and, quite soon, there was a hole two metres deep. At that point, the paws popped out of the hole they had made and started another hole right next to it. In a few moments, this second hole was as deep as the first and the pile of earth at the side of the rectangle was growing fast.

After twenty minutes, about a quarter of the rectangle had been dug down to a depth of two metres and Measle began to hope that, perhaps, his swimming pool project was actually going to work.

Then, quite suddenly, there was a popping sound, like a cork coming out of a bottle, and the two giant paws faded into a thin grey smoke which blew away on a little gust of wind.

'Well *done*, Needle,' said Mr Bland. 'You're showing a definite improvement, particularly in spell-duration, aren't you?'

'Thank you, Bland,' said Mr Needle. 'I must say, I'm quite pleased with the result. But you'll do *much* better, I'm sure.'

'Oh, I'm sure I won't,' said Mr Bland. 'But I shall do my best, of course.'

Mr Bland directed his gaze at the centre of the rectangle and said, '*Humfuss quadrickle effodium limitudinus!*' A pair of pale blue beams darted from his eyes and sizzled to the centre of the rectangle—and Measle watched with delight as another pair of giant paws appeared and started to dig furiously. These paws were a little different from the ones that Mr Needle had produced:

Mr Bland's paws were chocolate brown in colour and perhaps just a little larger. However, they seemed to dig at the same speed as Mr Needle's—and, quite soon, another quarter of the rectangle had been dug out to two metres in depth.

But all too soon there was that popping sound again and the giant paws turned to smoke and then drifted away in the breeze.

'Oh, *excellent*, Bland!' said Mr Needle. 'I do believe you were almost up to my time!'

'You're too kind, Needle,' said Mr Bland, gazing down at his handiwork with a look of pride. Then he turned to Measle and said, 'Well, Master Measle, that's all we can do for today, I'm afraid.'

'We can continue tomorrow, of course,' said Mr Needle.

'When our mana has recharged,' said Mr Bland.

'Thanks so much,' said Measle. 'That's fantastic!' And he meant it. Fully half the rectangle was now two metres deep—and it looked good enough to be turned into the deep end of a splendid swimming pool.

All three stared proudly down at the neatly dug pit in front of them.

Then Nanny Flannel's voice came drifting across the lawn.

'Measle! Measle, dear! Lord Octavo's on the telephone! He wants to talk to you—urgently!'

Too Little, Too Late

The sewer beneath the Wizards' Guild building was a horrible place for anybody or anything, except for the rats that lived there—and for the Slitherghoul, of course.

The Slitherghoul, in its primitive way, rather liked the darkness and the slimy wetness of the ancient tunnels. The rodent parts of its brain even recognized certain sections and felt quite at home down there—and the wrathmonk and the warlock parts of its mind were simply glad to be out of the Detention Centre, even if freedom meant slithering around in the darkness of these endless tunnels.

The question was—where to go?

The question was answered very quickly.

It was obvious really. Enough of the thinking

parts of the Slitherghoul's collective brain wanted things that were to be found in one place, and one place only. The creature itself hungered blindly for the great untapped source of mana that Sheepshank's shuttered brain had detected outside the cell; Griswold Gristle, Judge Cedric Hardscrabble, Buford Cudgel, and Frognell Flabbit hungered for revenge; so did Officer Offal—he hated Measle for the way he'd tricked him into his imprisonment; and Toby Jugg (while also interested in taking a cruel revenge on the Stubbs boy) still had the same ambitions that had landed him in prison in the first place—to control a Mallockee and marry a Manafount.

All these desires were to be found in only one location.

Merlin Manor.

But—how to get there? The Slitherghoul explored its available minds again.

From Buford Cudgel, Frognell Flabbit, and Griswold Gristle it learned the location of Merlin Manor. But here, in the darkness of the sewers, it needed a direction to take.

More minds were explored and discarded.

Finally, in the limited brain of a ginger-haired young wrathmonk with grotesquely protruding ears the Slitherghoul found what it needed. The young wrathmonk's name was Mungo MacToad. Mungo MacToad had a strange hobby. He liked drains. Mungo knew a lot about drains and, in particular, how to move about in them. He knew these city sewers like the back of his dirty hand.

This knowledge gave the Slitherghoul a rough direction to take.

Then, switching back to the superior brain of Toby Jugg, the Slitherghoul set off.

And, now that it had somewhere to go, it moved quickly.

Ten metres above it, up on the surface, something strange was happening. A very large rain cloud, black and dense and swirling, moved steadily through the streets of the city. It didn't behave like an ordinary rain cloud at all. For a start, it was so compressed that it looked almost solid—and it hovered only a few feet from the surface of the road. But the oddest thing about this unnatural cloud was the fact that, unlike ordinary clouds, it didn't seem to be governed by the speed or the direction of the wind. Every now and again, it changed direction quite sharply, turning left round a corner at the side of a building, or veering right at a set of traffic lights—just as if it was *following* something.

Which, since it was composed of the tightly compressed individual rain clouds of about a dozen or so even *more* tightly compressed wrathmonks, it was.

That was three days ago. It had taken the Slitherghoul a day and a half to reach the end of the underground pipelines. The sewer down which it had travelled ended at a sewage works out in the country and it was here that the Slitherghoul emerged, late at night under the cover of darkness. Once again, it searched the collective minds inside itself for a new direction.

Toby Jugg supplied it.

When Toby was a young man, he'd enjoyed sailing. Toby knew how to navigate by checking the positions of the stars in the night sky. That night, the sky above the sewage works was particularly clear—apart from a single large black cloud that poured its drenching load down on the Slitherghoul.

Armed now with a new set of directions, the Slitherghoul set off across the fields. On its way, it met—and ran over—a large number of living creatures. Thousands of insects ended up inside the great jellified mass—grasshoppers and beetles and earwigs and flies and many other tiny bugs of every description. Several more mice, a couple of voles, and a sleeping weasel were caught in its sticky folds but, when it came across a herd of cows, the Slitherghoul steered a path round them. Something told it that a cow or two might impede its progress too much, so the Slitherghoul was careful to avoid such large creatures. It also took pains to bypass all human habitation and, when daylight came, it lay quiet and still in a ditch by the side of a cornfield, looking so much like a long deposit of brown mud that, even if somebody had passed close by during that whole day, it was unlikely that the person would have taken any notice of the thing at all.

Then, as night returned, the Slitherghoul slimed its way out of the ditch and started off again.

It shouldn't be too long now, whispered the brain of Griswold Gristle, and Buford Cudgel's mind agreed and so did Frognell Flabbit's. The reason for their conclusion was simple— the Slitherghoul had been oozing its way along the edge of a field and had just passed close by a crossing of two small lanes. There was a signpost there, with the words, 'Dimwitch—2 miles' painted on it.

Griswold, Buford, and Frognell all knew from past experience that Merlin Manor was close to the village of Dimwitch. Judge Cedric Hardscrabble should have known as well but the poor old judge was too stupid to remember such things as directions, so he wasn't any help at all.

The Slitherghoul switched back to Toby's mind.

Go faster! it seemed to be whispering—and the Slitherghoul, sensing it was now near the end of its journey, began to glide quickly across a ploughed field, ignoring the ridges and the furrows in the earth beneath its huge, slimy body.

* * *

Measle took the telephone from Nanny Flannel's hand and put it to his ear.

'Hello?'

'Hello, young Measle,' said the familiar, gravelly old voice of Lord Octavo. 'How are things at Merlin Manor?'

'All right, thanks, Lord Octavo,' said Measle. Measle liked Lord Octavo a lot, and he was pretty sure that Lord Octavo liked him right back. The old wizard had been brilliantly helpful to the Stubbs family during the inquiry into the Dragodon adventure and, with Sam Stubbs down at the South Pole, he was now the most senior wizard around.

'Mr Needle and Mr Bland behaving themselves, are they?'

'Yes, they're being very nice. Very helpful, too.'

'Good. Now look, young fellow, you haven't seen anything unusual, have you?'

'What sort of unusual, Lord Octavo?'

'Oh, I don't know . . . people lurking about . . . strangers watching the place . . . odd noises. Anything like that been going on?'

'No. Why?'

'Well, something rather dreadful has happened, I'm afraid. All the prisoners in the Detention Centre seem to have disappeared.'

'*What?*' yelled Measle. 'But—but *how*? And—and *when*?'

'We don't know how. It happened at least three days ago and I'm sorry to say we've only just discovered it. But the point is, several of the escaped wrathmonks aren't exactly friendly towards the Stubbs family, are they? In fact, at least four of them have good reason to want to do you harm, Measle. And then there's Toby Jugg and that big prison guard—'

'*They've* escaped too?'

'I'm afraid so. And there's a creature called a Slitherghoul on the loose as well, but there's no particular reason why it should bother you, so I wouldn't worry about that. I am a bit concerned about those others, though. They know where you live, you see. Are you sure you haven't noticed anything suspicious?'

'Quite sure, Lord Octavo.'

'Good. Well, maybe they'll know better than to come anywhere near you. But if you hear or see anything even a little bit suspicious, I want you to call me immediately. Meanwhile, I'll try and get in touch with your parents; which won't be easy, I'm afraid. The South Pole doesn't have much in the way of a phone service and, what with the convention taking place deep inside a glacier, we haven't been able to make contact with anybody yet. But we'll keep trying. Now, I'd better have a word with Needle and Bland.'

Measle gave the telephone back to Nanny Flannel and went off in search of the two men. As he left the kitchen, he heard Nanny Flannel say, 'What's all this about, Lord Octavo?'

Mr Needle and Mr Bland took the call in Sam's study and, when they came out, their faces were serious.

'Well?' said Nanny Flannel, who had questioned Lord Octavo very closely while Measle was searching for them. What Lord Octavo had told her was making Nanny Flannel quite anxious.

'No cause for concern, Miss Flannel,' said Mr Needle. 'We shall be on special guard tonight.'

'Very special indeed,' said Mr Bland.

'Humph!' said Nanny Flannel, dismissively. 'And what, precisely, does that mean?'

'It means, Miss Flannel,' said Mr Bland, importantly, 'that one of us will be awake throughout the night and patrolling the house and grounds.'

'We shall take it in turns,' said Mr Needle.

'Humph!' said Nanny Flannel again. 'Well, that doesn't impress me at all—it's what you do already.' She shook her head firmly and said, 'No, there'll be no patrolling of the grounds, gentlemen. You can patrol *indoors*, if you must. I want all the doors and windows locked tight and I want everybody safe *inside* the house. Is that quite understood?'

Mr Needle and Mr Bland both opened their mouths to object but a second look at Nanny Flannel's determined face stopped them before they could speak. The two men nodded meekly and then set off round the house. They carefully checked every window and every door and Nanny

Flannel, Measle, and a curious Tinker followed them, watching their every move.

At last, when Nanny Flannel was satisfied that everything was safe and secure, she took them all into the kitchen, sat them down around the table, and dished out supper.

Supper was one of Nanny Flannel's specials—a wonderful steak-and-kidney pie, with mashed potatoes and peas and lots of rich brown gravy. Mr Needle and Mr Bland ate as if they hadn't had a proper meal in a week. Measle sat opposite them, with his back to the kitchen window, and he watched them out of the corner of his eye. In the soft light of the kitchen lamps, the Gloomstains on the tips of their ears were quite prominent, although they still weren't very dark, which meant that the warlock abilities of Mr Needle and Mr Bland were not yet fully developed. While he was thinking about this, it suddenly occurred to Measle that neither Mr Needle nor Mr Bland had, at this precise moment, any magical abilities at all! They'd used up all their mana digging out the swimming pool, which meant that, apart from their human abilities, they weren't going to be much use protecting him—at least, not for another twenty-four hours. Measle wondered briefly if either Mr Needle or Mr Bland had told Lord Octavo about this? Probably not—they wouldn't want to admit they'd used up their mana on something that had nothing to do with security.

It was at this moment that Mr Needle lifted his eyes from his plate and stared past Measle's right ear at the kitchen window behind him.

Mr Needle's face went white. He opened his mouth and screamed in sudden terror and Mr Bland jumped in his seat, looked up from his plate, and he too screamed in panic.

Measle's head whipped round.

There was something there! A horrible white thing, squashed against the glass of the window! The white thing had six pointed yellow teeth and a pair of mad, staring eyes—round eyes, like a dead fish—and some sort of disgusting pink ball seemed to be growing out of the top of its head.

Measle started to laugh. He turned back to see that both men had leaped to their feet, knocking over their chairs in the process. Now they were pressed tightly against the far wall and Mr Bland seemed to be moaning in terror.

'It's all right,' said Measle, trying to suppress his laughter. 'It's only Iggy. We forgot all about him. We usually leave the kitchen door open, you see, so that he can look inside.'

Mr Needle and Mr Bland relaxed visibly. They came forward rather sheepishly and picked up their fallen chairs and sat down on them, but neither man seemed to have much of an appetite left, because they left the rest of their food untouched.

'Can we let Iggy in, Nanny?' said Measle. 'Just for tonight? Just this once?'

'Well, all right,' said Nanny Flannel, reluctantly. 'But just this once, mind. And he's to keep his nasty wet head over a bucket—I'm not mopping up after a lazy little wrathmonk, thank you very much.'

Measle got up and went to the kitchen door and unlocked it. Then he poked his head out into the cool night air and called out, 'You can come inside, Iggy.'

Iggy took his face away from the window and came, a little cautiously, to the open kitchen door.

'I can come inssside, Mumps?'

'Yes, Iggy. Just for tonight, though.'

'Is she goin' to hit me wiv de mop again?' asked Iggy, peering anxiously over Measle's shoulder.

'No, Iggy,' said Measle. 'But you've got to sit with your head over a bucket, otherwise she might.'

'Okey-dokey,' said Iggy, nervously. Keeping a watchful eye on Nanny Flannel, he scuttled into the kitchen sideways, like a crab. Nanny Flannel set a big tin bucket down in one corner of the kitchen. She put it down with a definite CLANG! and Iggy jumped. Then Nanny Flannel fetched a spare kitchen chair and banged it down next to the bucket.

'There,' she said, pointing sternly at the chair and Iggy ducked his head, trotted obediently over, and sat down on it. Then he leaned over, tilting his head sideways so that he could look out into the room, and the drops from his little black rain cloud started to *plink! plink! plink!* into the bottom of the bucket.

There was a short silence while everybody except Measle glared severely at Iggy. Measle couldn't help grinning at him—Iggy looked so funny, bent over the bucket like that as if he was washing his hair.

Iggy, encouraged by being allowed into Nanny Flannel's domain, decided to start a conversation.

'I miss my little fing,' he announced, to nobody in particular. 'When's it comin' back?'

Measle saw Mr Bland and Mr Needle glance at each other, their eyebrows raised in query.

'He means Matilda,' he said. 'He likes Matilda.'

Iggy nodded vigorously, scattering drops of rainwater over the floor. Nanny Flannel cleared her throat loudly and Iggy froze again, holding his head stiffly motionless over the tin bucket.

'She is my ssspecial friend,' said Iggy, being careful not to move a muscle in his neck. 'When is she comin' home, Mumps?'

'Soon, Iggy,' said Measle.

'Good,' said Iggy. Then he said, 'Dere's a funny sssmell outside. It's quite a nice sssmell, actually. I dunno wot is makin' it.'

'A smell?' said Mr Needle, narrowing his eyes. 'What sort of smell?'

'A *nice* sssmell,' said Iggy.

Mr Needle's eyes stopped being narrow and he turned and smiled briefly at Mr Bland. 'The creature obviously likes Miss Flannel's excellent steak-and-kidney pie, Bland,' he said.

'No,' said Iggy, firmly, craning his head round to stare at Mr Needle. 'No, I don't like cake-and-ssskidly pie. Dat is 'orrible ssstuff, dat is. No, I mean anuvver sssmell, wot is *outsssside*.'

'What does it smell like, Iggy?' asked Measle, trying to keep this conversation going, because conversations with Iggy were often quite funny. He was having a bet with himself about whether or not either of these brisk, efficient men from the Wizards' Guild ever actually laughed out loud.

'It sssmells like nice dead fings,' said Iggy. 'It sssmells like nice dirty teeth—an' like nice dirty feet—an' like nice sssoggy Sssprussel bouts—an' like old bread all covered wiv dat nice green furry ssstuff—an' like ... er ... um ... uvver fings like dat. I sssmelled it before, once—but I can't 'member when.'

Measle's curiosity got the better of him. He went to the kitchen door and opened it. He stuck his nose out into the cool evening air and took a sniff.

Nothing—just the smell of the countryside at night.

No—there! The faintest whiff of something disgusting—something foul and dead—or perhaps not dead, because there were sharp chemical smells mixed in with all the other horrible stinks. The smell seemed to be coming from a long way off, because there was still only the mildest trace of it on the soft breeze—

Measle pulled his head back into the kitchen. Carefully and calmly, he closed the door and then reached up and slid the heavy iron bolt into place. Then he turned round and said, 'Iggy's right. There's something out there—and I think I know what it is.'

Nanny Flannel, Mr Bland, and Mr Needle all stared at him with looks of deep concern on their faces.

'What did you see, dear?' said Nanny Flannel.

'I didn't see anything, Nanny,' said Measle. 'But I smelt something. And the thing is—I've smelt it before. Like Iggy did—but I *remember* where I smelt it, you see.'

'Where?' asked Mr Needle, sharply.

'In the Detention Centre,' said Measle. 'In the High Security bit, where my mum and dad were locked up. There was something in one of the cells and it smelt just like—well, just like whatever is out there. It's a horrible smell and, if you smell it once, I don't think you could ever forget it.'

'Yeah!' said Iggy, eagerly. 'Yeah—*dat's* where I sssmelt it! In de uvver place where de bad wraffmonks go!'

'But, what is it, dear?' said Nanny Flannel.

'I think it's called a Slitherghoul, Nanny. That's what Lord Octavo called it.'

The blood drained from the cheeks of Mr Needle and Mr Bland. Nanny Flannel's face remained its usual pink but a little crease of worry appeared on her forehead.

'Lord Octavo didn't think we need to worry about that, dear. He seemed more concerned about the escaped wrathmonks.'

Measle didn't answer, because he became aware that Mr Needle and Mr Bland, their heads close together, were holding a frantic, whispered conversation. Measle strained his ears and heard, '... *but why would it come here?* ... *perhaps the boy is mistaken* ... *Lord Octavo mentioned the distinctive odour* ... *we should make sure* ...'

Mr Needle and Mr Bland got up from the kitchen table. Both men plastered sickly smiles on their faces, in an attempt (Measle supposed) to reassure everybody that there was nothing to worry about. Their smiles were so obviously artificial that they had the opposite effect and, for the first time, Measle felt a small knot of fear in his stomach. Mr Needle crossed casually to the kitchen window. He opened it a crack and sniffed. Then, hurriedly, he closed the window again. He turned and threw a nervous glance across the room to Mr Bland—and Measle saw Mr Needle make a tiny nodding motion with his head.

Mr Bland let out a short, nervous laugh.

'I'm sure there's nothing to worry about, Master Measle,' he said. 'It's probably something quite harmless. Now, if you will excuse us, we had better report this to Lord Octavo—just to be on the safe side, you understand.'

Mr Needle and Mr Bland bowed slightly in Nanny Flannel's direction. Mr Needle said, 'An excellent supper, Miss Flannel. Many thanks.' Then he and Mr Bland turned and walked silently out of the kitchen.

There was a moment of silence. Then Nanny Flannel said, very quietly, 'Go and see what they're doing, dear. But don't let them see *you*. Understand?'

Measle understood. He nodded and slipped out of the kitchen, making his way as quietly as he could to the dining room. He crept over to the big jar of jelly beans standing on the sideboard. He took off the glass lid and fished out a couple of yellow ones that lay on the top of the heap. He would have taken more, but there wasn't time to dig for buried yellow beans so, clutching the two tightly in one hand, he tiptoed out of the dining room. Standing in the dark corridor, Measle heard the sound of voices coming from Sam's study. Measle crept along the wall, towards the study door. The door was open and warm lamplight spilled out into the dark passage. Measle edged closer—and now the whispering voices of Mr Needle and Mr Bland were as clear as bells.

'But—what can we *say*, Needle? How can we explain the loss of our mana?'

'We don't explain anything, Bland! Why give ourselves trouble? We simply report the odour and state that we have everything under control! Besides, it's probably nothing more than the scent of a dead animal, in which case we have nothing to fear!'

'But what if it *isn't*, Needle? What if it is in fact this Slitherghoul? The boy seemed fairly sure and so did the wrathmonk—'

'A small boy and an idiotic little wrathmonk! Why believe either one, Bland?'

'But if—'

'But, *if* what they are saying is true, then we simply make sure that the thing stays *outside*, while we remain *inside*, safe and sound! The doors and windows are barred and, as I understand it, the creature is nothing more than a small lump of jelly. I can't see a lump of jelly getting past the locks of Merlin Manor, can you?'

'I suppose not, Needle.'

'Of course not, Bland! Then, tomorrow, when our mana has returned, we will deal with it! It's just a matter of waiting it out, that's all.'

'Then why should we report anything at all, Needle?'

'Because, my dear Bland, Miss Flannel and young Measle and even that ridiculous Niggle creature already know that there might be something amiss. If we don't at least make some sort of report, it might appear that we were neglecting our duties.'

'Yes—yes, I see.'

'Good. Now, we'd better close that door. We don't want anybody eavesdropping, do we?'

Quick as a flash, Measle lifted his hand and popped a yellow jelly bean into his mouth. He bit down on it then stepped silently into the open doorway. Mr Bland was just a few metres away, approaching the door with his hand outstretched towards the handle and Measle, now as invisible as air, stepped sideways, pressing his back against the study wall. Mr Bland's eyes passed over Measle and saw nothing, of course. But he came very close and Measle held his breath as the man closed the door beside him. Then Mr Bland crossed back to where Mr Needle was standing by Sam's desk.

From the moment he'd bitten down on the jelly bean, Measle had started counting down in his head. He'd begun at thirty and now had reached twenty—

Nineteen, eighteen, seventeen—

He watched as Mr Needle took a small black notebook out of his breast pocket.

Sixteen, fifteen, fourteen—

Mr Needle opened the notebook and ran his finger down the page.

Thirteen, twelve, eleven—

Mr Needle picked up the telephone and, consulting the notebook, punched in a number.

Ten, nine, eight—

Mr Needle lifted the telephone to his ear.

Seven, six, five—

A puzzled look crossed Mr Needle's face and he took the phone receiver away from his ear and shook it gently.

Four, three, two—

Measle popped the second jelly bean into his mouth and, with the thought that in exactly half a minute he'd be visible again, started counting down from thirty.

Twenty-nine, twenty-eight, twenty-seven—

Mr Needle was jiggling the phone rest.

'Is something wrong, Needle?' asked Mr Bland, licking his lips nervously.

Twenty-six, twenty-five, twenty-four—

'There appears to be no dialling tone,' said Mr Needle.

'No dialling tone?' Mr Bland's voice contained a tremor of fear.

'None. It's dead. Listen for yourself.'

Mr Needle passed the telephone receiver to Mr Bland, who held it tight to his ear. Then Measle watched as Mr Bland, with shaking hands, slowly put the receiver back on its rest.

Fourteen, thirteen, twelve—

'Perhaps a coincidence?' muttered Mr Bland.

'Perhaps,' said Mr Needle. 'But we should assume the worst, Bland. Come along—we must be extra vigilant now.'

Measle pressed himself against the wall by the door as Mr Needle and Mr Bland walked quickly across the room towards him. Mr Needle opened the door and the two men hurried out—and Measle heaved a big sigh of relief, because his invisibility wore off only a few seconds after the men had gone.

Measle quickly went to his father's desk. He picked up the phone and held it to his ear.

Nothing.

Sometimes, the sound of *nothing* can be rather frightening.

This, Measle decided, was one of those times.

And then he decided it was an even *more* frightening time when, thirty seconds later, all the lights went out and he was plunged into pitch darkness.

The Siege

It had been many months since Griswold Gristle, Buford Cudgel, and Frognell Flabbit had visited Merlin Manor, but they remembered it well.

After the Dragodon had been destroyed, together with his great dragon Arcturion, Griswold, Buford, Frognell, and Judge Cedric Hardscrabble had nothing left to lose. So, seeking revenge against the Stubbs family, they had ridden up Merlin Manor's long gravel drive on Cudgel's big black motorbike. They had attacked Sam Stubbs with every spell at their disposal. Shortly afterwards (and to their horrified surprise) they had found themselves bundled uncomfortably together in a magical silver net and carted away in a white van, which had driven them straight to the Detention Centre deep in the basement of the Wizards' Guild, where they'd stayed locked up ever since.

Their visit to Merlin Manor had been short and not at all sweet—but three of the wrathmonks had held a picture of the great house in their heads for all the long months of their imprisonment. Poor old Judge Cedric's mind was as fuzzy as ever, so he remembered almost nothing—but the others had minds that, while insane in their wrathmonk way, still worked reasonably well. Now, in front of them, the familiar shape of Merlin Manor was silhouetted against the night sky.

The Slitherghoul had stopped in a field about three hundred metres from the house, looking at the dark building through the eyes of Griswold, Buford, and Frognell and sensing the three wrathmonks' excitement at finally arriving at their destination. Then the Slitherghoul had switched to Toby Jugg's brain—and Toby Jugg was thinking something else entirely. Toby was thinking about how clever it would be to cut Merlin Manor off from the rest of the world.

The Slitherghoul had moved, using Toby's eyes to search. It started to look for a pole—a tall wooden pole, probably made from a pine tree, with many wires connected to the top of it.

There! At the edge of the field, where it ran by the side of the long gravel drive! A tall pole—

The Slitherghoul had slimed across the field at full speed. When it arrived at the base of the telephone pole, it reached up a long thin section of itself, stretching upwards towards the wires. It curled the tip of its jelly tentacle round the wires and pulled hard. For a moment, the wires strained and held—then they were wrenched out of their sockets with a twang! falling to the ground in a twisted heap.

Exactly a minute and a half later, Mr Needle had picked up the telephone in Sam Stubbs's study.

A dead telephone, because it was no longer connected to the outside world.

There were other cables up there at the top of the pine pole. Thicker cables. They would offer more resistance—*but they must come down too!* Under Toby's guidance, the Slitherghoul had reached for them—

First the telephone—now this! thought Measle, as he felt his way along the dark passage towards the kitchen. A little light from a full moon and a scattering of stars came through a skylight in the ceiling, so Measle could just about make out where he was, which meant he could hurry along a little faster than if the darkness had been total. By the time he got back to the kitchen, the ever-practical Nanny Flannel had lit several candles and stuck them in the necks of empty bottles and put them round the room. By their flickering light, Measle saw that Nanny Flannel was standing over Mr

Needle and Mr Bland, who were both sitting at the kitchen table, looking rather nervous.

'But what exactly *is* this creature?' Nanny Flannel was saying as Measle came into the room. 'And what is it doing here?'

Mr Needle and Mr Bland exchanged uncomfortable looks. Mr Needle was the first to speak.

'Nobody knows for sure what it is, Miss Flannel. Or what it does. However, I am certain that it poses no particular threat. It is, after all, quite small—'

'How small?' demanded Nanny Flannel, fiercely.

'As I understand, about the size of a coffee table, Miss Flannel. And made of some sort of jelly. Really nothing to fear.'

'Don't tell me what to fear and what not to fear, Mr Needle!' said Nanny Flannel sharply. 'There's an unknown something-or-other out there in the darkness, and now all the power is gone and we've no lights—'

Measle cleared his throat loudly and, when everybody had turned and was looking at him, he said, 'It's not just the lights, Nanny. The telephone doesn't work either.'

'What?' said Nanny Flannel, her eyes wide.

'Mr Bland and Mr Needle know,' said Measle. He turned to the two men and said, 'Don't you?'

'Um . . . there does appear to be a malfunction on the line,' admitted Mr Needle, reluctantly. 'I'm sure it's only temporary, though.'

'Nothing to worry about,' said Mr Bland, his eyes darting uneasily round the kitchen.

'Nuffink to worry about!' sang Iggy cheerfully, from his corner of the kitchen.

Then, without any warning, it began to rain heavily just outside the outer kitchen door. It didn't sound like ordinary rain. This rain sounded as if it was torrential—a steady, roaring sound of very big drops of water, very close together, hurtling through the night sky and crashing to the ground below. Before anybody could say anything, there came another sound—and it was just as frighteningly strange as the rain. A heavy, squelchy, sloppy-sounding THUMP! against the kitchen door. At exactly the same moment, the kitchen was flooded by the most horrible smell Nanny Flannel had ever smelt.

'Ugh!' she exclaimed. 'What on earth is that?'

'That's the Slitherghoul, Nanny!' yelled Measle. 'And I think it's a lot bigger than a coffee table!'

They all heard it now. Through the thunder of the rain, a slithering, sliding, grating sound came from outside as the Slitherghoul pressed its huge, slimy body against the outer wall of the kitchen. A yellowish-greenish-brownish slime spread across the window and the kitchen door creaked from the weight that was now pressing against it.

The Slitherghoul had started to look for a way in.

Mr Needle and Mr Bland jumped to their feet. They both had very frightened faces. Nanny

Flannel glared at them and said, 'Well, what are you doing just standing there? You're supposed to be guarding us all! *Do* something!'

'They can't, Nanny!' said Measle, raising his voice a little, because the slithering and the creaking sounds were getting louder. 'They can't—because they used up all their mana helping me with the swimming pool! They haven't got any magic left!'

Nanny Flannel's face darkened with fury. She took a couple of steps towards the men and Measle saw that she was going to give them one of her special scoldings. Nanny Flannel's special scoldings were very frightening. Only once had

Measle ever been on the receiving end of one—when he'd tried making pancakes on his own and had only succeeded in making a terrible mess of Nanny Flannel's kitchen—and he knew how awful they were. He felt suddenly a little sorry for Mr Needle and Mr Bland. Before Nanny Flannel could open her mouth and start, he blurted out, 'It's not their fault, Nanny! I asked them to help!'

Nanny Flannel took no notice. She lifted her finger and started to wag it under the noses of the two warlocks.

'You silly, silly little men!' she stormed. 'If you wanted to help, why didn't you just roll up your sleeves and dig in the ordinary way? How dare you waste your mana like that! How *dare* you!'

''Ow dare you!' yelled Iggy, who was getting wildly overexcited by all the noise and confusion. He had a big grin on his pale little face and the end of his long nose kept twitching—because the smell that was now flooding the kitchen was really, really *nice*! He'd lifted his head away from the bucket and now a little pool of water from his rain cloud was gathering on the kitchen floor.

Tinker was adding to the uproar by barking at the top of his lungs. He was facing the kitchen door, every hair on his body bristling with fury, every tooth in his head bared and gleaming. *Something out there! Something really, really smelly! Don't like it! Dangerous! Make it go away!*

'Miss Flannel—' said Mr Needle, wanting to start a long explanation about why it wasn't their fault that they had no mana—but the noise drowned out his voice. Outside, the Slitherghoul was starting to flex its great strength against the door and the window and now the timbers and the glass in both were creaking loudly at the strain. Inside, Tinker's barking was reaching fever pitch and Iggy had begun to prance around the kitchen in a strange, mad, hopping dance, shouting as loudly as he could, "OW DARE YOU! 'OW DARE YOU! 'OW *DARE* YOU!'

The last thing Nanny Flannel needed right now was a wet, overexcited wrathmonk dancing round her kitchen! She turned, marched over to where the mop was leaning against the kitchen wall and grabbed it.

'Stop this nonsense right now, Iggy!' she snapped.

Iggy was far too agitated to take any notice. He jumped up onto the kitchen table and started to hop about, his feet trampling all over the remains of supper. Several plates shattered and he kicked the pieces to the floor, all the time shouting, "OW DARE YOU! 'OW DARE YOU! *'OW DARE YOU!'*

Nanny Flannel realized that Iggy was so manic that he was out of control—and there was only one way to get him back to his senses. She marched across the kitchen, took careful aim, and swung the mop at Iggy's backside.

Whack! it went—and, with a yelp of surprise, Iggy jumped a metre into the air, clutching his bottom with both hands. A look of pure terror flooded his face. He stopped dancing and shouting. He dropped down from the table, scuttled to where Measle was standing and tried to hide behind him.

'You sssaid she wouldn't hit me wiv de mop, Mumps,' he whispered accusingly into Measle's ear. 'But she did—'an now I fink she is goin' to do it again!'

Nanny Flannel was glaring fiercely in their direction, the mop still held threateningly over her head, when suddenly the first pane of glass in the tall, floor-to-ceiling kitchen window cracked and splintered and fell to the floor with a shattering *crash!*

Everybody froze, staring with growing horror at the window. The whole frame was bending inwards, the wooden mouldings cracking, the panes of glass splintering—and the smell was now becoming almost more than anybody could bear without being sick.

Tinker's barking was becoming more and more frenzied, because *his* highly sensitive nose was being overwhelmed by the power of the stink. He couldn't believe anything could smell this strong! And this bad! Usually, Tinker didn't think anything smelt bad—just *interesting*. But this pong was beginning to choke him.

Mr Needle and Mr Bland put their hands to their faces and pinched their noses shut between finger and thumb. Apart from that, they didn't move. They were rooted to the spot and even their eyes seemed to be paralysed with terror.

Not so Nanny Flannel. The moment she heard the first pane of glass crash to the floor, she had turned and faced the horror, the mop held at the ready, as if it was a great two-handed sword.

'Measle dear!' she called, her old voice steady and firm. 'Measle, get out of here! Get out and lock the door behind you! Then run, dear! Run as fast as you can!'

Measle didn't move. He had no intention of leaving Nanny Flannel, or Iggy, or Tinker to their fates. He didn't mind so much about Mr Needle and Mr Bland, but he wasn't about to desert his friends! Besides, his curiosity was as strong as his fear. He wanted to see what this thing was—

He didn't have long to wait.

The pressure against the window was growing by the moment and, in the few seconds left before the whole frame gave way, Measle saw a very strange and horribly frightening thing.

He saw, by the light of the kitchen candles, that the whole of the outside of the window was covered by a thick film of yellowish-greenish-brownish slime which seemed to pulse and flex and slither against the weakening window. And then, without warning, a head—*a human head*—seemed to float past, buried deep within the transparent jelly—

And the head had eyes that seemed to be staring straight at Measle.

Eyes that glittered with a cold, calculating intelligence; the face framed by long, flowing hair and a short beard—

The face suddenly grinned at him. And, in that extraordinary moment, Measle knew who it was.

It was Toby Jugg.

THE WALLS ARE BREACHED!

There wasn't time for Measle to think about what this horrible sight meant, because a second later the entire window frame gave way with a creaking, splintering CRASH! It fell onto the kitchen floor in a jumble of broken wood and glass and the Slitherghoul fell in with it—or, at least, that part of the creature which had been pressing so hard against the glass. The rest of it was still outside but slowly it began to ooze its way through the gaping hole, adding to the slimy mass of jelly that lay in a great pile on top of the remains of the window.

Nanny Flannel took two paces forward, raised the mop high over her head and then brought it down hard on the leading edge of the Slitherghoul.

'Take that, you nasty thing!' she shouted. 'Take that! And that! And that!'

The stink inside the kitchen was overwhelming and Measle began to feel quite sick. Then he heard Iggy muttering in his ear.

'Coo! Dat sssmells ever ssso nice, don't it, Mumps? An' look at Miss Fwannel—she is bashin' de fing wiv de mop! I'm jussst glad she's not bashin' me!'

The Slitherghoul was getting bigger, as more and more of it slimed its way through the smashed window. It took no notice of Nanny Flannel's flailing mop, nor of Tinker's furious barking, not even when he darted forward and tried to nip at the very edge of the jelly. Instead, it simply oozed more and more of itself into the kitchen, lumping its enormous shape higher and higher, until the top of it brushed against the ceiling. Then, when most of it was inside the room, it acted—

Quick as a flash, before Nanny Flannel could react, the Slitherghoul whipped out a jelly tentacle and grabbed the old lady round her stout waist. It dragged her towards itself—

'Run, Measle! RUN!' yelled Nanny Flannel— then, a second later, the slime enveloped her and she was gone.

Measle stared with horror at the spot where Nanny Flannel had disappeared. It was the worst thing he'd ever seen—this great, stinking mound of jelly had simply swallowed his beloved Nanny

Flannel whole! She was gone—the one person other than his mum and dad whom he trusted with his life! And now all that was left between him and an identical fate were two useless warlocks, a wrathmonk who thought the smell of the monster was nice—and a faithful but very *small* dog!

Tinker kept up his furious barrage of barks and now had got up the courage to take several more nips at the leading edge of the jelly.

Poo! It tastes as bad as it smells! Horrible thing—get out of here!

Inside the Slitherghoul, something very interesting was taking place. For the last few moments, it had found itself using a different brain—

The reason the Slitherghoul was now looking out at the world through eyes that didn't belong to Toby Jugg was because of the extraordinary strength of Nanny Flannel's mind. The old lady had always been able to get everybody—even stubborn Sam Stubbs—to do exactly what she wanted them to do, so—after the initial shock of finding herself engulfed (*and then finding herself apparently still alive!*)—Nanny Flannel instantly tried to take charge.

For a few moments, she succeeded. She saw that Tinker was in imminent danger of being grabbed himself, because a finger of jelly was starting to extend towards him. Nanny Flannel, using all her power to overcome whatever was directing the creature, managed to pull the tentacle back and away from Tinker—

Instantly, she felt another mind—one at least as powerful as hers—push the tentacle forward again.

No! she thought. *No, I won't allow it!*

Once again, Nanny Flannel strained her brain—and, once again, the tentacle withdrew. Unfortunately, this action made Tinker even braver, because he assumed that the tentacle was pulling away from him because it was afraid, so he darted forward again, seized the smelly lump of jelly between his jaws and started to shake it furiously.

Instantly, Nanny Flannel's mind was overpowered —not just by Toby Jugg's but by several others' too. Nanny Flannel had no idea who these others could be, but Buford Cudgel, Griswold Gristle, Frognell Flabbit, and Officer Offal (all of whom had reason to hate the little terrier) joined their minds to Toby Jugg's and overwhelmed the thoughts of Nanny Flannel.

A second jelly tentacle whipped out and wrapped itself around Tinker. Tinker yelped and struggled—but then he too disappeared inside the Slitherghoul.

'NO!' screamed Measle.

It's not possible! he thought miserably. *My two best friends, gone! Just like that!*

Behind him, Measle heard Iggy snigger. Then he heard the little wrathmonk whisper, 'Coo! De nasssty old lady is gone! And de nasssty little doggie too! Coo! Disss is Iggy's lucky day!'

Measle was as unhappy as he'd ever been in his life, but he suddenly felt very angry too, particularly—at this precise moment—with Iggy Niggle. He was about to turn on the little wrathmonk when he saw what Mr Needle and Mr Bland were doing.

The two men were scrambling towards the door that led to the rest of the house. They each held a candle in a bottle. Mr Needle got to the door first. He grabbed the handle and wrenched it open, then he and Mr Bland, who was fighting to get past him, tumbled together out into the passage beyond. Measle saw Mr Needle push Mr Bland to one side—then he saw Mr Needle take hold of the edge of the door and, with one sweeping movement, slam it shut!

Measle reacted. He forced his legs into action—running quickly across the kitchen towards the door.

But, as he got close, he heard the distinct sound of a key turning in a lock—

Click.

Measle slammed against the door. He grasped the handle, turned it, and pulled hard—but the door didn't budge! He was trapped! Mr Needle and Mr Bland were so frantically desperate to get away from the monster in the kitchen that they had betrayed him!

'Open the door!' yelled Measle—but all he heard

was the pounding of two pairs of polished black shoes as Mr Needle and Mr Bland raced away down the corridor.

Measle turned round. If he was going to be swallowed by the Slitherghoul, he wanted to face it head-on.

The Slitherghoul seemed to be having some sort of problem. One minute it was pushing out a great jelly tentacle across the kitchen floor towards Measle, the next the same tentacle seemed to quiver and then withdraw, as if the huge, shapeless thing was unable to make up its mind.

Which was exactly what was happening.

Inside the Slitherghoul, a battle was raging. A battle of minds. On one side were the brains of Toby Jugg, Officer Offal, Griswold Gristle, Buford Cudgel, Frognell Flabbit, and Judge Cedric Hardscrabble—not to mention the rest of the wrathmonks from the Detention Centre, all of whom were quite happy to help in a venture, just as long as they were being really nasty and cruel to somebody.

On the other side of the battle stood Nanny Flannel. She wasn't entirely alone. Corky Pretzel, the young guard from the Detention Centre, was on her side. Corky was a good man but, unfortunately, he didn't possess a particularly strong mind. All the same, he knew instinctively which side he should be on and he matched his mind with Nanny Flannel's and, together, they fought as hard as they could—helped in no small way by the furious and determined doggy brain of Tinker, who certainly knew which side *he* was on.

But it was a losing battle. There were only three good minds on the friendly side and one of them belonged to a dog—with the result that, every time the Slitherghoul pulled itself back from attacking Measle, a moment later it would advance again. Each of these advances was twice the length of its retreats, which meant that the huge mound of jelly was moving, in a strange, jerky fashion, steadily across the kitchen floor towards Measle and Iggy Niggle.

There was no way out. The Slitherghoul's mass lay between them and the kitchen door and the *other* door—the one at his back which led to the rest of the house—was locked tight.

There must be something I can do! thought Measle desperately. *Or something Iggy can do—*

Of course! Iggy's got a spell! His lock-opening spell! It's the only one he can do, but it's perfect for this moment!

Measle whirled round and grabbed Iggy by the front of his old suit.

'Do your spell, Iggy! Do it now!'

Iggy wriggled uncomfortably in Measle's grip. 'Dat won't do nuffink on dat smelly fing,' he argued, his hooked nose twitching ecstatically.

'On the *door*, Iggy! Do your spell on the *door*!'

The Slitherghoul was inching closer and closer.

It extended a jelly tentacle towards Measle and Iggy, then, an instant later, it pulled it back inside itself again. The great mass jerked forward another half metre, then pulled back a little, before slithering forward again—

'On de door, Mumps?' said Iggy, in a puzzled voice. 'Wot door?'

'*This* one, Iggy!' yelled Measle, turning Iggy round and shoving him hard up against the wooden panels.

'Oh—dis one,' muttered Iggy. 'Okey-dokey. 'Ow many jelly beans will you give me?'

'A *squillion*!' shouted Measle, using Iggy's favourite number.

Iggy nodded eagerly and then looked expectantly at Measle.

'When you've done the spell, Iggy! I'll give them to you when you've done the spell!'

The stink in the kitchen was terrible. Measle glanced over his shoulder. The Slitherghoul was very close now and had, in fact, stopped moving forward. All it needed to do was extend a tentacle—

Inside the Slitherghoul, Nanny Flannel's brain screamed '*NO!*' It was a silent scream, of course—but a very powerful one. Corky Pretzel added his own thoughts and (in his own doggy way) so did Tinker—and the tentacle quivered and then withdrew again.

NO! GET HIM! shrieked Toby Jugg's mind and a

whole chorus of wrathmonk thoughts joined in: *Get him! Get him! Get him! Get him! GET HIM!*

And then Measle heard Iggy shout, '*Unka-ssssshhhriek gorgogasssshhh plurgholips!*'—and, without waiting a moment longer, Measle leaned past Iggy and grabbed the door handle. He twisted it hard and pulled even harder—and the door flew open! Measle pushed Iggy through the gap and then jumped through himself, and, as he did so, he thought he felt the lightest touch of something on his shoulder.

Once through, Measle turned and, grabbing the edge of the door, he pulled it as hard as he could. The door closed with a *bang!* right on the tip of a long jelly tentacle that was waving its way through the air, headed straight for Measle's head. The tip of the tentacle was cut cleanly away from the rest of the slimy thing. It fell to the floor with a squishy plop—then Measle watched as it turned away from him and Iggy. It slithered across the floor like a little worm and, flattening itself to the thickness of a slice of bread, it wriggled under the door and back into the kitchen.

Measle quickly turned the key in the lock and heard the bolt slide home with a satisfying click.

'Ssscuse me, Mumps,' said Iggy, in a whiny voice. 'Ssscuse *me*—but if you want dis door *locked*, den why did you make me do my ssspell to *open* it? Huh? Huh?'

'That thing was going to eat us, Iggy!' hissed Measle.

Iggy shook his head firmly. 'No, it wasn't,' he said, his big round fishy eyes glowing in the darkness of the passage. 'It only eats nasssty fings, like Miss Fwannel and de doggie. It won't eat us, coz we is *nice*.'

Iggy often made silly assertions like this and Measle had learned not to argue with him. Besides, there were more pressing matters to attend to—*literally*. There was a squishy thump against the door and Measle heard, quite distinctly, the sound of the timbers creaking.

'Come on, Iggy!' he said, grabbing the wrathmonk's damp hand. 'Come on—that door won't hold for long!'

Together, Measle and Iggy tore down the dark passage. They passed the open door of the dining room—

Measle skidded to a stop and Iggy bumped hard into his back.

'Ow!' said Iggy and was about to start a long, whiny complaint about how he didn't like it when people stopped suddenly without any warning, when Measle grabbed him and dragged him back to the dining room door. He pulled Iggy over to the sideboard. Then, letting go of him, Measle took hold of the glass jar full of jelly beans and yanked off the top.

'Hold out your hands, Iggy!' he said. 'I'm going to give you your squillion jelly beans!'

'Wot—now?' said Iggy, in a surprised voice. It wasn't often that he got what he asked for quite as quickly as this.

'Yes! Right now. We're going to fill your pockets full!'

'And dat is a sssquillion, is it?' asked Iggy, a little suspiciously.

'Yes! When your pockets are full, that's a squillion!'

Iggy grinned in the darkness. He'd always wanted to know just exactly how many a squillion was—and now he knew.

The little wrathmonk held out both his hands and Measle poured a stream of multi-coloured jelly beans into them. Iggy stuffed the beans into both his trouser pockets and then held out his hands for more.

Measle went on pouring—and Iggy went on pocket-stuffing—until there was no room in any of his clothes for more.

'That's it, Iggy,' said Measle firmly, because Iggy, with his pockets bulging, was holding his hands out again. 'That's your squillion jelly beans.'

From down the passage, there was the sound of wood cracking. The kitchen door was beginning to give way. Hurriedly, Measle tipped the small number of remaining jelly beans into his own hands and, as quickly as he could, he sorted out the paler yellow beans and stuffed them into his pockets.

'Come on, Iggy!'

Measle and Iggy darted out of the dining room. Measle took a quick look down the dark corridor. There, at the far end, was a little ragged circle of light. As he watched, the circle grew suddenly bigger and there was the noise of wood being torn apart. In a flash, Measle realized what was happening—the bolts and hinges on the kitchen door had held against the Slitherghoul's attack and now the monster was trying to rip a hole in the panels that would be large enough to let it squeeze through.

Measle grabbed Iggy's hand. It felt sticky. Measle peered at Iggy in the gloom and saw that the wrathmonk's mouth was stuffed full and Iggy's jaws were chomping up and down. The thin little face was wreathed in a blissful smile.

'Don't eat them all at once, Iggy!' hissed Measle. 'Save some for later!'

Iggy shrugged and then brought his other hand close to his face. Measle saw that it was full of jelly beans. Iggy peered at the heap and then started picking out one, then two, then a third bean from the pile. These he stuffed into the small outer breast pocket of his damp and shabby suit. Suddenly aware that Measle was staring at him, Iggy muttered, 'I is pickin' out de green ones, Mumps. I don't like de green ones.'

Measle wondered how Iggy could possibly see which ones were green and which ones weren't—in this gloom, all the jelly beans looked pretty much the same colour to him. But there was no time to ask, because at the far end of the corridor there was another ripping, wrenching, tearing sound—and Measle suddenly remembered that he'd heard that sound before, when Basil Tramplebone had become a giant cockroach and, using the creature's sharp, curved claws, had tried to dig his way into the plywood tunnel where Measle and his friends were hiding.

Then—as now—that sound meant it was time to go.

Measle pulled Iggy after him as they ran away towards the door of Sam Stubbs's study. The door was closed, but Measle saw a faint sliver of yellow light beneath it. Measle hurled himself against the door and it flew open and he and Iggy tumbled into the room.

Mr Needle and Mr Bland, clutching their two candles, were huddled together on the far side, behind Sam's big desk—and their eyes opened very wide when they saw Measle and Iggy Niggle.

'Why—M-Master M-Measle!' stammered Mr Bland. 'You've escaped! Er . . . m-may I b-be the first to offer m-my congratulations—'

'I s-second that!' announced Mr Needle, smiling insincerely.

'We—we were just trying to see if the telephone was working again,' said Mr Bland.

'Unfortunately, it doesn't appear to be,' said Mr Needle. He was about to say more but the look on Measle's face stopped him dead.

Measle took a step into the room and glared at the two men. Then he said, 'You locked me in there! You locked me and Iggy in the kitchen!'

'No, no,' said Mr Needle, in a shocked voice. 'We would never do that, would we, Bland?'

'Never, Needle!' said Mr Bland and he smiled a sickly smile and started to fiddle with the telephone.

Measle shook his head in disgust. No matter how nice these two men tried to be, they still were never to be trusted. He said, 'Well, I thought you'd like to know that the Slitherghoul is just about through the kitchen door and is going to be heading this way any second! So perhaps you ought not to stay in here, because this door won't hold it back either!'

'An' den it will eat you,' announced Iggy triumphantly. 'Dat old Sssquiffypoo will eat you *bofe*—coz you ain't nice!'

A waft of stinking air tickled Measle's nose. He darted to the open study door and peered down the passage. He could just make out a section of jelly that was starting to ooze its way through the ragged hole in the door. Measle turned and looked over his shoulder at the two frightened men.

'Iggy and I are going now,' he said, quite quietly. 'Do you want to come with us?'

Mr Needle looked at Mr Bland and Mr Bland looked at Mr Needle. Then they both looked at Measle and shook their heads in unison.

'You are welcome to join *us*, Master Measle,' said Mr Needle. 'We intend to barricade the door.'

'We shall use the available furniture,' said Mr Bland, pointing at the big desk.

'I don't think that'll stop it,' said Measle. 'Not for long.' He glanced again down the passage and saw that most of the Slitherghoul seemed to be through the hole in the door. Its jelly mass filled the end of the corridor right up to the ceiling.

'Well, good luck,' said Measle, knowing that he didn't really mean it. 'Come on, Iggy.' He and Iggy backed out into the corridor; Mr Needle crossed the room and, with a small, fearful smile, the man shut the door firmly in their faces.

Measle and Iggy ran further down the passage, until they reached the great staircase of Merlin Manor. There were a lot of windows here in the hallway and Measle could see everything quite clearly. The only question was—which way to go?

Up had always been the direction Measle had chosen in the past. He'd climbed the Ferris wheel at the Isle of Smiles, he and Toby had climbed the immensely tall spiral staircase inside the Wizards' Guild—*and perhaps this Slitherghoul thing can't climb stairs!*—but, even as he thought that, Measle guessed it probably wasn't true. All the same, up seemed better than sideways or forwards at this moment, so he grabbed Iggy's skinny elbow and said, 'We're going upstairs, Iggy! Come on!'

Iggy had never been upstairs at Merlin Manor. He'd hardly ever been inside Merlin Manor at all and the idea of actually going upstairs was very exciting. He reached into his trouser pocket, pulled out a handful of jelly beans and, making sure there were no green ones among them, he stuffed them into his mouth.

Together they hurried up the great curving staircase, and, all the time, Measle was wondering, *And then what? Where do we go next?*

The moment Mr Needle had closed the door in Measle's face, he and Mr Bland had started to build the barricade. They had shot the bolt at the top of the door and then, together, they had manhandled Sam's big desk across the room and shoved it tight against the door. Then they had moved everything else—the chairs, the filing cabinets, the bookshelves, and even the fine Persian rug—and had piled them up in a great jumbled heap on top of and round the base of the desk. When there was nothing left in the room that could be moved, Mr Needle and Mr Bland huddled together on the bare floor, their backs pressed against the wall. They held their candles in trembling hands and waited.

They didn't wait for long.

The Slitherghoul pulled the last of itself through the ragged hole in the kitchen door. Buford Cudgel's head—which was bigger than the head of anybody else inside the monster—had become stuck for a minute and this had slowed down the Slitherghoul a lot. But now the Slitherghoul was free and clear.

But a supporting beam over the kitchen door was now badly damaged.

This beam was made of oak and it was very old. Ever since Merlin Manor had been built, the beam had held up much of the stone wall above it. Over the years it had slowly weakened, and now, with the sudden stresses and strain put on it by the forceful blundering of the Slitherghoul, the beam quite suddenly gave way.

There was a creaking, cracking sound, quickly followed by a thunderous roar that lasted about three seconds—then a rattling noise as small stones fell and tumbled down a great mound of dusty rubble—then, silence.

The Slitherghoul ignored the whole event. It was intent on what was in *front* of it, not what was *behind*.

It moved on stickily down the dark passage. It saw, through Toby's eyes, the faint glowing line of light at the base of the study door.

Somebody's in there! thought Toby's brain. *Possibly the boy! Or perhaps even his baby sister, the fabulous Mallockee!*

The Slitherghoul pressed the great weight of its body against the door and felt it bend inwards. *This one will give way quickly*, thought the collective minds of Toby and the wrathmonks, because it's easier to break down a door that opens *away* from you.

Inside the study, Mr Needle and Mr Bland had heard the thunder when the kitchen beam gave way, and now they heard the creaking of the door timbers and they huddled a little closer.

'Why has it not gone after the boy?' hissed Mr Needle into Mr Bland's ear.

'The light!' whispered Mr Bland. 'It sees the light under the door!' Both men took deep breaths and blew out their candles, plunging the room into absolute darkness.

But it was too late. The Slitherghoul was now bracing the rear section of its body against the floor, walls, and ceiling of the corridor and was beginning to press harder against the door. The wood creaked and the nails in the frame began slowly to tear away from the wall with a squealing sound. A moment later, the whole structure broke free and was pushed forward into the room, shifting the desk backwards a metre and dislodging the piled-up furniture, so that it all crashed thunderously to the bare floor.

Mr Needle and Mr Bland crawled into the furthest corner of the study. The room, with its heavy curtains drawn, was pitch dark and they couldn't see a thing. But they could smell—and the stink was so terrible that it made Mr Bland suddenly cough and choke.

'Quiet, Bland!' whispered Mr Needle. 'It will hear us!'

The Slitherghoul didn't need to hear anything. It pushed the heavy desk to one side, as if it was no bigger than a matchbox. Then it extended a fat jelly tentacle and slid it across the room. Slowly, carefully, it felt its way along one wall—then another—*ah! There! Something alive!*

Mr Bland gasped as the tip of the tentacle touched his ankle. Then, in the pitch darkness, he screamed as the tentacle wrapped itself round his leg and started to drag him across the floor.

'Needle! Help me!' he shrieked. But Mr Needle didn't help him. Mr Needle pulled his own body into a tight, trembling ball and he crouched in the corner, shuddering with terror and trying to make himself as small as he possibly could. In his paralysed mind, there was a tiny spark of hope— *Perhaps the thing will be content with Bland? Perhaps it won't come after me as well? Perhaps it thinks that Bland was alone?*

Mr Needle heard Mr Bland scream steadily all the way across the room. Then there was a squelching sound and the screaming stopped abruptly. For a moment there was silence and Mr Needle's hopes rose a little. Then he heard it again—the unmistakable sound of a slimy, slithering tentacle, coming nearer and nearer and nearer—and suddenly Mr Needle lost all control of his mind and started screaming himself, well before the tip of the tentacle even touched him—

Standing at the top of the staircase and leaning over the banister, Measle and Iggy listened to the distant screaming. It was a horrible sound and it was something of a relief to Measle when it suddenly stopped. But Iggy needed an explanation.

'Wot's 'appening, Mumps?' he whispered, fearfully.

'I—I think it's got Mr Needle and Mr Bland,' said Measle.

'Oh, goody,' said Iggy. 'I don't like dose men. Dey is quite nasssty.'

Measle turned on Iggy and hissed angrily at him.

'Sometimes, Iggy, you make me so *cross*! Mr Needle and Mr Bland were guarding us! Well, they were *supposed* to be guarding us—and now they've gone! And so have Nanny and Tinker! Now there's nobody left but you and me! And that thing is going to come for us next! Don't you understand? It'll be coming for *us*!'

As the echoes of his voice died away, Measle became aware of another sound—a slushy, squelching, slithery noise, coming from somewhere below him. He leaned over the balcony and peered down into the gloomy stairwell.

The Slitherghoul had reached the foot of the stairs and was starting to slime its way up the first of the steps. Even in the dim light, Measle could see that it was now enormous. Not only that, but the thing seemed to be moving faster than before—it slid smoothly up the stairs, the individual steps causing its great jelly body to ripple as it passed over them.

'Come on, Iggy,' muttered Measle. 'It's moving quite fast. We've got to stay ahead of it.'

'Where is we goin'?' said Iggy, peering doubtfully over the banister at the approaching mound of jelly. 'Where *can* we go, Mumps?'

'I don't know, Iggy,' said Measle. And whether it was the terrible smell that wafted up the stairs, or whether it was the awful realization that he really had no idea what to do, Measle suddenly felt quite sick.

There was a cracking sound beneath them, then the landing on which they were standing shuddered and lurched sideways, nearly knocking Iggy and Measle off their feet. The cracking sound grew louder—then there was a deafening BANG! quickly followed by a thunderous CRASH! from far below. Both Measle and Iggy grabbed the railing and leaned over, staring downwards.

Most of the bottom half of the staircase was gone. It lay in a great, dusty pile on the floor of the hall. For a moment, Measle had the happy thought that the Slitherghoul had fallen with it. But then his eyes became accustomed to the darkness and he saw, to his horror, that the creature was only a few metres below him. At the moment when its great weight had caused the staircase to crack and then break (at its weakest point, which was right in the middle) the Slitherghoul had managed to shoot out two thick tentacles of jelly and wrap them around the remains of the banister rail above it. The stairs had fallen away beneath it, leaving the Slitherghoul hanging in mid-air—and now it was slowly but steadily dragging itself upwards. Once it reached safety, it lay still for a moment, as if to make sure that no sudden movement on its part would cause the rest of the staircase to fall as well. Then, when nothing happened, it began to slither upwards again.

Measle realized it would only be a matter of seconds before the Slitherghoul was on them—

and, in the same moment, he knew that there was really only one place they could go now. There were no doors on the upper floors of Merlin Manor that were strong enough to keep the Slitherghoul away—and now there was certainly no escape back down the stairs. Besides, the idea of endlessly running from the monster *inside* the house was obviously pointless; which left only one possible escape route.

Measle grabbed Iggy's skinny arm and dragged him away from the stair head. Together, they ran down the long corridor, arriving, a moment later, at another, narrower set of stairs. Measle raced up them, dragging Iggy behind him.

'Where is we goin', Mumps?' gasped Iggy, stumbling to keep up.

'The roof, Iggy!' panted Measle. 'We're going to climb out onto the roof!'

ON THE ROOF

Measle knew a good way onto the roof. It was through his bedroom window.

Measle's bedroom was right at the top of the house, which was how he was able to get onto the roof from there, by climbing out through its tall window.

He wasn't supposed to do this, but he did, a lot. Or rather, he *had* done, until Sam found out that he'd been going up there regularly. It was one of the few times that Measle had seen him angry.

'Merlin Manor's roof is very old and a lot of the tiles are probably loose,' Sam had scolded. 'You step on one of those and you could easily slide off! And, last time I looked, you couldn't fly, could you?'

Of course, by the time that Sam had found out

that Measle had been climbing about on the roof, Measle already knew every inch of it.

And now the roof could be an escape route—

Measle burst into his dark bedroom and instinctively he reached out and flipped the light switch on the wall. Nothing happened. The room remained dark, but there was enough moonlight coming through the tall window to let Measle see his way across the floor. He pulled Iggy in and then shut the door and locked it.

'Is dis where you sssleep, Mumps?' said Iggy, looking round the room, his big fishy eyes round with wonder.

'Yes, Iggy.'

Iggy sniffed. 'It ain't very nice, is it?' he said. 'Not as nice as my little 'ouse. Well, ssstands to reason, don't it? It's rainin' in 'ere, ain't it? An' it *never* rains inssside my little 'ouse!'

It was true. Iggy's rain cloud had followed them as they moved through Merlin Manor and was now positioned directly over Iggy's head and dribbling its tiny drops down onto Iggy's woollen hat.

Measle marched over to the window and heaved it upwards. Without hesitation, he swung one leg, then the other, over the windowsill. Then he held out his hand and said, 'Come on, Iggy. It's quite safe—you can climb out too.'

Iggy scrambled through the opening and then stood close to Measle. They were on a narrow ledge, with a low parapet on the far side. Up here, all the windows led out onto this ledge, which ran round the whole house. The roof itself slanted steeply up behind them—and the ledge was the only flat part of the whole structure.

Measle leaned past Iggy and slid the window down. Then he peered along the side of the building, his eyes straining in the gloom. He leaned out further, but he still couldn't see what he was looking for.

'Come on, Iggy,' he muttered, moving a couple of metres sideways along the ledge and then leaning both hands against the steep tiles of the roof. 'We've got to climb up there. Do you think you can manage it?'

Iggy wrinkled his long nose in derision. '*Manage* it? *Courssse* I can manage it, Mumps!' he said, dismissively. 'I was a *burglarider*, wasn't I? I was de *bessst* burglarider in de whole world! I could climb anyfink, couldn't I?'

Measle had forgotten about Iggy once being a burglar. He grinned at the little wrathmonk in the darkness and then patted his damp shoulder.

'Come on then,' he said. 'Race you to the top!'

Iggy won easily. By the time Measle reached the pointed top of the roof, Iggy was already there, sitting astride the sloping tiles as if he was on a horse. Measle, panting slightly, joined him, sitting close behind him. This wasn't the highest section of Merlin Manor's roof—on the other side of the house there was a tower room that was quite a bit higher—but, even so, Measle was able to see all the way across the roof in every direction.

And then he saw what he'd thought he might see.

There, about forty metres away, hung a large, dense, and very black cloud, releasing a steady downpour of torrential rain onto the old tiles. The water streamed down the steep slopes in all directions, gurgling and splashing into the gutters and, in places, overflowing the channels before disappearing, in little glittering waterfalls, down into the shadows below.

The cloud was moving.

Measle saw that it was coming steadily towards them.

Just because he'd been running away—and thinking miserably about the horrible thing that had happened to Nanny Flannel and to Tinker—that didn't mean that Measle's brain had stopped working. The thought process had started the moment he'd seen Toby Jugg floating inside the jelly mass of the Slitherghoul.

If Toby's in there, then perhaps there are others? Perhaps that's where all the wrathmonks from the Detention Centre went—inside *the Slitherghoul?*

Another clue to this idea had been the sudden downpour of rain outside the kitchen door, only seconds before the Slitherghoul had started to try and force its way in—and that was why Measle had expected to see a wrathmonk cloud hovering over the Slitherghoul's position. The fact that his guess had been right didn't make Measle feel any better. In fact, the sight of the great, black, billowing cloud made him feel much, much worse.

'Coo! Wossat, Mumps?' breathed Iggy into his ear.

'That's a wrathmonk rain cloud, Iggy.'

'Ooh,' said Iggy, uncertainly. 'Dat must be a very big wraffmonk, Mumps!'

'It's not just one wrathmonk. It's *lots* of them. And they're the *bad* wrathmonks! From the *Other Place*, Iggy!'

Iggy didn't really want to have anything to do with bad wrathmonks from the Other Place since he'd promised to be on his best behaviour. This was the main condition that the Wizards' Guild had imposed on him, if he wanted to go on living at Merlin Manor with the Stubbs family, that is. And Iggy *did* want to—very much.

'But—what are ssso many bad wraffmonks doin' 'ere, Mumps?' said Iggy, twisting his head over his shoulder and talking out of the side of his mouth.

'I'm pretty sure that they're all inside the Slitherghoul.'

This concept was a bit too complicated for Iggy—but his little brain just managed to reason that, if the wrathmonks were *inside* something, then that might mean that they couldn't get at him or Mumps, and this made him feel much better.

'Oh, well, dat's all right, den,' he said, cheerfully.

Measle had been watching the cloud carefully. It was much closer now but it kept delaying its forward movement by a number of shifts sideways —first left, then right, then left again—

Measle realized what was happening. The Slitherghoul was investigating each room on the long corridor. Most of the rooms were empty, or were used for storage, which explained why the Slitherghoul didn't seem to be wasting much time searching them.

Measle heard the distant sound of breaking wood.

And now the leading edge of the rain cloud drifted over Iggy's head, and first Iggy and then Measle found themselves sitting under a drenching torrent of cold rain.

Measle had to shout over the noise of the downpour. 'It's in my bedroom, Iggy!'

The Slitherghoul was, indeed, just entering Measle's room. The fact that *this* door—unlike the others on the corridor—was locked was of considerable interest, and it had taken only a moment to smash the door down. But the room was empty and the creature was about to slime its way back out into the passage when something inside itself caught at its attention.

The something was Tinker. Tinker recognized the room immediately. *It was where he and the smelly kid slept!*

For a fraction of a second, Tinker's doggy mind was the strongest one there and it was this surge of thought that the Slitherghoul detected. Quickly, it switched to Toby's mind.

This is the boy's room! Might the boy still be here?

The Slitherghoul spread its mass over Measle's carpet, using a dozen extended tentacles to feel into every corner. One tentacle yanked open Measle's wardrobe and rummaged stickily among his clothes. Another felt carefully under the bed—

Not here! The boy is not here! thought Toby, irritably. Besides, he wasn't all that interested in the boy. It wasn't the boy he'd come for—it was Lee Stubbs and her little girl, the Mallockee! *Why waste all this time searching for a boy?*

Toby began to force the Slitherghoul to leave the bedroom.

Nanny Flannel's eyes were the ones that saw the little crack at the bottom of the window frame. Nanny Flannel knew all about Measle's expeditions onto the roof and the moment she saw the narrow opening she guessed where Measle and Iggy might be. Quickly, she wiped the idea out of her mind and started to join with Toby's mind in urging the Slitherghoul out of the room.

But another mind had caught her thought—

Griswold Gristle was deeply resentful of the way Toby Jugg had taken over everything. That a mere warlock should think he should be the one to lead them all! *No matter that his brain is more powerful than mine*, thought Griswold, furiously. *I should be the one to control where this creature goes and what it does!*

And what about me? What about what I want? came another thought, and Griswold recognized the brutish stubbornness of Buford Cudgel.

And me? came another, and this time Griswold heard the whiny tones of Frognell Flabbit.

Last—and very much least—came a feeble little thought from Judge Cedric Hardscrabble. *Griswold, dear friend—don't leave me! Don't leave me!*

Griswold sent a powerful brainwave out to his three friends.

We mussst ssstick together! he cried. *We mussst stick together by* thinking *together! There are other minds here, my friends, powerful minds! But if we ssstick together, we can be the masters here! Are we agreed?*

Yes! came the rumbling thought from Buford Cudgel.

Yes! came the whiny, scratchy thought from Frognell Flabbit.

Yes! We musst ssstick together, dear friends! came the mumbling, muddled thought from what passed for Judge Cedric's brain.

Very well! cried Griswold's mind. *Now, what is it that we four want?*

The boy!

The boy!

Oh, is that what we want?—and Griswold realized that this last thought was from his foolish old friend, the judge.

Yesss, Cedric. We want the boy!

All four wrathmonk brains were now thinking the same thought—and it was the power of their collective minds that stopped the Slitherghoul in its tracks.

No! screamed Nanny Flannel's mind. *Leave this room! There is nothing here!*

There are other, more important matters! shouted Toby's brain—and, for a moment, these two powerful personalities became dominant inside the Slitherghoul.

Who else is with us? shrieked Griswold. *Who else wishes to hunt down the boy? That evil boy, who has done usss all ssso much harm! That ssson of Ssstubbs, the mossst wicked family in the world! Come—join usss! Join usss!*

Immediately, several of the wrathmonks who had been locked up alongside Griswold and Buford and Frognell and Judge Cedric sent silent cries through the jelly—*YESSS! We will join you! The boy—hunt for the boy!*

Griswold recognized the cocky voice of Mungo MacToad among them—and then an unexpected voice joined in:

I want to get that young fellow, too! Count me in as well!

The voice was familiar to Griswold but, for a

couple of seconds, he couldn't place its owner. Then he realized who it was.

It was the voice of Officer Offal.

Officer Offal was mortally afraid of the wrathmonks who had been in his charge—and now he found himself floating among them! He had no idea if they could harm him under these circumstances but it had occurred to him that perhaps by joining them in their hunt for the boy (a boy he thoroughly detested, of course) then maybe they might soften their attitude towards him?

Ho, yes! he boomed. *I'm with you, lads! I'm on your side, wrathies!*

Griswold Gristle heard Officer Offal's falsely friendly offer—an offer from a person he loathed with every fibre of his soft white body! But he loathed Officer Offal a lot less than he loathed Measle Stubbs.

Why, thank you, Officer Offal! cried Griswold, trying to inject as much sincerity into his thoughts as he possibly could. *With your help, we shall undoubtedly sssucceed!*

And now there were just too many minds in opposition to Toby and Nanny Flannel. Besides, Toby and Nanny Flannel had entirely *different* reasons for wanting the Slitherghoul to give up chasing Measle, and that weakened their wills a lot.

As for Corky Pretzel—apart from being utterly confused by everything that had happened to them, he was a simple man who was accustomed to being *told* what to do by his senior officers, with the result that he lay quiet and still inside the Slitherghoul, hoping that nobody would notice him.

And Mr Needle and Mr Bland were doing pretty much the same, since they were now surrounded by a group of wrathmonks, most of whom they had personally escorted down into the depths of the Detention Centre.

So, for the foreseeable future, the wrathmonks were in control.

It was Frognell Flabbit who noticed the open window. A sudden gust of wind blew a scattering of rain in through the opening—and the Slitherghoul turned and slithered across the floor towards it.

SLIPPERY SLOPES

'We've got to move, Iggy,' said Measle, through chattering teeth.

The pounding rain had soaked through their clothes and both he and Iggy were shivering with cold. And besides, the thought that the Slitherghoul must now be directly beneath him made Measle want to put some distance between them.

Together, they started to move along the ridge, inching their way slowly over the tiles. Soon they came out from under the rain cloud and Iggy stopped moving but Measle pushed him gently between his shoulder blades and said, 'Go on, Iggy—we've got to get further away.' Iggy started moving again and only when they reached the far end of the ridge did Measle tap him on the back and say, 'OK, Iggy—that's far enough.'

In fact, they couldn't go any further even if they wanted to. This section of the roof ended here and in front of Iggy was a sheer drop to the ground below.

Measle twisted his body and looked back over his shoulder and saw, to his horror, that a slow-moving mound of jelly was oozing its way up the tiles, towards the spot on the ridge where they had just rested. The Slitherghoul was a good thirty metres away but, at the speed the thing was moving, it wouldn't be all that long before it would catch up with them.

For the first time in a long while, Measle had no idea what to do next. He and Iggy were trapped— and it was all his fault! Why had he imagined that they would find safety up here on the roof? Now there was nowhere to go—and there was nothing they could do to save themselves—

Measle felt Iggy wriggling behind him and he turned his head back in time to see the wrathmonk scrambling to his knees. Without a word, Iggy took hold of Measle's shoulders and then, very carefully, he clambered over Measle, so that he was between him and the slow-moving pile of slime, which had reached the ridge of the roof and was beginning to slither steadily towards them both. Iggy sat down again, his spindly legs hanging on either side of the ridge. He leaned forward and began to scoot himself towards the Slitherghoul. Measle caught hold of the back of Iggy's coat.

'What are you doing?' he hissed.

'I'm goin' to breave on it,' said Iggy over his shoulder.

'*Breathe* on it? Why? What good will that do?'

'It won't do it *any* good, Mumps!' said Iggy, irritably. 'Coz it's a bug, see? An' my breaving sssspell kills bugs! Ssso I'm goin' to breave on it!'

'But, Iggy, that's not a bug!'

'Well, it *looks* like a bug, Mumps,' said Iggy. 'An' dat *makes* it a bug! Ssso *dere!*' The next moment, he moved forward with a powerful jerk, wrenching his coat out of Measle's grasp. Before Measle could lean out and grab the coat again, Iggy had managed to put a metre and a half between them and now was moving along the ridge as fast as he could.

'No, Iggy! Come back!' yelled Measle—but Iggy took no notice. If anything, he scooted along a little faster, rapidly closing the gap between himself and the Slitherghoul.

Using the eyes of Griswold Gristle, the Slitherghoul saw the strange little person coming steadily towards it. Griswold's mind was momentarily puzzled; he recognized the small wrathmonk from before and saw no particular danger from him. *If needs be, we shall absorb him*, he thought, *but we are after that boy! That boy, sitting there at the end of the ridge, so helpless! So exposed! We have him now!*

When Iggy got to within a couple of metres of the leading edge of the mass of jelly, he leaned forward, took a deep breath and breathed out as hard as he could. When nothing happened, he shouted, 'Ho! You want sssome more, you bad Sssquiffypoo, you!' And he took another breath and blew it out at the Slitherghoul—and the Slitherghoul simply kept moving forward—

Iggy took another breath—

The leading edge of the slime touched Iggy's knees—

From the far end of the ridge, Measle saw everything. He saw Iggy begin to try to scramble backwards. He saw the mass of the Slitherghoul rear upwards. He saw Iggy raise his arms to cover his head. He saw the jelly drop down and over the little wrathmonk, enveloping him completely. And then he saw that Iggy was gone and that the great slimy mass was advancing steadily towards him, much of its jelly body hanging down on either side of the ridge as it oozed its way along—

With Iggy swallowed up, Measle felt as alone as he'd ever felt in his whole life. More alone than when he was running from Basil Tramplebone! More alone than when facing the great dragon Arcturion! More alone than when he found himself betrayed by Toby Jugg! At least he'd had Tinker with him all those times! But now, he had nobody! All that stood between him and the Slitherghoul was a fast-diminishing length of roof!

I can't just sit here and wait for the end! thought Measle, desperately. *Perhaps—perhaps there's something I can throw at it!* Measle's hands scrabbled over the rough tiles, testing each in turn until he found one that felt a little loose. Measle pulled at it with all his strength. The tile shifted under the stress and, suddenly, it cracked in half. Measle felt a swift, searing pain across the palm of his hand. He looked down. There was a line of blood, oozing from what looked like a deep cut. Measle grimaced—*it really hurts!*

But there was no time to worry about a cut hand. The Slitherghoul was squelching closer and closer—

Measle lifted the broken tile. It felt heavy and solid. He raised it over his head and, using only his unhurt hand, he hurled the tile towards the Slitherghoul. It fell short, clattering onto the roof and then sliding rapidly down the steep angle. It hit the parapet and bounced, flying over the low wall and into the darkness below. Seconds later, Measle heard it break with a distant crash. Frantically, he pulled at another tile and, as he did so, the Slitherghoul suddenly paused in its forward motion. The back half of the thing lumped up against the front half and then, clumsily, slithered sideways, so that almost half of the mass of jelly was now draped over one side of the roof, with the front half still balanced across the ridge.

Measle, using both hands and ignoring the pain,

threw the second tile and this one struck the Slitherghoul square on its leading edge—and a little more of the mass of jelly slid sideways. Now, only a third of the creature clung to the ridge; the rest of it lay against the steep slope of one side of the roof. To his excitement, Measle saw that its great weight was slowly pulling it sideways and the torrential rain that poured down on the thing wasn't helping the situation either. The water was making the tiles slippery and the greater part of the Slitherghoul was having difficulty getting a grip on the slick surface.

Throwing stuff at it was working! Measle yanked at another tile and then threw it hard. It bounced off the Slitherghoul as if the thing was made of rubber and the Slitherghoul lost a little more of its grip on the ridge tiles, letting even more of its vast mass slide sideways.

There was a slow, rending, ripping sound, as the ridge tiles beneath the front third of the Slitherghoul were dragged out of their settings. They crumbled into fragments beneath the great weight of the creature and began to slide down the slope. With nothing to hold it in place, the mass of jelly lurched sideways and then slid, slowly at first but with gathering speed, down the steep and slippery slope of the roof. Measle watched with awe as it slithered—like a pat of butter in a hot frying pan—down towards the roof's edge. He saw it shoot out a number of jelly tentacles, waving them in a frantic bid to find something to cling to. Then he saw the whole huge mass pile up against the low wall of the parapet. More and more jelly gathered there in a growing heap, until the narrow ledge could contain no more. The excess jelly flowed over the top of the wall and, within three seconds, the rest followed, sliding soundlessly into the darkness below.

A moment later, there was a distant, squelching THUD!

Through all his feelings of misery and loneliness and pain, Measle couldn't help the sudden lightening of his heart. He'd done it! He'd saved himself!

And then the horror of the situation returned, plunging him back into frightened despair. There was no reason to think that the Slitherghoul was dead. A thing that could ooze its way through narrow holes, that could smash down heavy doors—a thing without a bone of its own in its entire body—a thing like that might easily survive a fall from a rooftop!

There was only one way to find out.

Measle sat quite still and watched the rolling billows of the nearby rain cloud. For half a minute it hung quite still in the night air, dropping its heavy fall of rain down onto the spot where the Slitherghoul had landed far below.

Then, with a sick feeling growing in the pit of his stomach, Measle saw the cloud start to drift slowly sideways. He watched as it moved along the side of the house, then it turned a corner and drifted out of sight behind the tall tower.

It could mean only one thing. The Slitherghoul was still alive!

What would it do now?

Trying not to use his cut hand, Measle scooted himself back along the ridge. When he got to the section where the tiles had been torn away, he found himself crawling along on the rough wood of an ancient beam. Measle could feel slime and his face wrinkled in disgust. Even the sticky trail that the Slitherghoul left behind stank to high heaven!

Soon, he was back at the point directly above his bedroom. Carefully, he turned onto his stomach and inched his way backwards down the steep slope of the roof. His toes touched the flat part of the ledge and he pushed himself upright. There, a couple of metres away, was the open window. Measle quickly stepped over the sill and dropped down onto the bedroom floor. In the gloom, he could make out the shattered remains of his door—and he could smell the terrible stink of the Slitherghoul's slime, which lay all over the floor in a thin film.

Measle shivered. He was soaked through and very cold. He pulled off his wet clothes and took clean dry ones from his wardrobe. He wrapped a

handkerchief round his injured hand and tied it, using his teeth and his good hand to get the knot tight. He was just finishing dressing when he heard a sound from beyond the open window.

A scrabbling, scrambling, pushing, pulling, heaving sound.

To Measle's ears, it sounded as if something was climbing steadily up the outer wall of Merlin Manor.

Since there was nobody left at Merlin Manor but him, Measle realized what it must be.

His heart was thumping in his chest like a wheezy old pump and his legs felt weak. Slowly, without taking his eyes off the window, Measle started to shuffle backwards towards the smashed remains of his bedroom door.

Where can I possibly go this time? There's nowhere to hide, there's nowhere that's safe!

Measle's slow backward progress was halted suddenly when his heel caught against a smashed piece of wood on the floor. He staggered for a second, then lost his balance and sat down heavily among the remains of the door.

Something rose up above the parapet and filled the open window. A dark shadow blotted out the moonlight and loomed over Measle—it smelt really bad!—then it moved over the sill and flopped down onto the bedroom floor with a thud.

'Oh, dere you are, Mumps! I fort you might be 'ere ssstill—and you is! Dat was clever of me to fink dat, wasn't it? Huh? Huh?'

BRUISED FEELINGS

'Iggy?'

'Wot you doin', Mumps? Sssittin' dere in de dark. An' wot you done to de door, huh? It's all sssmashed up. Coo—your dad's goin' to be ever ssso cross!'

Measle scrambled to his feet, ran across the room, threw both his arms round Iggy's neck, and hugged him fiercely.

'Iggy! I don't believe it! You—you were swallowed up! And now you're here! But *how*? How did you get out of the Slitherghoul?'

Iggy took hold of Measle's wrists and gently disentangled himself. Then he lifted his long hooked nose in the air, closed his eyes, and took on the air of somebody who was deeply offended.

'I did not *get* out of de Sssquiffypoo,' he said, in a pained voice. 'De Sssquiffypoo *ssspitted* me out! Jusst like dat! Like I didn't tassste nice, or sssumfink! Jussst fink of dat, Mumps! Me, wot tastes luvverly! And dat ssstupid old Sssquiffypoo, it jussst spitted me out!'

Iggy took a deep breath and sighed heavily at the injustice of it all. Then he said, sorrowfully, 'It hurt my feelin's, Mumps. I never been ssspitted out before!'

Measle's happiness at finding Iggy alive and well and *outside* the Slitherghoul was tempered a little by the discovery that Iggy was covered from head to toe in a thin layer of smelly slime—and a lot of that slime had come off on him, too. Using his wet shirt, which he'd dropped on the floor, Measle started wiping the slime from both of them.

'But, Iggy—don't you see—it's *wonderful* that the Slitherghoul spat you out!'

'Huh!' said Iggy, dismissively. 'Well, *I* fink it was very rude!'

It took a while to persuade Iggy to get over his hurt feelings, but eventually Measle managed to get the story out of him. At the end of its long fall, the Slitherghoul had landed with a great squelching thump on the ground and had lain there, not moving, for several seconds. Iggy himself suffered no ill effects from the long fall and, in fact, felt rather comfortable floating about in the soft jelly. He'd sensed a number of minds reach out to him, but he'd pretty much ignored them—he was too busy wondering whether or not he liked this new experience. Apart from the vague thought that, if he was going to spend a lot of time inside this thing, then he might start to miss Mumps a bit, and then the stronger thought that he'd *certainly* miss Matilda a lot more, apart from those hazy feelings of loss, on the whole he was rather enjoying himself.

And then, quite suddenly, he'd felt a constriction round his body, a sudden shoving sensation against the top of his head, and, a moment later, he'd found himself squeezed, like toothpaste from a tube, out onto the cold wet ground. Iggy had sat there, a little dazed, and had watched the Slitherghoul turn away from him and then slime its way off alongside the wall of the great house, until at last it turned the distant corner and was lost to sight.

Like most people who have fallen a fair distance and survived, Iggy had looked up towards the roof high above him. His eye had been caught by a stout-looking iron drainpipe that ran from the gutters all the way down the wall to an open spout at the bottom. It was the type of drainpipe that Iggy had often used when he was a burglar—he could shin up one of those as easily as a monkey— and it crossed his fuddled mind that perhaps his buddy Mumps was still up there on the roof, waiting for him? Feeling more and more offended at the way he'd been so ignominiously ejected, Iggy had started to climb the drainpipe. It was more difficult than usual, because of the slime that covered his hands and feet. That made things terribly slippery and several times Iggy had slithered a metre or two back down the pipe. But he was stronger than he looked and his grip on the iron pipe was like a steel vice and, quite soon, he reached the parapet. From there, it was a quick hop over the windowsill and into Mumps's bedroom.

'But—but why did the Slitherghoul spit you out, Iggy?' asked Measle, wiping the last of the slime from Iggy's coat.

'Coz it's got no *manners*, dat's why!' said Iggy, firmly.

Measle threw the smelly, slimy shirt into the far corner of the dark room. He was thinking furiously.

There must be a reason! There must be a reason why the Slitherghoul swallowed everybody else and kept them inside it, but not Iggy! Why? Why did it reject him and not any of the others?

Another thought occurred to Measle. It was to do with how he'd dislodged the Slitherghoul from the roof. It was all too *easy*! Surely a creature like that, which could change its shape, which could fall all that way without hurting itself, which could smash down doors and swallow any number of people whole—surely a monster as powerful as that wouldn't be bothered by a few roof tiles? And yet it had suddenly slumped to one side—

Then Measle remembered that it had slumped to one side *before* he'd ever hit it with a tile! Something other than a hurled tile had caused it to lose its grip. When it had slithered down the roof and piled its jelly mass against the low parapet, why hadn't it used its tentacles and grabbed hold, and hung on tight? Why had it simply allowed itself to flow over the top of the low wall and then plummet to the ground? It couldn't have been because of a few tiles.

Click, click, click, went Measle's agile brain.

The Slitherghoul had started to behave oddly immediately after it had swallowed Iggy . . .

'I think you made it feel sick, Iggy!'

Iggy's eyebrows shot to the top of his head. He stared at Measle, a look of outrage plastered across his face.

'Wot? *Wot?* I did *WOT*?'

'Er . . . I think you made it feel sick.'

Iggy glared at Measle for several silent seconds. Then he lifted his long, bent nose in the air and, staring haughtily up at the ceiling, he said, 'Ho! Dat is *charmin'*, dat is! Dat is de *nicessst* fing wot you 'ave ever sssaid to me, Mumps! Dat I make people sssick! Fank you! Fank you *ssso* much!'

It was strange how easily Iggy's feelings could be hurt. Measle realized he was going to have to do some fast talking if he wanted any co-operation from the little wrathmonk.

'Oh, I didn't mean you make *people* sick! We all love you, you know that!'

'No, I don't,' muttered Iggy, still staring up at the ceiling.

'Well, we *do*, Iggy! Look, what I meant was . . . um . . . the Slitherghoul spat you out because I think you tasted of something it doesn't like! And that makes you special, you see?'

'Ssspecial?'

'Yes! Very special! The Slitherghoul swallowed up a whole lot of people—good people as well as bad people—but it spat you out because you're special!'

Iggy lowered his gaze and looked at Measle out of the corner of one fishy eye. 'An' bein' ssspecial like dat—dat is a *good* fing, is it?'

'Yes! It's a *very* good thing! It means that you're safe from it! It means that it won't swallow you up, even if it wants to! It means . . . it means . . . it means that you're *stronger* than it is!'

Iggy—who in many ways was rather like a little boy—enjoyed being told how strong he was. He relaxed his stiff posture and nodded smugly.

'Well, *courssse* I is stronger dan dat old Sssquiffypoo, Mumps. I is ssstronger dan everyfing! I is ssstronger dan a Squiffypoo, I is ssstronger dan a car, I is ssstronger dan a train, I is ssstronger dan a . . . dan a . . . dan a—'

While Iggy was desperately trying to think what else he was stronger than, his hand crept to one of his pockets, dived in and came out with a fistful of jelly beans. Iggy poked around, removing the green ones and depositing them in his breast pocket. Then he threw the rest straight into his open mouth.

Iggy's mouth was smeared with sugar.

Click, click, click, went Measle's mind.

Can that be it? he wondered. *Could it be Iggy's awful diet of nothing but sugar that made the Slitherghoul spit him out? There are other wrathmonks inside the monster and it hasn't rejected any of them, and there are other ordinary people in there too, including a dog, and they haven't been spat out, either! Only Iggy—and the only thing different about Iggy that I can think of is what he eats, which I'm pretty sure isn't what any of the others trapped inside the Slitherghoul eat . . .*

'Maybe you taste too sweet, Iggy!'

The muscles in Iggy's face went into one of their wriggling, writhing contortions, as Iggy tried desperately to work out if Measle had said something nice, or something insulting. Eventually, Iggy decided that Measle was being complimentary.

'Ho—well, fank you, Mumps. I *is* quite sssweet, actually.'

Click, click, click . . .

'So, Iggy, if the Slitherghoul doesn't like sweet things, maybe we can find a way of making it go away! Of stopping it eating us!'

''Ow?' said Iggy, doubtfully.

'I don't know. Maybe . . . maybe we could throw sugar at it!'

The thought of throwing perfectly good sugar away was almost more than Iggy could bear and he started his facial contortions again. Then, seeing Measle's eager eyes staring at him, with excitement written all over them, Iggy's face muscles settled down and he said, 'Well, maybe we could throw jussst a *little* bit at it? Dat way, we could find out if it don't like it—an' if it don't care, den we won't throw any more, right?'

'Right!' said Measle, who was well aware of how important it was to Iggy that there was a plentiful supply of sugar at Merlin Manor.

'But all de sugar is in de kitchen,' said Iggy, in a pensive voice. In the back of his very small mind was the thought that, if they couldn't *get* to the distant kitchen, then they wouldn't be able to get to the *sugar*, which meant that there wouldn't be any sugar-throwing at all, which meant—

'Yes, Iggy,' said Measle. 'So, we're going to have to find a way down there, aren't we?'

'I come up de pipe fingy,' said Iggy smugly. 'Bet you can't do dat, Mumps.'

Measle walked quickly over to the window and leaned out as far as he could. He stretched his body across the narrow ledge and then looked down, over the low parapet. The thick, black, cast-iron pipe was right there and Measle peered along its length, seeing how the distance made it seem narrower and narrower the closer it got to the ground.

The ground was a very long way off.

The drainpipe looked smooth and slippery.

His hand was throbbing.

Normally, Measle was game to try pretty much anything, as long as it looked as if it might be fun. He even liked doing quite dangerous things, like climbing about on old roofs and going for motorbike rides with Nanny Flannel—but he also knew his limitations. While Iggy, a once-professional burglar wrathmonk, might be able to shin up and down drainpipes with ease, a twelve-year-old boy with a hurt hand was probably going to find it impossible.

Measle withdrew his head and rejoined Iggy, who was chomping away at another mouthful of jelly beans.

'You're right, Iggy. I don't think I can climb down that way. I've hurt my hand, too.'

Since he was a wrathmonk, Iggy didn't care a jot about people getting hurt, as long as it wasn't him. Or Matilda. He didn't like it when Matilda got hurt, but a lot of his concern for her was because of the terrible noise her powerful lungs could produce when she was upset about something. Iggy glanced briefly at Measle's bandaged hand and said, 'Huh! Dat is nuffink! Now, when Miss Fwannel hit me wiv de mop—dat *really* hurt!'

Measle knew better than to argue with Iggy. 'I bet it did,' he said. 'But the thing is—we've got to get down to the kitchen and, if I can't climb down, how are we going to do it?'

Iggy thought for a moment, his face muscles doing their usual contortions. Then he said, brightly, 'I could frow you off de roof?'

Measle sighed. 'Good idea—except that would kill me.'

'Not if I didn't frow you very hard.'

Measle shook his head, but Iggy's idiotic idea was leading him on to one that might just work.

'We could make a rope, Iggy! We could make a rope out of all the bedclothes, like escaping prisoners do! And then—then you could lower me down!'

'I could do *wot?*' said Iggy, doubtfully.

'You could lower me down to the ground, Iggy! You're very strong! Don't you remember rescuing me from that suit of armour that time? You pulled me up by my hair, didn't you?'

Iggy's face cleared. 'I did, didn't I?' he said, in a smug voice. 'Okey-dokey, Mumps. Let's do dat!'

For the next half hour, Measle and Iggy were very busy. They started with the bedclothes from Measle's bed—stripping off the two sheets and knotting the ends tightly together. Iggy couldn't help with the knotting, that was far too complicated for him, but he was quite happy trotting down the narrow stairs that led to the floor below and pulling the sheets off Sam and Lee's bed—and then another pair from Nanny Flannel's. He carried the bundle of linen back up to Measle's room and dumped it on the floor in a heap.

'Dat old Squiffypoo is back,' he said, carelessly, just as if he was announcing the arrival of a rain shower.

'What? *Where?*' said Measle, his eyes darting nervously round the room.

'Down at de bottom,' said Iggy. 'Where de ssstairs is all broked.'

'What's it doing?'

'It's not doin' nuffink,' said Iggy, stuffing yet another handful of jelly beans in his mouth. 'It's jussst lyin' dere, sssmelling *nice*, dat's all.'

Measle didn't really trust Iggy to know what the Slitherghoul was doing, so he hurriedly knotted the rest of the sheets together and then gathered them all up in his arms and headed for the door.

'Where is you goin', Mumps?' said Iggy, not budging.

'Down to the floor below. There's no point lowering me from up here, not if we can do it from down there! It won't be so far, you see?'

Iggy shrugged his skinny shoulders and followed Measle out of the bedroom. They walked quickly to the head of the narrow staircase, where Measle stopped. He listened for any noises from below. There was silence—apart from a faint drumming sound of heavy rain falling on a distant part of the roof.

Iggy's right! thought Measle. *The Slitherghoul is inside the house again!*

Careful not to make a sound, Measle and Iggy crept down the short flight of stairs. When they reached the landing below, Measle caught a faint whiff of the Slitherghoul's stench.

Measle put his mouth near Iggy's ear and whispered, 'Are you sure it was just lying still, Iggy? Are you sure it wasn't trying to climb up here?'

Iggy pulled his head away from Measle, stuck a finger in his ear, and waggled it irritably. 'I told you, Mumps! It wasn't doin' nuffink!'

Measle was about to move off again, when he heard it—a distant scraping, grating sound, of something heavy being pushed, or pulled, across a stone floor. Putting his finger to his lips, Measle grabbed Iggy's hand and together they tiptoed along the dark corridor, heading for the top of the great staircase. As they got nearer, the smell became stronger and stronger—and so did the scraping, grating noises.

Then, the noises stopped.

Measle and Iggy crept forward until they were able to peer down into the hall below.

The enormous pine table from the kitchen was now directly beneath them!

Measle frowned in puzzlement. What on earth was it doing there?

A moment later, the scraping sound started up again and Measle and Iggy watched as, slowly, another piece of furniture was pushed into position beneath them. This time, it was the polished mahogany table from the dining room—and now Measle and Iggy could see the dark, shifting shape of the Slitherghoul pushing its burden into place next to the pine table, making a kind of broad, uneven platform right below them.

And then Measle realized what the Slitherghoul was doing.

'It's trying to build a way to get up here!' he hissed.

Iggy stared down at the tables in admiration. He'd never think of anything as clever as that! 'Coo—dat mussst be a very sssmart Sssquiffypoo!' he whispered.

Yes, it must! thought Measle. *And that's kind of weird for a lump of slime!*

There was no time to do any more wondering.

Already, another large piece of furniture was being shoved into position. This time it was a sofa from Merlin Manor's living room.

The base of the Slitherghoul's structure was getting bigger by the second.

DEFENCE!

'Come on, Iggy! We'd better hurry!'

Measle and Iggy ran silently back along the passage, this time heading for Sam and Lee's bedroom. When they got there, Measle didn't linger. Instead, he walked quickly past his parents' bed—now stripped of its sheets—and pulled open the bathroom door. He went to the window, opened it, and leaned out as far as he could without falling.

'Here, Iggy!' he said, excitedly. 'We're going to get down to the kitchen from here!'

Measle made a loop at the end of the knotted sheets and wrapped it round his middle, tying it with a tight knot. Then he took the other end of the improvised rope and tied that round the base of the toilet. He pulled hard, to make sure that it wouldn't come loose. It seemed strong enough.

Measle turned to Iggy, who had been staring at his preparations with his eyes wide and his mouth hanging open.

'Right, Iggy,' said Measle, speaking in the slow, gentle voice he used whenever he wanted Iggy to do something. 'I'm going to climb out of the window and you're going to be holding tight to the rope—'

'Dat's not a rope,' said Iggy. 'Dat's just stuff you make cloves out of.'

'Yes, Iggy,' said Measle carefully, 'it is what you make clothes out of—but at the moment, it's *pretending* to be a rope, you see?'

Iggy's face cleared. *Pretending* was something he understood.

'Okey-dokey, Mumps. Ssso—wot was I doin' again?'

'You hold tight to the rope and, when I say, "Go, Iggy!" you start to let me down. Nice and slow—and, whatever you do, don't let go of the rope, right?'

Iggy nodded seriously. 'Don't let go. Right.' Then he frowned and said, 'Er . . . why don't I let go, Mumps?'

Measle sighed. Getting Iggy to do things could be very difficult and you never knew if he really understood or not.

'You mustn't let go because, if you do, I will fall all the way down and probably *die*! All right?'

This explanation seemed to satisfy Iggy, because he nodded again, more seriously than before. Then he picked up the knotted sheets and grasped them tightly with his strong, bony hands.

'Dere, Mumps,' he said. 'I is holdin' de rope.'

Measle said, 'Well done!' Then he swung his legs over the windowsill. He could feel the cool night air wash over his face. He looked down—the ground seemed a long way off. Measle took a deep breath and felt his fluttering nerves settle down a little.

'All right, Iggy,' he called, softly. 'You can start lowering me down!'

In the bathroom, Iggy, concentrating for all he was worth, slowly began to pay out the rope and, outside, Measle found himself slithering, centimetre by centimetre, down the rough brick wall.

Please don't let Iggy be distracted by something! thought Measle, knowing quite well that, if Iggy should suddenly feel the need for another mouthful of jelly beans, it was very likely that he'd simply stop whatever he was doing and—*and well, that would be a very bad thing!*

'You're doing great, Iggy!' Measle hissed, as loudly as he dared.

'I know, Mumps!' came Iggy's voice, floating out through the bathroom window.

Measle had obviously done a good job with the sheet-knotting, because the rope held and, sooner than he thought possible, Measle felt his toes touch down on the ground.

He slipped the loop of sheeting down over his hips and stepped out of it. Then, he hurried to the kitchen door and turned the handle. It didn't budge—

Of course! It's still locked!

It didn't matter. Getting into the kitchen was easy—Measle simply climbed through the shattered window, his feet crunching on the broken glass. There were several candles still burning and, by their light, he walked quickly to the pantry door and opened it.

Merlin Manor's pantry was big. Inside, stacked tightly on shelves, were packets and packets of sugar. There must have been several hundred of them—and they were all there just so that Nanny Flannel could supply Iggy with his daily ration of two hundred red jelly beans.

Measle stood there, staring at the bags and thinking hard. He realized that he hadn't thought this through—what exactly was he going to *do* with the sugar? What were the chances that his guess was right? How long could he stand here, wondering what to do, before the Slitherghoul completed its climbing platform?

Measle shook himself, clearing his head.

He saw a packet, nestling on a shelf down near the floor, which looked a little different from the others. He peered closer.

Sugar lumps.

Nanny Flannel must have bought them by mistake one day.

The thing about sugar lumps which makes them different from just plain sugar is the fact that you can carry them in your pockets.

They are also hard.

And square.

And exactly the right shape—

Click click click—

Measle grabbed the packet of sugar lumps and ran out of the pantry. Quickly, he hopped through the remains of the kitchen window. The sheet rope was still there, hanging from the bathroom window. Measle stuffed the packet of sugar lumps into the front of his jacket, then stepped into the loop that was coiled on the ground. He pulled it up round his chest. Then he looked up and called, 'Iggy! Iggy, are you there?'

Iggy's head popped out of the bathroom window and Measle could see his big round fishy eyes staring down at him.

'Wot d'you want?'

'I want you to pull me up.'

Iggy's face muscles started to wriggle and writhe and Measle sighed inwardly. Iggy was obviously *thinking* again—and, when Iggy thought, an awful lot of effort was expended with very few results.

Finally, Iggy's face settled down. He leaned out a little further and said, 'If you want to come back up, Mumps, den why did you go down in de firssst place? Huh? Huh?'

'I've got sugar, Iggy!' said Measle, knowing that the word 'sugar' would get rid of any objections Iggy might come up with.

Iggy's face split into a big grin.

'Okey-dokey, Mumps!' he hissed. 'I is goin' to pull you up now!'

Iggy's head disappeared and, a moment later, Measle felt the rope tighten round his chest.

It was amazing how strong Iggy could be when he wanted. Measle shot up the side of Merlin Manor as if he was in a lift. A few seconds later, he was scrambling over the windowsill and dropping down onto the bathroom floor.

'Where is de sugar, den?' said Iggy, his eyes glittering with greed.

Measle took the packet out and opened it. He gave a single sugar cube to Iggy who stuffed it into his mouth and crunched it up quickly with his sharp wrathmonk teeth.

'Gimme annuvver one, Mumps!' said Iggy, holding out a clawlike hand.

Measle shook his head. 'No, Iggy, not now. Remember, we're going to throw them at the Slitherghoul and see if that makes it go away.'

Iggy's face fell but he didn't take his eyes off the packet. Measle knew that he was going to have to keep a tight hold on it, or Iggy would simply grab it and then refuse to give it back. To keep Iggy from thinking of that idea, Measle took out another sugar lump and gave it to him.

'There, you can have one every now and then but we've got to save most of them for the Slitherghoul, and this is the only packet. All right?'

Iggy nodded slowly and without any conviction.

'How is we goin' to frow dem?' he said, his jaws crunching busily.

Measle didn't reply. He was busy searching in his chest of drawers.

It's in here, somewhere, I know it is! Now, where did I put it?

With a cry of triumph, Measle yanked something from the bottom of one of the drawers and held it up for Iggy to see.

'Wossat, Mumps?'

'It's my catapult! See, you put a sugar lump into this leather bit—like that, see—and then you pull it backwards like this and those bits get all stretchy, and then you take aim, and then you let go—'

The sugar lump whizzed across the bathroom, out through the open doorway and cracked against the door of Sam and Lee's wardrobe in the bedroom.

Iggy stared in amazement. Then he said, 'Can I 'ave a go wiv dat, Mumps?'

Reluctantly—because he knew that Iggy would nag him until he gave way—Measle handed Iggy the catapult and another sugar lump. Iggy raised the sugar lump to his mouth and Measle said, 'No, Iggy, remember, it goes in the pouch, doesn't it?'

'Ho, yesss, sssilly me.'

Iggy managed everything fairly well, until it came time to release the missile. Copying Measle, he took careful aim at the open doorway—then, instead of letting go of the pouch, he let go of the catapult's handle. The catapult flew backwards and smacked Iggy hard on his beaky nose.

'Owwwwww!' he squeaked, dropping the catapult and putting both hands to his bruised face. 'Ooooooooohhh! Dat cattybull fing is *'stremely* dangerous!'

Measle was sorry that Iggy was hurt—but he was also relieved, because now Iggy wouldn't want to have anything to do with operating the catapult. Measle had often found that it was best to let Iggy try something because, when he failed (and Iggy always failed), the chances were that he would never try again. This meant that Iggy would never again try to drive the big black motorbike; he would never again try to eat raw eggs; he would never again try to put his fingers in Tinker's ears; and would never, ever, be rude to Nanny Flannel. There were a lot of other things that Iggy would never try again—and now playing with Measle's catapult was one of them.

Measle had a quick look at Iggy's nose. There was no blood, so he gave Iggy six more sugar lumps to make him feel better and said, 'You're so brave, Iggy. I would have screamed my head off.'

Iggy looked pleased with himself and stopped snivelling and rubbing his nose. Measle realized that they really couldn't waste any more time. There was no telling how the Slitherghoul's platform was progressing—not without taking a look.

'Come on,' said Measle. 'Let's go and shoot at something, shall we?'

They left the dark bathroom, scurried silently over the thick carpet of the bedroom and out into the corridor. The Slitherghoul smell was strong out here. Measle took Iggy's bony hand and together they crept along the passage. As they neared the head of the stairs, they could hear the sounds of heavy objects being moved.

Carefully, Measle and Iggy craned their heads over the top of the banister rail.

The Slitherghoul was right beneath them, its stinking mass not more than a few metres away. It lay sprawled over the top of a great jumble of piled-up furniture and, even as they watched, it began to extend two thick jelly tentacles up towards them. Measle glanced over his shoulder and saw that the tentacles were aiming for a pair of massive stone pillars that stood at the top of the broken staircase. He knew, in that instant, that the pillars were going to be easily strong enough to support the creature's great weight—which meant there were only seconds before the Slitherghoul would be on their level! And, after that, where could they go?

Measle didn't waste another moment. He pulled out a sugar cube, fitted it into the leather pouch of his catapult, took aim, and fired.

The sugar lump struck halfway along the first of the two tentacles. It hit the outer skin of the Slitherghoul and then disappeared into the jelly, leaving no entry hole behind.

For a moment, nothing much happened, except that the tentacle stopped its upward movement and simply hung, quivering slightly, in the dark air. Measle quickly loaded another sugar lump and let fly—this time at the other tentacle.

Again, the little white cube just disappeared into the greenish-brownish-yellowish mass—and again, the tentacle paused.

Measle took careful aim and let go—and this sugar cube flew down and hit the main body of the Slitherghoul right between the bases of the two tentacles.

The effect was remarkable. The Slitherghoul seemed to shudder convulsively. Its two extended tentacles retracted at high speed, disappearing back into the slimy mass, which shifted uneasily on the great mound of furniture. The structure swayed with the Slitherghoul's sudden movement and there were several ominous creaking sounds from deep within the jumbled heap.

Measle fitted another sugar lump into the leather pouch and let fly.

The Slitherghoul shuddered again—and then it began to slide slowly down the stack of furniture. Its great weight slithered to one side, the stack swayed and creaked and swayed again—and then collapsed, with a thundering crash of splintering wood, down onto the stone floor of the hallway. The Slitherghoul could do nothing but ride the falling furniture mound all the way to the bottom. It thudded to the floor with a soggy, squelching *thump!* and then lay there, among the mass of broken furniture, quivering like a jelly.

It worked! thought Measle, excitedly. *Now, let's see if I can make it retreat even more!*

Measle started to shoot sugar lumps, one after the other, straight down at the great stinking mass and, to his great relief, the Slitherghoul began to heave its body out of the way of the missiles. It slimed over the remains of the furniture and moved away to the doorway of the living room, where it paused. But it was still in range of the whizzing sugar lumps—three hit it in quick succession—and it was forced to retreat even further, moving backwards into the dark living room until Measle lost sight of it in the shadows.

Iggy tugged at Measle's sleeve. 'Can we ssstop shooting de sugar now?' he asked, plaintively. 'Now dat de Sssquiffypoo has gone away?'

Measle took one last look down into the

darkness. Then he nodded and stuffed the catapult into his back pocket.

'An' can I have a sugar lump, Mumps?' whined Iggy. 'I'm ever ssso 'ungry.'

Measle felt in his pockets and pulled out the remaining lumps. There were very few left.

'We've got to save them, Iggy. It's the only way to keep the Slitherghoul away, you see.'

'Why can't you get sssome more from de kitchen?' muttered Iggy, anxiously.

Measle shook his head. 'I told you—there *aren't* any more. I looked. There was just that one packet. I think Nanny Flannel made a mistake when she bought them. There's plenty of sugar, just not any more in lumps.'

'Pl-plenty of sugar?' said Iggy, hopefully. He'd never been allowed into Nanny Flannel's kitchen, and so had never seen the pantry shelves sagging under the weight of bag after bag of sugar. The idea was terribly exciting.

'Can we go dere, den? To de kitchen? I wanna sssee all dat sugar, Mumps!'

Measle thought about this for a moment. It would mean returning to the ground floor, which was the same level as the Slitherghoul, and that was dangerous. On the other hand, they couldn't stay up here for ever and perhaps there was something they could do with that great store of sugar. Obviously, they weren't going to be able to shoot it at the Slitherghoul but perhaps there was some other way of using the stuff against the monster?

Measle was good at making up his mind in the shortest possible time. Briskly, he nodded and then got to his feet.

'Come on then, Iggy,' he said. 'We'll both have to go down the rope this time.'

They left the gaping hole in the landing that had once been the great staircase of Merlin Manor and went quickly back to Sam and Lee's bathroom. Measle explained to Iggy how he was to lower him down again and then, having done that, Iggy was to make sure that the sheet rope was securely fastened to the base of the toilet and then he was to climb down the rope and join Measle on the ground.

'Okey-dokey, Mumps.'

Two minutes later, Measle and Iggy were standing on the ground, close by the shattered kitchen window. They picked their way carefully over the windowsill and crunched across the broken glass to the pantry door. Measle fetched a candle from the mantelpiece and held it up, so that Iggy could see the glorious sight of all those bulging bags of sugar.

'It's all for you, Iggy,' said Measle and Iggy's face split into an enormous grin.

'All mine?'

'This is what Nanny Flannel makes your jelly beans out of. Well, mostly—I think there's some other stuff in them as well and of course there's the strawberry juice, too, but it's more sugar than anything else.'

Iggy couldn't take his eyes off the floor-to-ceiling stacks of sugar bags. He stared, entranced, with greedy eyes, and then he said, 'Can I eat sssome, Mumps?'

Measle shrugged. He couldn't think of a reason why not, and Iggy took his shrug as a 'yes'. He reached out one bony hand and pulled a bag right from the very middle of a stack. Instantly, the whole pile collapsed, several of the bags bursting and spilling their contents over the floor.

'Oops,' said Iggy, in a voice that sounded as if he didn't care a bit about the mess. He poked a hole in his paper bag with one sharp fingernail and then, holding the bag high in the air, he let a stream of sugar fall into his open mouth.

Measle stared at the glittering grains that lay scattered all over the floor. His first thought was— *Nanny is going to be furious at this mess!*—but then he remembered, with a sickening feeling, that Nanny Flannel wasn't going to be *anything* any more.

The sickening feeling turned quite suddenly into anger. Whatever this foul, stinking creature was, it had swallowed up two of his best friends in all the world and now seemed intent on swallowing up him and Iggy as well. Well, he wouldn't let it! *There must be something else I can do to it, besides shooting sugar lumps at it!*

Measle's mind started to work furiously.

All that sugar lying there—what if the Slithergboul got completely covered with the stuff? What would that do to it? Would it do anything? And how could we get the Slithergboul to cover itself with it in the first place? There's no question that it hates sugar! It hurts it somehow—so, the more sugar we can get on it, the more it'll be hurt! Maybe, with enough sugar, we might even be able to kill the thing! But, how to do it?

Iggy suddenly stopped pouring sugar into his mouth. He dropped the almost empty bag on the floor and the small amount of remaining sugar spilled out, adding to the mess already there. Iggy gulped, his fishy eyes wide. Measle thought the little wrathmonk's pale face looked even paler than usual and there was a sheen of sweat across Iggy's forehead.

'I is feelin' a bit sssick,' muttered Iggy.

Measle wasn't at all surprised—not with the huge amount of sugar that Iggy had consumed so far. Normally, Iggy was rationed to just two hundred red jelly beans a day and that would make most ordinary people feel pretty ill. But Iggy wasn't an ordinary person. He was a greedy wrathmonk who had eaten his entire ration of strawberry-flavoured jelly beans within a few minutes of getting them that morning, and since then he'd stuffed himself with many handfuls of other jelly beans from the jar in the dining room, plus poured almost a whole bag of sugar granules down his throat in one go. It was no wonder he was feeling queasy.

'Drink some water, Iggy,' said Measle and Iggy shambled over to the kitchen sink, turned on the tap and stuck his mouth under it. He'd turned the tap full on and the cold water shot out with some force, gurgling into Iggy's open mouth and splashing over his face, soaking his whole head. Iggy straightened up sharply and banged his head against the tap.

'Urrrgh! Owwww!' he squeaked, pulling off his woolly hat and dropping it into the sink. He rubbed his head with both hands.

Measle was about to sympathize and tell Iggy how brave he was being (which was something he always did when Iggy hurt himself, otherwise Iggy would complain for the rest of the day) when the smell hit him.

It must have been a sudden change in the wind direction outside, because one minute the stink wasn't there and the next it was—and it was very strong.

Quickly and silently, Measle stepped out of the pantry, his feet crunching on the spilled sugar. Beyond the broken window the darkness lay heavy against the house. Measle ran to the jagged opening and carefully peered out—

The Slitherghoul was sliding fast across the kitchen yard and now Measle heard the thunder of its massive rain cloud overhead.

Measle turned away from the window, his eyes searching desperately for a way out. His first thought was for the door that led to the corridor and he dashed across the kitchen and grabbed Iggy by one wet hand. He dragged the little wrathmonk towards the shadows on the far side of the kitchen. His candle guttered in his hand, the dim flame lighting up the doorway—

Which was completely blocked by a great pile of rubble that reached from floor to ceiling.

No Way Out

They were caught like rats in a trap.

When the old oak beam had given way, it had brought down a whole section of the kitchen wall and part of the passage ceiling too. The pile of plaster, bricks, and wood was jammed tight in the opening. The only other way out of the kitchen was through the shattered window—and now the Slitherghoul must be almost directly outside.

There was only one thing that Measle and Iggy could do.

Measle blew out his candle and dropped it to the floor. Then he dragged Iggy back to the pantry and together they pressed themselves into the shadows of the back wall.

Measle reached into his pocket and took out a

yellow jelly bean. Then he grabbed Iggy by the lapels of his mouldy old jacket and pulled him close. Before Iggy could say a word, Measle stuck his hand deep into the breast pocket of the mouldy jacket and extracted a green jelly bean. He held the green bean in front of Iggy's face and hissed, 'Eat it, Iggy!'

Iggy was still rubbing the bruised spot on his head. He blinked a couple of times and then said, 'I told you, Mumps, I don't like de green ones!'

'I don't care, Iggy!' hissed Measle. 'You've got to eat it!'

Stubbornly, Iggy shook his head and, at the same moment, he compressed his lips tightly, showing clearly that he had no intention of letting the nasty green thing anywhere near his mouth.

Measle peered desperately over Iggy's shoulder. Beyond the broken window, a dark shape moved in the shadows. The smell of the Slitherghoul flooded the kitchen.

Measle made a fist out of the hand that was holding the green jelly bean and then, quite gently, he bopped Iggy right on the end of his bent and beaky nose.

'Owww!' yelped Iggy, opening his mouth wide to wail. Instantly, Measle opened his fist and crammed the jelly bean into Iggy's mouth. Measle put one hand on the top of Iggy's soggy head, the other under Iggy's bottom jaw and then pushed both hands hard together.

Iggy's mouth closed with a snap and, right before Measle's eyes, the little wrathmonk disappeared.

Measle couldn't see Iggy, but he could feel him. He could feel Iggy's chest lift, as Iggy filled it full of air—and he knew in that moment that Iggy was going to yell out some sort of protest at this cruel treatment. Measle instantly put his hand over Iggy's mouth. At the same moment, he popped the yellow jelly bean into his own mouth and bit down hard.

If anybody had looked into the kitchen then, they would have thought that nobody was there, apart from some faint, gurgling, grunting noises coming from deep inside the pantry. The noises sounded exactly as if somebody was trying to say something but couldn't because somebody *else* had their hand pressed tightly across their mouth.

The Slitherghoul slimed up to the jagged opening of the kitchen window and, using several wrathmonk eyes, it peered into the room. It had been attracted here by a light flickering in the distant shadows and several of the wrathmonk minds had cried, *He's there! The horrid boy is there!*

In the dim light of the remaining candles, all the Slitherghoul could see was an empty room and the dark rectangle of the pantry door. It was about to turn away and search somewhere else when the sound of running water reached the ears of every one of its victims. Iggy had left the tap running at full force and the water in the sink wasn't draining away. Iggy's woolly hat was lying where he'd dropped it—at the bottom of the sink, blocking the drain hole, and the water was rising fast. Soon it would spill over the edge.

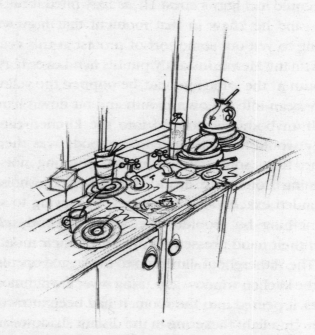

The Slitherghoul paused and then peered into the flickering shadows and Toby Jugg's mind cried out, *Why? Why is the water running?* And then Griswold Gristle's mind joined in and hissed, *I think the boy is there!*

We don't sssee anything! came a chorus of other wrathmonk voices, and the weight of their opinions began to turn the Slitherghoul away from the window again—but Griswold's mind shrieked, *No! He's there, I tell you! We have ssseen thisss trick before! The boy has the ability to disappear into thin air! We mussst feel for him!*

The vast, stinking bulk of the Slitherghoul pressed up against the hole where the window had been and part of its body bulged through the opening and spilled onto the broken glass on the kitchen floor. Measle and Iggy, pressed hard against the back wall of the pantry, watched through their invisible eyes as a fat tentacle of slime extruded from the body of the creature. Slowly the tentacle started to stretch out across the floor, its tip sweeping backwards and forwards in wide arcs. Slowly, horribly, the tentacle came nearer and nearer.

Measle and Iggy didn't move a muscle. Iggy had frozen into a statue at Measle's side and Measle had felt confident enough to take his hand away from the wrathmonk's mouth. He needed one hand to get another green jelly bean out of Iggy's pocket and he needed his *other* hand to get a yellow one out of his *own* pocket and hold them in readiness.

This time, Measle had been too scared to count down from thirty, so he was forced to guess how much longer they had. Well before the half minute was up, he slipped his yellow jelly bean between his lips. Then he felt for Iggy's mouth and pressed the green jelly bean past Iggy's unresisting teeth, quickly clamping his hand over the wrathmonk's jaw.

This time, Iggy seemed to understand why he was being made to eat the nasty green ones, because Measle felt him bite down on the jelly bean without any protest at all.

But invisibility wasn't going to help them. Not this time. Four of the wrathmonks had experienced Measle's disappearing trick twice before and it was they who were leading this search, causing the tentacle to slither back and forth across the whole width of the kitchen, a hunt which Measle knew would end in their discovery.

The sound of running water changed from the roar of a wide open tap to something more splashy, as the sink suddenly overflowed. The water cascaded over the lip of the basin and dropped, in a miniature Niagara Falls, onto the kitchen floor. Quickly it spread across the tiles in an ever-widening puddle. The tip of the tentacle swept through it, brushing the water from side to side and sending little tidal waves rolling towards the pantry.

Measle and Iggy huddled together, watching helplessly as the fat, wriggling tentacle came nearer and nearer.

A tiny wave of water, no more than a couple of centimetres high, washed through the open pantry door. It reached almost to the feet of Measle and Iggy, flowing over the crystals of sugar on the floor—and the grains melted and dissolved.

The tentacle had felt its way all across the kitchen floor and now only the dark pantry was left. There was an absolute certainty in Griswold

Gristle's mind—*We have him, dear friends!* he cried. *There is only one place he can be! Push on—push on into the darkness!*

The tentacle wriggled its tip through the opening of the pantry door and slithered across the floor, its tip sliding from side to side through the shallow puddle of water.

The Slitherghoul felt a sudden, stinging pain.

None of its internal victims felt the pain and, when the tentacle stopped its forward motion and started hurriedly to reverse out of the pantry, the minds of Griswold and Buford and Frognell and Judge Cedric all cried out, *No! Don't ssstop! Go forward! He's there, we tell you! He's there!*

But the Slitherghoul paid no attention. Its own brain was small and crude and pathetic next to the minds of its victims, but when it felt pain, or suspected its existence was in any sort of danger, it reacted instinctively, overpowering any alien thoughts that might try to control it.

None of its victims understood the reason for the extraordinary retreat from the dark pantry and the Slitherghoul's hurried exit back out through the kitchen window.

No! No! NO! screamed the thoughts of the four wrathmonks—and now several other minds joined in and tried to make the Slitherghoul return to its search. The creature ignored them all and slithered away over the gravel path by the side of the house. Cooling drops from the rain cloud fell heavily onto its heaving body, slowly washing away whatever it was that had caused the stinging sensation. The Slitherghoul paused in its flight and lay still, letting the rain thunder down. In its primitive mind, a new sense—a sense of *danger*—lay like a lead weight, and it was a sense the Slitherghoul had never experienced before. If a brain as small and as crude as the Slitherghoul's could be said to feel uneasiness, then that was what the Slitherghoul was now feeling—and no amount of urging from the minds of its victims was going to budge it until that feeling went away.

Inside the pantry, the effects of the jelly beans were wearing off. Measle and Iggy reappeared in the darkness. Both turned to stare at the other in wonder and Measle saw that Iggy's eyes were even rounder and fishier than ever.

'Coo,' said Iggy, quietly. 'Dat old Sssquiffypoo just went away. Why did it do dat, Mumps?'

Measle knew why. It was the sugar, of course. The water from the sink had dissolved the crystals that were scattered over the pantry floor, making a sweet solution which the Slitherghoul had found unpleasant to the touch—perhaps even painful! Certainly the creature seemed desperate not to have any further contact with the stuff . . .

Click, click, click, went Measle's brain.

A vague idea for a trap formed in his head. It was a big idea, full of doubts and uncertainties, and certainly very hard to achieve, but it was the only one he'd got at the moment—*and it must be better to do something than just wait around for the creature to catch up with them! The only question was, where could they set the trap?*

'Is—is dat old Sssquiffypoo comin' back, Mumps?' asked Iggy, peering out into the kitchen.

'I don't know, Iggy. I hope not, anyway. But look, I've got an idea and I'm going to need your help.'

Iggy sniffed suspiciously. Sometimes Mumps's ideas meant a lot of hard work. 'Do we have to dig again?' he said. 'Coz, if we do, den I'm not helpin', and dat's final!'

Measle didn't reply. He stepped out into the kitchen, sloshing through the water on the floor. He reached out and turned off the kitchen tap, then he fished in the water and pulled Iggy's sodden hat out. The drain gurgled and the water began to drain away. Measle watched as the level in the sink fell and he didn't take his eyes away until the last of the water had disappeared down the hole.

Click.

I know where the trap can be!

Measle turned excitedly to Iggy but, before he could say anything, Iggy grabbed at the sodden hat in Measle's hands and said, 'Ooh, I was wonderin' where dat was, Mumps! Fanks!'

Iggy stuck the cap on his head and the water dribbled down his face and neck.

'There's no digging, Iggy,' said Measle, thoughtfully.

Iggy's face brightened. 'Okey-dokey, den.'

Stepping as silently as possible across the debris on the kitchen floor, Measle and Iggy went to the window and peered out into the darkness. The smell of the Slitherghoul was faint. Measle looked from side to side, his eyes searching the dark sky. *There!* About fifty metres away, the dense rain cloud hung close to the side of the house and, beneath it, Measle could just make out the low hump of the Slitherghoul. It didn't seem to be moving.

Measle grabbed Iggy and dragged him back to the pantry. He positioned the little wrathmonk next to the shelves and pulled Iggy's arms straight out in front of him.

'Now, look, Iggy, this is what we're going to do. We're going to load you up with bags of sugar and we're going to see how many you can carry, OK?'

'Ooh, is dis a game, Mumps?'

'Well, it's a *sort* of game. A very special sort of game, which is going to help us get rid of that old Squiffypoo. So you're not going to complain if you have to carry rather a lot, are you?'

Iggy shook his head firmly, sending drops of water flying. He liked doing things which showed off how strong he could be. Digging, he'd decided, wasn't one of them, but carrying heavy stuff probably was. He held his arms stiffly in front of him and Measle started grabbing bags of sugar off the shelves and piling them high against Iggy's chest. Quite soon, the stack was up to Iggy's eyes.

'Right!' said Measle. 'That's enough for one load.'

He took hold of Iggy's elbow and led him out of the pantry and across the kitchen. A couple of times Iggy almost fell, tripping over some of the fallen bricks and plaster that littered the floor, but Measle steadied him each time and they reached the shattered window without dropping a single bag.

Measle paused at the window and peered out. The Slitherghoul was still there, a dark hump under a torrent of rain. There was no way of telling in which direction the creature was looking, so Measle wasn't going to take the risk. He reached into his pocket and took out a yellow jelly bean. Then he did the same to Iggy, pushing his hand past the stack of sugar bags and wriggling it into Iggy's breast pocket. He pinched a green jelly bean between his finger and thumb and pulled it out.

'Now then, Iggy,' he whispered, 'when I say go, we're going to eat our jelly beans, all right?'

'All right, Mumps,' said Iggy, reluctantly. 'But I ssstill don't like de green ones.'

'Well, I don't like my yellow ones much either, but that's part of this game, you see. When we're invisible, we're going to run as fast as we can. And we're going to try and not drop a single bag.'

'Dat is easy-peasy for you to sssay,' said Iggy, scornfully. 'Coz you isn't *carryin'* any bags, is you?'

'No, I'm not,' said Measle carefully. He didn't want to start an argument with Iggy—not at this moment, certainly. 'But I'm in charge of these jelly beans, you see. I've got to be able to get them out of our pockets quickly, and I need both hands for that, don't I?'

Iggy nodded. Even his little brain could see the logic of that.

'Ssso—where is we goin' to run to, Mumps?'

'There,' said Measle, pointing out into the darkness. 'We're going to run out there.'

Baiting the Trap

'Er . . . dat's where de old Sssquiffypoo is, Mumps,' said Iggy, a little nervously.

'I know, Iggy. That's why we're going to eat our special jelly beans. We'll be invisible and the Squiffypoo won't see us, will it?'

Iggy's face cleared and he grinned. 'Okey-dokey, Mumps.'

'But we'll have to be very quiet, otherwise the Squiffypoo might hear us, and that would be almost as bad as it seeing us, Iggy. So, we have to run like little mice, all right?'

'Okey-dokey, Mumps.'

'Now, when we run out there, you won't be able to see me and I won't be able to see you. So I'm going to keep hold of your collar, Iggy, all the way.'

'All de way *where*?'

'All the way to our swimming pool.'

Iggy's eyes narrowed suspiciously. 'I fort you sssaid we wasn't goin' to do no more diggin'?'

'We're not. In fact, what we're going to do is see if we can fill it up again.'

Iggy's face started its wild grimacing so, to prevent an endless discussion about nothing, Measle said, hurriedly, 'Just do whatever I tell you to do, and everything will be fine. And, if we get separated, just run as fast as you can back to the kitchen, understand?'

Iggy's face settled down and he nodded, slowly.

Measle held up the green jelly bean and said, 'Now, I'm going to stick this in your mouth, but don't bite on it yet. Wait until I say "GO!"'

Iggy nodded again and opened his mouth and Measle put the green jelly bean on Iggy's tongue. Then he popped his yellow bean into his own mouth and tucked it into his cheek.

'Ready?' he said, reaching out and taking hold of Iggy's damp collar.

Iggy nodded again, his eyes wide with the effort of not biting into a jelly bean, even if it was one of the green ones.

Measle took a deep breath.

'GO!'

Measle watched as Iggy's jaws clamped down on the jelly bean. At the same instant, Measle slipped his own jelly bean out of his cheek and bit down hard—and, together, he and Iggy disappeared in wisps of grey smoke.

'Right, Iggy, now let's run!'

Measle, clutching tight to an invisible collar, scrambled over the jagged windowsill. He could feel Iggy moving next to him as they dropped down onto the stones of the kitchen yard and, the moment Measle sensed that Iggy was with him on the solid ground, he started to run as fast as he could, dragging Iggy along beside him.

The edge of the lawn was just a few metres away but a good seven seconds had passed before Measle's feet touched the grass. Keeping hold of an invisible little wrathmonk who was staggering under a heavy load of sugar bags was slowing him down badly.

Out of the corner of one eye, Measle was watching the distant hump that was the Slitherghoul. It still wasn't moving.

Just let it stay there! thought Measle, beginning to pant a little now. He and Iggy stumbled silently over the grass, towards the dark rectangle of their swimming pool and, by the time they reached the edge of it, another ten seconds had passed.

They were more than halfway through their invisibility.

Measle skidded to a halt on the damp grass and he felt Iggy do the same at his side. The muddy pit was directly in front of them.

'Throw the bags in, Iggy!' hissed Measle.

'*Wot?*' came Iggy's voice, from somewhere near Measle's left ear.

'The bags, Iggy! Throw them in the hole!'

'*Frow dem in de hole? Frow dem in de hole?* Are you *potty*, Mumps?'

Measle felt Iggy's body stiffen, as if the little wrathmonk was about to utter a strong protest—*but there isn't time for that, Iggy!*—so Measle, still firmly clutching the back of Iggy's collar, reached out with his other hand and began to scrabble at the bags in Iggy's outstretched arms. He couldn't see them, but he could *feel* them, and a moment later his scrabbling took effect as several of the topmost ones slipped from the pile. Measle heard them fall, with soggy thumps, into the muddy bottom of the pit.

Iggy gasped and Measle felt him take a step backwards, away from the edge of the pit. *That's no good!* thought Measle desperately. There was only one thing to do, and Measle did it. He grabbed Iggy's collar with both hands and pushed hard, forcing Iggy back to the edge and almost shoving him over, and Iggy, desperate not to fall in, forgot all about the load he was carrying and started to flail his arms about, just like people do when they feel their balance going. Immediately, Measle heard the sound of a large number of invisible sugar bags thumping down into the pit—and, at the same moment, came a wail of despair from Iggy.

'Noooo!'

Measle moved his hands off Iggy's collar and up over his invisible mouth and Iggy's wail was instantly cut back to a muffled moan.

'Sshhhh, Iggy! Not a sound!' Measle hissed. 'We don't want the Squiffypoo to hear us!'

To Measle's horror, right front of his eyes, a long, pointed ear started to take shape out of grey smoke. The jelly beans were wearing off! Measle took one hand away from Iggy's mouth and fumbled for Iggy's front pocket. He yanked out a still invisible jelly bean and stuffed it into Iggy's mouth.

'Bite it, Iggy!'

As Iggy chomped down on the jelly bean, Measle was already pulling one of his own from his pocket and popping it into his mouth.

They were only just in time. The grey smoke took only moments to solidify and by the time the second jelly beans took effect, both Iggy and Measle could be seen quite clearly, looking like a pair of grey ghosts out in the middle of the vast lawn.

Measle peered towards the lump in the shadows. Neither it, nor its rain cloud, seemed to be moving.

'We were lucky that time, Iggy,' he whispered into the darkness, and, out of the darkness, came Iggy's plaintive whisper back at him, '*Lucky?* We ain't lucky, Mumps! We jussst frew away all dat puffickly good sugar!'

'And we're going to do it again, Iggy. Lots more

times, in fact! Come on, let's get back to the kitchen before our jelly beans wear off again.'

Getting from the pit back to the kitchen was a quicker business than getting from the kitchen to the pit, because now Iggy wasn't burdened by armfuls of sugar bags but, even so, they only just made it back inside the relative safety of the kitchen before both of them materialized out of grey smoke.

The moment Iggy appeared in front of him, Measle realized that the little wrathmonk was upset. Iggy's face was wriggling and contorting more wildly than usual and he was even paler than normal. His fishy eyes were huge and almost completely round and he was glaring at Measle with an expression of bewildered fury.

'Wot—wot does you fink you is *doin'*, Mumps?' he sputtered, angrily. 'Miss Fwannel will kill usss! Frowin' away puffickly good sugar like dat! Dat is not funny!'

Measle kept his voice calm and quiet. 'Nanny Flannel has gone, Iggy. So has Tinker. So have Mr Needle and Mr Bland. Mum and Dad and Tilly are all a squillion miles away. We're all alone here, and we have to try to save ourselves.'

'Dat is all very well, but frowin' away puffickly good sugar—'

'We're not throwing it away, Iggy. We're building a trap.'

'A trap?'

'Yes, a *sugar* trap.'

Iggy's face was as blank as a sheet of white paper and Measle knew that there was no point in trying to explain things to him—not now. Later perhaps, but right now he just needed Iggy's strength.

'Look, Iggy, you've just got to trust me,' said Measle, gently. 'I know what I'm doing, but I can't do it without your help. So, will you help me, without asking any questions and without getting all cross?'

Measle's calm and soothing voice had a remarkable effect on Iggy. His wriggling face muscles settled down, his eyes got a little less round, and his whole skinny body seemed to relax a fraction. He sniffed and said, 'No diggin'?'

'No digging, Iggy. Just more throwing sugar. Lots more. All right?'

Iggy was very, very silly, but, deep in his heart (and not caring to admit it) he knew that Measle was clever. He knew that Measle was cleverer than he was, which was why, most of the time, he would let Measle take charge of things during their adventures at Merlin Manor. And now his friend had a very serious look on his face and, in that instant, Iggy decided to do what Measle was asking.

'Okey-dokey, Mumps.'

They made that hurried trip ten more times and, now that Iggy knew what was expected of him, they did it faster and faster.

By the time the pantry shelves were bare, both

Measle and Iggy were very tired. And, while Iggy's breast pocket still bulged with green jelly beans, Measle's pocket was almost empty of yellow ones.

'I fink I like diggin' better, Mumps,' panted Iggy, leaning against an empty shelf. He was staring at the floor, bent double, with both hands grasping his knees, in an attempt to catch his breath. 'All dis runnin' about,' he grumbled, 'bein' ingrizzible, frowin' away puffickly good sugar. Ho, yesss, I definitely likes diggin' better!'

'Well, we don't have to do either any more, Iggy,' gasped Measle. He too was bent over, his hands on his knees, panting for breath. 'Now, we've got to do something else, but I promise it won't be *nearly* so tiring.'

SETTING THE TRAP

When Measle and Iggy had got their breath back, Measle crept to the kitchen window and peered out. The dark lump of the Slitherghoul was there, fifty metres away but now it was moving again, slowly sliming its way across the lawn, the rain cloud hovering overhead.

With a sickening feeling in the pit of his stomach, Measle saw that it was heading straight for the swimming pool.

Not yet! thought Measle, panic rising in his chest. *The trap's not ready yet! It mustn't see it! It mustn't see what we've done!*

Measle's mind raced.

Distract it! We've got to distract it!

Measle came to a sudden decision. He knew

what he had to do. At the back of his mind, he knew it was a hideously *dangerous* thing to do but they had no choice.

Measle darted back to the pantry and seized Iggy's hand. Dragging him across the littered kitchen floor, he hissed, 'Come on, Iggy! We've got to do some more running!'

Iggy opened his mouth to object, but then he remembered that he'd decided to be helpful. He allowed himself to be pulled along and, at the same time, he dipped his fingers into his breast pocket and pulled out one of the few remaining green jelly beans. He was about to pop it into his mouth, when Measle saw what he was doing.

'No, Iggy! Not this time! This time, we have to be *visible*!'

Iggy got as far as saying, 'Grizzible? *Grizzible?* But, if we is *grizzible*, den dat old Sssquiffypoo is goin' to sssee usss, and den—'

He didn't get any more out, because Measle dragged him through the broken window. Once outside, Measle started to jump up and down, waving his free arm and yelling, 'OVER HERE! OVER HERE! COME AND GET US—WE'RE OVER HERE!'

Out on the dark lawn, the Slitherghoul slowed and then stopped, a good three metres short of the edge of the swimming pool pit. Ponderously, it moved its huge slimy body round. Measle yelled even harder.

'COME ON, YOU HORRIBLE OLD SQUIFFYPOO, YOU! COME AND GET US!'

The Slitherghoul seemed to pause for a moment. In fact, a small battle was going on inside it. Nanny Flannel was trying to hold the Slitherghoul back, but the four evil wrathmonks joined their minds to Toby Jugg's and, with the help of several of the other released prisoners, they were urging the Slitherghoul to give chase.

Nanny Flannel did her best, but the others were too strong for her. The Slitherghoul began, slowly at first, to slime its way across the lawn towards the kitchen yard. Gradually it gathered speed.

'Come on, Iggy!' hissed Measle. 'Now we've really got to run!'

Together, Measle and Iggy raced down the long side wall of Merlin Manor. Their feet crunch-crunched on the gravel path. Halfway along the wall, Measle dared a quick glance over his shoulder.

I—I don't believe it! That great slug thing is gaining on us! How can it move so fast?

Indeed, the Slitherghoul was catching up—and catching up fast. Measle remembered the time when Basil Tramplebone, in the guise of a giant black cockroach, had been chasing him and Tinker along the railway lines of the great table-top train set. Basil the cockroach had been about the same size as this terrible creature and *he'd* been able to move fast, too.

Measle remembered another thing: if a great mass such as this wanted to stop suddenly, or change direction, it took time and space to do it. So, the trick was to dodge and weave—

Measle and Iggy reached the corner of the house and they darted round it. Here was the front of the house, with its great circle of gravel driveway. For a moment, Measle and Iggy paused, gulping in lungfuls of breath.

Across the driveway, set in an enormous area of closely-cropped grass, was one of the glories of Merlin Manor.

The main rose garden.

Partly because of the great pride that Sam took in them, and the care he lavished on their upkeep—but mostly because of Iggy's breathing spell, which killed the bugs that threatened to harm them—the roses of Merlin Manor were spectacular. Bushy and dense and healthy, every summer their stems were heavy with flowers of every colour and every scent. They grew tall and very wide and overhung the narrow grass paths that intersected the beds, so that, at first glance, the rose garden looked almost like an impenetrable jungle. But the paths were there and Measle knew them well. If there was dodging and weaving to be done, the paths in the rose garden were the spots to do it.

A soft night breeze brought the stink of the Slitherghoul to Measle's nostrils. He looked back over his shoulder again—the monstrous mound of slime was slithering over the gravel path at an impossible speed. It was no more than a few metres away!

Measle leapt forward, pulling Iggy with him. Silently, they ran across the drive, then onto the lawn. The rose garden loomed dark in front of them. There was just enough light for Measle to see the beginning of one of the paths that led towards the centre of the garden and he headed for it as fast as his legs—and the weight of a dragging wrathmonk—would let him.

They made it just in time. Only seconds after Measle and Iggy darted between the first of the overhanging rose bushes, they heard the sound of the Slitherghoul barging into the same gap. There was the sound of breaking branches.

Measle and Iggy ran deeper and deeper into the rose garden. They dodged left—then right—then left again—their heads slung low and their backs bent as they scurried between the overhanging plants. Behind them came a terrible noise of ripping stems as the Slitherghoul forced its giant body along the same paths. But it was slowing down. Measle could hear the sounds slowly diminishing.

'It can't turn corners like we can!' he panted in Iggy's ear. 'It's slowing down! Come on—round here!'

He hardly needed to give Iggy directions. The

little wrathmonk knew the rose gardens better than anybody, since he spent so much time there. At first, Iggy hadn't liked the roses much. It's not in the nature of a wrathmonk to like nice things, particularly nice things that smell so good; wrathmonks prefer the stink of rotting meat to the scent of roses. But slowly Iggy had got used to his job and, while he never really liked the flowers much, he did get quite fond of the *thorns*. The longer and the sharper the thorns were on any particular rose bush the better as far as Iggy was concerned. He always spent a little longer breathing on those rose bushes that grew the best set of thorns than on those whose thorns were smaller and blunter—with the result that the biggest and best rose bushes in the gardens of Merlin Manor also possessed the biggest and best thorns.

The sound of breaking branches behind Measle and Iggy not only grew quieter as they put more and more distance between themselves and the Slitherghoul, the noise itself also seemed to have stopped moving at all. Now, the only sound they could hear was a distant thrashing, thumping, ripping.

Measle paused for a moment and turned round. He stood on his tiptoes and tried to see over the tops of the rose bushes, but they were too high.

'Come on, Iggy, let's get to the sundial!'

The sundial was made of brass and it stood on an old stone pillar in the centre of the great rose garden. A few more twists and turns brought Measle and Iggy to the circular bed, where the sundial stood.

'Quick, Iggy, lift me up!'

Iggy hastily stuffed the jelly beans he'd just taken out of his pocket into his mouth and, chewing busily, he hoisted Measle up, so that Measle was high enough to pull himself onto the top of the stone pillar. He carefully stood upright on the small platform and then stared out across the rose gardens.

It was pretty dark, but he could just about make out the dark lump of the Slitherghoul. It appeared to be about six metres within the border of the rose garden—and it appeared to be stuck. Measle watched as the lump heaved and rippled and he saw, to his puzzled satisfaction, that the lump didn't seem to be advancing by even a centimetre.

His puzzlement only lasted another second.

'It's stuck, Iggy!' Measle called down. 'And I think it's the thorns that are sticking it!'

Anybody who has tried to walk among rose bushes knows just how grabby a rose thorn can be. They stick in your clothes and you really have to pull hard to get free. There were a thousand thorns sticking in the soft, slimy jelly of the Slitherghoul's body and, while the creature felt no pain, it found itself making almost no headway whatsoever. It strained and pulled—and a hundred thorns popped away from its sides—but a hundred more fastened into the soft substance, so that its forward motion was slowed down to mere centimetres a minute.

It looked to Measle as if it was going to be stuck there for quite a time.

'Dat is a clever plan, Mumps,' said Iggy, standing at the base of the pedestal and staring up at Measle with a look of admiration on his pale face. '*Ssstreemely* clever, ssstickin' dat old Sssquiffypoo wiv de prickles.'

Getting the Slitherghoul stuck in the rose bushes hadn't actually been part of Measle's plan, but he decided to let Iggy think it had been. Right now, he needed all the admiration he could get, if only to persuade Iggy to do whatever he said, without any of the usual arguments.

Measle jumped down from the pedestal.

'Right,' he said, firmly, 'I think we've got a little

time before that old Squiffypoo gets free. Come on, we've got work to do!'

'Not diggin' again, Mumps?' said Iggy suspiciously.

'No, Iggy, *not* digging! *Fun* work! Come on!'

Together, Measle and Iggy ran quickly through the rest of the rose garden, putting more and more distance between themselves and the sounds of the thrashing Slitherghoul. Soon, they were out the other side, racing towards the far wing of Merlin Manor. They rounded the corner and ran on, down the long side of the house, then round another corner, and there lay the back lawn of the house and, right in the middle of it, the darker shadow of the swimming pool pit.

'Coo!' panted Iggy, running fast at Measle's side. 'We has gone all round de *whole* house!'

Measle led Iggy back to the kitchen yard. There, on the wall close by the door, was a tap. Fastened to the tap was a garden hose. It was coiled over a hook and Measle, using all his strength, lifted the whole coil off the hook and dropped it to the ground. Then he grabbed hold of the brass nozzle and started to drag it across the yard.

'Come on, Iggy!' he yelled. 'Give me a hand with this!'

'What is you doin' wiv dat pipe fing?' said Iggy, standing there and not helping at all.

'We've got to get this end all the way to the swimming pool! Come on, help me pull!'

Iggy didn't move. He sniffed and put his nose

in the air and said, 'Huh! Dat pipe fing won't reach.'

'Yes it will, Iggy! I measured before! When we were doing the digging! It reaches fine! Now, come *on*!'

Reluctantly, Iggy took hold of the hose and together they dragged it all across the kitchen yard, then onto the grass. The further they pulled it, the heavier it became, but finally they reached the edge of the pit. Both of them were breathing hard.

'Iggy, I want you to run back and turn on the tap. Can you do that?'

Iggy sniffed scornfully. 'Of courssse I can do dat!' he said. 'Wot do you fink I am—a ssstoopidy-poopidy?'

'No, I don't think you're a stoopidy-poopidy.'

'Good,' said Iggy, firmly. 'Den I will do it.' He paused, his face wriggling in thought. Then he said, 'Er . . . wot was it you wanted me to do, Mumps?'

'Turn on the tap, please.'

'Ho, yesss. Okey-dokey.'

Iggy shambled away towards the house and Measle bent down and put his hand on the brass nozzle. A few moments later, he felt the whole hose move and stiffen as it filled with water. Using both hands, Measle twisted the brass nozzle and a hard jet of water blasted out of it. He directed the stream down into the bottom of the pit and heard the water spray across the scattered bags of sugar. It made a sort of *blatting* sound as it smashed against the paper bags.

'Wot is you doin' *now*?' squealed Iggy, who had trotted back to Measle's side and was staring, with horror, down into the dark pit. 'Wot is you *doin'*? You is makin' all dat lovely sugar all *wet*! And den we won't be able to *eat* it, Mumps!'

'I'm filling up our swimming pool, Iggy!' said Measle, putting all the enthusiasm he could muster into his voice. 'And it will be lovely to swim in, won't it? Because, you see, the water will taste all sweet, like your jelly beans! In fact, it'll be like *swimming* in jelly beans!'

Measle saw Iggy's face break into a wide smile.

'Coo, dat will be nice, doin' swimmin' in jelly beans!'

The water roared down into the hole. The seconds, then the minutes, ticked by and Measle began to realize that filling a large hole in the ground with water was going to take quite a long time. The *blatting* sound of water smashing against paper bags had changed to a loud splashing noise, so Measle guessed that the level of the water must have risen just higher than the scattered sacks, but even so, at this rate, it was going to take an age to fill the pit.

'Iggy, could you go and see what that old Squiffypoo is doing?'

'Wot, now?' said Iggy.

'Yes, now! It may have got free—and we've got to get a lot more water into the pool before we can have our swim!'

'Okey-dokey,' said Iggy, and he trotted off into the darkness.

'Be careful!' yelled Measle, but Iggy didn't reply.

Measle held tight to the brass nozzle and directed the jet of water into the black pit. He didn't dare let go of the thing—he knew what happened when you let go of a hose when water was running through it. He and Iggy had been playing with it one day, seeing how high they could make the jet go and then, when they got bored with doing that, squirting water at each other—and Iggy had made the mistake of dropping the hose. Spraying water everywhere, the hose had started to wriggle and writhe all over the lawn, like a crazy snake, and it had taken Measle and Iggy a good three minutes to catch the thing again. By the time they did, they were both soaking wet.

Measle's hand started throbbing. He'd forgotten all about it in the excitement and terror of the chase but now, with the fingers of both hands clutched tightly around the brass nozzle of the hose, he could feel the pain. All of a sudden the discomfort, the darkness, the loneliness, and the danger of his situation seemed to lump together in a great heavy weight—and the weight settled on his shoulders like a big black slab of misery and fear that pressed him down towards the muddy ground.

Where's Iggy? Is he doing what I asked him

to do—or has he forgotten all about me and is off somewhere, gobbling the rest of his jelly beans?

I wish he'd come back.

I wish Tinker was here.

I wish Nanny was here.

I wish Mum and Dad were here.

But they're not.

And—I'm scared.

The minutes ticked away. The splashing sound had a deeper note to it now, as if the water itself was getting deeper. It was too dark to see into the pit, so Measle had no way of knowing just exactly how high the level of the water was, but he knew it couldn't be very high. Not yet at least.

''Ello, Mumps.'

Measle almost dropped the hose. He twisted his head round and here was Iggy, his face gleaming pale in the surrounding darkness.

'Iggy! You nearly gave me a heart attack!'

'Did I?' said Iggy, his face splitting into a proud grin. He had no idea what a heart attack was but it sounded a pretty important thing to give people and, since Mumps was his best friend, he was pleased he'd nearly given him one.

'Did you see the Slithergh— I mean, the Squiffypoo?' Measle asked.

'Ho, yesss,' said Iggy, his eyes wandering over the dark rectangle of the pit. 'I saw 'im all right. Can we ssswim yet?'

'Soon, Iggy. What was the Squiffypoo doing? Is it still stuck in the rose garden?'

Iggy shook his head. 'No, it's not ssstuck. Not no more, no how.'

'It's not? Well, what's it doing, Iggy?'

'It ssstarted to follow me, ssso I runned away, didn't I?'

'That was sensible, Iggy. So—where is it now?'

'Wot, de old Sssquiffypoo?' Iggy jerked his thumb over his shoulder. 'It's right behind me.'

Sugar and Slime

Even as Iggy spoke, Measle caught the first faint whiff of the horrendous Slitherghoul stench. He looked over Iggy's shoulder and there—rounding the far corner of the house and slithering over the gravel of the kitchen yard—it came.

The Slitherghoul seemed to pause for a moment. Then, it obviously saw Measle and Iggy, because it jerked forward towards the edge of the lawn, gathering speed as it slimed its way towards them.

Just for a second, Measle found himself paralysed with fear. He and Iggy were out in the open, with nowhere to hide—and the trap wasn't ready yet! The only weapon he had was the hose—and it wasn't much of a weapon, not against a creature that seemed oblivious to the drenching rain that cascaded against its body! Instinctively, Measle turned the nozzle away from the pit and aimed it straight at the fast-advancing creature.

The water blasted out in a great glittering arc but the Slitherghoul was still well out of range. Measle lifted the nozzle higher—

Then suddenly, the pressure in the hose relaxed and the jet of water from the nozzle died away to a trickle.

Measle stared down at the hose in disbelief. At the same moment, he heard the distant sound of water splashing down hard against gravel.

He looked up and saw that the Slitherghoul was speeding in a direct line towards him and Iggy, and the direct line lay exactly over the top of the hose that was stretched along the grass. The weight of the Slitherghoul must have forcibly yanked the other end of the hose clean off the tap.

Measle dropped the nozzle and took a step backwards. Immediately he felt the muddy ground crumble beneath his feet. He waved both arms wildly, in an attempt to keep his balance, but it was no good. The edge of the pit slipped away, carrying Measle with it, down into the darkness.

SPLASH!

Measle landed on his back, sending a great spray of water up into the air. The water quickly flooded through his clothes. He struggled and his feet found the muddy bottom. He stood up. The water came to just above his knees. Something pale floated by.

'Dat old Sssquiffypoo is comin', Mumps!' called Iggy's voice from somewhere above him. 'It's comin' fassst! It's nearly here! I don't fink dis is a good time to go ssswimmin'!'

Measle floundered in the icy water. The bottom of the pit was slippery with mud and there were lots of the pale, floating things scattered across the dark surface—the sodden remains of the paper sugar bags.

Then, without warning, there was a tremendous SPLASH! right at Measle's side and Measle received a great wave of water directly in his face. Sputtering, he cleared his eyes.

In the dimness, he could just make out Iggy, who was sitting in the mud looking crossly at the water that reached halfway up his chest.

''Ere—I do not *like* dis ssswimmin', Mumps,' Iggy announced, making no effort to get to his feet. 'I is all wet—*all over*! I don't like bein' all wet— not all *over*!'

Measle lunged and grabbed Iggy's sleeve.

'Come on, Iggy, we've got to get out of here!'

Iggy didn't respond. He was thoughtfully sucking one of his claw-like fingers.

'Dat's funny,' he mumbled. 'Dis swimmin' water tastes quite nice. Maybe dis ssswimmin' ain't ssso bad after all.'

It was obvious Iggy had completely forgotten everything Measle had told him about the plan and there was no time to explain it all over again.

207

Measle pulled hard at Iggy's sleeve, causing the finger to pop out of the little wrathmonk's mouth.

''Ang, on Mumps! I wasn't finished!'

'Come *on*, Iggy!'

His feet slipping and sliding on the muddy bottom of the pit, Measle started to drag Iggy towards the sloping shallow end. Together, they sloshed their way through the black water, the masses of sodden, floating paper bags making their progress even harder. They'd only got about halfway there, when Measle once again caught the dreadful stench of the Slitherghoul. He whipped his head around.

There, at the far end—where the pit was deepest—silhouetted against the dark sky, loomed the Slitherghoul. Measle could see that it was poised right at the edge of the pit and, even without any visible eyes, appeared to be staring down at them.

It had never been part of the plan to be in the pit themselves but Measle realized in that instant that the accident that had put him there was probably a bit of unlooked-for luck. The problem of getting the Slitherghoul into the pit was something that had bothered him and he'd pushed the whole thing to the back of his mind, in the hope that, when the time actually came, he'd have a solution. But here—cold and wet and muddy though it might be—*was* a solution! And it was so *obvious*.

Measle let go of Iggy's sleeve and started to

wave both his arms frantically over his head. He jumped and splashed and screamed as loud as he could.

'Here! I'm down here, you old Squiffypoo! Come and get me, you stinky thing! Last one in the pool's a weedy sissy!'

The dark mass of the Slitherghoul seemed to shiver. Then, without a sound, it heaved itself forward, over the crumbling edge of the pit. The entire creature half fell, half slithered down into the water, making a wave that almost knocked Measle off his feet. For a moment, the Slitherghoul seemed to disappear beneath the surface but then, a second later, Measle saw the great mound of slime rear itself up again. Sodden scraps of paper bags festooned its jelly sides.

'Come on, Iggy! RUN!'

Iggy had been bending over, his face close to the muddy water, surreptitiously slurping the sweet stuff into his mouth when Measle grabbed him and started to drag him away. He slipped and fell but Measle kept on dragging him through the water and Iggy, lying prone, took the opportunity to swallow a few more mouthfuls. He felt himself being hauled up a slope, and now it was hard for his mouth to reach the surface of the water, because the water was getting shallower and shallower.

Measle was almost at the top of the slope and his feet were clear of the water. Held tight by one sleeve, Iggy was still lying there, his head bent sideways in a final attempt to get just one more swallow. With a last effort, Measle heaved Iggy clear of the water.

Measle paused for a second, panting hard.

They both heard the hissing sound at the same moment. Measle turned and Iggy lifted his head and they both stared down into the pit.

The hissing sound came from the Slitherghoul —or rather, it came from the Slitherghoul's skin. The creature made no sound, but plumes of steam seemed to be rising from the muddy water that surrounded it. The monster itself was writhing and rippling and shuddering and floundering, causing a succession of large waves to splash against the sides of the pit—and those same waves, rebounding off the walls, swept back and over the top of the struggling mound of jelly, *which was gradually getting smaller*.

There was no doubt about it. As it flopped and struggled in the muddy water, Measle could see that the Slitherghoul was slowly shrinking.

Then a very strange thing—even stranger than the shrinking—happened.

Two yellow bubbles, like nasty zits only much, much bigger, swelled up on the outer surface of the Slitherghoul. As Measle and Iggy watched, the bubbles grew and then burst wetly, exposing a pair of slime-covered heads. The heads twisted and turned in what looked like an effort to drag themselves clear, and the attempt seemed to work, because, next, two pairs of shoulders were exposed, then four arms. A moment later, he and Iggy could see two waists, then four legs.

Mr Needle and Mr Bland fell, with a double splash, away from the quivering surface of the Slitherghoul and into the muddy water. Both men disappeared beneath the surface for a second or two, then their heads rose back out. Mr Needle and Mr Bland coughed and spluttered and wiped the slime from their eyes. Then they turned and saw the great quaking mound of jelly behind them.

Mr Needle screamed—and so did Mr Bland. Slipping and sliding and bumping into each other in their panic, they scrambled away from the creature as fast as they could. They stumbled up the slope, seeming not to see Measle and Iggy at all. They simply blundered past them, their clothes and hair soggy with muddy water and stinking slime. When they reached the top, both men stared wildly in all directions, then ran away into the darkness.

Measle pulled Iggy to his feet and they both stared down at the slowly diminishing monster. It was still enormous—it filled the deep end of the pit completely—and it displaced a huge amount of water, so much so that the level of the sweetened liquid reached about three quarters up its rippling sides. It seemed incapable of forward movement, because it made no effort to drag itself out of the stuff that was hurting it so badly, and Measle wondered if, somehow, it was paralysed. But, whatever else was happening to it, the gradual shrivelling continued.

Another bubble appeared on the skin of the Slitherghoul. This time, the shape of the bubble wasn't round, like the ones that had contained the heads of Needle and Bland. This bubble was smaller and roughly rectangular. When it burst, it exposed something that, beneath the slime, seemed to be covered in hair—white and fuzzy hair.

With a yelp, Tinker's little body slipped out of the slime, slid down the flank of the Slitherghoul, and splashed into the water. His nose bobbed up and he sneezed twice and shook his head furiously—then, seeing Measle and Iggy standing at the top of a long, muddy slope, he dog-paddled towards them. A moment later, his paws touched down on solid ground and he raced up the incline and jumped into Measle's arms.

Like all dogs, Tinker had—in the past—done his fair share of finding disgusting things to roll in and then, having worked as much of the disgusting stinky stuff into his fur as he possibly could, had run indoors to show off his new smell to everybody. Measle had always felt sorry for him when Nanny Flannel had dragged him off for a forced bath. This time, Tinker could smell as bad as he liked, because Measle's joy at finding the little dog alive and well knew no bounds. And Tinker stank. He stank really badly, and his fuzzy white fur was matted with slime—but Measle didn't care.

Even as his face was being licked frantically by a doggy tongue, Measle's mind was working overtime. The Slitherghoul seemed to be giving up its victims! *First, Mr Needle and Mr Bland, then Tinker, so, who'll be next to emerge?* He remembered the sequence—*the Slitherghoul swallowed Nanny Flannel first, then Tinker, then Needle and Bland—and it was letting them out in reverse order, which meant that the next victim to appear ought to be—*

Even as he was working it out, the stout shape of Nanny Flannel was rising up out of the shrivelling jelly. Her glasses were askew and her hair had come loose—and the moment her feet were free, she rolled and tumbled down the side of the Slitherghoul and splashed into the muddy water. But there was no pause for spluttering—not from Nanny Flannel. She found her feet and, without a backward glance, strode firmly through the sloshing water and up the slope to Measle's side.

'Oh! Look at the state of me!' she said, smiling cheerfully into Measle's eyes and trying to wipe some of the slime from the front of her dress. 'I won't try to kiss you, dear—I see Tinker's already doing that and the last thing you need is to be covered with any *more* of this foul stuff. Now, I don't know how you did it, Measle, but I can't tell you how nice it is to be outside that disgusting thing!'

Measle was speechless with happiness. He couldn't do much of anything except grin with delight. Nanny Flannel seemed to understand his silence, because she began to try to clean her glasses on her dress, but all she managed to do was transfer slime from one surface to another. She gave up and popped the smeary spectacles into her pocket.

'I can't see a thing, dear,' she said. 'What's happening?' She peered short-sightedly down into the darkness of the pit.

Measle and Iggy peered too. There was movement—a lot of movement—down there. It was too dark to make out exactly what was happening, but all over the shuddering slimy body of the Slitherghoul small bubbles were forming, some no bigger than the head of a pin, some as large as a man's fist—and, as Measle and Iggy watched and Nanny Flannel squinted in horrified wonder, the bubbles began to burst, releasing whatever was inside. It was too dark to make out the small objects that were now streaming down the flanks of the Slitherghoul—but within a few moments, the surface of the surrounding water started to bubble and heave with activity.

'Whatever is going on?' said Nanny Flannel. A

moment later, Measle understood what was going on, because some of the larger objects that were disturbing the water in the pit began to move towards the shallow end. Once they found solid ground, they pulled themselves out of the water and ran up the slope, rushing past Measle's feet.

Rats. Mice. Several voles. Some tiny shrews. Three rabbits. A weasel—

'They've all come out of the Slitherghoul!' said Measle. 'It must have swallowed them too!'

They all looked back at the shrinking creature flopping and floundering in the muddy water. The surface of the pool was still alive with activity, but whatever the animals were that were causing the movement, they didn't seem to be moving anywhere in particular.

'Insects!' whispered Measle. 'They don't know which way to go. The Slitherghoul must have swallowed up thousands of them!'

'Time to go, dear,' said Nanny Flannel firmly. She took Measle's hand and pulled him gently, and Measle dragged his eyes away from the extraordinary spectacle down in the bottom of the pit and allowed himself to be led out onto the grass. Iggy shambled after them.

'Now then, Measle,' said Nanny Flannel, 'there are other creatures inside that nasty thing and I imagine it won't be long before they escape too. I don't know what or who they were, because inside that monster I could only *sense* their presence, but I know that most of them mean you harm—'

'I think I know who they are, Nanny,' said Measle. 'Toby Jugg is in there—I know that because I saw him—and I think all the wrathmonks from the Detention Centre are in there too, including the four who hate me most—Griswold Gristle and Buford Cudgel and Frognell Flabbit and that stupid Judge, too—'

Nanny Flannel interrupted him. 'Then, dear, let's get away from here as fast as possible,' she said. 'Because, if you're right, then they should be making their appearances any minute now!'

Even as Nanny Flannel stopped speaking, a larger bubble was forming on the top of the Slitherghoul and, a second later, the head of a young wrathmonk with red hair and protruding ears popped out. All over the Slitherghoul's body, other lumps and bubbles were rising out of the slime.

'Come on, dear!' said Nanny Flannel, raising her voice—and Measle and Iggy didn't need any further encouragement. Measle put Tinker down on the grass and, together, the four of them ran quickly across the lawn, towards the looming shadow of the house. When they got to the kitchen yard, the sound of splashing water reached their ears. The tap in the wall was still running at full force and Nanny Flannel marched over to it. She took her filthy spectacles from her pocket and held them under the stream. Then she shook the water off the lenses and turned the tap off.

'No point wasting water,' she muttered to herself. She reached deeper into her pocket and took out a handkerchief and dried the glasses. Then, perching the glasses on the end of her nose, she turned to Measle and said, 'Now then, dear, you're usually very good in this sort of situation. Any idea what we do now?'

For once, Measle was at a loss. So many things had happened so quickly over the last few minutes he hadn't had time to plan ahead. And plan for what? What was going to happen next anyway? Gloomily, he shook his head and said, 'Haven't a clue, Nanny.'

'Pity,' said Nanny and Measle detected a note of grimness in her voice. 'A great pity,' she repeated, 'because I can just about make out a couple of shapes coming out of your swimming pool—and they both look quite human, I'm sorry to say.'

Measle whipped his head round and peered out across the expanse of grass. Dimly, he could make out two figures on their hands and knees crawling up out of the pit. It was too dark to see who they were.

Measle squinted, trying desperately to pierce the gloom. As he strained his eyes, he saw a third figure emerge from the pit—and this figure was huge and hulking and Measle remembered only one huge and hulking figure from the Detention Centre.

'I think one of them is Mr Cudgel!' he whispered urgently. 'And that means—'

'And that means the other brutes won't be far behind!' said Nanny Flannel. 'We must find somewhere safe. Not the house—that's the first place they'll look!'

As if they all had the same thought, Measle, Iggy, and Nanny Flannel crept as silently as they could to the corner of the kitchen yard, putting a little more distance between themselves and the distant pool. By the time they reached the spot, two more shapes had crawled out of the pit and had joined the others. At the moment, all of them were still on their hands and knees, their heads hung low, and Measle could just make out the faint sounds of gasping and coughing and spluttering.

Nanny Flannel tapped him on the arm. 'Measle, dear, the big question is—have they still got their wrathrings on?'

It dawned on Measle that this was indeed the Big Question. Without their wrathrings, the escaped prisoners were absolutely deadly. But, if they still had their wrathrings round their necks, some of the danger they threatened was reduced. The wrathrings would stop their major enchantments—but it would do nothing for their breathing spells. However, for a wrathmonk to perform his breathing spell, he had to be very close to his victim. There was no way of telling if the distant figures had dull silver rings around their throats and Measle had no intention of going any closer to them than he was right now.

'I don't know about the wrathrings, Nanny,' he said. 'But, either way, we've got to get away from here. I know Mr Gristle and Mr Cudgel would both like to try out their breathing spells on me and I'd rather they didn't get the chance.'

'Come on then, dear,' said Nanny Flannel. 'You too, Iggy. Stay with us, mind. They may be wrathmonks just like you but they're much, *much* nastier and you're not to go anywhere near them. Do you understand?'

'Yes, Miss Fwannel,' muttered Iggy obediently.

'Where are we going, Nanny?' asked Measle, relieved that, from now on, somebody else would be making the decisions.

'I don't like the idea of being caught out in the open, Measle. So I think we ought to barricade ourselves in somewhere. The garage, perhaps? That's got a good strong door and no windows. Assuming they have their wrathrings on—and let's hope they do!—we ought to be able to hold out in there for quite a while—and, with any luck, they won't find us anyway.'

Measle nodded slowly. There really was nowhere else to go.

'Good,' said Nanny Flannel, decisively. 'Let's go! Quickly now!'

Hurriedly, they turned the corner and ran along the side of the house, towards the distant garage.

THE SLIMY BUNCH

Under a steady downpour of icy cold rain, a crowd of wrathmonks was gathering on the muddy grass by the side of the pit.

Most of them were on their knees, coughing and spluttering and spitting and not taking notice of anything much, other than concentrating on clearing their eyes and noses and throats of the stinking slime that covered them from head to foot. They all felt strangely weak as well, with arms and legs that seemed to be made of softened wax. The wrathmonks had been cradled in the comfort of the Slitherghoul for several days now, without being able to move even a fingertip, and the result was that their muscles had become flabby with disuse. They felt sick and confused as well.

Griswold Gristle was the first to recover his senses. He sat on the damp lawn and looked around in the darkness. He could see Buford Cudgel, a few metres away, bent double and gasping for air. Frognell Flabbit knelt nearby, scraping slime from his head and wiping his hands on the grass. Judge Cedric Hardscrabble lay on his back by the very edge of the pit, his bowler hat over his face. He seemed to be fast asleep.

The rest of the wrathmonks were slowly dragging themselves up and out. In the darkness, they looked like dead people rising from their graves—or, in this case, from one giant communal grave.

'Mr Cudgel! Mr Cudgel!' croaked Griswold, climbing unsteadily to his feet.

'What?' growled Cudgel, lifting his big, bullet head and glaring angrily at Griswold.

'Would you be ssso kind and look down into the hole and sssee what has become of the creature? I would not care to be ssswallowed up inssside it again!'

Cudgel grunted and then crawled to the edge of the pit and looked down. He was quite still for several seconds and Griswold began to wonder what was keeping him so interested. Then Cudgel swung his head and rumbled, 'It's got sssmall, Griswold. Not much bigger than a table.'

'And what is it doing, dear Mr Cudgel?'

'Sssplashing about. It looks a bit feeble, if you asssk me.'

'Not moving out of the water?'

'No.'

Griswold shivered. His clothes were soaked with slime and water and he was getting very cold.

'Mr Flabbit! Cedric! Come to me, please! You too, Mr Cudgel, if you would be ssso kind?'

Buford and Frognell shambled over to where Griswold was standing. Judge Cedric stayed where he was. He raised his bowler hat off his face and said, in a faint voice, 'What a mossst extraordinary dream I've just had, dear Griswold! Let me tell you all about it! There was thisss enormous lump, mossst peculiar it was, of what I can only dessscribe as yellowish-brownish-greenish jelly—'

'Cedric!' snapped Griswold. 'Be quiet and come here!'

Slowly, his ancient bones creaking with the effort, Judge Cedric Hardscrabble dragged himself to his feet and, his legs wobbling unsteadily beneath him, he stumbled over to join the group.

The other wrathmonks from the Detention Centre simply sat about on the grass and stared round with bewilderment. Never having been to Merlin Manor before, they had no idea where they were. They noticed, vaguely, that there was a small group of four wrathmonks over to one side, who seemed to be engaged in an urgent, whispered conversation.

Separated from them were two figures who seemed, somehow, different from the rest.

Toby Jugg huddled on a pile of mud, his knees drawn tight against his chest, both arms wrapped round his legs. He was gazing wild-eyed down at the edge of the pit. Nearby, Officer Offal was squatting on his haunches, having a hard time wiping the slime from his broad, pink face.

Toby's long hair was soggy with slime and water and it lay plastered flat against his head, exposing both of Toby's ears. The Gloomstains—those dark, greyish-blackish discolourations that showed the world that he was a powerful warlock—had disappeared from the tips of his ears and now, instead, Toby had a brand new and impressively large rain cloud hovering a few metres above his head. He appeared not to notice the drenching rain that beat down on him, but Officer Offal, with one eye finally cleared of the stinking slime, noticed it. Offal peered a little closer at the figure under the cloud and saw, with a sudden start of fear, that Toby's ears were clear of the Gloomstains. He experienced a sudden, sick feeling. The evidence was right before his eyes and Officer Offal knew exactly what it meant.

Toby Jugg was no longer a very powerful warlock who had been reasonably friendly towards him.

Toby Jugg was now a very powerful *wrathmonk* —and who knew what the insane creature's attitude would be now?

Officer Offal didn't want to wait to find out. He shuffled backwards hurriedly.

The movement caught Toby's eyes. They were now an unpleasant shade of yellow. Slowly, Toby turned his head and his yellow eyes rested on the figure of Offal as he tried, as unobtrusively as possible, to edge away into the shadows.

'Ah—there you are, Offal,' said Toby, gently, and Offal stopped trying to shuffle away and sat, as still as a statue, a weak little smile hovering on his mouth.

'I feel sssomewhat ssstrange,' said Toby, hissing like a snake. His eyebrows rose in surprise at the sounds he was making. Then he lifted his big, lion head and stared upwards at the black cloud that hovered overhead.

'Ah,' he said, slowly. 'Now I undersssstand. How very interesssting. I wonder—'

Toby broke off. Tentatively, he reached up and touched the dull silver wrathring round his neck. His eyes narrowed with anger and frustration. Then his face relaxed. He opened his mouth, took in a small breath and puffed it out—and a tiny cloud of glittering particles appeared in the still night air. Toby smiled a small, secretive smile. Then he said, 'Officer Offal, would you be ssso kind and come over here? I have missed you ssso much. I would like you to sssit bessside me. Come, Officer Offal.'

Offal licked his fat lips nervously and Toby said, 'I won't hurt you, Officer Offal. I promise I won't hurt you.'

Offal smiled a sickly smile. Knowing there was

nothing else he could do, he crawled slowly and reluctantly across the wet grass and sat down a metre from Toby's side.

'Thank you, Officer Offal,' said Toby. He grinned wolfishly at Offal and Offal saw, quite clearly, the two sets of pointed teeth on either side of Toby's mouth glowing white in the darkness.

And then Toby broke his promise. He whispered, 'You're my own little guinea pig, Officer Offal. My own, fat little guinea pig. And I'm a wicked liar.' He took a deep breath, leaned towards the tubby ex-guard, and *blew* at him.

Toby's breath glittered white in the darkness. It was a pale, gleaming cone of vapour that spread out from his lips and washed over Officer Offal's head like a wave crashing over a rock.

Instantly, Offal's face froze; not only in the sense that it stopped moving, but also quite *literally*. His sickly grin remained plastered across his face as a fine layer of frost spread across his pink cheeks, turning them a ghostly white. Tiny icicles formed on his bushy eyebrows and his dying eyes shone with a thin sheet of ice film. Toby went on breathing softly over Offal and his frigid breath spread the freezing effect over the whole of the guard's body, until he was completely covered with a layer of frost, and icicles hung from his chin. Beneath the film of white, Offal's skin had turned a pale, ghostly blue.

Toby stopped breathing. He stuck out one finger

and prodded Offal's chest. It was as hard as stone. Toby pushed a little harder. Slowly, the frozen body of the guard toppled sideways and fell, with a solid-sounding *clunk!* onto the grass. Toby peered closer. There was no movement at all, not even the rise and fall from the man's chest, that would show he was still breathing. Offal might as well have been made of granite.

Toby smiled. Then he muttered, 'Hmm. Remarkable. Inssstant death by freezing! Not at all a bad exhalation enchantment! A sssplendid one, in fact! But no less than was to be expected with a warlock of my ssstanding!'

He turned his handsome head, sweeping his yellow eyes over the wretched collection of wet, shivering wrathmonks. Then his gaze centred on a group of four wrathmonks, a little separated from the rest, their heads huddled together. There was something about them that was vaguely familiar to Toby, as if he'd seen them somewhere before, but couldn't quite work out where. One of them was a great giant of a man, with a bullet head and a massive, bulldog jaw; one was small, with tiny black eyes and a shiny, billiard-ball head. The third had a red, lumpy face and a long hank of greasy hair combed over his forehead to disguise his baldness; the fourth was very old, with a great bush of frizzy white hair sticking out from under an ancient bowler hat. All four wrathmonks wore white prison jumpsuits, which meant that they, too, had been captives in some section of the Detention Centre.

Toby shook his head, trying to remember where he might have seen them before but there seemed to be something wrong with his brain. He didn't usually have this trouble with thinking or remembering—and then he realized what he was. *I'm a wrathmonk! Which means I'm insane! Which means my mind won't work as well as before—but perhaps the advantages will outweigh the disadvantages! But, first things first—I shall need some friends!*

Staggering a little on weak and wobbly legs, Toby rose to his feet and stumbled towards the four huddled wrathmonks.

Down at the bottom of the pit, the thrashing, writhing, rippling movements of the Slitherghoul were weakening. Buford Cudgel had been right: it was now no bigger than a dining table. The muddy water that surrounded it now sometimes washed clear over the top of the mound of jelly, sloshing round yet another bubble of slime that was rising out of the creature. The bubble popped—and Corky Pretzel's head emerged, quickly followed by Corky Pretzel's big, muscle-bound body. There was now no distance for Corky to fall—he simply flopped sideways, hitting the water with a gentle splash.

Corky—just like everybody else—was keen to get as far away from the foul creature as he possibly could. But, even as he began to struggle towards the shallow end, Corky heard voices from somewhere up above.

They were voices he recognized: two of his prisoners from the Detention Centre.

'But—dear Griswold—' bleated the quavering voice of Judge Cedric Hardscrabble, and instantly came back, 'No, Cedric!' in the oily, irritated tones of Griswold Gristle. 'I cannot provide you with an umbrella and, even if I could, I wouldn't bother! We have more pressing matters to attend to, than finding you a ssstupid umbrella!'

Corky froze. He pressed himself tight up against the muddy wall of the pit, as far away from the Slitherghoul as possible, with only his head showing above the water. While he'd been considerably kinder and more sensitive than Officer Offal had ever been, he was still the Detention Centre guard and the voices that were floating down to him were the voices of his prisoner wrathmonks, every single one of whom would be happy to see him dead.

The Slitherghoul itself took no notice of him. It simply continued to flounder and thrash, its movements becoming progressively weaker and weaker. It was now no bigger than a coffee table.

'Gentlemen,' came another voice from above and Corky listened even more intently than before because there was something odd about the voice. He *thought* he recognized it but there was something a little different about it, something he couldn't quite put his finger on—

'Gentlemen—forgive me for interrupting you, but you four sssseem to have collected your wits about you sssomewhat more quickly than those other poor wretches over there. And, sssince I too appear to have a greater undersssstanding of our circumstances than they do, I thought I would approach you and introduce myssself. I am Toby Jugg—at your ssservice, gentlemen!'

Corky wasn't clever but he knew the difference between a warlock and a wrathmonk. He'd also been down in the bowels of the Wizards' Guild long enough to know all his prisoners by name and it wasn't longer than five seconds before Corky worked out that the hissing sounds he could hear in Toby Jugg's voice meant only one thing. Corky didn't need to see Toby's rain cloud—he knew with a certainty that it would be there, hovering a few metres over Toby's head.

'What do you want with usss?' said Griswold, coldly—and Corky remembered that wrathmonks were not naturally drawn towards others of their kind, unless those others could somehow be of benefit to them. Indeed, Corky knew that wrathmonks often heartily detested each other.

'I would like to know if it was any of you that was interesssted in the Ssstubbs boy,' said Toby, his voice relaxed and genial. 'If ssso, then you should know that it was I who joined my mind with yours and helped you in the pursuit.'

'Really?' said Griswold, his voice still sneery with distrust. 'And why should we believe you?'

'Were you not aware that another mind—and a ssstrong one, too—was allied to your efforts?'

Reluctantly, Griswold conceded that they had felt a certain encouraging presence and Judge Cedric said that, to him, the additional mind intruding on his thoughts had felt a bit like having a scratchy little kitten inside his head.

'Yesss, yesss, Cedric!' snapped Griswold, irritably. 'We don't wish to hear about kittens! Thisss fellow is claiming an interessst in the Ssstubbs boy. Well, what is ssso different about that, may I asssk? Any wrathmonk worth his sssalt would have the sssame interessst—a desire to wreak revenge on the Ssstubbs family! What makes you ssso different, Missster Jugg? And another thing—why were you not in the Detention Centre, along with the ressst of usss, eh?'

Corky strained his ears. He knew the answer, of course, but he wanted to hear it from Toby Jugg himself.

'I am new to your ranks, gentlemen,' came Toby's easy-going, friendly voice. 'Until very recently, I was but a lowly warlock, imprisoned in the High Sssecurity block of the Detention Centre, along with a fellow I am sure you remember. A fellow by the name of Officer Offal?'

There was a hate-filled hissing from the four wrathmonks. Toby's voice came again, drowning out the sounds of enraged snakes. 'You'll be happy to hear that I have dealt with him on your behalf. He's over there, closely resembling a frozen Chrissstmas turkey—the result of my newly-discovered exhalation enchantment. Please feel free to examine him.'

Corky heard shuffling sounds as the wrathmonks moved away. He was about to move himself— about to get himself out of this freezing, filthy water, about to get away from the wriggling mound of jelly—when a sudden gust of wind swept across the lawns of Merlin Manor, driving rain from the various wrathmonk clouds sideways. Corky received a splattering of drops on his upturned face and, immediately, he huddled back against the muddy wall of the pit, staring anxiously upwards. The rain on his face meant that there was still a wrathmonk nearby. Then he heard a strange little noise. It took him several moments to work out what it was—Toby Jugg was humming cheerfully to himself.

There were three small splashes in the water next to the Slitherghoul and Corky switched his gaze from the rectangle of dark sky above his head. Three little creatures were swimming towards the shallow end of the pool and Corky could just about make out what they were.

Two rats and a mouse. The mouse seemed to be

having difficulty steering towards the shallows and, once or twice, it even went in small circles—almost as if there was something wrong with its eyesight. All three animals swam slowly, their legs moving stiffly and weakly through the water but, eventually, all three made it to shallow water and, once their paws found solid ground beneath them, all three staggered—like little drunk men—up the muddy slope and out of sight.

Then came the sounds of the four wrathmonks returning and Corky, switching his gaze back up to the rectangle of night sky, shrank further back into the shadows and tried hard to stop his teeth from chattering.

'Not bad, Missster Jugg,' came Griswold's oily voice, and now there was a note of respect in it. 'Not bad at all. Of courssse, we four were hoping to have the pleasure of dealing with that oaf Offal in our own ways but you ssseem to have done the job for usss—in a fairly effective manner, I sssuppose. Ssso—that is your exhalation enchantment, is it? Breath of ice?'

'It ssseems to be,' said Toby.

'Hmm. You should consider yoursssself fortunate,' said Griswold. 'Only a very few wrathmonks are possessed of *fatal* breathing spells.'

'Is that ssso?' said Toby. 'Then I am indeed fortunate! And what, may I ask, are yours?'

'Boils!' came Judge Cedric's reedy voice. 'Sssplendid boils and ssspots and pimples, all over!'

'Toothache!' said Frognell Flabbit, in his pompous, important voice. '*Agonizing* toothache. Mossst effective, if I do sssay ssso myssself!'

'Mine is of the more *fatal* variety,' drawled Griswold, in a superior tone. 'My exhalation enchantment has the effect of rapid and total dehydration. It dries out all the body's natural fluids, leaving behind—I'm delighted to sssay—nothing more than a little, shrivelled, desiccated corpse!'

There was a pause and then Corky heard Toby say, 'And you, sssir? Although, I must sssay, your great sssize and ssstrength would almost be all that you need, I should imagine.'

'Mine is fatal, too,' came Buford Cudgel's rumbling voice.

'Unfortunately for Mr Cudgel,' squeaked Griswold, 'and jussst between oursssselves, you undersssstand, he is quite unable to use it!'

'Shut your mouth, Gristle!' barked Cudgel and Griswold's voice stopped dead. Corky strained his ears harder. This was the first he'd heard about Buford Cudgel being unable to use his exhalation enchantment and he hoped he'd hear more. He wasn't disappointed.

'I'm ssso sssorry to hear that,' said Toby. 'Why, it mussst be an *extraordinary* enchantment indeed! I am mossst interesssted—do *please* tell me about it.' And Toby used such a friendly, concerned, and interested voice that Buford Cudgel appeared to soften towards him, because Corky heard the giant wrathmonk mutter, 'It's because it's too dangerousss, even for me, sssee?'

'Too dangerousss? How amazing! How is it too dangerousss?'

'It makes all the germs and bacteria in my victim grow to the sssize of inssssects,' said Cudgel, and Corky detected a note of pride in the voice that sounded like distant thunder.

'And,' interrupted Griswold Gristle, 'poor Mr Cudgel has only ever used it once—when he first achieved wrathmonkhood—and that was on a little bluebottle which was buzzing round his head. He breathed on it—and what do you sssuppose happened next?'

'Who's telling thisss ssstory, Gristle—you or me?' rumbled Cudgel.

'Why, *you* are, my dear Missster Cudgel,' said Griswold in a wheedling voice. Then he added, in a voice that was tinged with sarcasm, 'But, perhapsss you might do it *quickly*, sssince we are all sssomewhat cold and wet and I for one would prefer that to be otherwise!'

'Right. Well, I found out how many germs a fly has on it—and *in* it,' said Cudgel, his enormous frame shuddering at the memory. 'It's billions—*trillions* even! The whole room filled up with these horrible things and then they overflowed into the hall and up the ssstairs. They were crawling everywhere, biting and ssstinging and chewing—I only jussst got out of there alive. The whole house burssst open like a rotten apple and they ssstarted filling up the back yard—'

'It was lucky that their life sssspan outside their host is quite short,' interrupted Griswold. 'Also, there happened to be a cave nearby, full of bats! There must have been a couple of million of the dear furry creatures! They came out and ssstarted to eat the germs as fassst as they could. It took them a whole week and at the end they were the fattest bats you've ever ssseen—'

'They could hardly fly at all!' said Cudgel, gloomily. 'Sssince then, I never dared use my breathing ssspell.'

'Sssuch a pity,' breathed Griswold. 'One would ssso like to sssee it in action.'

'Ssso would I,' whispered Toby, respectfully. 'Ssso would I!'

There was a long silence, while the wrathmonks savoured the thought of Buford Cudgel's unusable spell. Then Toby, injecting an even more respectful tone into his voice, said, 'How wonderful, to be wrathmonks of sssuch great experience! How I should be honoured to learn from you all!'

This seemed to have the right effect, because Griswold said, in a brisk, business-like voice, 'Missster Jugg, you mentioned earlier you were interesssted in the Ssstubbs boy meeting an unpleasant end. Ssso are we. Perhapsss you would care to join forces with us? In an inferior capacity, of coursse—but perhapsss we can teach you sssomething of our wrathmonk ways!'

'I would be ssso very grateful,' said Toby. 'Perhaps —dare I sssuggessst this—we might move to sssomewhere a little drier? Perhaps we could find a room in that house there, where we could dissscuss matters?'

This suggestion obviously met with approval, because Corky heard a rumble of agreement and immediately the group of wrathmonks moved away, out of his earshot. Corky waited. When he'd heard nothing from above for several minutes, he was about to wade through the muddy water towards the shallow end when a sudden splashing sound reached his ears. The noise was quite different from the floundering sounds of the Slitherghoul, which seemed to have stopped altogether.

Corky looked into the shadows and saw, to his surprise, that the Slitherghoul had disappeared. In its place was the figure of a pale, skinny young man, in a long black robe. The young man was splashing feebly in the water, his eyes tight closed, his mouth opening and closing like a dying fish. He had long, stringy black hair and a nose that was so big it seemed to be crowding out all his other features. Corky watched as the young man's head suddenly disappeared under the water, then rose again, coughing and spluttering. He was obviously so weak as to be in danger of drowning and, while he was rather an unpleasant looking specimen of humanity, Corky had no intention of letting that happen.

Corky waded over and scooped the thin body out of the water, cradling it in his arms. The young man's eyes opened momentarily, then closed just as fast. A soft moan emerged from his mouth, then his head flopped sideways and he stopped moving. Corky bent and pressed an ear to the man's skinny chest. The beating of his heart was there—slow and very faint—but it was regular and, with the small rise and fall of the man's chest, Corky thought that there was a good chance the man might simply have fainted away.

'Come on, then, you,' muttered Corky, hoisting the slimy little body onto one shoulder with no more effort than if it had been an empty sack. 'Come on, whoever you are. Let's see if we can get ourselves up and out of here, eh?'

Corky waded silently to the shallow end. He stepped carefully on the slick, slippery mud, moving up the slope until his eyes could peek over the top. He turned slowly, peering into the empty darkness. The lawn appeared to be deserted. *No! There! Over by the looming shadow of the great house—a bunch of white-suited wrathmonks! It looks like most of 'em! And they're just about far enough away not to see us if I'm careful.*

Corky crept up the slope and out onto the grass. Then, hunched low, he began to move quickly away from Merlin Manor and towards a distant line of trees.

THE GARAGE

The garage of Merlin Manor had once been a great stone barn, where the hay that had been cut at the end of the summer months was stored. It had been converted into a garage many years ago, by a predecessor of Sam Stubbs—a predecessor with lots of money, a passion for rare cars, and an equally strong passion for security. It had huge steel doors across the front, and no windows for a car-thief to climb through, other than a small, heavily-barred skylight set high up on the roof. Inside, Sam's predecessor had kept his splendid collection of new and antique automobiles—all fifty of them—so now there was more than enough room for the long, green Stubbs car *and* Nanny Flannel's motorbike. In fact, there was enough space inside the building for two or three school buses and a small plane as well. Like all garages, there was the usual sort of clutter around the walls. There were shelves with tools and old oil cans and rusty pitchforks and, running the length of the back wall, there was a sort of loft high up under the sloping roof, which could only be reached by climbing a rickety ladder.

In almost total darkness, Measle, Nanny Flannel, Iggy, and Tinker were huddled together up in the loft, half concealed in a pile of dusty hay. Their clothes were slowly drying out and their teeth were no longer chattering but they still felt cold and damp and uncomfortable. The slime was stiffening in Tinker's wiry fur, itching as it contracted, and the little dog was scratching himself busily with a back paw.

'Can you hear anything out there, dear?' asked Nanny Flannel, in a hoarse whisper.

'No, Nanny—Tink, keep still!—no, not a sound.'

'Where can they all have got to?' muttered Nanny Flannel.

'Well, I know where dey is *not*, Miss Fwannel,' hissed Iggy. 'Dey is not in *'ere*!'

Not yet, thought Measle.

The enemy wasn't very far away.

Toby had led Griswold Gristle, Buford Cudgel, Frognell Flabbit, and Judge Cedric Hardscrabble

242

away from the pit and across the grass to the kitchen yard. When the other wrathmonks saw this party of five walking with purpose towards the house, it had seemed like a good idea for them to follow, if only to see what the group had in mind. What Toby had in mind was, first, get out of the incessant rain and, second, go in search of Measle—because Measle was the most likely person to know where the Mallockee was. And when Measle had told Toby where she was, then there was no further reason to keep the boy alive . . . *But I mussst tread carefully*, he thought, *I mussst let the Gristle fellow think he is in charge—at leassst for the time being . . .*

The crowd of wrathmonks almost filled the ruined kitchen, but at least they were out of their rain. Some drops occasionally splashed in through the broken window, but the wrathmonks were already so wet, they didn't notice. They huddled together and listened while Griswold outlined his plan. When he'd finished, there was a silence.

'I don't sssee why we should help,' said Mungo MacToad, defiantly. His ginger hair was matted against his head, making his protruding ears look more pronounced than ever. 'It's nuthin' to do with usss.'

'I ssseem to remember that you were quite keen to join usss while we were all inssside that horrible creature,' said Griswold severely. He glared at the young wrathmonk through his tiny black eyes, his pasty white forehead furrowed in a frown.

'Yeah, well,' muttered Mungo, staring at the kitchen floor, 'that was when we was inssside, wasn't it? We was ssstuck, wasn't we? Nothing else to do. But now we're *free*, ain't we? And I for one ain't got no time to go hunting no boy.'

'Not even a *Ssstubbs* boy?' rumbled Buford Cudgel, clenching and unclenching his enormous fists.

Mungo sniffed and said nothing. He was mortally afraid of the giant wrathmonk.

'What about the ressst of you?' called Griswold, looking round at the crowd. 'Who among you would be ready to join usss in our hunt?'

There was a lot of shuffling of feet and staring at the littered kitchen floor, but not a single wrathmonk said a word.

Then Toby, in a small, humble voice, began to speak—and there was something about this big, broad-shouldered wrathmonk, with his yellow eyes and his great mane of grey-flecked hair, which made each member of that huddled crowd listen to every word. He spoke quietly and reasonably and his eyes made contact with each member of his audience in turn, so that every single wrathmonk felt that Toby was speaking to him, and him alone. And what Toby said made sense. He talked about the monstrous Stubbs family, and how it was the *duty* of every self-respecting wrathmonk in the world to exact revenge against every member of that family. He told them a little about the Mallockee, and how incredibly valuable she would be to the Wrathmonk cause. But mostly he spoke about Measle Stubbs, that terrible boy, who seemed to take pleasure in destroying their kind—he even ticked off the names of those whom Measle had killed. 'Our old friend Basil Tramplebone and his pet, Cuddlebug, Mr and Mrs Zagreb, young Ssscab Draggle—they all met terrible deaths at the hands of that unnatural boy!' Toby followed that with the list of those whom Measle had caused to be imprisoned. '*Wise* Judge Cedric Hardscrabble, *intrepid* Frognell Flabbit, the *great* Buford Cudgel, and the *brilliant* Griswold Gristle, not to mention myssself and perhapsss sssome of you as well? And, if it wasn't the boy who caught you, then it was mossst likely the foul Sssam Ssstubbs, was it not?'

At first, Griswold Gristle was annoyed that this newcomer to their ranks should take it upon himself to do all the persuading. But the more Griswold listened, the more he fell under Toby Jugg's spell and, by the time Toby finished speaking, Griswold had (without being fully aware of the fact) pretty much resigned the leadership of his group.

In fact, there wasn't a wrathmonk there who *didn't* fall under the spell of Toby's cheerful, persuasive voice and, when he fell silent, every fishy wrathmonk eye was staring at him with awe and admiration.

'Ssso, what do you want usss to do?' rumbled Buford Cudgel.

'Find Measle Ssstubbs,' said Toby, leaning elegantly against the cold kitchen stove. 'It shouldn't be difficult.'

'He is a ssslippery child,' said Griswold. 'He's very good at hiding, Missster Jugg.'

Toby eased himself off the stove. 'I don't doubt it, Missster Gristle. But tell me this—' And here Toby raised his nose and sniffed delicately at the still air—'am I wrong in thinking that, with the onset of thisss glorious wrathmonkhood, my sssense of sssmell has improved dramatically?'

'That's true enough,' said Frognell Flabbit. 'Your sssense of sssmell does get a lot better. Why?'

'Because,' said Toby, grinning cheerfully, 'using our noses, it would ssseem an easy matter to dissstinguish between Measle and all the ressst of us. Am I not right in thinking that Measle is the only living creature around here who has *not* been ssswallowed by the monster? And, if that is ssso, then am I not right in thinking that he will be the only living creature around here who will not sssmell of this ssstinking ssslime that covers usss all from head to foot?'

Several of the younger wrathmonks gave small, embarrassed grins. They thought the smell of the Slitherghoul quite pleasant on the whole . . .

'And therefore,' continued Toby, 'would it not be a sssimple affair to detect the sssmell of a fairly clean human boy, from the ssstench of all the ressst of us?'

There was a murmur of admiring assent from the wrathmonks. Logical thought was something very few wrathmonks went in for—mostly, they just did the first thing that came into their heads. Toby, sensing he now had them all in his power, herded them out to the kitchen yard, where they stood in a circle, under a downpour of rain, sniffing the night air.

'I got a whiff of sssomething jussst then,' said Mungo MacToad. 'I think it came from over there.' He pointed off to the side of the house. Toby said, 'Come, let usss follow our noses!' He set off in a purposeful, commanding manner and the wrathmonks fell in behind him, sniffing furiously. As they got closer to the distant garage, more and more wrathmonks picked up the scent—and now the excitement among them was rising.

'There, Missster Jugg!' exclaimed Griswold, pointing at the dark shape of the garage. 'I do believe he might be in there!'

Mungo MacToad sniffed harder than anybody. He said, 'No quessstion about it! He's in there!'

When they got to within five metres of the building, Toby paused and the rest of the wrathmonks came to a halt behind him. Toby scanned the tall stone wall, taking in the giant steel doors, with their massive hinges. Carefully, he walked all the way round the building and the crowd of wrathmonks followed respectfully in his footsteps. When he got back round to the front, Toby nodded in satisfaction. There were no other doors in the garage, and no windows at the back either. There was a small skylight set high in the slanting roof, but there was no way that any of them were going to be able to reach that. The only way in and out was in front of him. He approached the spot where the doors joined together. There was a pair of handles on either side of the join and Toby grasped them in his big hands and tried to pull the doors apart. He grunted with the effort, but the doors wouldn't budge.

'Let me try,' said Buford Cudgel, elbowing his way through the crowd. Toby stepped aside and Buford took hold of the handles, bunched the muscles in his broad back and strained—

The doors didn't even creak.

Toby motioned all the wrathmonks to move back several paces. Then he bent his head close to the door and called, 'Look, Measle, old ssson, I know you're in there! Now, don't be afraid, I don't mean you any harm. I jussst want to know where the Mallockee is, that's all! And your mother, of course! You tell me where the Mallockee is, and where your mother is, and I'll leave you alone! I'll leave all of you alone!'

Inside the garage, high up in the gallery, Iggy shivered under the hay. That was the voice of his old master, Toby Jugg! He'd always done what Toby

Jugg told him to do. For a moment, Iggy forgot all about the fact that Toby had been found guilty by the Court of Magistri and had been sent to rot deep in the bowels of the Wizards' Guild and that therefore he—Iggy—no longer owed any loyalty or obedience to his old master.

Iggy cupped his hands round his mouth and before either Measle or Nanny Flannel could stop him, he yelled, 'DE LITTLE FING AIN'T 'ERE, MISSSTER JUGG, SSSIR! DE LITTLE FING IS FAR, FAR AWAY, DOWN IN DE SSSOUTH HOLE! SHE'S— mmmmmph! mmmmmmph! mmmmmmph!'

Measle had managed to get his hand over Iggy's mouth just after Iggy had yelled 'Sssouth Hole!' but the damage was done. Toby's voice came back through the iron doors—

'Is that you, Missster Niggle? How interesssting to hear your voice again! And thank you ssso very much for the information!'

Outside, Toby straightened up, his face a mask of disappointment. He believed what Iggy had told him. There was no reason not to. Besides, he'd heard something about the upcoming South Pole conference from his guard, Corky Pretzel, and it made perfect sense that Sam Stubbs, the new Prime Magus of the Wizards' Guild, would take his magically-gifted daughter with him. And that meant that Lee Stubbs had most probably gone with them.

No Mallockee. No Manafount. This entire expedition was a waste of his time!

Griswold Gristle was tugging at his sleeve and Toby looked down at the small, bald wrathmonk with distaste.

'What do you want, Missster Gristle?'

'That perssson who ssspoke,' Griswold bleated, 'there are sssome among usss who believe he might be a wrathmonk—'

Toby shook off Griswold's clutching hand. 'He *is* a wrathmonk. His name is Ignatius Niggle, and he is a *traitor*, Missster Gristle! He is in league with the boy! He helped to imprison me! He's a weak, pathetic little turncoat! And, if you're going to kill Measle Ssstubbs, then I think he should die as well!'

Griswold Gristle shuddered with delight. The prospect of the imminent death of Measle Stubbs was just too wonderful for words, and, if that meant killing a treacherous little wrathmonk too— well, that hardly mattered at all!

'You will help usss, Missster Jugg? You will help us break down the doors?'

Toby stared up at the tall, windowless walls and the massive steel doors. It looked impossible, but a leader gives orders when his followers ask for them.

'Find tools. Hammers. The heavier the better.'

Griswold Gristle gathered the wrathmonks and explained what was needed. They scattered in all directions, searching the nearby outbuildings. Within minutes, they were back, clutching what they had found. Buford Cudgel held a big sledgehammer, the kind used for smashing concrete.

The rest of them had found a variety of tools, mostly quite useless. Toby curled his lip in contempt when he saw that Frognell Flabbit was carrying a small electrical screwdriver and he almost laughed out loud at Judge Cedric's find—a large tin of white paint.

The wrathmonks stood around, looking at Toby expectantly. He waved a hand at the steel doors and immediately the wrathmonks started to attack them with everything they'd got. Only Buford's hammer made any impression at all—a series of dents in the thick metal. Mungo MacToad scraped an old chisel viciously across the doors and Griswold Gristle pounded at them with a small spanner. Judge Cedric banged his tin of paint weakly against the barrier until the lid flew off and a great splash of white flew out and cascaded over his head.

Judge Cedric wailed and dropped his paint can and Mungo MacToad sneered and said, 'Oh, yeah, a definite improvement, I don't think!'

After five minutes of useless exercise, the wrathmonks gave up. Panting, they fell back from the doors and stared at them in disgust. Only Toby, who had taken no part in the attack, still breathed easily. He was mildly amused at the pathetic efforts of his little band of followers, but enough was enough. They would be expecting results from their leader and he must not disappoint.

Toby stepped near to the battered, paint-splashed

doors. He peered closer and saw for the first time that, in one of them, there was a large keyhole at waist level. There was no key in it. Toby bent and put his eye to the hole. He saw nothing but blackness. There was a piece of straw by his foot. Toby picked it up and pushed it into the keyhole. The straw met no resistance.

Toby straightened up. He turned to the clustered crowd of wrathmonks and his eyes singled out the hulking figure of Buford Cudgel.

'Missster Cudgel? A word, please?'

Buford lumbered forward, elbowing his way through the crowd.

'Yeah—what?'

Toby pointed to the keyhole. 'It occurred to me that your devassstating exhalation enchantment might jussst work in thisss sssituation, Missster Cudgel. Sssee, there is a sssmall hole through which you can blow—'

Buford shook his head. 'No, it's no good. I told you—it's too dangerousss! There's ssso many germs, the weight of 'em sssmashes down walls and breaks through doors—'

'I doubt *these* walls, Missster Cudgel,' said Toby, pointing upwards at the massive blocks of stone that comprised the walls of the old barn. 'And not these doors either. I think we have proved jussst how ssstrong they are. Besides, we shall ssstand well back, ready for flight should the need arise.'

'I dunno—' said Buford, uneasily.

Toby grasped Buford's arm. It was like grabbing hold of a tree trunk. 'But Missster Cudgel, wouldn't you like to try out your amazing exhalation enchantment once again? Especially on sssuch deserving victims!' Toby turned and looked out at the pale faces of the other wrathmonks. In a few words, he described the effects of Buford Cudgel's breathing spell and, by the time he'd finished, every face had taken on a look of respect and anticipation.

'I daresssay that would be sssomething we would all like to sssee!' said Toby and every head nodded vigorously. Nobody had such a devastating breathing spell as that!

'Go on then, Missster Cudgel!' said Mungo MacToad, whose own exhalation enchantment was little more than the ability to turn everything he breathed on a nasty shade of purple. 'Give usss an exhibition!'

Buford glanced at Griswold Gristle and Griswold nodded excitedly. 'A grand way to dessstroy our enemies, Missster Cudgel,' he squeaked. 'Imagine the potential devasssstation of thisss whole area! Merlin Manor and its lands will be ruined for ever! And, if we all ssstand well back and are prepared to flee, as Missster Jugg has sssuggested, I sssee no real danger for us thisss time.'

Buford nodded his great bullet head. 'All right, then,' he rumbled. 'But I dunno if it'll work. You're sssupposed to be really close to your victims and I don't even know where they are, do I? Ssso, if it goes wrong, don't blame me.'

He approached the door and bent double and put his mouth to the keyhole.

'Ho there, Measle Ssstubbs!' shouted Buford, his voice like a splitting clap of thunder. 'Remember me? It's Buford Cudgel! I've come to sssay goodbye! We've all come to sssay goodbye— Missster Gristle and Missster Flabbit and the judge and me—and a whole lot of other wrathmonks, too! Do you remember my breathing spell, Measle? If ssso, then you know what happens next, don't you? And here it comes! Goodbye, Measle Ssstubbs, from all of usss! HAVE A NICE DEATH!'

Mungo MacToad sniggered. 'Good one, Missster Cudgel!' he yelled from a safe distance.

Buford took a deep, deep breath and started to blow steadily through the keyhole.

GERMS!

The pounding against the steel doors had been deafening for those huddled inside the garage and it had gone on for what seemed an age before finally stopping. Ever since, there had been an eerie silence from outside.

Until now.

Tinker heard it first.

His fuzzy ears cocked forward and he turned his head in the direction of the sound and growled softly deep in his throat. Iggy's long, pointed ears were the next to pick up the faint noise of somebody blowing through a keyhole and then Measle heard it too. It sounded like wind whistling round distant chimneys. Only Nanny Flannel, who was beginning to go a little deaf, didn't hear anything at all.

Measle froze. He'd recognized the voice of the giant wrathmonk and he remembered the moment, back at the Isle of Smiles Theme Park when he was surrounded by his enemies and Buford Cudgel had described the awful effects of his breathing spell.

Germs and bacteria, that lived inside the victim's body, growing in an instant to the size of small insects—

'What's happening, Measle?' whispered Nanny Flannel. Measle shook his head, pretending he didn't know. It was probably best that nobody knew but him. He braced himself and waited for the horror that was coming.

The interior of the garage at Merlin Manor was a huge space and the stinking breath of Buford Cudgel was almost immediately diffused in the surrounding air, losing much of its potency and failing, as yet, to reach the nostrils of any living creature, let alone the noses of Measle, Iggy, Tinker, and Nanny Flannel, who were huddled together high in a distant corner of the loft, just about as far from the garage door as it was possible to be.

But, eventually, the foul but diluted air had to find *something* alive and it did—in the shape of a small, black beetle, which was scurrying across the concrete floor in search of something to eat.

The beetle didn't have nostrils, but it did have primitive organs that could absorb and react to the filthy, magical breath of Buford Cudgel. The effect was immediate. The beetle stopped dead in its tracks, as if it had walked into a wall. Then its legs curled up under its body and it slumped, dead, on the floor, and, at the same time, it started to swell. It was only a second or two before the pressure inside its corpse caused the outer shell to split open.

A mass of wriggling, shapeless *growing* things spilled out onto the concrete floor. More and more of them burst through the split in the insect's body and, within moments, the beetle's corpse had disappeared under a mounting pile of squirming, writhing movement.

From his vantage point up in the loft, all Measle could see was that something appeared to be moving down on the concrete below. What it was, he had no idea but it was definitely growing—it was spreading over the floor and rising up in the air and, all the time, its dark surface was shifting and rippling, as if it was somehow alive—

It's germs! thought Measle. *It's bacteria—and they're growing, just like Cudgel said! And any second now, they're going to reach us!* Panic caught at him, like a giant hand squeezing his chest and, for a moment, he couldn't breathe. He felt Iggy crawl closer to him in order to peer down at the dark mass below them, and he heard Tinker's familiar growl a little further off. Nanny Flannel was lying by his other side and she tapped him on the arm and said, 'What on earth *is* that down there, Measle?'

But Measle was so frozen with terror that he couldn't even open his mouth to tell her.

Outside, Buford had finally run out of breath. He straightened up, turned, and said, with a shrug of his massive shoulders, 'Well, that didn't work, did it? I told you ssso—you've got to be right next to your victim for these things.'

'Ssso, what now, Missster Jugg?' squeaked Griswold, who by now had utterly relinquished the role of leader.

Toby peered up at the tall building. While not particularly interested any more in what became of Measle Stubbs, he was still intrigued by a challenge. Of course, there were any number of ways of getting into the barn—they could drive a tank through those doors, or blow them up with a small bomb, or even cut down a tree and have Buford Cudgel use it as a battering ram—but all these solutions would take time and trouble. Besides, they seemed so *clumsy*.

There had to be a more—well—*interesting* way of breaking through.

Inside the garage, the entire floor was now covered by a heaving, seething sea of blackness—

and the sea was getting deeper every second, the shifting, squirming surface rising fast towards the loft. Already, the Stubbs family car and the motorcycle and sidecar combination were out of sight. There was a soft hissing sound as millions of shapeless things moved against each other.

'Coo, dat is funny lookin' ssstuff, Mumps,' muttered Iggy, and Measle caught a whiff of wrathmonk breath from Iggy's lips.

The idea popped in his head like a bursting bubble.

Of course! Why didn't I think of that before?

'Iggy—breathe on it!'

'You wot?'

'Breathe on it, Iggy! It's *bugs*! Billions and squillions of bugs! And your breath kills bugs, doesn't it?'

'Ho, yesss,' said Iggy proudly. 'My breaf is de *bessst* breaf for killin' bugs! My breaf is ssso 'orrible, it can kill bugs de sssize of *eggylumps*! De sssize of houses! De sssize of mountains! De sssize of—'

Measle knew that, once Iggy started on one of his lists detailing how brilliant he was, it was difficult to stop him, so he grabbed Iggy's damp collar, pulled him close and yelled directly in his face.

'No time, Iggy! Tell me later! Right now, I need you to breathe on them! Breathe on them *NOW*!'

Iggy had heard that tone from Measle before and he knew better than to argue with him. He leaned over the edge of the loft floor and took a deep, deep breath. Measle could hear the long, drawn-out sound of air being sucked into wrathmonk lungs. Puffing his cheeks, Iggy blew out hard, spraying his breath downwards towards the rising surface that seemed to boil with movement.

Outside, an idea had occurred to Toby Jugg.

He was staring closely at the giant hinge that held the lower half of the left-hand door to the stone wall of the garage. The hinge was dusted with a light coating of rust. Toby reached out and dragged a forefinger across it—the surface wasn't smooth, like formed steel. It was slightly rough, as if the metal had been shaped in a mould.

Cast-iron!

A possibility!

Toby beckoned to Buford Cudgel and the giant shambled to his side.

'Missster Cudgel, dear fellow, I need your great ssstrength, and your great hammer, too.'

'What's the point?' grumbled Buford. 'Didn't work the last time.'

'But it might *thisss* time, Missster Cudgel. Now, if you would be ssso kind as to raise that hammer and then bring it down as hard as you can against thisss hinge—*no!* Not *yet*, Missster Cudgel! When I sssay, and not before! There is sssomething I mussst do firssst!'

Buford paused, the sledgehammer held in beefy hands high over his head. He watched as Toby bent his head close to the hinge—and then he frowned in puzzlement as Toby took a deep breath and began to blow gently against the ironwork.

Instantly, the brown rust colour that covered the hinge turned white, as a fine layer of frost congealed on the surface. Toby went on blowing—but nothing else happened.

Nothing that could be seen, at least.

In fact, what was happening was this: the chilling cold from Toby's exhalation enchantment was penetrating deeper and deeper into the cast-iron hinge, bringing the temperature of the metal lower and lower and lower, until the whole thing was colder than the coldest part of the deepest of deep freezers—

And Toby went on blowing.

'What's 'e doing, Missster Cudgel?' said Mungo MacToad, who had sidled up close to Buford's side.

'I dunno, do I?' said Cudgel, edging away from the red-haired wrathmonk. He'd never cared for Mungo MacToad—a nasty, know-it-all piece of work in Buford's opinion.

'All right, Missster Cudgel,' called Toby, straightening up and wiping his mouth with the back of his hand. Buford noticed that Toby's lips had turned a pale shade of blue. Toby said, 'Now, hit that hinge as hard as you can, please!'

Buford raised his sledgehammer and brought it down with all the force that his enormous muscles could muster.

The iron hinge shattered into a thousand pieces, little shards of ice-cold metal whizzing off in all directions, like shrapnel from an exploding grenade. One of them struck Frognell Flabbit's leg and he yelped and moved away to a safer distance.

''Ere—that's clever, that is!' said Mungo MacToad, admiringly. He stepped closer and stared down at the remains of the hinge. ''Ow did you do that, Missster Jugg?'

'If metal gets very cold, it becomes brittle,' said Toby. 'Ssspecially cast-iron. I thought everybody knew that.'

'*I* knew that, Missster Jugg,' said Griswold Gristle, eagerly, although in fact he didn't.

Toby wasn't listening. He had moved across to the other door and was blowing down at the lower hinge there. After a short while, he beckoned to Buford Cudgel and, a second later, that hinge was shattered too. Now, with their lower supports gone, both doors sagged a little. Toby looked up at the top hinges. They were out of his reach. Once again, he beckoned to Buford.

'Can you lift me on your shoulders, Missster Cudgel?'

Buford put down his hammer and hoisted Toby up onto his shoulders as if he was no heavier than a toddler. Wobbling slightly, Toby leaned forward and started to breathe against the third hinge.

Up in the loft, everybody was holding their nose against a terrible stench that rose in waves from below. With her free hand, Nanny Flannel was holding tight to Measle's wrist and she was speaking as quietly as possible, with her firm, no-nonsense voice.

'You *must*, dear,' she said, and Measle shook his head for the third time. Nanny Flannel tightened her grip.

'Don't shake your head at me, young man. You have no choice. Those doors aren't going to hold much longer.'

'But—'

'No buts, Measle. It's you they're after and we can't help you—so you have to run, don't you see?'

'But—but I can't just leave you, Nanny!'

'Yes, you can, dear. Now, how many yellow ones have you got?'

Measle reached in his pocket and pulled out the few jelly beans that were left. It was hard to see the different colours in the dim light that filtered through the skylight but he could just about make out a few that were paler than the rest.

'A couple, I think, Nanny.'

'And you, Iggy?'

Iggy tapped the front pocket of his jacket and said, 'I got about a sssquillion, Miss Fwannel.'

'Good. So, when the time comes, I want you both to use them and get away, if you can. Is that understood?'

There was a thunderous *CRASH!* from outside and the left-hand door shuddered and slipped sideways by half a metre. Now its whole weight was resting on the ground, held in place only by the central locking device.

Measle thought of something. 'Why can't you do the same thing, Nanny?' he asked, excitedly. 'What's *your* least favourite jelly bean?'

'That's no good, dear,' said Nanny Flannel, sadly. 'You see, I don't like *any* of them—and you've got to have a clear least-favourite for the magic to work.'

'What about Tinker? He probably likes jelly beans, doesn't he?'

Nanny shrugged her narrow shoulders. 'The trouble with Tinker is he likes them *all*, so it doesn't work for him either, for the same reason. And no, dear, you can't carry him. He'll slow you down and that's the last thing you need right now. Tinker and I will be fine—won't we, Tinker?'

Tinker wagged his stubby tail a couple of times and crawled a little closer to Nanny Flannel's side. His mind was taken up with other matters though—

So many really big smells! Really, really BIG ones! And the fact is—and I never thought I'd say this—but a dog can have too much of a good thing . . .

Toby had finished breathing on the final hinge. He tapped the top of Buford Cudgel's bullet head and Buford reached up and lifted him off his shoulders and put him back on the ground.

Toby looked up at the tall doors, noting the new, sagging angle of both of them. Thoughtfully, he moved sideways, positioning himself well to the right of the doors—and Griswold Gristle saw him do it. Not knowing quite why he should feel the need to copy Toby, Griswold went and stood at his side, like a trusty lieutenant. He turned and motioned to Frognell Flabbit and Judge Cedric, gesturing that they too should move closer to him. When Judge Cedric hesitated, Frognell grabbed the old wrathmonk's skinny arm and hustled him to Griswold's side. The rest of the wrathmonks, mesmerized by what was going on, simply stood in a huddled group directly in front of the doors and gaped up at the last remaining hinge.

Buford raised his hammer high—

'Hit it from the side, Missster Cudgel!' squeaked Griswold, for he had suddenly seen the possible danger to them all—a danger that Toby Jugg had also obviously realized, because he had been the first to station himself off to one side. *And yet, he said nothing!* thought Griswold. In that instant, he realized that Toby Jugg was not to be trusted a jot.

Buford stepped to one side and raised his hammer high. He swung his arm back and then swung it forward with all his might. The hammer head connected with the final frozen hinge, shattering it with a CRASH!

For a moment, nothing happened. Then there was a creaking, groaning sound of protesting metal and the tops of the doors separated from the stone lintel and began to fall fast away from the garage walls.

It all happened too quickly for the small group of gawking wrathmonks who were standing directly in the path of the falling doors. Before any of them could think of moving out of the way, the great steel panels were upon them.

There were no screams, no crunching of bones —just a pair of dull THUMPS! as the doors hit the ground, obliterating the group of gaping wrathmonks beneath them.

In the very next moment, the great doors themselves were obliterated. A tidal wave of black, slimy sludge poured out of the opening, washed sluggishly over the flattened doors and then spread out across the yard in a stinking layer several centimetres thick.

'What—what on *earth* is this ssstuff?' said Griswold, stepping back hurriedly to avoid any of the black sludge touching his shoes. He and Toby —and Frognell Flabbit, Buford Cudgel, and Judge Cedric Hardscrabble—stationed as they were on either side of the garage doors, had experienced nothing worse than a quick blast of air as the doors fell past them. The black sludge, after its first wave had been released, flowed slowly, giving them time to move backwards and away from its path; but all of them peered in puzzlement as it ran past, and all of them wrinkled their noses in disgust at the stench—a swampy mixture of bad eggs, rotten meat, and mud.

'It would appear that your exhalation enchantment worked after all, Missster Cudgel,' said Toby, straightening up from examining the black tide. 'Thisss material, unless I'm missstaken, is dead bacteria. Dead bacteria grown to extraordinary sssize. The only question is—why are they dead ssso sssoon? Didn't you sssay it took sssome time for them to expire?'

Buford nodded. 'And who did it kill? That's what I want to know.'

'That's what we *all* want to know, Missster Cudgel,' muttered Toby. He glanced down at the spot where the small mob of wrathmonks had been standing. All that could be seen of the two metal doors, which had crushed them flatter than pancakes, were the vague shapes of a pair of huge, slime-covered, rectangular slabs.

'It would ssseem that your—ah—your *great strength* has killed a few *other* unfortunates too,' went on Toby, without a trace of sympathy in his voice. 'Entirely by *accident*, of course,' he added hurriedly, because Buford was glaring angrily in his direction.

'Well, they will hardly be missed,' sniffed Griswold disdainfully. 'A very low-grade ssselection of wrathmonks, in my opinion. Frankly, we will be better off without them.'

And that was the last thought, of *any* kind, that they gave to their former fellow wrathmonks.

Iggy's breathing spell had worked and the bacteria hadn't stood a chance. His breath had washed over the rising sea of germs, killing them instantly. Iggy, with the extraordinary lung capacity that wrathmonks possessed, had kept on blowing down at the rising, seething black mass below him until the mass had stopped rising and stopped seething and become, instead, a sludgy lake of dissolving, decomposing matter, held back only by the great steel doors, which acted like a dam across a river.

The black sludge had finally stopped flowing. Toby and the rest of the wrathmonks peered cautiously round the sides of the opening and into the darkness of the garage. The smell was very strong. They could just make out the shapes of the Stubbs car—and the motorcycle and sidecar—half buried under a thick layer of black slime.

'Is anybody there?' called Toby, and his voice echoed round the great interior of the garage. 'Anybody *alive*, that is?'

Up in the loft, Nanny Flannel took her hand away from Measle's wrist and put it on his shoulder. She put her other hand on the back of Iggy's scrawny neck.

'Now, dear!' she hissed. 'And you, Iggy! NOW!'

Measle and Iggy bit down on their jelly beans. The moment they were both invisible, Nanny Flannel pushed them, giving them the impetus they needed. Measle couldn't see Iggy and, as he stepped out into space, all he could hope for was that Iggy wouldn't jump towards the same spot that he was aiming for—the sludge-covered roof of the family car, several metres below.

Measle landed, with a squelchy thump, on his hands and knees. The layer of black slime on the top of the car was about ten centimetres thick—

too thin to cushion his fall much. It was also very slippery and Measle found himself sliding forward across the roof, then down over the windscreen and onto the long, rakish bonnet. He flailed in the darkness, just managing to grab hold of what he thought must be one of the windscreen wipers, halting his forward movement with a jerk. Off to one side, and from somewhere lower than where he was, he heard a soggy splash and then, a moment later, a muffled 'Oooowwww!' from an invisible Iggy. He had obviously miscalculated his jump, a jump which should have taken him to the top of a stack of shelves, but which instead had let him drop all the way down to the floor, where the slime was deepest.

But there was no time to worry about Iggy. Already, a whole lot of wrathmonk heads were visible on either side of the opening and Measle knew that twice as many wrathmonk eyes were busy scanning the shadows for the cause of the two distinct sounds they had just heard.

'Is that you, Measle, dear boy?' called Griswold Gristle, his voice eager with anticipation. 'Are you still among the living? If ssso, how lovely for you! And how lovely for all of usss too! All your old friends, Measle—all jussst *dying* to sssee you!'

It was lucky for Measle that not one of the surviving wrathmonks was prepared to start wading through the black sludge in order to investigate the interior of the garage. Instead, their heads remained quite still, poking round the two sides of the opening. Measle slipped soundlessly off the bonnet of the car and down onto the garage floor. He could hear Iggy off to one side, muttering miserably to himself, 'Ooooh! Dis is disssgussstin', dis is!' Measle waded through the muck towards the sound, feeling in the darkness with his hands. But Iggy must have moved away from the spot where he'd fallen, because Measle heard him again, his muttering, grumbling little voice now coming from the other side of the motorcycle.

'*Nasssty* ssstuff! Not nice, like de Sssquiffypoo ssstuff! Dis is '*orrible* ssstuff!'

'Iggy!' hissed Measle into the darkness. 'Get out of here! Run, Iggy! Run!'

The muttering stopped suddenly and a moment later Measle heard the sound of legs wading hurriedly through sludge. The sound was heading towards the open air—*and that's where I ought to be heading too!* thought Measle, turning quickly and pushing his way through the slimy mess. He guessed that he had a few seconds of invisibility left.

There was no point trying to be quiet. His movement though the sludge could be seen quite clearly—a pair of troughs disturbing the black surface, two furrows that moved steadily out of the garage and past the wrathmonks' puzzled gazes.

'It's him!' squealed Griswold, pointing a pudgy,

trembling finger at the moving furrows. 'The boy! He's *invisible*—an old trick from Measle Ssstubbs!'

'And—and there's another one!' howled Frognell Flabbit, his long comb-over hanging lankly down onto his shoulder. His finger was pointing too, at another set of tracks that were sloshing past them through the muck.

Mesmerized by the strange sight, none of the wrathmonks moved. Instead, they simply stood on the sidelines, watching the progress of the two sets of furrows crossing the garage yard. As the furrows neared the edge of the sludge, they seemed to separate—one set moving off in the direction of the long driveway, the other heading towards the back of Merlin Manor.

'Quickly!' shouted Toby suddenly, galvanizing the other wrathmonks out of their paralysis. 'We mussst catch them! Sssplit up. Missster Cudgel and Missster Flabbit, you come with me! Missster Gristle and the judge—follow that ssset! Quick—after them!'

When really frightened, Iggy could run fast. Iggy ran fast now. He scuttled like an invisible spider towards the only place he really knew—the rose garden at the front of Merlin Manor. Every few seconds, as instructed by Measle and Nanny Flannel, he reached into his top pocket, pulled out a green jelly bean and swallowed it and so remained invisible all the way to the rose garden. Once he reached its outer edge, Iggy plunged deep into the heart of it, finding a spot where the bushes grew thickest. Then he crawled on his stomach, beneath the clinging thorns, finding his way to a little space he knew about, right in the very centre. It was a place where he hid sometimes, when Nanny Flannel was cross with him, and it was the one place he felt reasonably safe. His little black rain cloud didn't give him away, either—it was so small, it hovered close above his head, so there was nothing for his pursuers to see, other than the dark shapes of hundreds of rose bushes covering most of the huge lawn in front of Merlin Manor.

Toby, Frognell, and Buford had been following a trail of small, black, slimy footsteps, which Iggy had left behind him. The trail grew fainter and fainter as the slime wore off Iggy's shoes, and it petered out altogether just short of the rose garden, bringing the three wrathmonks to a halt.

'Use your noses!' barked Toby, sniffing wildly at the night air. Buford and Frognell obeyed, lifting their noses and smelling for all they were worth.

'Well?'

'All I can sssmell is thisss ssslime,' muttered Frognell, trying unsuccessfully to smooth back his drooping hank of hair. 'And that could jussst be usss, couldn't it?'

'You don't sssmell the boy?'

'Flowers!' rumbled Buford. 'Jussst ssstinking flowers! And ssslime! That's all! There's nobody here, I tell you!'

Toby stared long and hard at the rose garden then, reluctantly, he turned away.

Deep inside a thicket of thorns, Iggy went on chewing his green jelly beans.

Dat's funny, he thought to himself, *dey don't taste all dat bad, actually*.

If anything, Measle ran even faster than Iggy, because he was in the greater danger. He had only one jelly bean left.

As they'd hurriedly planned it up in the loft, the idea was that—once outside—he and Iggy should run in opposite directions, in the hope that their pursuers would then split up into two smaller groups, which might give both of them a slight advantage.

Measle had reached the kitchen yard and now he paused, wondering frantically which way to go next. He had only a few moments of invisibility left before he'd be forced to swallow his last bean—and then what? He glanced up at the dark shape of the house. There was nowhere he could hide in there, not with the staircase gone, the upper storeys out of reach and the kitchen little more than a cave.

Where? Where to go now?

Measle turned away from the house and looked out across the enormous lawn. *There! On the far side—the line of trees where the forest begins—perhaps I could hide in there!*

Without giving it another thought, he raced away from the house, heading across the lawn towards the distant trees. Behind him, he heard the crunch of feet on gravel. Frantically, he burrowed in his trousers for the last jelly bean.

His fingers met a small, sticky mess at the bottom of his pocket. *Oh no! It must have dissolved in my wet clothes!* Wildly, he scraped at it with his fingernails, managing only to get a small amount on the ends of his fingers. Running as fast as he could, he stuck the fingers into his mouth and sucked hard.

He knew he wouldn't make it, because the outline of his hand started to materialize right before his eyes—and the line of trees was still a long, long way away and here he was, right out in the open.

The black rectangle of the swimming pool appeared in the ground a few metres in front of him and Measle began to dodge sideways, with the intention of skirting round it. The last place he wanted to be was anywhere near the Slitherghoul, which he guessed was still down there in the wet darkness. But then his feet stumbled against something that was lying on the grass—something hard and unyielding—and Measle tripped and lost his balance. In the split second before he fell, he glanced down at the obstruction and saw, to his amazement, Officer Offal lying on his back and staring up at him through glassy eyes.

Measle had been running too fast for the fall to be a simple stumble. Instead, his momentum sent him flying through the air, directly into the yawning black rectangle of the pit. He landed at the bottom with a tremendous splash, falling to his hands and knees, his fingers sinking into the mud at the bottom. For a moment, he was too shaken up to take in his surroundings. But then he remembered the Slitherghoul—

Measle froze, his eyes darting wildly around the enclosed area and scanning the surface of the muddy water. There was no sign of the Slitherghoul. But that was hardly any comfort—Officer Offal had seen Measle quite clearly and would be raising the alarm any second now.

There was silence from above. Now that Measle came to think about it, there had been something very odd about the moment when his feet had made contact with the big guard's body. It had felt hard, like a log of wood, and Offal's eyes, while wide open, had looked strangely blind. *Well, whatever that means, I can't risk moving again—not with no jelly beans left—let's just hope nobody else saw me.*

But the outline of Measle's ghostly form *had* been seen. Griswold Gristle had rounded the corner of Merlin Manor and was waiting for his old friend to catch up with him. Panting heavily, Griswold scanned the darkness with his beady black eyes. Across the lawn, and for a brief instant, he saw something that looked like grey smoke, in the rough shape of a small boy. And then the little grey figure dropped down, vanishing from view.

Something sharp and bony bumped hard into Griswold's back and he heard the wheezing of his friend's ancient lungs, pumping like a pair of cracked bellows. Impatiently Griswold turned round and grabbed Judge Cedric's skinny old arms.

'He's there, Cedric!' he squeaked. 'The boy! I sssaw him—he is in the pit!'

'What pit?' panted Judge Cedric. 'There's a pit? Where? Where?'

Griswold didn't bother to answer. Instead, he transferred his grip to Judge Cedric's hand and started to drag the old wrathmonk towards the distant pool.

GRISWOLD BREATHES!

Measle shivered with cold. He huddled in the shallow water, his back pressed tightly into a muddy corner. Soggy paper bags floated on the surface—*but at least that Slitherghoul thing has gone! Now, if only they don't think to look in here*—

He heard the sounds of pounding feet getting nearer and nearer and nearer, and he knew that, whoever was after him, the pit was going to be the first place they would search.

He would be found unless—

There was only one thing left to do. Measle took a deep breath, filling his lungs with as much air as they could hold. Then, pinching his nose between finger and thumb, and closing both eyes tight shut, he ducked the whole top half of his body under the surface of the icy water.

A slight, swirling eddy rippled over Measle's head.

A second later, Griswold and Judge Cedric, both gasping for breath, skidded to a stop at the muddy edge of the pit.

'Oh, *thisss* pit,' huffed Judge Cedric, clutching his side where a sharp pain was stabbing him in the ribs. 'But—but I sssee no boy, Griswold.'

'He's here, I tell you!' hissed Griswold, staring down into the darkness. 'I sssaw him jump—and there is nowhere else he can be! And thisss time, Cedric, we really have him. There can be no essscape from usss now.'

'But where is he?'

Even as Judge Cedric spoke, Griswold knew the answer. A bubble broke on the dark surface of the water—then another—

'He is under water, Cedric!' squeaked Griswold. 'Well, I know how to deal with that!' Hurriedly, he stepped down onto the mud of the shallow end and then slithered down to the water's edge. Once there, he bent down and took a deep, deep breath.

Measle was almost at his last gasp. His lungs were beginning to hurt and he knew that he had only a few more seconds of breath left. He was going to have to surface—or drown.

* * *

Griswold began to blow his stinking wrathmonk breath directly at the surface of the water. At first, nothing seemed to be happening, but the steady falling of the water level, creeping down the mud walls centimetre by centimetre, showed clearly that Griswold Gristle's drying-up spell was working just fine. Exactly where all that water was going was impossible to know, but the effect was as if somebody had pulled a plug out of the bottom of the pit and the water was simply draining away.

Up on the grassy bank, Judge Cedric was hopping excitedly from side to side, clapping his hands and crying, 'Oh, sssplendid, *sssplendid*, Griswold! We shall have him now!'

Measle had no idea what was going on somewhere above his head. The water was too muddy and the night was too dark to see anything, even if Measle had had his eyes open, which he hadn't. But his time was up and, whatever was going on at the surface, Measle was going to find out. His lungs at bursting point, Measle uncurled his body. In one explosive movement, he lifted his head and then his torso out of the water and took an enormous lungful of cool night air—cool night air that was tinged with the scent of dead fish, old mattresses, and the insides of ancient sneakers.

Instantly, the whole upper part of his body, which was clear of the water, dried out. His hair, his face, his leather jacket, the remains of a sodden paper bag that had draped itself over his right shoulder—everything was as dry as if it had just come out of a tumble dryer.

Measle's sudden appearance from under the surface of the muddy water took Griswold a little by surprise. He had been expecting the waters to sink and then reveal Measle's huddled form, but here was the boy, suddenly rearing up out of the depths like a breaching whale.

Griswold snapped his mouth shut, cutting off his horrible breath. It was probably the single luckiest break in Measle's short but eventful life. In the instant before Griswold stopped, his exhalation enchantment had dried off every drop of surface water that was clinging to Measle's upper half and, had Griswold gone *on* breathing, the process would have continued with the rapid dehydration of Measle's body itself. But, instead of continuing with his devastating spell, Griswold chose to gloat. He smiled a wolfish smile and said, 'Ah, there you are, dear boy. Have a nice ssswim, did we? Now, come along out of there—there are ssso many people who want to meet you!'

'My boils!' screamed Judge Cedric from above. 'You promised I could do my boils on him, Griswold!'

'And ssso you shall, Cedric!' said Griswold, beckoning to Measle with a stubby finger.

Measle stood his ground and shook his head. He

wasn't going to go anywhere. Especially anywhere that Griswold Gristle wanted him to go.

Griswold frowned. He said, 'Why do you think your top half is dry, Measle? Eh? It's because I was breathing. I was performing my exhalation enchantment on all thisss water, drying it out mossst sssuccessfully, I might add! And then, up you popped, and the ssspell worked on you, too—and it can go *on* working, if I ssso choose! All I need to do is take another breath and ssstart blowing it out again. Let me tell you, the results are *mossst* unpleasant for the victim. Ssso, why don't you do as you're told. Come out of there and join Judge Cedric and myssself up on the grass and perhaps I will allow you a few more moments of life, eh?'

Measle paused for a moment. Griswold took a sudden, swift intake of breath—

'All right,' said Measle, miserably. 'All right. I'm coming.'

He sloshed through the shallow water and then tramped up the muddy slope and onto the grass at the top. When he got there, he took a quick look at the still form of Officer Offal, lying by the side of the pit. Now he could see what he'd missed the first time. Officer Offal's body seemed to be coated with a thin covering of ice. His short red hair was white with frost and an icicle stuck out from the end of his nose like a little sword.

Officer Offal was frozen stiff.

Griswold and Judge Cedric came and stood

close to Measle, both glaring down at him with red, angry eyes. The rain from their two black wrathmonk clouds dribbled down on Measle, making a *tip-tapping* sound as the drops pattered against the dry paper bag that was still draped across his shoulder.

'Now, Griswold?' said Judge Cedric, his long beaky nose twitching with excitement. 'Can I breathe on him now?'

'Why not?' said Griswold, in a fat and oily voice. 'A little unpleasantness before the finality of death! Jussst the ticket, Cedric! But let me move out of the way firssst!'

Griswold stepped away, making sure he was well out of range of Judge Cedric's poisonous breath.

Judge Cedric was determined to savour the moment. He licked his thin, cracked lips and glared down at Measle.

'Any minute now, my boy!' he snarled. 'Any minute now! Spots ... and boils ... and pimples, all pussy and painful and putrid—'

'Oh, do get *on* with it, Cedric!' called Griswold.

Patter, patter, patter went the raindrops against the paper bag on Measle's shoulder. The bag was getting wetter and wetter—and soggier and soggier.

And then a raindrop fell onto something other than just the paper.

It fell onto something that was already *on* the paper.

It fell onto a little glistening glob of snot.

THROUGH MEASLE'S EYES

The drop of rain water that fell onto the glob of glistening snot instantly washed away all trace of the diluted sugar that had, up to that moment, coated the thing's slimy surface.

There was a reason why the Slitherghoul reacted so badly to sweet substances. It was all to do with the character of the wizard that had created it in the first place. Sheepshank was a bitter person, and sweetness is the opposite of bitterness, which was why the Slitherghoul, finding itself floating in a solution of sugar and muddy water, became progressively weaker and weaker. As it weakened, it gave up all its victims. It couldn't die—there was only one thing that could kill it, and sugar wasn't it. But it could be reduced to its original size, and now, empty of all its inhabitants, and coated with a mild solution of sugar and water, which kept it weak and ineffective, the Slitherghoul had reverted to its original form—a yellowish-brownish-greenish globule of snot.

But when the raindrop washed away all traces of sugar that coated its surface, the Slitherghoul became itself again—and the first thing it looked for was Life.

It found it immediately—right next to itself, in fact. Even as Judge Cedric gloated, grinning evilly down at Measle and rubbing his dry old hands together with the sound of sandpaper on wood, the Slitherghoul moved across the paper bag and, extending a tiny tentacle of itself, touched Measle's neck.

By the time Measle realized what was happening, it was too late. The moment the tip of the tiny tentacle touched bare skin, the Slitherghoul slid as fast as lightning off the paper and onto Measle. Once there, it spread out its sticky, jelly body, so that it was thinner than the thinnest paper. It slimed fast up Measle's neck and slid over his right ear, and now Measle could feel a strange sensation as this fine, sticky film rapidly covered his head, then his eyes, then his nose.

Measle opened his mouth to yell out, but the Slitherghoul covered it up before he could even take a breath. Its body spread impossibly thin, it slid down and over the rest of him, absorbing Measle, changing his shape to suit itself, until at last there was no more small boy, just a pile of quivering jelly about the size of a large suitcase.

It was a strange sensation, being inside the Slitherghoul. It wasn't unpleasant: there was no pain, because Measle couldn't feel anything. He couldn't hear anything, either, all he could do was see and think. He could see because his were the only eyes the Slitherghoul had available, and he could think because the Slitherghoul allowed him to.

At first, Measle couldn't think of anything much. He was too horrified by what had happened to him to do anything other than stare at the startled figure of Judge Cedric who—since the Slitherghoul was now a small mound of jelly less than half a metre tall—looked to Measle like a tall tree. The old judge was staring down with a look of blank astonishment at what was lying at his feet, and he made no move to get away when the Slitherghoul, acting on its instincts, made a sudden, slithering lunge in his direction.

No! thought Measle wildly. Even in his dismay and confusion, he knew one thing for sure: he didn't want any wrathmonks in here with him!

The Slitherghoul stopped dead. It stayed quite still for several seconds, then—in a tentative sort of way—it extended a small, stubby tentacle towards Judge Cedric's skinny ankles.

No! shrieked Measle's mind again and,

immediately, the tentacle drew back. Measle concentrated his mind and tried to turn the Slitherghoul away from Judge Cedric—but there was a limit to the control he seemed to have over the creature, because the Slitherghoul didn't move.

Why doesn't that stupid old man get out of the way? thought Measle, and just as if Judge Cedric had heard his thoughts, the old man suddenly came to what little sense he had and stumbled hurriedly backwards.

The Slitherghoul made another, instinctive lunge across the grass and Measle had to use all his mental power to bring it to a halt again. To his relief, Judge Cedric shambled away towards the waiting figure of Griswold Gristle. Griswold's lips moved. Measle couldn't hear what was being said but, from the looks of panic on both the wrathmonks' faces, it was clear what they were thinking. Measle saw Griswold grab Judge Cedric's arm and he watched as both wrathmonks set off, running as fast as a pair of short fat legs, and a pair of old thin ones, would let them. They seemed to be heading towards the line of trees on the far side of the great sweeping lawn . . .

Corky Pretzel was sitting with his broad back leaning against an old oak tree, staring down at the pathetic little figure of Sheepshank. The young chap with the enormous nose was lying on the ground at

Corky's feet, his head pillowed on Corky's rolled up uniform jacket. He was unconscious but he was still shivering with cold. It was hardly surprising. The black robe—made of some sort of coarse wool—was the only thing the fellow was wearing, apart from a length of rough rope knotted round his middle and a pair of old leather sandals on a pair of very dirty feet. Corky thought he looked like a monk from the Middle Ages.

Well, apart from the Gloomstains, that is.

Corky had seen them the moment he laid the man down on the dry leaves of the forest floor. Sheepshank's long stringy black hair had fallen away from his ears, revealing the dark stains that extended all the way from the tips to the lobes.

'So, you're a warlock, are you?' muttered Corky. He got no reply.

Corky had taken off his shirt as well as his uniform jacket and had placed it over Sheepshank's body. Corky didn't know what else to do with the little fellow, who was obviously in a pretty bad way. Every few seconds, Sheepshank's head would roll from side to side and weak moaning sounds would come from his pale lips. His eyelids fluttered and his hands made little pushing movements, rustling among the fallen leaves of the forest floor.

Corky was very confused. So much had happened, so many inexplicable events had taken place, and now here he was, with a very sick young warlock, and no idea who he was, or what to do with him, or how to take care of him. There was no going back towards the house, that was for certain. There were just too many wrathmonks out there for him to handle on his own.

The sound of footsteps, crashing through the undergrowth, took his attention away from Sheepshank. The sounds were coming nearer. Corky could hear the noise of breaking twigs and panting breaths. Cautiously, he stood up and poked his head round the tree trunk.

Twenty metres away were the figures of a pair of rascally wrathmonks he knew only too well. Griswold Gristle and Judge Cedric were stumbling through the wood, running as if all the monsters in the world were after them—and they were running in his direction.

Runaway wrathmonks! This was exactly the sort of situation that Corky was trained to handle.

He pulled his head back, pressed himself against the tree, and waited. A few seconds later, Griswold Gristle and Judge Cedric, gasping for breath, staggered past him, on either side of the oak tree. They didn't see Corky, or the huddled figure at Corky's feet, but they did feel Corky's two massive hands grab them both. One hand seized Griswold's left ear and the other hand seized Judge Cedric's right ear and, before either startled wrathmonk could make a sound, other than utter a horrified gasp of pain, Corky swung both hands towards each other, slamming the two wrathmonk heads together with a *CRACK!* that echoed through the forest.

The Slitherghoul was gliding over the grass towards the line of trees. It moved slowly, because Measle was using all his mental powers to delay it as much as he could. If he had to be inside this horrible creature, he wanted to be the only occupier. But Measle could do nothing about the Slitherghoul's basic instincts, so, following its basic instincts, the creature simply trailed in the footsteps of the last living things it had come across—Griswold Gristle and Judge Cedric Hardscrabble.

It soon found them.

The two wrathmonks were slumped, groggily shaking their aching heads, against the bases of two stout trees. Both had their arms stretched behind their backs, encircling the tree trunks as far as they would go. Round each wrist was a strong nylon strap, and the straps were connected together by yet another length of nylon, so neither wrathmonk was going anywhere, at least not for the time being. The narrow nylon straps looked thin and not very strong, but police forces all over the world use them on their prisoners, because they are impossible to break and the only way to get out of them is to cut them with a sharp knife. Corky Pretzel knew this as well as any policeman and, being a trained Detention Centre guard, always carried a bundle of these straps in a leather pouch on his belt. Tying up two unconscious wrathmonks was a simple job and, once done, Corky knew that there was nothing much to fear from either of them. He had put his shirt on again, wrapping his uniform jacket tightly round Sheepshank's body. Then he'd hefted the little man onto his shoulders and, with one last look at his prisoners, he'd marched off through the woods.

The Slitherghoul slimed its way across the forest floor towards the two bound wrathmonks. It paused in front of Griswold Gristle. The tubby wrathmonk became aware that something very smelly was next to him. Slowly, he raised his aching head—then he screamed loudly.

Inside the Slitherghoul, Measle was doing his best to pull the creature away. But his mind simply wasn't strong enough to overcome the thing's instincts. He managed to force the Slitherghoul to retract its tentacle once, then twice, but, the third time, the tentacle ignored Measle's howling mind and reached out and touched Griswold's terror-filled face. In a smooth movement, it enveloped the wrathmonk. Once Griswold was inside, it started to slither across to the other tree, where Judge Cedric's bony frame was already wriggling and heaving with panic.

The Slitherghoul didn't get very far. Griswold was tied to a tree, which meant that, as long as he was inside the creature, the Slitherghoul was *also* tied to a tree. The tree was a young oak, very strong, with roots that extended deeply into the ground, and no amount of heaving on the part of the Slitherghoul was going to budge it. At last, dimly realizing that, if it ever wanted to move anywhere else, it would have to give up its prey, the Slitherghoul extruded, like a length of toothpaste, a slimy, slippery, and smelly Griswold Gristle from its jelly interior, leaving him coughing and wheezing on the ground by his tree. Then it slithered over to Judge Cedric and attempted exactly the same thing on him.

Measle gave up trying to control it. It was going to do what it wanted to do and there was nothing—other than in the short term—that he could do to stop it. He waited while the Slitherghoul swallowed a whimpering Judge Cedric and then—after a few moments of futile pulling and heaving—pushed the old wrathmonk back out onto the ground again. Then the Slitherghoul sat there, halfway between the two wrathmonks, its jelly sides rippling slowly, as if undecided as to what to do next—which, given the fact that Measle had stopped trying to direct it, was exactly what it was.

Judge Cedric blinked the slime from his eyes. His bowler hat was tilted sideways and his normally bushy white hair hung in gooey clumps on either side of his face.

'Griswold!' he bleated. 'Griswold, dear friend, my head hurts and I appear to be ssstuck! I cannot move my hands, Griswold! Please come and help me, dear friend, before this frightful thing ssswallows me again!'

Griswold gritted his teeth and hissed, 'I too am fassstened to a tree, Cedric! I cannot help you!'

'What shall we do, Griswold?' wailed Judge Cedric. 'What shall we *do*?' He stopped struggling against his bonds because the nylon straps were cutting into his wrists.

'We should breathe on it, Cedric!' hissed Griswold. 'Perhaps, together, we can kill it! Are you ready?'

'Yesss, Griswold!'

'On my count, then. One . . . two . . . three . . . *breathe*, Cedric!'

Both wrathmonks leaned as far forward as their straps would let them and breathed out their stinking wrathmonk breaths over the Slitherghoul—

Nothing happened. No boils appeared on its slimy sides, no hint of dryness dulled its wet exterior, but still the two wrathmonks breathed, until Judge Cedric's face turned a strange shade of purple and Griswold's pigeon chest grew narrower and narrower and narrower. At last, with a final puff, they ran out of air—and the Slitherghoul just sat there, rippling gently, as if nothing whatsoever had happened to it.

If Griswold and Judge Cedric had known of the

futile efforts, over many centuries, of the countless wizards and warlocks who had attempted to destroy the Slitherghoul, they probably wouldn't have bothered to try for themselves. But now, with the evidence of just how useless their exhalation enchantments were against a magical monster like this, they simply huddled against their trees and stared, with wonder and fear and loathing, at the mound of jelly between them. Measle, looking at them from deep inside the Slitherghoul, couldn't help feeling a stab of pleasure at their helplessness.

Then, without warning—and without Measle making any such mental suggestion—the Slitherghoul started to slime its way out of the forest, back towards the dark shape of Merlin Manor in the distance.

GOING FOR HELP!

Nanny Flannel and Tinker had lain low up in the loft of the garage, listening to the various sounds of the hunters and the hunted. There hadn't been any noises for some time now and Nanny Flannel decided that they couldn't just lie here for ever. Anything was better than hiding up in this foul-smelling loft. Measle and Iggy were off on their own somewhere—*please let them be safe. But there's nothing I can do to help them now, unless—unless I go for help! Yes! And the way to do it is sitting there, right beneath me!*

'Come on, Tinker,' she whispered. 'Time to go.'

Tinker crawled close to the old lady, his stubby tail flipping busily from side to side. Nanny Flannel gathered up the little dog in her arms, tucked him into the front of her apron and then, slowly and cautiously, she climbed down the ladder. At the bottom, her feet sank deep into the black sludge and she wrinkled her nose in disgust.

'We'll be cleaning this up *for ever*,' she muttered. The smell was horrible too and, every time she took a step, her feet stirred the black goo, releasing even more of the stink than before.

Nanny Flannel waded across the floor to where the motorcycle and its sidecar stood, still half buried under the sludge. Trying not to breathe, she scooped armfuls of the foul stuff off the machine, until it began to look more like a motorcycle and sidecar and less like an uneven lump in a sea of black gunk. She threw handfuls of the muck out of the sidecar, until there was room for Tinker to sit in it. Then she put Tinker firmly into the sidecar seat and said, 'Stay, Tinker. I know it's not very nice, but stay!'

To Tinker's doggy mind, this black stuff was *exactly* the kind of interesting smelly substance a sensible dog would roll in if he found a little patch of it out on a walk through the woods somewhere. The trouble with it was that there was just so *much* of it. *All a fellow needs is a little tiny patch, not a ruddy great bog of the stuff! Besides, rolling in it is pointless now because I'm pretty much covered from head to paws—and all a fellow really needs is a little dab behind the ears! Oh well, a ride in the sidecar is always fun!*

Nanny Flannel swung her leg over and settled down into the saddle with a thump. She turned the key in the ignition and the green neutral light on the headlamp shone through the film of goo.

'That's a good sign, Tinker,' muttered Nanny Flannel. 'Now, let's hope she starts!'

Nanny Flannel pressed the starter button, and the engine wheezed . . . coughed . . . belched . . . wheezed again, and roared into life.

'Good!' shouted Nanny Flannel over the steady thumping beat of the motor. 'Now, let's get out of here!'

Toby Jugg, Buford Cudgel, and Frognell Flabbit were trudging back from the rose garden, crossing the gravel drive back towards the garage, when they heard the distinctive sound of a twin-engined motorcycle heading in their direction. Buford froze, straining his ears. Then he growled, 'That sssounds like my old bike! Who's riding my old bike, I should like to know!'

'I daresssay we shall sssoon find out, Missster Cudgel,' said Toby. 'It ssseems to be heading in our direction!'

The three wrathmonks waited, their faces gleaming white in the darkness, as the sound of the thumping engine drew nearer.

* * *

Corky Pretzel heard the sounds too. He had skirted the edge of the wood, keeping the distant shape of Merlin Manor always in sight. Now he was halfway across a field that bordered the front drive. Sheepshank's head lolled against Corky's broad chest and the little wizard was muttering to himself. Corky couldn't make out the words but at least the man was showing some more signs of life.

Meanwhile, there was that thumping noise in the distance. Corky thought it sounded just like a big motorbike. A big motorbike could be very useful right now—very useful for both of them.

Corky began to pound across the field towards the long driveway, and Sheepshank's head bounced against his chest with every step he took.

Bounce, bump! Bounce, bump! Bounce, bump!

Dimly, and as if his body was many miles away, Sheepshank's brain began to stir. Sensations flooded through his frame. He was uncomfortable. He was cold. He was damp. His head was banging rhythmically against something smooth and smelly. He seemed to be upside down—or, at least, his head was. He could hear the sound of running footsteps and, close to his ears, panting noises of somebody out of breath. Further off—much further off—was a sound he didn't recognize. It was a horrible sound! A steady, thudding noise, like . . . like the beating of a great heart! An enormous heart, to be heard at such a distance! A heart that could belong only to an awful monster! A dragon, perhaps!

Bounce, thump! Bounce, thump! Bounce, thump!

Sheepshank struggled to move, but he was still too weak. He tried to open his eyes, but some kind of glue seemed to be holding them shut. He tried to speak, but his tongue felt heavy and too big for his mouth. The sounds his ears were hearing were too awful to contemplate. The only sense he felt he could rely on was his brain.

Think, Sheepshank! Remember!

The last thing he could remember was—*what was it? In what action was I engaged? Ah yes! Searching for my little dead spider! I was in my cell, secure from prying eyes, searching for my little dead spider! And now—this? How could I venture from that to this with no conscious thought in between?*

Sheepshank's still sluggish brain struggled to connect the two events. One minute he was in the silence and privacy of his cell, the next—well, what exactly was happening at this precise moment? There was no way of understanding, unless he could see! He must open his eyes! Sheepshank screwed up his eyelids and then strained to pull them apart, and the dried slime that covered one of his eyes split—

Darkness! But just enough light to make out—*what?* Rough grass flying by! A pair of boots—*black* boots—pounding along! And close to his open eye, covering a broad chest, was a tunic of some sort, made of a fine cloth he didn't recognize, against which his head was bouncing at every step.

And that noise! That terrible noise! It was getting closer—

Nanny Flannel and Tinker roared round the corner of the house and almost ran straight into three wrathmonks who were standing stock still in the middle of the circular drive. Nanny Flannel wrenched at the handlebars and the motorbike and sidecar skidded sideways in the gravel, missing Frognell Flabbit by a whisker, before thundering on towards the first bend in the driveway. It all happened so quickly that none of the wrathmonks got even a glimpse of who was on board the bike. All they saw was a blinding beam from the headlamp and, as the machine skidded past, a vague human shape in the saddle, and another, smaller shape in the sidecar, both dimly lit from behind by the red glow of the rear light. Toby Jugg managed to get off a single blast of breath at the retreating machine—and Nanny Flannel felt a sudden, icy chill up and down her spine. She gritted her teeth, leaned forward and twisted the accelerator grip as far as it would go. The engine roared even louder and the motorbike spun its back wheel and raced off down the drive.

Corky Pretzel reached a barbed-wire fence, which ran along the edge of the field. On the other side of the fence was a shallow ditch and, just beyond that, ran the driveway of Merlin Manor. Corky could see a single headlight in the distance and he could hear the roar of the powerful motorbike, and both were getting nearer and nearer.

Corky climbed easily over the wire, with Sheepshank slung over his shoulder like a sack of letters. He stepped across the ditch and stood by the side of the drive, his eyes straining in the darkness. He came to a decision: whoever was coming his way, he would do his best to stop them.

There was a risk, of course, but Corky reasoned that if the motorbike was being driven by wrathmonks—*and who else was there around here?*—it could, at the most, carry only *two* of them—and two was a number Corky could certainly cope with, assuming that their wrathrings were still round their necks, of course.

Corky lowered Sheepshank's limp body gently down onto the grass verge and walked to the middle of the drive and stood, facing in the direction of the approaching motorbike.

Nanny Flannel steered the bike round a long corner and then centred the handlebars, because ahead of her was the long, straight-as-an-arrow stretch of driveway that led all the way to the front gate. The pins holding her hair in its neat bun on the back of her head were blown loose by the wind, and her long grey tresses streamed out, like a plume of smoke, behind her. Next to her in the sidecar—grinning from ear to ear—sat Tinker, his ears flapping in the wind.

Nanny Flannel saw a figure of a man—a big, muscular young man—standing about a hundred metres away, right in the middle of the drive. He seemed to be holding out his arms, as if he wanted her to stop.

Nanny Flannel had no intention of stopping— particularly not for somebody she didn't recognize.

The young man was a complete stranger and this was hardly the moment to be picking up unknown hitchhikers! He'd just have to get out of the way—because she wasn't stopping for anything! Nanny Flannel pressed her left thumb to a button on the handlebar and the two big trumpet-shaped air horns blasted out in a deafening wail that pierced the still night air like the cry of an enraged banshee.

Sheepshank lay quite still in the long grass. The one eye he had managed to open was now closed again and he'd curled himself into a tight ball, in the desperate hope that the approaching monster wouldn't notice him in this darkness. The sound of its advance was terrifying enough but now the monster was screaming in rage and the steady pounding of its great heart was getting louder and louder—and *faster and faster!* Sheepshank whimpered in terror and huddled down against the damp ground.

Let it not spy me! Let it not spy me!

Corky stood his ground, watching the blazing headlight race directly towards him. When it didn't look as if the motorbike was going to stop, Corky began to wave his arms up and down. It didn't help. The blaring of the twin horns went on and the bike was almost on top of him!

Corky wasn't very bright but he wasn't a

complete fool either. When the bike was ten metres away, he stepped quickly to one side—at exactly the same moment that Nanny Flannel (who wasn't a fool either) wrenched the bike's handlebars to the left, away from the strange young man, and away from the ditch, too—and the barbed-wire fence—and away from the small bundle of what looked like dark clothing that lay in the grass at the edge of the drive. Nanny Flannel knew there was no ditch to the left of the roadway, just lumpy, uncut grass, so she knew she was safe to veer hard left. For twenty metres the motorbike bounced across the uneven surface. Then, once she was sure they were past the danger, Nanny Flannel took her thumb off the horn button and steered to the right again and the motorbike roared back onto the driveway and headed fast towards the distant gates.

Sheepshank shivered with relief. The monster had not noticed him! It had passed him by!

Sheepshank had opened his one good eye and had caught a quick glimpse as the terrible creature had flown by. It was definitely a dragon of some sort, with a single blazing eye right in the middle of its head. This strange, one-eyed dragon even had its Dragodon astride its back and Sheepshank had quaked at the sight of the dragon master's long grey hair, streaming in the wind. This Dragodon must be a very great wizard indeed, because the dragon was allowing the dragon master's wolf companion to ride at his side! Sheepshank had quickly closed his eye again; the sight was too frightening to behold. At the same time, Sheepshank couldn't help thinking that, as dragons went, this one had been surprisingly *small*, and the wizard's companion had looked more like a *puppy* than a full-grown wolf. All this was very strange.

Yet, he thought, *for all its smallness, the creature is still a monster to be feared and avoided at all costs.* He could still hear it, the sound of its thudding heart diminishing into the distance. It had stopped screaming at last. Had its Dragodon finally quietened its savage voice? At all events, he was safe for the time being.

Sheepshank allowed his skinny body to relax, uncurling it from the tight ball he'd squeezed himself into. Carefully, he opened one eye again.

'Hello there, matey,' said Corky, who had seen the movement and was now squatting down next to Sheepshank. 'Feeling any better, are we?'

The gates of Merlin Manor loomed ahead of Nanny Flannel. They were wide open and, knowing that directly beyond them lay the main road, Nanny Flannel slowed the motorbike before driving between the stone pillars on either side of the entrance. Once past them, she was about to come to a full stop when she became horribly aware that an enormous *something* was almost on top of her.

Huge, twin headlights blazed into her eyes, almost blinding her, and the blast from a powerful horn almost knocked her out of the saddle. Nanny Flannel grabbed the brake lever and hauled the motorbike to a skidding stop. The big, shiny, single-decker bus, which had been about to turn into the Merlin Manor entrance, slid ponderously to a halt itself, its huge chrome bumper only an inch from the front wheel of the motorbike.

There was a hiss of air brakes, then a second hiss as the door of the bus slid open. Somebody stepped down and hurried to Nanny Flannel's side.

'Miss Flannel! Are you all right?'

The voice was familiar. Nanny Flannel blinked several times, until her eyes lost their temporary blindness. She peered into the darkness at the slight figure that stood beside her, and then she smiled in relief.

'Oh, Lord Octavo!' she cried. 'Oh, you have no idea how happy I am to see you!'

Tinker, his stubby tail a blur, barked once in full agreement.

Measle on the Warpath

Toby Jugg, Buford Cudgel, and Frognell Flabbit were still at the front of Merlin Manor, standing right in the middle of the circular driveway, when Measle came slithering up behind them.

They had been bickering amongst themselves about what they should do next. Buford was all for chasing after his motorbike and clobbering the thieving rider with his huge fists. Frognell saw no point in running after something they could never catch. His interest lay more in the desire to get away from this dark and dangerous place and find somewhere warm and comfortable, with lots of beer and a nice new hairbrush. His comb-over was so heavy with dried Slitherghoul slime, it was stubbornly refusing to stay in place and Frognell Flabbit couldn't bear that.

Toby Jugg wanted to stay. He'd got over his initial disappointment at not finding either the Mallockee or the Manafount at Merlin Manor and had worked out the idea that, if he simply waited long enough, then they would be sure to turn up here. And then—well, now that he was a powerful wrathmonk, with a Mallockee and a Manafount under his control there was no limit to what he might do!

So, ever since Nanny Flannel had roared past them on the motorbike, all three wrathmonks had stood under their rain clouds, furiously hissing their demands at each other.

Toby smelt the stink of the Slitherghoul first. He whipped round and saw the awful creature, only a few metres away, sliming fast over the gravel towards them. The Slitherghoul was still quite small, but Toby knew that size made no difference to this thing. It had only been the size of a small dining table when it had swallowed him and Officer Offal.

'*RUN!*' screamed Toby, grabbing Buford's enormous arm in one hand and Frognell's flabby arm in the other. Buford and Frognell paused only long enough to glimpse what was coming up behind them, before all three of them took off at high speed towards the house.

It was extraordinary under the circumstances,

but Measle actually had a vague plan in his head. At first, being inside the Slitherghoul had been such an odd, disconcerting sensation that he'd had a hard time thinking at all. But for some time now, he'd been able to gather his thoughts together and quite interesting thoughts they had been, too. On his way back from the wood, he had passed close by the swimming pool pit. It had occurred to him that perhaps he could urge the Slitherghoul towards the pit and then down into it. Assuming the sweetened water was still there and hadn't yet filtered away through the muddy bottom, logically, once immersed in the stuff, the creature would be forced to give him up, just like it had given up all its other victims. So Measle had used all the power of his mind to try to direct the Slitherghoul towards the gaping hole in the grass—but the Slitherghoul would have none of it. All Measle had managed to do was steer the slimy blob a little closer to the edge, but the creature had sensed what Measle wanted it to do, and instinctively it remembered the unpleasant effect from before. It resisted the order easily, flowing stickily past the pit with several centimetres to spare.

It seemed intent on moving back towards Merlin Manor and Measle was forced to just float within the creature, letting it do whatever it wanted. Quite soon, they were back in the deeper shadows that surrounded the great house. The Slitherghoul slimed its way steadily along the side of the building and then out onto the circular driveway. There, standing in the middle of the gravel, were Toby Jugg, Buford Cudgel, and Frognell Flabbit. Where the rest of the escaped wrathmonks were, Measle hadn't a clue. Besides, wherever they were, they posed no threat to him—not while he was inside this mound of magical jelly! He'd realized at once when Griswold and Judge Cedric had breathed their exhalation enchantments over the Slitherghoul that, encased inside it, he was safe from all of that kind of thing.

In fact, he thought, *I'm pretty much invincible! Which means I can do whatever I like in here!* Then Measle's rational mind took over, reminding him that the control he could exercise over his host was minimal and, if the Slitherghoul didn't want what he wanted, then he had no control over it at all.

Ah, but what if it does *want the same thing I do?*

Right now, it seemed that the Slitherghoul wanted exactly the same thing Measle did. Well, perhaps not exactly; the Slitherghoul wanted to *absorb* the three wrathmonks, Measle wanted to *chase* them. At this stage, that amounted to the same thing.

It was extraordinary how fast the Slitherghoul could move, when all the various parts of its brains were in agreement. Toby, Buford, and Frognell ran as fast as they could and the Slitherghoul slimed rapidly in their wake, not gaining on them, but not losing them either. Measle saw, to his satisfaction, that his initial approach behind them had been the right thing to do, because all three wrathmonks were running fast towards the house, which was exactly the direction he wanted them to run.

Toby was the first to reach the front door. He wrenched at the handle and dived into the hallway beyond. He tried to close the door behind him, but Buford and Frognell—in their panic-stricken attempt to get away from the monster on their tails—managed to jam themselves together in the opening. They were only stuck there for a moment, but it was long enough for the Slitherghoul to close the gap between them. Now there was no time to get the door closed; it was all Buford and Frognell could manage just to get themselves unstuck. They popped free, with only a second or two to spare, and stumbled into the dark hallway, their eyes searching desperately for Toby Jugg.

He was nowhere to be seen.

They turned in time to see the Slitherghoul squeezing itself through the doorway. Frantically, Buford and Frognell dashed around the enormous hall, searching for an exit. Their movements were hampered by the mound of broken wood, plaster, and iron which was piled high right in the middle.

Measle pushed hard at the Slitherghoul's mind, urging it to his bidding, and the Slitherghoul obeyed. It glided rapidly after the two wrathmonks (the thought, *Where is Toby?* flitted through Measle's mind), following the panic-stricken pair as they skirted round the hallway.

Then Buford and Frognell ran into a dead end. With the collapse of the staircase—and then the further collapse of the great pile of furniture—a section of the rubble had slipped sideways, right across their escape route! There was no way they could scramble over this mess of plaster and wood and bricks and upholstery. The only way was back.

Buford and Flabbit turned—and there was the monster, almost upon them!

Buford saw the door first. It was quite small, set into the side of the hall and cleverly concealed, painted to look just like the wall that framed it. Buford reached out and grabbed the handle and pulled it open. It was a heavy door but Buford hardly noticed that. There was a dark rectangle beyond, and no way to tell where it led, but neither Buford nor Frognell had any choice in the matter. Seizing Frognell by the back of his neck and shoving him hard in front of him, Buford plunged through the opening.

The Slitherghoul lunged forward and Measle, using every fibre of his mind, screamed silently at it to *hold back*! For a brief moment, the Slitherghoul paused. It was just long enough for Buford to slam the heavy door shut, shutting himself and Frognell safely (as he thought) behind ten centimetres of ironwood, heavily reinforced with steel bars.

It was exactly what Measle wanted him to do.

Unfortunately for Buford, there was no lock or bolt on the inside of the door and Measle imagined the giant wrathmonk holding tight to the handle and using all his strength to stop it being opened again. In fact, Measle was unable to prevent the Slitherghoul from grabbing the door with an extended jelly tentacle and giving it a long, hard pull. But the Slitherghoul was now too small and too weak—and Buford Cudgel too big and strong —so the door remained firmly closed.

The concealed door in the hall of Merlin Manor led to a very interesting place. Just beyond it was a steep stone staircase. At the bottom was a small room, with walls and floor of thick granite. Being below ground level, there were no windows. Once, long ago, it had been a sort of dungeon, in which wrathmonk bounty hunters held their prisoners until they could get word to the Wizards' Guild to come and take them away. But in modern times, with the invention of the telephone and fast cars, the wrathmonk hunters had little use for the place as a jail and, for some time, Sam Stubbs had used it to store his wine. But the mechanics of the little prison had never been changed. Right beside the door, and painted the same colour as the surrounding walls, making it hard to see at first, was a heavy iron bar, on a pivot. On the other side of the door was an iron slot. Measle waited until the Slitherghoul's small brain decided that pulling at the door was futile. The moment the Slitherghoul relaxed its tentacle grip on the handle, Measle, using all the force of his brain, screamed, *Keep them in there! We can come back for them later! Keep them in there! Use the bar! USE THE BAR!*

The tentacle wavered for a moment, then it reached out, took hold of the iron bar and swung it into place across the door. The bar made a solid sounding *thunk!* as it slammed home, and Measle knew that neither Buford Cudgel nor Frognell Flabbit were going anywhere. Not until somebody came and let them out, at least.

Now all we've got to deal with is Toby, thought Measle. *He's easily the most dangerous one—but there's nothing he can do to me, not inside this thing*.

There was a sudden commotion from somewhere on the other side of the mound of broken furniture as three smashed dining room chairs slid to the floor with a crash. The Slitherghoul instantly turned away from the barred door and sped round the pile, and Measle saw the back of Toby Jugg's head, his mane of greying hair streaming behind him, as he raced for the open front door. Obviously Toby had managed to conceal himself in the heaped-up rubble and had then waited until both hunter and prey were past him. But, in emerging from his hiding place, he'd disturbed the three broken chairs, and they had slid to the floor.

Measle caught a glimpse of Toby's terror-filled face as the burly wrathmonk threw a hasty look over his shoulder and saw the Slitherghoul close behind him. Then Toby was through the front door, his feet pounding over the gravel drive, running as fast as he could towards the distant front gates.

The Measle-Slitherghoul slimed rapidly after him.

SHEEPSHANK TRANSFORMS

Corky Pretzel had dragged Sheepshank into a sitting position, with his back leaning against one of the fence posts. Sheepshank had managed to get his other eye open and he was staring, with utter bewilderment, at his surroundings. Although it was dark, he could clearly see that he was in the countryside. And what strange countryside it was! The fence post he was leaning on held strands of some kind of metal wire, with cunning, sharpened points at regular intervals along their lengths. And the wooden posts that supported these wondrous wires were marvels in themselves, carved square with fabulous precision! And there were other, even more extraordinary, things to see—the young man who was bending over him was adorned with clothes the like of which Sheepshank had never seen! Most peculiar were the shoes—with thick flexible soles, engraved with a wondrous pattern of grooves! A new fashion, no doubt.

There was something encircling the young man's wrist. A band of silvery metal, with a round disc set in the band. There were pointers in the disc, beneath a fine window of glass. It looked a little like the great clock set high in the front wall of the Wizards' Guild building, but it couldn't be a clock, of course, for it was far too small. Cunning pouches were sewn into the man's nether garment, in which one might place various objects—*removing the need for a money purse*, thought Sheepshank. And the young man himself was something of a wonder, too. He looked far fitter and stronger than anybody Sheepshank had ever known. His skin was clear and clean—and that was odd because there wasn't a soul in Sheepshank's circle who didn't have some sort of blemish or boil or spot on their faces. His teeth were straight and white and, what was even more surprising, he seemed to have all of them still in his head! Oddest of all was the look on the young man's face. Nobody had ever looked at Sheepshank with that expression—an expression of friendly and interested concern!

Sheepshank could only stare and wonder.

Corky smiled and said, 'What's your name, matey?'

'Sheepshank, sir,' whispered the little warlock, in a hoarse and shaky voice.

'Sheepshank, eh? Righty-ho. Where did you come from, Mr Sheepshank?'

For the life of him, Sheepshank couldn't remember. It all seemed so very long ago. He tried to search his memories but they were all blank, like plain white sheets of paper with nothing yet written on them. Everything had gone, apart from the clear memory of that moment, searching for his dead spider, then something wet and slimy on his thumb. Then something horrible happened—

But what?

Sheepshank's poor, overwhelmed brain was interrupted in its struggles by a new sound from somewhere off in the distance. This sound was even more terrifying than the awful noise of the passing flight of the small dragon. This sound was a low, steady rumbling roar, which was getting closer and closer.

Corky turned his head and looked away from Sheepshank, down the drive. Sheepshank looked too and saw, to his mounting horror, that there were now *two* dragons approaching them! The small dragon, with the single glowing eye, was in the front, and it was leading a much, much larger dragon. This second monster had *two* glowing eyes and it rumbled and roared as it approached, but it still couldn't drown out the sound of the smaller dragon's beating heart.

Sheepshank reached out and grabbed Corky's sleeve.

'Let them not devour me, master!' he bleated. 'I beg you—if you have a morsel of human kindness—let them not devour me!'

'Nobody's going to devour you, matey,' said Corky, wondering if the little fellow had, perhaps, lost his mind. But he had no time to think about that, there were more pressing questions to be answered. Quite what a bus was doing coming up a private driveway at this time of the morning was anybody's guess, but Corky had a vague thought that it was unlikely to contain any wrathmonks. Buses weren't the kind of vehicles you'd expect to find wrathmonks riding in—but then, who, exactly, had chosen a *bus* to come to visit this place? For a moment, Corky thought they might be a bunch of tourists who had taken a wrong turning, but tourists didn't go sight-seeing at three o'clock in the morning, surely? And another thing—was the bus *chasing* the motorbike, or was the motorbike simply leading it up towards the house?

There was only one way to find out. Once again, Corky Pretzel stepped out into the middle of the drive and held his arms out wide.

It was the bravest thing that Sheepshank had ever seen. The young man didn't have a sword and he wore no armour, yet he was prepared to challenge not just one dragon, but two! He watched as the light from the leading monster swept across

Corky's body, then he shuddered in fear as the twin lights from the eyes of the greater of the two terrible creatures washed over the young man, turning him in an instant as white as snow.

Corky threw one hand up and shielded his eyes from the three blinding headlights. A moment later, both the motorbike and the bus ground to a halt about ten metres from where he stood. A few seconds went by while both vehicles kept their engines running, then there was a hiss as the bus door slid open.

To Sheepshank's ears, the hiss was that of an enraged Great Worm, about to lunge for its prey. Once again, he whimpered with terror, but he couldn't take his eyes off the awful sight.

Lord Octavo hurried past Nanny Flannel and Tinker on the stationary motorbike. Now he too was bathed in the lights of the two vehicles. To Corky, he was just a small black silhouette in a sea of blinding whiteness.

'Officer Pretzel?'

'Yeah—and who are you?' replied Corky, straining to make out who was in front of him.

'It's I, Lord Octavo!'

Corky had never felt such relief until that moment. Apart from the Prime Magus, Lord Octavo was certainly the most important member of the Wizards' Guild and one of the most powerful, too. If Lord Octavo was here, well, everything was going to be all right!

'Oh, very glad you're here, your lordship!' stammered Corky. 'Although I don't rightly know where *here* is, I'm sorry to say—'

'We're at Merlin Manor, Pretzel,' said Lord Octavo, briskly. 'The house of the Prime Magus. Now, Miss Flannel has filled me in with most of what has been going on here—'

'*Who's* filled you in, sir?' said Corky.

'Never mind, Pretzel,' said Lord Octavo. 'Suffice to say, I get the picture—or at least most of it. The big question is—where's the Slitherghoul?'

'I'm afraid I dunno, sir,' said Corky. 'There's been a lot of argy-bargy. It had all the prisoners inside it, would you believe, and me, too—'

Corky broke off because he became aware of a lot of movement coming up behind Lord Octavo. Silhouettes wavered in the beams of the headlights and he called out, 'Who's there?'

'Reinforcements, Pretzel,' said Lord Octavo. He turned and waved in the direction of the bus and, a moment later, the engine was switched off and the headlights died. Nanny Flannel had seen the gesture too, because she leaned forward and turned the motorbike's ignition key. The *thump, thump, thump* of the motor coughed to a halt and the big single headlight dimmed to darkness.

Corky—no longer blinded by the vehicles' headlights—could see that a group of about fifteen assorted wizards and warlocks were clustered in a group behind Lord Octavo.

324

The old wizard patted Corky on his arm. 'You didn't think I'd come on my own, did you? The moment I discovered that the telephone line to Merlin Manor was out of order, I suspected trouble, so I gathered together a few colleagues and this splendid bus and, well—here we are! I just hope we're not too late. Good gracious—who is that?'

Corky turned round and saw Sheepshank staggering towards him. There was a strange look on the little man's face. It was a mixture of blind terror and fierce determination—and something else, too.

There was madness in Sheepshank's eyes.

There was also an extremely dark and solid-looking rain cloud hovering over Sheepshank's head, and it was releasing a steady, drenching downpour onto his shoulders. The little man was already soaking wet. Sheepshank appeared not to notice this. He simply staggered forward, his eyes now definitely round and fishy, his face even paler than it was before, one bony finger outstretched towards the motorbike and the bus. Sheepshank's hand was shaking wildly and his mouth was working, as if he was trying to say something.

Lord Octavo called out, 'Careful, everybody! That's a wrathmonk! And he has no wrathring round his neck!'

Lord Octavo stepped forward and, in a voice that seemed to crackle with some strange, commanding power, he shouted, 'WRATHMONK!

STOP WHERE YOU ARE! COME NO FURTHER, WRATHMONK!'

Sheepshank stopped walking forward at the sound of Lord Octavo's voice. He stood there, swaying slightly, and getting steadily wetter and wetter. He stared with wonder at the old wizard—and then he bowed low.

'Great magic!' he muttered. 'Great magic indeed! To ssslay not one, but *two* great dragons, with a mere wave of the hand! Thou art truly a massster, my lord!'

'Dragons? What dragons?'

Sheepshank's finger trembled as he pointed over Lord Octavo's shoulder. 'Those Great Worms, my lord! Thou hast sssilenced their roaring voices, their beating hearts! And thou hast dimmed their terrible, glowing eyes! 'Tis a wonder to behold!'

Lord Octavo—and all the wizards and warlocks grouped at his back—turned round and stared at the bus and the motorbike behind them. Then Lord Octavo turned back, a small, puzzled smile on his face.

'Who are you?' asked Lord Octavo, carefully.

'He says his name is Sheepshank, sir,' said Corky,

glaring suspiciously at the little man. Corky was used to dealing with wrathmonks but this was different. For one thing, Sheepshank wasn't wearing a wrathring. For another—well, he didn't like the look of Sheepshank's rain cloud. It was altogether too dark and too heavy and unpleasantly menacing as well. This one was going to take some careful handling. Corky was relieved that Lord Octavo—and a small mob of wizards—were right beside him.

There was a long silence, broken only by the sound of Sheepshank's torrential rain and the steady tick ... tick ... ticking sound of the hot metal of the motorbike engine cooling in the night air.

'Sheepshank?' whispered Lord Octavo, a look of wonder flooding his old face. '*Sheepshank?* It's ... it's not possible!'

Measle had lost Toby Jugg. The man was powerful and athletic and he'd fled though the front door and into the darkness at tremendous speed. For a short distance, the Slitherghoul had followed him, across the gravel driveway, over the grass verge, across the ditch, and then over the barbed wire fence that ringed the field beyond. Toby had taken the fence in one bound, but the Slitherghoul had been forced to flow over the top of it and several of the sharp barbs had caught in its jelly sides, slowing it down enough for Toby to get a good distance ahead. By the time the Slitherghoul had lifted itself away from the fence, Toby was nowhere in sight.

But other attractions *were* in sight and the Slitherghoul's attention was drawn to them. There, in the distance, about three-quarters of the way down the drive, was a group of three bright lights. Dark figures moved through these lights, casting impossibly long shadows across the ground—and the Slitherghoul sensed that these figures were almost certainly human.

Why chase one, when there are many?

Measle's mind tugged at the Slitherghoul's but it was no use. The Slitherghoul started to slide along the edge of the field, towards the distant lights. Halfway there, the lights went out but the dark, shifting figures remained.

The Slitherghoul slimed along a little faster.

Lord Octavo stepped a little closer to Sheepshank, staying just outside the range of the pelting raindrops. Sheepshank smiled uncertainly, exposing his new teeth—two sets of three, on either side of his mouth—and all coming to sharp points, like arrow heads. At the same moment, he seemed to become aware of the fact that he was standing under a cold shower of water and he turned his head and looked up at his hovering rain cloud. He frowned, squinting his eyes against the drops that were falling into them. Then he lowered his gaze and stared back at Lord Octavo, with the beginning of a sly little smile on his face.

'Am I become a Wrathful Monk, my massster?' he asked, his eyes gleaming in the darkness.

'You are indeed, Master Sheepshank,' said Lord Octavo. 'And a powerful one too, as no doubt you have realized. But I suggest you attempt none of your spells at this moment. I am a great Master Wizard—you saw me slay the dragons, did you not?—and here too is a whole host of powerful mages. If you should attempt to harm any one of us, we will all combine against you and, no matter how powerful you are, we shall prevail.'

Sheepshank shook his head, his long stringy hair whipping wetly round his face. 'I shall not, my massster,' he muttered. His voice sounded sincere but, in the shadows, nobody—not even Lord Octavo, who was standing closest to him—saw the gleam of cunning in his fishy eyes.

'For a wrathmonk, you are wise,' said Lord Octavo. He nodded slowly to himself, as if deep in thought. Then said, 'I have a question for you, Master Sheepshank. What year is it?'

'*Year*, my lord?'

'Aye, Master Sheepshank. What year?'

'Why, it is the year twelve hundred and six, my lord.'

There was a collective gasp from the crowd of wizards, and several muttered comments that the fellow must be even madder than the average wrathmonk. Lord Octavo turned to them and said, 'Do you not understand who this is, my friends?'

Nobody spoke. Lord Octavo sighed. 'I do wish somebody would *occasionally* read a book these days,' he muttered. 'So, nobody here knows the story of Sheepshank, the apprentice wizard?'

Again, nobody spoke. This time, the silence had a slightly embarrassed feeling about it.

Lord Octavo sighed again. Then, so quietly that it was almost a whisper, he said, 'Well, gentlemen and ladies, what we have here is a very remarkable person. He has, to all intents and purposes, invented a Time Machine. Master Sheepshank has come to us from the distant past—from the year twelve hundred and six, to be exact about it—and quite what we're going to do with him is anybody's guess.'

A chubby, middle-aged female wizard opened her mouth to speak, but Lord Octavo put a finger to his lips and shook his head firmly. 'Later,' he muttered. 'I will explain later. Now is not the time.'

He felt a tap on his shoulder. Nanny Flannel, with Tinker at her feet, was by his side. She said, 'We have to find Measle, Lord Octavo!'

Lord Octavo nodded. 'Indeed, we do, Miss Flannel.' He turned to his forces and called out, 'I will take care of Master Sheepshank. The rest of you—everybody in pairs! Support each other! Spells only when necessary. And if you come across the Slitherghoul, don't waste them on the creature, because they'll have no effect—'

He was interrupted by a squeaky, excited voice calling out from the shadows of the line of trees that bordered the drive.

'Coo! Is dat you, Lord Octopus? It is I—Missster Ignatius Niggle, sssir!'

SHEEPSHANK'S SPELL

Iggy had become bored, lying all alone under his rose bush. He'd worked his way through the rest of his jelly beans, which had congealed into a sticky lump at the bottom of his pocket, but which tasted just fine, as far as Iggy was concerned. There were still a few green ones in his top pocket, but as he didn't like them as much as the others he didn't eat them. He'd kept one pointed ear cocked for any sounds, but he'd heard nothing for quite a long time, other than the pattering drops from his tiny rain cloud as they fell onto the leaves of the rose bush.

Deciding to take a risk, Iggy had crawled out from his cover and then worked his way, as silently as he could, through the rose garden. Once he reached the open lawn, he saw the lights near the end of the drive. All wrathmonks are naturally suspicious, and even Iggy (a more trusting one than normal) had his doubts about everybody until he knew them really well and felt quite comfortable being around them. So, instead of simply trotting down the long gravel road and saying hello, he worked his way through the scattered trees that bordered the left-hand side of the drive.

When he was halfway there, the lights had gone out.

Iggy had crept closer and closer, scuttling from tree to tree, until he came near enough to hear voices. The voice he heard first was one that belonged to somebody with whom he felt very comfortable indeed, which is why he dropped his skulking attitude and called out to his old friend.

'Ah, Mr Niggle,' came Lord Octavo's friendly voice. 'We meet again.'

Iggy trotted out of the shadows, grinning from ear to ear. He stopped in front of Lord Octavo and gave him a low bow. 'Jussst in case you was wonderin'', Lord Octopus, sssir,' he said, straightening up and beaming into Lord Octavo's wise old eyes, 'jussst in case you was wonderin'', I been behavin' myssself, jussst like you told me to! I been *ssstremely* good, Lord Octopus!'

'I have no doubt about it, Mr Niggle,' said Lord Octavo. 'Now, however, we have an very urgent matter to take care of. Do you know where Measle is?'

Before Iggy could reply, Tinker started to bark.

Everybody looked at him. The dog was crouched by Nanny Flannel's feet, glaring furiously at the shadowy figure of Sheepshank who was still standing at the spot where Lord Octavo's voice had rooted him. The hair on Tinker's back stood up in a bristly ridge, his ears were flat to his head, and his tail was tucked firmly between his short legs.

Tinker had caught a whiff of wrathmonk breath. What with having Iggy around all the time, Tinker was used to a wrathmonk's smell and no longer reacted when he sniffed it. But this smell was subtly different.

The scent of *this* breath was old and mouldy, like something dug up from a graveyard. And there was something else, as well, and it was this something else that had made Tinker turn in the direction of its source and begin to bark his defiance.

Evil. Powerful, destructive evil.

I don't know who he is—and I don't want to, neither! thought Tinker, every fibre of his stocky body bunched and ready for action. *He's up to something—something no good! And he's dangerous, too! Anythin' that smells like that has got to be dead dangerous—and dead nasty, too!*

All eyes had swung to Sheepshank. The skinny young man gazed back at everybody from under hooded eyelids. Without warning, he lifted his head, took a deep breath, and blew it out hard.

What happened next was thoroughly unexpected.

Wrathmonks have a single exhalation enchantment and they're all different. Most are hurtful and some are lethal. All are unpleasant.

Sheepshank's breath was none of these.

At first, neither Sheepshank nor any of the other wizards understood what, exactly, was happening. A metre from his pursed lips, Sheepshank's breath stopped as if it had run up against a wall. Then it congealed into a shimmering, silvery fog that spread quickly up, down, left and right, curving back on itself so that in a few seconds it had formed an egg-shaped container that completely enveloped Sheepshank's skinny frame. The fog was transparent, so that Sheepshank was still clearly visible in the middle of the egg. Everybody watched as he reached out a finger and prodded the inner wall of the shimmering shell, and they saw Sheepshank's finger push the transparent skin out into a point, as if it was made of thin rubber. But the fingertip didn't break through, so Sheepshank withdrew his finger and took a couple of steps backwards—and the shell went with him.

Lord Octavo came to a decision. He muttered to himself, 'We really have no time for this, whatever *this* is.' Then, raising his voice, he called, 'Master Sheepshank! Whatever this manifestation means, I fear we shall have to make you fast until such time as you can be examined properly. So, forgive me, but I am taking you prisoner.'

Lord Octavo waved his hands and shouted, *'Circumfretio Infragilistum Bolenda!'* Nanny Flannel, standing nearby, recognized the incantation immediately. It was the same one that Sam Stubbs had used when he'd netted Griswold, Buford, Frognell, and Judge Cedric on the steps of Merlin Manor. Indeed, here came the same net, materializing out of thin air and dropping neatly over and around the silver egg that encased the wrathmonk.

Then something very odd happened.

The moment the net touched the shimmering egg, its strands simply melted away, like ice under a blowtorch. A moment later, it was as if the net had never existed at all. Even its edges which had never even *touched* the egg fizzled away into nothing.

There was an incredulous murmuring from the wizards and Lord Octavo said, 'How very extraordinary.'

Inside his shell, Sheepshank watched with a detached air, as if he'd known exactly what was going to happen. Then he grinned, exposing his pointed sets of teeth.

'Hah!' he yelled, his voice sounding as if it came from a long way away. 'You have no power over me, wizard! For I am Sheepshank, the Wrathful Monk, and my magic is ssstronger by far! No one may touch me now!'

Lord Octavo turned to the cluster of wizards and warlocks and muttered, 'We shall have to put him to sleep. Quickly now, does anybody here have a Stupor Spell?'

An ancient warlock stepped forward. He was almost as old as Lord Octavo, with an abstracted air, a pair of bent wire spectacles on the end of his nose, and a wildly disordered mane of white hair, which didn't cover his ears at all. His Gloomstains were very dark and extended from the tips to the lobes, making his ears look as if they had been dipped in ink. He pointed a finger at Sheepshank and called out, in a quavery old voice, *'Norcoleppo Abstracta Instantium!'*

A sizzling bolt of light streamed out of the old warlock's finger and flashed across the space between himself and Sheepshank. When the bolt of light reached the outer shell of the egg, it ricocheted off it, like a bullet hitting a concrete wall. There was a whistling sound, like a dying firework and then—nothing.

Sheepshank grinned more broadly than ever and his eyes glinted red.

'It would ssseem that I am protected from you all, my masters!' he sneered from inside his shell. 'But be not dissscouraged—perhaps there is another who would try his ssstrength against mine?'

Several wizards and warlocks stepped forward, their hands raised, but Lord Octavo shook his head and said, quietly, 'Don't waste your time, my friends. That is a very powerful force field and I doubt that anything will get through it. All we can hope is that Master Sheepshank won't be able to get anything through it either.'

Iggy sidled close to Lord Octavo and touched his sleeve. 'I could do mine, Lord Octopus,' he said, eagerly. 'You know de one, don't you? It's de only one I got. De opening fings ssspell. P'raps I can open dat old eggy fing, eh?'

Lord Octavo smiled down at Iggy and said, 'An interesting thought, Mr Niggle. One wrathmonk against another. Go ahead.'

Iggy stared hard at Sheepshank and then yelled, '*Unkassssbbhriek gorgogassssshhh plurgholips!*'

A pair of lavender-coloured beams of light streamed from Iggy's eyes, shot across the intervening space and smacked against the rounded wall of the egg. They splashed outwards and then dribbled, in streams of purple water, harmlessly down the sides of the shell.

Lord Octavo patted Iggy kindly on his damp shoulder. 'Never mind, Mr Niggle,' he whispered. 'It was a good idea, though.'

Sheepshank threw back his head and cackled wildly.

'Do you not comprehend?' he shrieked. 'I am invincible! None can harm me! Come—more may try! Cast your magic. I, Sheepshank the Wrathful Monk, am ready!'

Then, out of the shadows of the trees that lined the driveway, slimed the Slitherghoul.

WHEN SPELLS COLLIDE

The Slitherghoul headed straight for the shimmering, egg-shaped object, with the small figure of Sheepshank encased inside it.

Measle—without realizing why or how—was making it do it.

The reason the Slitherghoul was speeding towards Sheepshank, and ignoring the cluster of human figures that stood nearby, was because the force field that surrounded Sheepshank shone with an eerie, silver light, which in the surrounding darkness was the most visible thing that stood in the Slitherghoul's path. Since the Slitherghoul was using the only pair of eyes it possessed at the moment—the eyes of Measle Stubbs—it was heading fast in the direction they were staring, and

Measle's eyes were staring with puzzlement at the shimmering egg and wondering what on earth it could be.

Lord Octavo, Nanny Flannel, and Tinker saw the Slitherghoul approaching Sheepshank from behind and, when Tinker turned his attention—and his frenzied barking—away from the wrathmonk and towards the slithering horror, the eyes of all the wizards and warlocks turned in that direction too. Sheepshank, suddenly aware that he was no longer the centre of attention, twisted round to see what was so interesting.

Oddly, it was in fact the first time Sheepshank had ever really seen the Slitherghoul—in its enlarged form, that is. The effect on him was electrifying, particularly since the revolting lump of slimy, dripping jelly seemed to be heading straight for him. In that moment of sudden, panicky fear, Sheepshank lost his head. Oh, he knew how to deal with a bunch of old wizards and warlocks all right, but this was something different. This was something that looked so alien, so horrible, that Sheepshank lost all faith in his shield and decided, on the spur of the moment, to do one of his spells. It flashed through his mind that the old wizard had managed to kill two dragons with one simple wave of his hand—well, here was his opportunity to demonstrate *his* powers on a foul fiend that was approaching fast.

Inside the Slitherghoul, Measle was doing his

best to stop the creature for a few seconds, if only to give the strange man encased in a shimmering, transparent egg a chance to escape. He did manage to slow the Slitherghoul down just a little, adding a few precious moments of freedom to the Slitherghoul's prey.

Why doesn't he move? thought Measle. *Why doesn't he run? Maybe he can't—maybe that egg thing is holding him to one spot!* Measle struggled with the primitive brain of the Slitherghoul, but the creature pushed onwards.

Sheepshank had only a few seconds to pick a spell out of his head. The one he chose was his most devastating and, since he had invented it, only he could perform it! It was his illegal, and massively-destructive, fire-shooting enchantment.

Sheepshank raised his hands and pointed his index fingers directly at the approaching mound of slime. He opened his mouth, took a deep breath, and screamed, '*CALORIBUT!—REGRAMINA!— NUNCIFLAM!—FULMITA!—CARBOREG!— EXPEDICAL!*'

Only Nanny Flannel heard what Lord Octavo then muttered under his breath. She heard it quite distinctly.

'Oh, *no*!'

What happened next was extraordinary and horrible but it happened so quickly that, mercifully, the horror lasted only a few seconds.

A sphere of white-hot flame, about the size of a

tennis ball, appeared at the ends of Sheepshank's extended fingers. It hovered there for half a second and then shot away from the wrathmonk, heading straight as an arrow for the dead centre of the Slitherghoul.

It didn't get very far. It travelled all of a metre before it met the inner surface of Sheepshank's shimmering shield.

When two spells of equal power meet, something bad usually happens. This was no exception. The white-hot sphere smacked against the inner skin—and then simply bounced back off it at the same speed it had left Sheepshank's fingertips. When it met his body—a soft, defenceless little bag of skin and bones—it simply went straight through it and out the other side. A fraction of a second later, the sphere hit the opposite wall of the shield and, once again, bounced away, back towards Sheepshank, making another neat hole through his frail body.

This happened faster than the eye could see. The only thing the horrified spectators could make out was a ball of blindingly white light, flashing so brightly that they had to shield their eyes against the glare. The globe of light seemed to be bouncing, at a staggeringly high velocity, around the inside of the egg.

Next, the shimmering egg collapsed in on itself and the ball of blinding light snapped out, plunging everything into what seemed to the onlookers like inky blackness. Spots of colour danced around in their eyes and they all blinked, trying to get used to the sudden darkness. A panicky voice from the middle of the cluster of wizards called out, 'I can't see a thing! Where's the Slitherghoul?'

Tinker was as temporarily blinded as the rest of them, but he didn't need his eyes—not while he had his nose. The little dog lifted his head and sniffed the night air.

Yup! Definitely—the smelly kid's out there somewhere. Quite close, too. Cor, he's even smellier than ever! Right—let's go and say hello!

Tinker trotted into the shadows, his nose leading the way. Nanny Flannel's eyes adjusted to the darkness in time to catch a glimpse of his stubby white tail heading away into the shadows, directly towards the Slitherghoul—*which she could no longer see*.

'Tinker! No! Come back!'

Then everybody heard it. The sound of somebody out there in the shadows coughing and spluttering and choking.

Tinker found him quickly. The smelly kid was sitting on the grass, surrounded by a wide puddle of slime. He was bent double, his hands clasped tight to his stomach, and he was coughing and spitting in an interesting way—so Tinker trotted up to him and swiped his tongue across Measle's face.

Eeeuooogh! Not a nice taste! Really quite nasty—well, that'll teach me to smell first and lick later ...

Measle grabbed Tinker and hugged him tightly. Then he got stiffly to his feet.

'Mumps? Is dat you, Mumps?' Iggy shambled out of the darkness and stood peering curiously at Measle.

'Oh, hello, Iggy. Are you all right?'

'*Courssse* I is all right!' sighed Iggy, impatiently. 'I is *talkin'* to you, ain't I? If I *wasn't* all right, den I wouldn't be talking to you, would I? I would be goin' all like, "*AAARGH—OOOGH—EEEGH*", wouldn't I? Or, if I was all like dead, den I wouldn't be going all like *anyfing*, would I? Coz I wouldn't be able to sssay anyfing at all, not if I was all like dead—'

Measle felt a sudden need to sit down again. He swayed, nearly losing his balance. A pair of strong arms took him by the shoulders, steadying him. He looked round and saw the kind, wrinkled old face of Lord Octavo.

'Oh, hello, sir,' he said, faintly.

'Hello, young Measle,' said Lord Octavo. 'We do meet under the oddest circumstances, don't we?'

PICKING UP THE PIECES

Somehow, Nanny Flannel had managed to make tea for everybody in the ruined kitchen. Several of the younger wizards had scoured the rest of Merlin Manor for usable chairs and now the kitchen was crowded with people, all sitting in a wide circle, listening attentively to Lord Octavo, Measle, and Corky Pretzel, who were having a very interesting conversation.

'And where, at this precise moment, are those two wrathmonks you hunted down, Measle?' said Lord Octavo, his eyes twinkling.

'Locked in the cellar, sir. It's Buford Cudgel and Frognell Flabbit.'

'A nasty pair. Splendid. And the other two, Officer Pretzel?'

'In the wood, sir,' said Corky. 'Tied to trees.'

'That's Griswold Gristle and Judge Cedric, sir,' said Measle. It was quite difficult to talk, because Nanny Flannel had a wet face-cloth in one hand and a bar of soap in the other, and she was trying to clean the dried, encrusted Slitherghoul slime off Measle's head.

'Splendider and splendider!' said Lord Octavo. 'And Toby Jugg?'

'I'm afraid he got away, sir,' mumbled Measle, through a faceful of flannel.

'Ah well, never mind. You can't win them all, can you? I daresay we shall catch up with him soon enough. Yes—what is it?'

A young wizard had climbed through the shattered window, approached Lord Octavo, and was whispering in his ear. Lord Octavo's eyebrows rose and an appalled expression flitted across his old face.

'Under *what*?' he asked.

'Under the garage doors, sir,' whispered the young wizard. 'Huge iron things, they are. They're squashed flat, I'm afraid. And I think it's the whole lot of them.'

'Oh dear, what a frightful thing,' said Lord Octavo, not sounding sorry at all. 'And what about Needle and Bland, Measle? What happened to them, eh?'

'They ran away, sir.'

Lord Octavo's face darkened with anger and a

deep frown-line creased his wrinkled forehead. 'Did they now?' he growled. '*Disgraceful* behaviour by two officers of the Wizards' Guild. Well, rest assured, Measle, they will be dealt with.'

Nanny Flannel decided that there was nothing more she could do about getting Measle clean, short of running him a hot bath—which was going to be difficult, since Merlin Manor no longer had a staircase. Clucking disapprovingly to herself like a peevish chicken, she went back to inspecting the ruins of her kitchen.

Free from the face-cloth, Measle said, 'There's one thing I don't understand, Lord Octavo—'

'Only *one* thing, Measle?' said Lord Octavo, smiling.

'I think so, sir. It's . . . what happened to the Slitherghoul? It just sort of melted away, didn't it? I thought it was indestructible?'

Lord Octavo nodded, gravely. 'Well, for eight hundred years it *was* indestructible, Measle.' He looked around at the assembled wizards and then raised his voice a little, so that everybody could hear. 'The Slitherghoul was created by Sheepshank. Whether it was an accident, or whether he did it on purpose, we shall never know, because sadly Sheepshank is no longer with us. As we all saw, that ball-of-fire spell of his—a most lethal and illegal-looking incantation, I must say!—converted him into a heap of ash in a matter of seconds. I don't think the poor fellow felt a thing, it happened so fast. Anyway, as we all know, once a wizard dies, his spells die with him—which was why that force field of Sheepshank's disappeared at the very moment of his death. And that's why the Slitherghoul was destroyed at long last, too. With the death of its creator, it died as well. And, ladies and gentlemen, what is so fascinating about the whole story is this: in the eight hundred years of the creature's miserable life, the only way the Slitherghoul could ever have been destroyed was if Sheepshank himself had died. But Sheepshank was *inside his own indestructible creation*, protected by it and held in suspended animation within its magical body. As long as Sheepshank was there, the Slitherghoul could live for ever.'

Lord Octavo paused, his old eyes scanning the rapt faces of his audience. Then he turned and looked at Measle and smiled.

'Eight hundred years of trying to eradicate the horrible thing and young Measle here—who, by the way, ladies and gentlemen, doesn't have a morsel of magic about him—does it with some sugar lumps and a puddle of sweetened water.'

Measle felt his face go pink. Everybody was looking at him with admiration and Corky Pretzel was gaping at him with his mouth hanging open. Measle decided to off-load some of this awe onto somebody else.

'Well, it was Iggy, really,' he gulped. 'If he hadn't eaten all those jelly beans—'

Iggy jumped out of the chair he'd been sitting in

and bounced crazily round the kitchen, hopping about like a mad kangaroo.

'Hee hee! I did it! It was me! Hee hee! All by myssself I did it! Hee hee! I made dat old Sssquiffypoo be deaded! I am de big hero, Lord Octopus! Me! All by myssself—no help from *anybody*—me, me, *ME*—'

'That's quite enough of that, Iggy!' Nanny Flannel's mop whacked down on the top of Iggy's head and Iggy stopped dancing and yelling immediately and went and sat down again, rubbing his head, a nervous look in his fishy eyes.

'Thank you, Mr Niggle,' murmured Lord Octavo, only just managing to suppress a little bubble of laughter that threatened to erupt from his chest. 'Your . . . um . . . your *contribution* has been noted and is appreciated by all of us.'

All Iggy understood out of that were the words 'thank you'—but that was enough. To be thanked by the great Lord Octopus was more than any small, damp, and pathetic wrathmonk could possibly wish for.

Nanny Flannel put down her mop and picked up a dustpan and brush. Shaking her head at the immensity of the task before her, she started to sweep up some of the debris on the floor. Measle thought, *It's going to take a million years to get this place cleaned up!*

Lord Octavo must have seen the despairing look in Measle's eyes, because he rose stiffly from his chair and using his commanding voice, called out, 'Ladies and gentlemen, we have work to do! This place is a mess! The Prime Magus and his wife—and the Mallockee, too, let's not forget her—will be returning in the next couple of days. We really cannot allow them to see their house in this appalling state. So, to work, everybody. I take it you all have reconstructive spells? Yes? Excellent! Perhaps, Miss Flannel, you could supervise the repairs? We must make sure everything is put back exactly the way it was before. Good—well, let's make a start!'

Everybody got up and Nanny Flannel, after a moment of deliberation, announced, 'The great staircase first, I think. Without that, we can't even get upstairs so let's start there.'

She began to lead the way out of the kitchen, but was stopped almost at once by the mound of rubble that blocked the door out to the passage. A beefy looking wizard with a cheerful red face stepped forward and muttered something under his breath. A couple of hand gestures, and, immediately, the pile of rubble started to reform itself, timbers rising off the floor, brick piling onto brick, plaster smoothing itself across the surface, until the doorway was back the way it was. Nanny Flannel cocked a critical eye at the result and said, 'Very nice, dear. The moulding round the door isn't quite right, but at least we can get through now. All right, everybody—follow me!'

Measle started after the small mob of wizards as they streamed out of the kitchen in Nanny Flannel's wake, but Lord Octavo said, 'No, Measle— I want you to come with me. You too, Mr Niggle. There's something we have to do together—since it was the two of you who started it.'

Lord Octavo winked. Then, beaming broadly, he climbed out through the kitchen window and, with Measle and Iggy at his heels, set off across the lawn.

Toby Jugg crouched in the darkness of the wood, watching with cold, angry eyes the flurry of activity around the great house.

His big, muscular hands held tightly to the necks of Mr Needle and Mr Bland. Neither man made any attempt to resist. They simply stood there, shivering slightly, and waiting to see what awful thing would happen to them next.

What had *already* happened was this: they had been hiding deep in the shadows of the woods, quaking with terror and hoping that nobody would find them ever again. Unfortunately for Needle and Bland, Toby Jugg—who had been steadily making his way round the house, keeping a good distance away from the building while he scouted out the situation—had stumbled across them. Immediately he'd seized them both, turning them upside down and shaking them hard—a bit like you shake a beach towel to get the sand off. Several objects had fallen from the pockets of Mr Needle and Mr Bland but Toby was interested in only one of them. A small brass key. He'd snatched that up, inserted the business end into the latch of his wrathring, and with a single twist, had freed himself from the metal band round his neck. He hurled the wrathring away into the bushes and then grabbed the necks of the unfortunate Needle and Bland. Holding them both painfully tightly, he snarled, 'One peep out of either of you, and you're a pair of dead wizards! I've got a collection of very nasssty ssspells up my ssssleeve and my exhalation enchantment is sssomething to sssee—it'll send chills up and down your ssspines, I promise! Ssso, are you going to be good little wizards and do exactly as I tell you or are you going to be ssstupid little wizards who end up *dead* little wizards?'

Mr Needle and Mr Bland—who could recognize a super-powerful wrathmonk when they met one—both expressed fervent promises that they were going to be good and obedient little wizards for as long as Mr Jugg *wanted* them to be good and obedient little wizards.

'Excellent!' hissed Toby, forcing their heads round so that he could stare into their frightened faces. He glared evilly at them with his yellow eyes.

'Yesss,' he hissed, sounding like an angry snake. 'Yesss, I think there's a possibility I could find a use for the pair of you. Ssso, for the foressseable future, you are going to do *exactly* what I tell you to do—and nothing else. Is that underssstood?'

Mr Needle and Mr Bland couldn't move their heads to nod, so they both whispered, in squeaky, frightened voices, 'Y-y-yes, sir.'

With that, Toby Jugg cast one last angry look back at Merlin Manor and, tucking Mr Needle under one massive arm and Mr Bland under the other, marched away into the night.

Measle and Tinker were splashing about in the swimming pool—and Iggy was sitting on a rock watching them—when Sam and Lee and Matilda came home, which was why they weren't on the steps to greet them when they all piled out of the Prime Magus's official car. The first moment Measle knew his parents and sister were home was when a shadow fell across his eyes and, looking up, he saw the tall silhouette of his father, standing by the edge of the pool.

'Oh—hi, Dad!' said Measle, shielding his eyes against the sun. 'Did you have a nice time?'

'Not really,' said Sam. 'It was dead boring, actually.'

'Oh dear. Well, it wasn't boring here.'

'Yes, so I gather. We got a call from the Guild. Lord Octavo told me all about it. It . . . er . . . it sounds like quite an adventure.'

'It . . . er . . . it was,' Measle grinned. Then he said, 'How do you like our swimming pool?'

'Mm. Not bad.'

Measle stopped grinning. He squinted up at Sam, trying to see if his father was joking or not but the bright sunlight behind Sam's head made that impossible, so Measle decided to take him seriously. 'Not bad? *Not bad?*' he squealed, in outrage. '*Look* at it, Dad! It's completely *brilliant*! It's got rocks all around it, so it looks like a real pool in the mountains somewhere! And look at the island in the middle. That's a real palm tree on it! And look at the deep end—look at the waterfall. If you swim through the waterfall, there's a real cave behind it! And if you climb up on those rocks, there's a slide that shoots you out over the waterfall! Not bad? It's *brilliant*, Dad!'

'Mm,' said Sam, trying to hide his smile behind the hand that covered his mouth. 'And you and Iggy did it all, I suppose?'

Iggy jumped up off the rock he'd been sitting on and bounced around, yelling, 'It was me, Missster Ssstubbs, sssir! I did it! All by mysssself! I digged it an' I filled it full of water an' I made de mountain fingy—'

'It was Lord Octavo, really, Dad,' said Measle. 'He finished it for us.'

'But the slide and the cave and the waterfall—I imagine those were your ideas, Measle?'

'Er . . . well . . . mine and Iggy's, Dad.'

A second silhouette came and stood close by Sam Stubbs and Measle yelled, 'Hi, Mum! Welcome home! How do you like our pool?'

'It's *fabulous*, darling,' said Lee. 'I love it! And so

does Tilly, don't you, sweetheart?' She lifted Matilda off her hip and held her up for Measle to wave at.

'Hi, Tilly!' shouted Measle.

'Dwiggy booda-gumbum,' replied Matilda, brandishing a chubby fist.

'I see she's not talking yet,' said Measle, treading water.

'Well, we've only been away five days,' said Lee. 'Give her a chance.'

Quite suddenly, the pool around Measle started to get rather hot. In a couple of seconds, it reached the temperature of bath water! Not only that, the colour turned from no-colour-at-all to a pale shade of greenish-yellowish-brown! And not only that— suddenly, there were lots of strange little slimy bits that looked like short white worms floating up on the surface! Not only that—now there was a strong and rather familiar smell.

Measle sighed and said, 'Tilly, that is very nasty, what you just did. And please, don't ever do it again—at least, not while I'm trying to have a swim, all right?'

'Oh dear,' said Lee. Measle could quite clearly hear the catch of laughter in her voice. 'What's Tilly done now?'

'It's not funny, Mum,' muttered Measle, trying to push away some of the white slimy things that were floating nearby.

'No, of *course* it isn't,' gurgled Lee, failing utterly to stifle her laughter. 'But what, exactly—?'

'She's gone and changed the water,' said Measle, deciding to get out of the pool before things got any worse. He swam quickly to the shallow end and then stepped up onto dry land.

'But changed it into what?' said Lee.

'I'm not sure,' muttered Measle, scraping slimy white bits off his chest. 'But I *think* it's chicken noodle soup.'

How about another MEASLE treat?

A small boy,
an even smaller dog, and the
biggest monster ever . . .

MEASLE AND THE DRAGODON

IAN OGILVY

Things are looking up for Measle. He's been
reunited with his parents and they're making up
for lost time and having lots of fun.
It seems too good to last.

And it is. The mysterious Dragodon and his gang
of wicked Wrathmonks have cast a spell on Measle's dad
and snatched his mum. Measle and his dog, Tinker,
have only one clue, and it leads them to the deserted
theme park—The Isle of Smiles.

Being hunted down by horrors in a dark, wet
funfair is anything but fun! Measle is on a mission
with more ups and downs than any rollercoaster—
can he save the day once again?

There's more **MEASLE** adventure in store with:

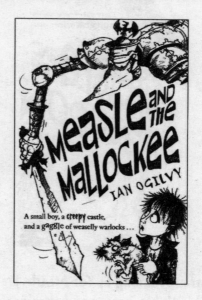

Measle's on his own again. Some double-crossing wizards have locked up his mum and dad and now they're after Measle.

He's got his baby sister with him—a baby sister with amazing magical powers—and every warlock in the place wants to get his hands on her.

Measle has to hide, and Caltrop Castle seems safe. But there's something strange about it. The creepy castle can keep the wizards and warlocks out ... but what is locked inside with Measle and the mallockee ... ?

Ian Ogilvy is best known as an actor—in particular for his takeover of the role of The Saint from Roger Moore. He has appeared in countless television productions, both here and in the United States, has made a number of films, and starred often on the West End stage. His first children's book was *Measle and the Wrathmonk*, followed by *Measle and the Dragodon* and *Measle and the Mallockee*—and he has written a couple of novels for grown-ups too: *Loose Chippings* and *The Polkerton Giant*, both published by Headline. His play, *A Slight Hangover*, is published by Samuel French. He lives in Southern California with his wife Kitty and two stepsons.

Measle Stubbs is best known as a bit of a hero—in particular for his triumphant role as the charge of the evil wrathmonk, Basil Tramplebone, and his defeat of the last of the Dragodons. Measle's last adventure was his struggles against the scary monsters at Caltrop Castle with only his baby sister and a very small wrathmonk to help him. Now he has defeated the slimy Slitherghoul he can relax at home with his family—for a while, at least.

To Pamela

Contents

List of illustrations

List of Illustrations

1 What is design?

One of the most curious features of the modern world is the manner is which design has been widely transformed into something banal and inconsequential. In contrast, I want to argue that, if considered seriously and used responsibly, design should be the crucial anvil on which the human environment, in all its detail, is shaped and constructed for the betterment and delight of all.

To suggest that design is a serious matter in that sense, however, is problematic. It runs counter to widespread media coverage assigning it to a lightweight, decorative role of little consequence: fun and entertaining—possibly; useful in a marginal manner—maybe; profitable in economic sectors dominated by rapid cycles of modishness and redundancy; but of no real substance in basic questions of existence.

Not surprisingly, in the absence of widespread agreement about its significance and value, much confusion surrounds design practice. In some subject areas, authors can assume common ground with readers; in an introduction to architecture or history, for example, although the precise degree of readers' knowledge might vary substantially, a reasonably accurate concept of what constitutes the subject can be relied on. Other subjects, such as nuclear physics, can be so esoteric that no such mutual understanding exists and approaches from first principles become necessary.

Design sits uncomfortably between these two extremes. As a word it is common enough, but it is full of incongruities, has innumerable manifestations, and lacks boundaries that give clarity and definition. As a practice, design generates vast quantities of material, much of it ephemeral, only a small proportion of which has enduring quality.

Clearly, a substantial body of people exist who know something about design, or are interested in it, but little agreement will probably exist about exactly what is understood by the term. The most obvious reference point is fields such as fashion, interiors, packaging, or cars, in which concepts of form and style are transient and highly variable, dependent upon levels of individual taste in the absence of any fixed canons. These do indeed constitute a significant part of contemporary design practice, and are the subject of much commentary and a substantial proportion of advertising expenditure. Other points of emphasis might be on technical practice, or on the crafts. Although substantial, however, these are all facets of an underlying totality, and the parts should not be mistaken for the whole.

So how can design be understood in a meaningful, holistic sense? Beyond all the confusion created by the froth and bubble of advertising and publicity, beyond the visual pyrotechnics of virtuoso designers seeking stardom, beyond the pronouncements of design gurus and the snake-oil salesmen of lifestyles, lies a simple truth. Design is one of the basic characteristics of what it is to be human, and an essential determinant of the quality of human life. It affects everyone in every detail of every aspect of what they do throughout each day. As such, it matters profoundly. Very few aspects of the material environment are incapable of improvement in some significant way by greater attention being paid to their design. Inadequate lighting, machines that are not user-friendly, badly formatted information, are just a few examples of bad design that create cumulative problems and tensions. It is therefore worth asking: if these things are a necessary part of our existence, why are they often done so badly? There is no simple answer. Cost factors are sometimes advanced in justification, but the margin between doing something well or badly can be exceedingly small, and cost factors can in fact be reduced by appropriate design inputs. The use of the term 'appropriate', however, is an important qualification. The spectrum of capabilities covered by the term 'design' requires that means be carefully adapted to ends. A solution to a practical problem which ignores all aspects of its use can be disastrous, as would, say, medical equipment if it were treated as a vehicle for individual expression of fashionable imagery.

This book is based on a belief that design matters profoundly to us all in innumerable ways and represents an area of huge, underutilized potential in life. It sets out to explore some reasons why this is so and to suggest some possibilities of change. The intention is not to negate any aspect of the spectrum of activity covered by the term 'design', but to extend the spectrum of what is understood by the term; examine the breadth of design practice as it affects everyday life in a diversity of cultures. To do so, however, some ground clearing is necessary to cut through the confusion surrounding the subject.

Discussion of design is complicated by an initial problem presented by the word itself. 'Design' has so many levels of meaning that it is itself a source of confusion. It is rather like the word 'love', the meaning of which radically shifts dependent upon who is using it, to whom it is applied, and in what context. Consider, for example, the shifts of meaning when using the word 'design' in English, illustrated by a seemingly nonsensical sentence:

'Design is to design a design to produce a design.'

Yet every use of the word is grammatically correct. The first is a noun indicating a general concept of a field as a whole, as in: 'Design is important to the national economy'. The second is a verb, indicating action or process: 'She is commissioned to design a new kitchen blender'. The third is also a noun, meaning a concept or proposal: 'The design was presented to the client for approval'. The final use is again a noun, indicating a finished product of some kind, the concept made actual: 'The new VW Beetle revives a classic design.'

Further confusion is caused by the wide spectrum of design practice and terminology. Consider, for example, the range of practice included under the rubric of design—to name just a few: craft design, industrial art, commercial art, engineering design, product design, graphic design, fashion design, and interactive design. In a weekly series called 'Designer Ireland' in its Irish Culture section, the Sunday Times of London publishes a brief, well-written analysis of a specific aspect of design. In a six-week period, during August and September 2000, the succession of subjects was: the insignia of the Garda Siochanna, the Irish national police; Louise Kennedy, a fashion designer; the Party Grill stove for outdoor cooking; the packaging for Carrolls Number One, a brand of cigarettes; Costelloe cutlery; and the corporate identity of Ryan Air, a low-cost airline. The range of subjects addressed in the whole series is even more bewildering in its diversity.

To that list can be added activities that appropriate the word 'design' to create an aura of competence, as in: hair design, nail design, floral design, and even funeral design. Why not hair engineering, or funeral architecture? Part of the reason why design can be used in this arbitrary manner is that it has never cohered into a unified profession, such as law, medicine, or architecture, where a licence or similar qualification is required to practise, with standards established and protected by self-regulating institutions, and use of the professional descriptor limited to those who have gained admittance through regulated procedures. Instead, design has splintered into ever-greater subdivisions of practice without any overarching concept or organization, and so can be appropriated by anyone.

Discussion of design on a level that seeks a pattern in such confusion leads in two directions: first, defining generic patterns of activity underlying the proliferation, in order to establish some sense of structure and meaning; secondly, tracing these patterns through history to understand how and why the present confusion exists.

To address the first point: design, stripped to its essence, can be defined as the human capacity to shape and make our environment in ways without precedent in nature, to serve our needs and give meaning to our lives.

Understanding the scale and extent of this capacity can be tested by observing the environment in which anyone may be reading these lines—it might be while browsing in a bookstore, at home, in a library, in an office, on a train, and so on. The odds are that almost nothing in that environment will be completely natural—even plants will have been shaped and positioned by human intervention and, indeed, their genus may even be a considerable modification of natural forms. The capacity to shape our world has now reached such a pitch that few aspects of the planet are left in pristine condition, and, on a detailed level, life is entirely conditioned by designed outcomes of one kind or another.

It is perhaps a statement of the obvious, but worth emphasizing, that the forms or structures of the immediate world we inhabit are overwhelmingly the outcome of human design. They are not inevitable or immutable and are open to examination and discussion. Whether executed well or badly (on whatever basis this is judged,) designs are not determined by technological processes, social structures, or economic systems, or any other objective source. They result from the decisions and choices of human beings. While the influence of context and circumstance may be considerable, the human factor is present in decisions taken at all levels in design practice.

With choice comes responsibility. Choice implies alternatives in how ends can be achieved, for what purposes, and for whose advantage. It means that design is not only about initial decisions or concepts by designers, but also about how these are implemented and by what means we can evaluate their effect or benefit.

The capacity to design, in short, is in innumerable ways at the very core of our existence as a species. No other creatures on the planet have this same capacity. It enables us to construct our habitat in unique ways, without which we would be unable to distinguish civilization from nature. Design matters because, together with language, it is a defining characteristic of what it is to be human, which puts it on a level far beyond the trivial.

This basic capacity can, of course, be manifested in a huge diversity of ways, some of which have become specialized activities in their own right, such as architecture, civil engineering, landscape architecture, and fashion design. To give some focus in a short volume, the emphasis here will be on the two- and three-dimensional aspects of everyday life—in other words, the objects, communications, environments, and systems that surround people at home and at work, at leisure and at prayer, on the streets, in public spaces, and when travelling. Even within this focus, the range is still huge and we need only examine a limited range of examples, rather than attempting a compressed coverage of the whole.

If this human capacity for design is manifested in so many ways, how can we understand this diversity? This brings us back to the second point mentioned above: design's historical development. Design is sometimes explained as a subdivision of art historical narratives emphasizing a neat chronological succession of movements and styles, with new manifestations replacing what went before. The history of design, however, can be described more appropriately as a process of layering, in which new developments are added over time to what already exists. This layering, moreover, is not just a process of accumulation or aggregation, but a dynamic interaction in which each new innovative stage changes the role, significance, and function of what survives. For example, innumerable crafts around the world have been widely displaced by industrial manufactures from their central role in cultures and economies, but have also found new roles, such as providing goods for the tourist trade or supplying the particular global market segment known as Arts and Crafts. Rapid developments in computers and information technology are not only creating exciting new possibilities in interactive design, but are also transforming the ways in which products and services are conceived and produced, in ways that supplement, rather than replace, the old.

Neither is it possible to describe a process with an essential pattern followed everywhere. There are significant variations in how the process of change occurs in different societies and also in the specific consequences change entails. Whatever the exact details, however, there is a widespread pattern for what existed before to continue in some form. It is this that helps explain much of the dense and complex texture of design, and the varied modes of practice under the rubric that confront us today. To ancient crafts and forms that survive and adapt are continually added new competencies and applications. A great deal of confusion in understanding design, therefore, stems from this pattern of historical evolution. What is confusing, however, can also be regarded as a rich and adaptable resource, provided that a framework exists enabling the diversity to be comprehended. A brief outline of the historical development of designing—that is, the practice and activity of creating forms—is therefore necessary.

2 The Historical
Evolution of Design

There has been change and evolution on multiple levels throughout the history of mankind, but human nature has remained remarkably unaltered. We are much the same kind of people who inhabited ancient China, Sumeria, or Egypt. It is easy for us to identity with human dilemmas represented in widely different sources, such as Greek tragedy or Norse sagas.

The evidence too is that the human capacity to design has remained constant, although its means and methods have altered, parallel to technological, organizational, and cultural changes. The argument here, therefore, is that design, although a unique and unchanging human capability, has manifested itself in a variety of ways through history.

Any brief description of such a diverse spectrum of practice must inevitably be an outline, using broad brushstrokes and avoiding becoming enmeshed in detail, with the intention of indicating major changes that have occurred in order to understand the resultant complexity existing today.

An initial problem in delving into the origins of the human capacity to design is the difficulty in determining exactly where and when human beings first began to change their environment to a significant degree—it engenders continual debate that shifts with each major archaeological discovery. It is clear, however, that in this process a crucial instrument was the human hand, which is a remarkably flexible and versatile limb, capable of varying configurations and functions. It can push, or pull, exerting power with considerable strength or fine control; among its capabilities, it can grasp, cup, clench, knead, press, pat, chop, poke, punch, claw, or stroke, and so on. In their origins, tools were undoubtedly extensions of these functions of the hand, increasing their power, delicacy, and subtlety.

From a broad range of early cultures, extending back to about a million years, natural objects began to be used as tools and implements to supplement or enhance the capacities of the hand. For example, the hand is capable of clawing soil to dig out an edible root, but a digging stick or clam shell is also capable of being grasped to do the job more easily, in a sustainable manner, reducing damage to fingers and nails. The task is made easier still if a shell is lashed with hide or fibre at a right angle to the end of a stick, to make a simple hoe. It can then be used more effectively in wider circles from an erect working position. Similarly, the hand can be cupped in order to drink water, but a deep shell forms the same shape permanently and more effectively to function without leakage as a dipper. Even at this level, the process of adaptation involves the capacity of the human brain to understand the relationship between forms and functions.

In these, and innumerable other ways, the natural world provided a diverse source of available, pre-existing materials and models, full of potential for adaptation to the solution of problems. Once adapted, however, a further problem emerged, such as how to make a hoe more durable, less fragile, and less liable to fracture than a seashell. Another dimension set in, beyond simply adapting what was available in ready-made form—that of transforming natural materials into forms without precedent in nature.

Another feature of much early innovation was the adaptation of techniques, forms, and patterns to new purposes and applications. An example was seen in the discovery in 1993 at an archaeological dig at Cayonu, a prehistoric agricultural village site in southern Turkey, of what is believed to be the oldest textile fragment extant, dating from around 7000 BC. The fragment was of linen cloth woven from domesticated flax, and the weave was clearly an adaptation of pre-existing basket-weaving techniques.

Other continuities are also clearly evident. Frequently, natural forms continued to be the ideal model for a particular purpose, with early artefacts made from metal or clay often shaped in forms identical to the natural models from which they originated, such as dippers being made of metal in the form of conch shells.

Humans, from earliest times, have created stereotypes of forms, fixed concepts of what forms are appropriate for particular purposes, as a counterpoint to their contrasting capacity for innovation. Indeed, forms frequently became so closely adapted to the needs of societies that they became interwoven with a way of life, an integral element of its traditions. In circumstances where life was precarious and people were highly vulnerable, the accumulated experience embodied in and represented by such forms was not lightly abandoned.

Nevertheless, over time, forms were adapted by intent or by accident, became refined, or were transformed by new technological possibilities, and new stereotypes would emerge to be adopted as a standard. These in turn would be adapted to specific local circumstances. In West Greenland, for example, each major Eskimo settlement had different versions of sea-going kayaks.

Emphasizing manual dexterity as a dominant feature of the crafts tends to underestimate two other developments crucial to enhancing human ability to transform an environment. Each represents a capacity to reach beyond innate human limitations. One was harnessing natural forces, the superior physical strength of animals and resources such as wind and water, to provide a supplemental level of power greater than the human body, and selecting superior strains of plants and animals for cultivation to provide greater yields. This required a process of enquiry and the accumulation of knowledge and understanding that could be applied to processes of improvement, in which writing and visual representation played a crucial role.

1. Greenland Eskimo kayak

Linked to this, and, in the long run, of increasing significance, was the ability to move beyond an accumulation of pragmatic experience into the realm of ideas as abstractions, with the evolution of tools moving beyond their origins in nature, to forms that were totally new and uniquely human in origin. Abstraction enables capacities to be separated from specific problems, to be generalized, and flexibly adapted to other problems.

Perhaps the greatest example of abstraction is language. Words have no innate meaning in themselves and are arbitrary in their application. For example, the words house, maison, and casa, in English, French, and Italian respectively, all refer to the same physical reality of a human dwelling and take on meaning only by tacit agreement within their society. The capacity to abstract into language, above all, allows ideas, knowledge, processes, and values to be accumulated, preserved, and transmitted to subsequent generations. It is also an integral element in understanding any process of making. In other words, mental skills and thought processes—the ability to use 'mind tools', which represent and articulate concepts of what might be—are as essential in any productive process as the physical skills of the hand and its tools, such as hammer, axe, or chisel.

In terms of design, abstraction has also led to inventions that are purely cultural, with no reference point in human physical form or motor skills, or in nature. Many concepts of geometric form probably derived from accumulated experience in practical work, before being codified and, in turn, fed back into other applications. The evolution of spear-throwers, such as the woomera of Australian aborigines, represents such an abstraction. It gave much greater power and accuracy in hunting and must have evolved in a long process of trial and error. The form of the wheel, however, has no immediately discernible precedent —human limbs cannot rotate upon their own axis and possible stimuli in nature are rare. The concept of infinite rotation is therefore an innovation without precedent. In other words, objects are not just expressions of a solution to a particular problem at any point in time, but can extend much further, into embodying ideas about how life can be lived in a dynamic process of innovation and refinement beyond the constraints of time and place.

Therefore, neither the hand alone, nor the hand allied to the other human senses, can be viewed as the source of design capability. Instead it is the hand allied to the senses and the mind that forms the coordinated trinity of powers by which human beings have asserted ever-greater control over the world. From the origins of human life, flexibility and adaptation resulted in a proliferation of means and ends, with individuals and societies adapting forms and processes to specific needs and circumstances.

Early human societies were nomadic, based on hunting and gathering, and, in a shifting pattern of life in search of new

2. Simple weapons embodying technical sophistication: the
Australian aboriginal woomera

sources of food, qualities such as lightness, portability, and adaptability were dominant criteria. With the evolution of more settled rural societies based on agriculture, other characteristics, other traditions of form appropriate to the new patterns of life, rapidly emerged. It must be emphasized, however, that tradition was not static, but constantly subject to minute variations appropriate to people and their circumstances. Although traditional forms encapsulated the experience of social groups, specific manifestations could be adapted in various minute and subtle ways to suit individual users' needs. A scythe or a chair could keep its basic, accepted characteristics while still being closely shaped in detail to the physique and proportions of a specific person. This basic principle of customization allowed a constant stream of incremental modifications to be introduced, which, if demonstrated by experience to be advantageous, could be integrated back into the mainstream of tradition.

The emergence of agricultural societies living a fixed pattern of life was also capable of supporting concentrations of populations, allowing a greater degree of specialization in crafts. In many cultures, monasteries were founded that not only emphasized meditation and prayer, but also had more practical members who had considerable freedom to experiment and were often at the forefront of technological innovation.

More widespread were concentrations of population in urban

communities, where more specialized, highly skilled craftsmen were attracted by the demand for luxuries created by accumulations of wealth. A frequent consequence was the emergence of associations of skilled craftsmen, in guilds and similar organizations, which, for example, already existed in Indian cities around 600 BC. Social and economic stability in an uncertain world was generally the main aim of guilds, whatever their variations across cultures. A widespread function was the maintenance of standards of work and conduct, and, in the levels of control some of them exerted, they prefigured the characteristics of many modern professional associations and represented an early form of licensing designers.

Guilds could often grow in status and wealth to exert enormous influence over the communities in which they were located. During the Renaissance, for example, Augsburg in southern Germany was famous for the exquisite skills of the gold- and silversmiths who were a major force in city life, with one of their number, David Zorer, becoming mayor in the early 1600s.

Ultimately, however, the influence and control of the guilds were undermined from several directions. Where trade between distant centres began to open up, it was entrepreneurial middlemen, taking enormous risks in pursuit of equally enormous profits, who began to dominate production. Industries based on handwork, often using surplus labour in rural areas, undercut

3. Craft, wealth, and status: Guild houses, Grand Palace, Brussels

guild standards and placed control of forms in the hands of entre-preneurs. In China, the ceramic kilns of Jingdezhen produced huge quantities of porcelain for export to India, Persia, and Arabia, and, from the sixteenth century onwards, to Europe. With distances opening up between maker and market, concepts had to be represented before being produced. Drawings and models sent to China from Europe specified forms and decora-tions to be shipped for particular markets or customers. With the diffusion of the printing press in late-fifteenth-century Europe, the circulation of drawings and prints allowed concepts of form to have wide currency. Individual designers published folios of drawings for forms and decoration that enabled practitioners to break with guild control of what could be produced and adapt a wide repertory of images for product concepts.

Efforts by governments to control and use design for its own purposes also reduced the power of guilds. In the early seven-teenth century, the French monarchy used privileged status and luxurious facilities to attract the finest craftsmen to Paris in order to establish international dominance in the production and trade of luxury goods. Laws were introduced to promote exports and restrict imports. Craftsmen became highly privileged and often very wealthy in catering for the aristocratic market, and in the process were freed by monarchs from guild restrictions.

The most sweeping changes, however, came with the onset of

4. Elegance as display: commode attributed to André Charles Boulle,
Paris, c. 1710

industrialization in the mid-eighteenth century. The sheer scale of products generated by mechanized processes created a dilemma for producers. Craftsmen were generally unable or unwilling to adapt to the demands of industry. In addition, new sources of form had to be found to entice potential purchasers in the markets that were opening, especially for middle-class customers who represented the new wealth of the age. With competition becoming fiercer as more producers with greater capacity entered markets, and with varying tastes in fashion being necessary to pique the taste of customers, a flow of new ideas was required. Academically trained artists, as the only people trained in drawing, were increasingly commissioned by manufacturers to generate concepts of form and decoration in prevailing taste. The English painter, John Flaxman, worked on several such projects for Josiah Wedgwood's ceramic manufactory.

However, artists had little or no idea of how aesthetic concepts could be converted into products, and new circumstances, as ever, demanded the evolution of new skills. On one level, manufacturing required a completely new breed of engineering designers, who took the craft knowledge of clock- and instrument-making and rapidly extended it to solve technical problems involved in building machines to ensure their basic functionality—building steam-engine cylinders to finer tolerances, for example, yielding greater pressure and power.

Where matters of form were concerned, two new groups emerged as influential. The first functioned on the basis of constantly seeking out new concepts that would be acceptable in markets, who were later to become known as style consultants. The second was a new generation of draughtsmen who became the design workhorses of the first industrial age. Working in factories to directions from style consultants, or from entrepreneurs or engineers, or using artists' drawings or pattern books, draughtsmen increasingly provided the necessary drawing skills for production specifications. Often, they were responsible for generating concepts of forms, based predominantly on copying historical styles or the products of successful competitors.

This specialization of function was a further stage in the separation between how product concepts or plans were generated and their actual production. Creating forms without understanding the context of manufacture, however, increasingly resulted in the separation of decorative concerns from function in many household wares, which led to a deep reaction against what many saw as the debasement of art, taste, and creativity by the excesses of industry. In Britain, the cradle of the Industrial Revolution, figures such as John Ruskin and William Morris established a critique of industrial society that had a profound effect in many countries. Their influence culminated in late-nineteenth-century

5. Functional simplicity: lidded jug by Christopher Dresser, Sheffield, 1885

Britain, with the establishment of the Arts and Crafts Movement, which promulgated the role of the craftsman-designer as a means of reviving a lost unity of design practice and social standards. The outbreak of the First World War in 1914, however, was such a bitter reminder of the savage power unleashed by modern industry that nostalgic images of a romanticized medieval idyll appeared increasingly indulgent.

Nevertheless, a belief in asserting the power of art over industry continued—a concept that many idealistic artists hoped to realize in the aftermath of the Russian Revolution of 1917, using art through the medium of industry, as a means of transforming Soviet society. The idea also had a powerful role in the doctrines of the Bauhaus, a school founded in post-First World War Germany to address the problems of how society could and should be changed by harnessing mechanical production to spread the power of art throughout all levels of society. As an ideal, it resonated in the consciousness of generations of twentieth-century designers educated in the tenets of the Bauhaus, but the captains of industry were not ready to abandon their authority. The ideal of the artist-designer remains a significant element of modern design approaches, with virtuoso designers such as Michael Graves or Philippe Starck attracting wide attention. However, the ideal of the artist-designer as change-master of modern society has been little realized in practice.

The Historical Evolution of Design

If Europe stimulated a profound body of design theory that stressed the role of art and craft, in the United States, a new scale of industrial technology and organization evolved by the 1920s and profoundly changed design practices. Through mass production based on huge capital investments, giant businesses generated a wave of innovative products that fundamentally changed every aspect of life and culture in America, with reverberations across the globe. To stimulate markets, products needed to be changed constantly, with mass advertising campaigns exhorting consumers to buy with abandon.

A key example is the automobile, which was first developed in Europe as a custom-built plaything for the wealthy, but which with Henry Ford's Model T, first produced in 1907, became accessible to the masses at ever-decreasing cost. Ford, following the logic of mass production, believed his single model was appropriate to all needs. All that was necessary was to produce it more cheaply in ever-greater quantities. In contrast, Alfred P. Sloan, who became President of General Motors, believed new production methods must adapt to different market levels. In 1924 he introduced a policy to reconcile mass manufacture of automobiles with variety in product. By using basic components across several lines, it was possible to give products a different surface appearance to appeal to different market segments. The outcome was the emergence of designers as stylists, specialists in

6. Styling becomes mainstream: 1936 Oldsmobile convertible

generating visual forms that above all had to be visibly differentiated from those of competitors.

Some leading designers, however, such as Henry Dreyfuss, began to evolve a concept of their role encompassing a vision of social improvement by working in concert with industry. After the Second World War, designers extended their expertise beyond concerns with form and began to address problems of more fundamental importance to clients' businesses. Donald Deskey, who came from a background as furniture designer to head a large New York-based consultancy specializing in branding and packaging, and even an arch-stylist such as Raymond Loewy, argued that declining American manufacturing quality disillusioned purchasers who, after being attracted by external style, found products unsatisfactory in use. They expressed concern about the decline of design awareness in American firms that preferred echoing competitors' products. As an alternative, they advocated design as a high-level strategic planning activity vital to the competitive future of corporations.

Awareness of change was generated by the American market becoming a competitive arena for products from around the world from the 1960s onwards. Large segments of American industry were subsequently decimated by imports from countries like Japan and Germany, where greater attention to production quality and a more holistic approach to design were the norm.

Yet these design approaches, so successful for a time, are also being superseded. Change is evident on many levels. By the 1980s, there began a sharp turn away from the geometrical simplicities of modernism, in a trend generally grouped under the title of postmodernism. This essentially and accurately describes what it is not, rather than what it is, since its main characteristic is an eclectic plethora of frequently arbitrary forms bearing no relation to utility. Much of this is justified by the concept of product semantics, drawing heavily on linguistic theory of signs and meanings. In other words, the meaning of a design is asserted to be more important than any practical purpose, although, since meaning bears little relation to any values, other than the personal inclinations of designers, confusion can ensue.

Another important trend is the effect of new technologies, such as information technology and flexible manufacturing, opening up possibilities of customized products designed in detail for small niche markets. In response, some designers are pioneering new approaches, evolving methodologies that base products on user behaviour, linking hardware and software, and working as strategic planners in the design of complex systems. Interactive design for electronic media is also confronting new problems of enabling users to navigate large and complex bodies of information. Such work is vital in interpreting new technology for potential users.

The Historical Evolution of Design

These changes are part of a repetitive historical pattern. As described earlier, the evolution of a new stage in design does not entirely replace what has gone before, but, instead, is layered over the old. This has been a recurrent pattern throughout the history of design. It not only helps explain why there is such a diversity of concepts and practices about what constitutes design in contemporary society, but also raises a question about the extent to which similar changes will confront us in the future. Exactly what will transpire is uncertain, but the signs are unmistakable—new technologies, new markets, new forms of business organization are fundamentally altering our world, and, without doubt, new design ideas and practices will be required to meet new circumstances. The greatest degree of uncertainty, however, revolves around the question: whose interests will they serve?

3 Utility and Significance

Although design in all its manifestations profoundly influences life on many levels, it does so in diverse ways. Again, it is necessary to find some bedrock of basic explanation in order to create a sense of order from the apparent confusion. A useful tool to this end is a distinction between utility and significance, which is an attempt to clarify the enormous confusion in discussion of design surrounding the term 'function'.

In 1896, in an essay entitled 'Tall Office Building Artistically Considered', the American architect Louis Sullivan wrote: 'It is the pervading law of all things organic, and inorganic, of all things physical and metaphysical, of all things human and all things super-human, of all true manifestations of the head, of the heart, of the soul, that life is recognisable in its expression, that form ever follows function. This is the law.'

These ideas were heavily conditioned by Darwin's theory of evolution with its emphasis on the survival of the fittest. By the late nineteenth century, ideas that the forms of fish or birds had evolved in response to their elements and that animals and plants were closely adapted to their environment were commonplace. In that context, it could be argued, form must indeed follow function, to the extent that the stripes of a zebra or the brilliant plumage of a parrot have a distinct purpose in the immutable laws of survival. Similarly, Sullivan's concept of function encompassed the use of decoration as an integral element in design.

Sullivan's concept became encapsulated in the dictum 'Form follows function', and became part of the vocabulary of design, although it underwent something of a transformation in the process. Function in design became widely interpreted in terms of practical utility, with the conclusion that how something is made and its intended use should inevitably be expressed in the form. This omitted the role of decoration and how patterns of meaning can be expressed through or attached to forms. In this respect, it is possible to speak of an alternative dictum: 'Form follows fiction'. In other words, in contrast to the world of nature, human life is frequently inspired and motivated by dreams and aspirations rather than just practicality.

As a consequence, the concept of function has been one of the most hotly disputed terms in design. In the early twentieth century, a broad body of ideas, generally grouped under the umbrella term 'functionalism', articulated design concepts that rejected the florid decoration so typical of the nineteenth century. This could mean several things. For some designers, such as Peter Behrens, who was active in Germany in the early years of the twentieth century, classical architecture and design were a source of inspiration. Stripped of decoration, these could yield forms that were clean and geometrical, qualities considered desirable in contrast to the heady repertoire of styles typical of the nineteenth century that had been adopted indiscriminately from every canon and culture of history. In like manner, traditional forms could similarly be simplified and refined, as in the work of W. R. Lethaby and Gordon Russell, contemporaries of Behrens, and heirs to the English Arts and Crafts tradition. Both tendencies could simultaneously claim to be contemporary while still retaining continuity through references to the past.

Another more radical tendency that totally rejected the past was articulated after the First World War in Europe. It was primarily associated with such figures as Theo van Doesburg, a Dutch theorist and leading member of the De Stijl group, Walter Gropius, the head of the Bauhaus school in Germany, and Le Corbusier in France. They evolved a repertoire of abstract geometric forms that in theory claimed to be the most suitable for the processes of standardized industrial production. Mass-manufacturing techniques, however, were equally capable of turning out complex, decorated forms, and indeed, in production terms, decoration could be advantageous. In the manufacture of plastic casings for radios in the 1930s, for example, heavy presses were used that made it difficult to produce a simple box-like shape. The problem was that, in the pressing, 'flow-lines' could appear as a consequence of the intense pressure applied, which marred large, plain surfaces. It was, therefore, better to use some means of breaking up large planes, by, for example, introducing steps into surfaces, or treatments such as stippling or hatching. The claim for clean, geometric form was in fact more significant as an ideology of the role of design in industrial society, rather than reflecting any innate characteristics of production methods. Instead of geometric form being the most suitable in practical terms, it was instead a powerful metaphor of what form in a mechanized age should ideally be. In this it was only one of several concepts that emerged—similar claims could be made with equal validity for the concept of streamlining, with its organic tear-drop curves and speed lines.

In place of dogmatic assertions that limit consideration of what form is considered permissible, a more inclusive definition of function is needed, which can be opened up by breaking the concept of function into a twofold division: the key concepts of utility and significance.

Utility can be defined as the quality of appropriateness in use. This means it is concerned with how things work, of the degree to which designs serve practical purposes and provide affordances or capabilities (and the consequences when they do not). A simple example is a professional kitchen knife used to prepare food: its primary utility value is as a cutting tool. In order for it to work effectively, the blade needs to possess material qualities enabling a sharp edge to be maintained and for it to remain stable in use. (A blade that is too thin will wobble when pressure is applied, which not only is inefficient but can be highly dangerous.) The processes of use also require that the knife handle fits comfortably in the hand, providing a good, firm grip. On this level, utility is concerned primarily with efficiency, derived from technological and material factors. However, in use, such efficiency can also be a source of great pleasure. When all the detailed aspects are well integrated, the best kitchen knives become an extension of the senses, with a satisfying sense of rightness, fitting into the hand almost inevitably and giving a fine degree of balance and control. In such terms, efficiency moves into a different level of response and meaning, and, indeed, it is sometimes very difficult to separate utility and significance precisely, since in practice they can be closely interwoven.

Significance, as a concept in design, explains how forms assume meaning in the ways they are used, or the roles and meaning assigned them, often becoming powerful symbols or icons in patterns of habit and ritual. In contrast to the emphasis on efficiency, significance has more to do with expression and meaning. Two simple examples of wooden toothpicks (and few forms are more basic) can illustrate the distinction between utility and significance, and also the ways in which they frequently overlap.

The first toothpick—or dental stick, as it is marketed—is produced by a Norwegian company, Jordan, a specialist in dental products. Under two inches long, it has a highly effective wedge form for the task of cleaning both teeth and gums, not only after a meal, but as part of an ongoing oral hygiene programme. This tiny object encapsulates a high degree of utility that is carefully designed in great detail for its intended task.

The second example is a traditional Japanese toothpick. Circular in form and longer by half an inch than the Jordan example, it has only one end sharpened. The other is a bevelled cone, below which are turned incisions around the shaft. The pointed end is clearly concerned with the primary utility of the object, that of removing food caught between teeth, and at first sight the other end might appear to be purely decorative, its form having no readily discernible purpose. An explanation for this form, however, can be found in traditional patterns of dining in Japanese society. This became an expression of sensibility and refinement, with diners kneeling on tatami mats at lacquered tables. The vessels and artefacts used were frequently works of art in their own right, and none more so than the table, which could have exquisite patterns inlaid or painted on its lacquered surface. Laying chopsticks on such fine surfaces while eating was considered indelicate and so chopstick rests (another combination of utility and significance) evolved, enabling chopsticks to be laid down without the part that had been in the mouth coming into contact

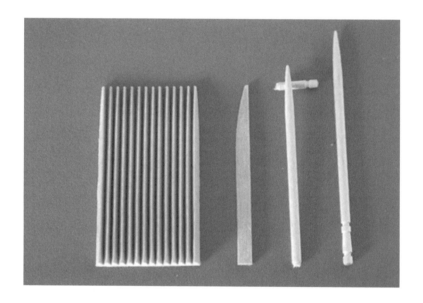

7. Toothpicks

with the table surface. With the toothpicks, however, the solution was built in. The turned incisions of the toothpick enabled one end to be easily broken off, which could then serve as a rest for the pointed end after use. It demonstrates how even the smallest utilitarian objects are capable of simultaneously embodying values.

It is possible to find designs of many kinds defined solely in terms of utility or significance. Many examples of the former are products related to the performance of professional services, tools with highly specific purposes, such as a hand saw or a lathe, or medical equipment, such as an ultrasound machine. Where information has to perform a highly specific task, as in a railway timetable, the layout and type forms should be clean, simple, and directed wholly to imparting essential facts. A primary condition of utilitarian design is that it must effectively execute or support certain tasks. In contrast, a piece of jewellery, a porcelain figurine, or a frame for a family photograph has no such specific purpose—instead their purpose can be described in terms of contemplative pleasure or adornment. Whether their meaning stems from the social taste of a particular fashion or age, or an intensely personal evocation of relationship and meaning, their significance is intrinsic and not dependent upon any specific affordance.

In addition, between the poles where utility and significance can be clearly identified as the dominant characteristic, there are innumerable products that unite efficiency and expression in an astonishing range of combinations. A lighting fixture can be on one level a utilitarian means of illumination, but at the same time expressive in sculptural form of a highly individualistic, even idiosyncratic, nature. Tableware, cutlery, and glassware serve specific purposes while dining, but again can be manifested in a huge variety of forms, often with complex decorative patterns. Perhaps the classic example of our age is the automobile, which, besides having the very utilitarian task of carrying people and luggage from place to place, has from its early years been an extension of ego and personal lifestyle. Rolls-Royce automobiles, for example, are not only superb examples of technical craftsmanship, but are a symbol of achievement in societies around the globe.

The significance of objects, the precise values imputed to them, however, will often vary considerably between different cultures. In the example of the Japanese toothpick given above, it is important to acknowledge the particular associations with sophisticated courtesy as an expression of Japanese culture. This raises important questions of how cultures evolve patterns of behaviour that become codified as rules or norms, with different cultures expressing values in their own specific way.

Meaning is not necessarily permanently fixed, however, since the significance of products can vary over time and space. A clas-

8. The symbol of achievement: Rolls-Royce Park Ward 2000

sic example was the Volkswagen Beetle, developed in 1930s Germany on the direct orders of Adolf Hitler, himself a motoring enthusiast. With production of the first prototypes in 1937, by the 'Strength through Joy' section of the German Labour Front, the official workers' organization, it was promoted as an icon of the achievements of the Nazi Party. When production recommenced on a large scale after the Second World War, the VW was successfully exported to the United States in the 1950s and became a cult object. The design was virtually identical across this period of time, but the significance of the product underwent a remarkable transformation: from an icon of fascism in the 1930s—the 'Strength through Joy car'—to the loveable 'Bug' and hero of Walt Disney's Herbie films in 1960s America. The transformation went further with the redesigned Beetle that appeared in 1997, which also rapidly acquired cult status in the United States.

Basically, concepts of culture can be divided into two broad categories: first, the idea of culture as cultivation, resulting in the acquisition of ideas or faculties expressed in certain styles or behaviour believed to have particular value. A certain hierarchy is involved, in that a concert of classical music is considered more significant than a rock concert, or a piece of sculpture more than a work of industrial design. To some extent, design has begun to be drawn into this sphere, as evident by the number of art museums that have developed collections and held major exhibitions of design. Incorporating design into concepts of exclusivity, often under the term 'decorative art', however, has often more to do with museums' search for contemporary justification than with understanding the role of design in modern life.

The second major concept of culture, and the one underlying this book, is based on a more generalized view of culture as the shared values of a community. In this sense, culture is the distinctive way of life of social groups—the learned behaviour patterns expressed through such aspects, as values, communications, organizations, and artefacts. It encompasses the fabric of everyday life and how it is lived in all its aspects and allows consideration of a broader range of design and its role in people's lives. It has the virtue of including more elite definitions, but as part of a broader range of discussion.

The influence of cultural values, as manifested in interpretations and meanings of designed objects, is felt at many levels. In the past, and continuing to some extent, very different objects for broadly similar functions evolved around the world, resulting in great diversity. If one examines, for example, how food is prepared, in China it is still widely cooked in a wok, compared to a range of specialized pans used in European kitchens. The food prepared in the former is eaten with chopsticks, the latter with an array of often very specialized cutlery. In these and innumerable other ways, the specific forms are the expressions of particular cultural contexts, habits, and values that have evolved in their particularity over time.

Two main levels of difficulty occur in confronting the specific characteristics of time and place. The first arises from the need to conform to existing cultural patterns, to integrate or assimilate in ways that cause no disruption or offence. The second involves navigating unavoidable changes in such patterns, which becomes infinitely more complex.

Problems seem to be fewer and of lesser intensity if products are simple and utilitarian, which minimizes the possibility of cultural conflict. World markets for a vast array of luxury products, such as Hermes leather goods, that are inherently simple even though expensive can be treated in an undifferentiated manner.

The consequences of not acknowledging the power of cultural diversity can be surprising. In the early 1980s a Harvard marketing expert, Theodor Levitt, achieved considerable prominence with his ideas on globalization, among which he argued that differences were lessening and standard products across the globe were the marketing tools of the future. It was perhaps coincidence, but, at the same time, the management of the appliance manufacturer Electrolux became convinced that Europe should become a single market for refrigerator/freezer units, like the USA, where a few large manufacturers make a limited range of designs. A policy introduced in 1983 to push towards this end proved costly, however, as the divergent cultures of Europe intransigently failed to follow the American pattern. In Northern Europe, for example, people shop weekly and need equal freezer and refrigerator space. Southern Europeans still tend to shop daily in small local markets and need smaller units. The British eat more frozen vegetables than elsewhere in the world and need 60 per cent freezer space. Some want the freezer on top, some on the bottom. Electrolux attempted to streamline operations but seven years later the company still produced 120 basic designs with 1,500 variants and had found it necessary to launch new refrigerators designed to appeal to specific market niches.

Packaging and visual imagery can also be a minefield. The former CEO of Coca-Cola, Roberto Goizueta, recounted that, when his company entered the Chinese market, it was discovered that the phonetic pronunciation of the company name translated as 'Bite the wax tadpole'. The problem was identified before major production began and the ideograms on packaging were sensibly adapted to mean 'Tasty and evoking happiness'.

In another example from East Asia, one of the stranger illustrations of the cultural perils of globalization was a leading brand of toothpaste, marketed for decades under the brand name of 'Darkie'. Its packaging had a cartoon-like illustration of a stereotyped, black-face minstrel with top hat, and teeth gleaming pearly white. In its market of origin nobody apparently found this troublesome, but Colgate-Palmolive's purchase of the Hong Kong manufacturer of this product in 1989 brought unexpected problems at home. A rumour rapidly spread in the USA that the company was selling a racist product and banner-carrying pickets appeared outside its New York headquarters. To appease American critics without destroying a well-known brand in Asia, Colgate-Palmolive sought to redefine the brand name as 'Darlie', with a visual redesign to match. The packaging image was modified to show an elegant man about town of indeterminate ethnic origin, but still in white tie and top hat and with gleaming teeth.

Globalization, however, should not be considered only in terms of problems of adaptation or conformity. Theodor Levitt was indeed partly right in pointing out ways in which trends in technology and communications were linking the globe together and in some respects radically altering notions of culture. The influence of globalization means that culture does not necessarily remain dependent on a specific environment, with everyone adhering to the same broad, homogeneous set of values and beliefs. It raises the possibility of having a culture different from those around us. Cultural multiplicity rather than homogeneity and an emphasis on cultural creation rather than cultural inheritance would appear on many levels to be patterns for the future. Any such transition, however, will not be simple or easy.

The role of design substantially contributes to such developments by creating change in values across national or ethnic boundaries. This can be on the level of products, such as motor cycles and television sets, but probably more powerfully from the constant imagery associated with global television broadcasts and advertising, as with CNN, the configuration of an online interactive site, such as Amazon.com, or the corporate identity of McDonald's or Coca-Cola. Their ubiquity and widespread appeal can create substantial friction and have attracted attacks from divergent sources, among them French nationalism, Russian fascism, and Hindu and Islamic fundamentalism. These all differ in origins and rationale, but have in common a resentment of new patterns of cosmopolitanism presented by the imagery of global design, in the name of protecting cultural identity. It would be a mistake, however, to identify all reactions to globalization with those of extreme groups. Many people are genuinely concerned about the loss of local control and identity to forces that frequently appear remote and not answerable for their actions. The utility of being able to watch new broadcasts from the other side of the world may not compensate for children being profoundly influenced by imagery and behaviour that can appear alien and threatening. Even on a more mundane level, it is easy to give offence. A major advertising campaign in Japan for an American brand of soap had a man entering the bathroom while his wife was in the bathtub, behaviour that might be thought to express sexual attraction in the USA, but which was considered ill-mannered and unacceptable in Japan.

These reactions cannot be dismissed as the inevitable consequences of change. The role and power of technology are indeed a problem when the ability to communicate simultaneously around the world, a marvellous development by any standards, is regarded as a threat. There are also far too many products and services being placed on world markets in which little or no concern is evident about whether they are comprehensible or usable. An assumption of uniformity in global designs as a basis for solutions can indeed create new problems, when a little forethought could have ensured appropriate adaptation to local conditions.

Obviously, the ability of human beings to create meaningful form spans a very broad spectrum of possibilities. At their most profound level, forms can embody metaphysical significance, going beyond the boundaries of tangible form to become symbols of belief and faith, expressing the deepest beliefs and aspirations of humankind. Nothing in the specific form of totems from Pacific Island tribes or the North American plains, or of statues of Buddha or Shiva, or the Christian cross can even hint at the complexity of the beliefs and values they represent. Yet the significance of such symbols becomes regarded as an objective social fact, understood by all who share the beliefs they symbolize. At the same time, it is also possible for people to invest objects with

intense personal meaning that need not conflict with broader patterns of belief in a culture.

In 1981, two Chicago sociologists, Mihaly Csikszentmihalyi
and Eugene Rochberg-Halton, published the conclusions of a
research project on the role of objects in people's lives, entitled
The Meaning of Things. They wrote of

the enormous flexibility with which people can attach meanings to
objects, and therefore derive meanings from them. Almost anything can
be made to represent a set of meanings. It is not as if the physical characteristics of an object dictated the kind of significations it can convey,
although these characteristics often lend themselves certain meanings
in preference to others; nor do the symbolic conventions of the culture
absolutely decree what meaning can or cannot be obtained from interaction with a particular object. At least potentially, each person can discover and cultivate a network of meanings out of the experiences of his
or her own life.

The capacity of people to invest objects with meaning, to
become imaginatively involved in creating from an object or communication a sense of significance that can reach far beyond what
designers or manufacturers envisage, has not been given much
credence in the age of mass production and advertising. All too
often the emphasis is on imposing patterns of meaning and conformity from the standpoint of producers. However, this human
capacity to invest psychic energy in objects is immensely power-

ful, with significant ramifications for the study and appreciation of design. In an important sense, it can be argued that the outcomes of design processes, the end result, should not be the central concern of the study and understanding of design, but rather the end result should be considered in terms of an interplay between designers' intentions and users' needs and perceptions. It is at the interface of the two that meaning and significance in design are created. For this reason, subsequent chapters exploring the outcomes of design in more detail will not be organized according to the categories widely used to define professional design practice, such as graphic or industrial design (although it will be necessary to discuss such terms). Instead, the chapters are grouped in terms of generic concepts: objects, communications, environments, systems, and identities, in which the concept of users', as well as designers', response and involvement can be further explored.

4 Objects

The term 'objects' is used to describe a huge spectrum of three-dimensional artefacts encountered in everyday activities in such contexts as the home, public spaces, work, schools, places of entertainment, and transport systems. They range from simple single-purpose items, such as a saltshaker, to complex mechanisms, such as a high-speed train. Some are an expression of human fantasy, others of high technology.

Objects are a crucial expression of ideas of how we could or should live, put into tangible form. As such, they communicate with an immediacy and directness that is not just visual, but can involve other senses. Our experience of an automobile is not solely through how it looks, but also through the feel of seats and controls, the sound of the engine, the scent of upholstery, how it rides upon the road. The orchestration of sensual effects on several levels can have a powerful cumulative impact. Such diversity in how objects are conceived, designed, perceived, and used also provides multiple perspectives from which they can be understood and interpreted.

The terminology of the professional practices involved is an additional complication. 'Product designer' and 'industrial designer' are in reality virtually interchangeable and both claim a role in thinking about product form in terms of the relationship between technology and users. 'Stylist' is more limited, a term describing a preoccupation with aesthetic differentiation of product form, usually under the control of marketers. 'Industrial artist' is an older term that is still occasionally used, emphasizing again a focus on form in aesthetic terms. Many architects can also work as designers, employing a variety of approaches. For particularly complex objects, perhaps with highly specific performance requirements, the form may be determined by engineering designers on the basis of technological criteria. An additional complication is that complex objects can require multidisciplinary teams involving many disciplines working in close cooperation.

Within the framework set out at the end of the previous chapter on the interplay between designers' and users' concerns, it is clear that there are some designers who, on balance, are more preoccupied with their own ideas, rather than with those of their users. Reinforcing such approaches are theoretical ideas grouped under the heading of postmodernism, which emerged in the 1980s, emphasizing the semantic value of design, rather than its utilitarian qualities. In other words, it is the meaning of a product, rather than the uses to which it is put, that is the primary criterion in its conception and use. It is not users, however, who are the focus of these concepts, but designers, which opens the door to products taking on arbitrary forms that may have little or nothing to do with use, but are justified by their 'meaning'. An example is the Italian company Alessi, which, in addition to a long-established range of household items of great simplicity, has in recent years offers a stream of products epitomizing this tendency. Perhaps the most well known is the lemon squeezer designed by Philippe Starck, under the name 'Juicy Salif'. Starck has a great talent for designing striking, unusual forms, as is obvious in this object. It is, however, signally deficient in the practical purpose it purports to fulfil and is instead intended to function as a 'household icon'. To have this item of fashionable taste adorn a kitchen, however, costs some twenty times that of a simple and infinitely more efficient squeezer—in fact, the term 'squeezer' should perhaps be more appropriately applied to profit leverage, rather than functionality for users.

This particular approach to design has been avidly adopted by innumerable companies looking to inject added value into products on which profits margins are low. As a result, postmodernist ideas in design have been widely appropriated for commercial purposes in order to convert efficient, inexpensive, and accessible products into new manifestations that are useless, expensive, and exclusive. The emphasis on meaning, moreover, unlocks a vista of unlimited possibilities for the elaboration of ever-new forms requiring little or no relationship to purpose, enabling

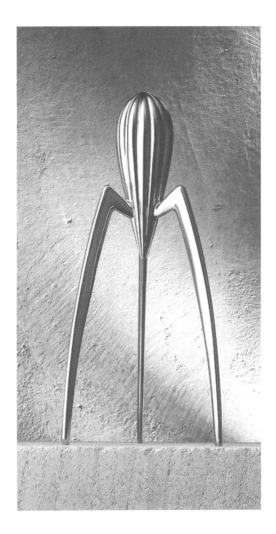

9. Pricey inefficiency as high style: 'Juicy Salif' by Philippe Starck, for Alessi

products to be drawn into cycles of fashionable change for the primary benefit of manufacturers.

Fashion, basically, depends upon many people's concepts of suitability being heavily influenced by what they see others doing and purchasing. As such, it is an innate characteristic of human nature. From this perspective, goods are indicators of social and cultural status. As disposable income has been more widely available for larger proportions of populations in advanced industrial countries, the potential for conspicuous consumption and so the demand for distinctive products have undoubtedly expanded and been subject to intense manipulation. Among the responses to this phenomenon has been the emergence of 'designer-brands', which have proved to be powerful devices, particularly in the more expensive sectors of the product spectrum.

An example is Ferdinand Porsche, grandson of the designer of the original Volkswagen 'Beetle', who began work in the family car company and set up his own design studio in 1972. His design activity includes work on large-scale products, such as trains for the Bangkok Mass Transit System, street trams for Vienna, and speedboats, which have a strong utilitarian element. He is best known, however, for small, exclusive personal items, such as tobacco pipes and sunglasses, made in cooperation with leading manufacturers. Even though these latter firms have a high reputation in their own right, such as Faber-Castell or Siemens, prod-

10. Access and convenience for all: Vienna streetcar designed by Porsche

ucts are marketed as a Porsche Design, which has become a fashionable identifier in its own right for luxury products.

It would be misleading to imply that all such 'designer-centred' approaches are focused solely on differentiating form as a means of adding value. Some individuals evolve insights into people's lives, with the results that they design radically new solutions to problems that might seem obvious once manifested in tangible form—in other words, giving users what they never knew they wanted—one of the most innovative roles design can play.

One of the greatest influences on form in the modern world, in this sense, has been Giorgetto Giugiaro. He also started out as an automobile stylist, working for FIAT, Carrozzeria Bertone, and Ghia, before founding Italdesign with two colleagues in 1968. No one has more influenced the direction of automobile styling around the world than Giugiaro. His concept of the Volkswagen Golf of 1974 set the pattern for subsequent generations of small, hatchback cars and a 1978 design for Lancia was the first minivan. Clean contours and lines, without superfluous decoration, typify his work. Italdesign worked on some industrial design projects, but in 1981 an offshoot, Guigiaro Design, was established to concentrate specifically on a broader range of products. These have included cameras, watches, express trains (even these have his signature), subway trains, motor scooters, housewares, aircraft

11. The hatchback sets a new pattern: VW Golf by Giorgetto Giugiaro, 1974

interiors, and street furniture. More recently he, too, has introduced a range of personal and fashion goods.

For some designers, retaining a degree of control over their work in order to guarantee its integrity is an essential dimension of practice. Being able to do so while being highly successful commercially demands creative skills and business acumen of a high order. Stephen Peart, whose company, Vent Design, is based in California, has such a reputation for innovative concepts and high-quality designs that marketing his services is unnecessary and a string of major companies have beaten a path to his door. He has rejected growth in order to keep overheads low and maintain the possibility of choice in the clients whose commissions he accepts. The integrity of his work is maintained by insisting on agreements stipulating that a contract is void if his design concepts are changed without his consent.

There are also companies where the influence of individuals can be decisive, particularly in establishing a philosophy about the role objects should play in people's lives. An example is in the field of domestic electrical appliances, such as toasters, kitchen mixers, and hair dryers. These are in fact used for only a few minutes in any day and the question of what role the forms should play in the long intervals when they are not used is pertinent.

The German designer Dieter Rams used the metaphor of a good English butler: products should provide quiet, efficient service when required and otherwise fade unobtrusively into the background. (A former butler from Buckingham Palace advising the actor Anthony Hopkins on his role in the film *Remains of the Day* commented: 'When you are in a room it should be even more empty.') Rams's designs for Braun over a forty-year period through to the mid-1990s used simple, geometric forms and basic non-colours, predominantly white, with black and grey used for details, and primary colours applied only for small and highly specific purposes, such as on/off switches. The consistent aesthetic cumulatively established by Braun was one of most formative influences on houseware design in the late twentieth century and established instant recognition for the company that many have sought to copy but few have equalled.

In contrast, similar appliances produced by the Dutch company Philips, under the design direction of Stefano Marzano, have tended to be more assertive visual statements, with a range of organic forms and bright colours, implying that such objects serve a more prominent visual role in the home when not in use.

Highly individual and innovative approaches to form can be particularly successful when allied to genuine improvements in product performance. Apple's iMac computer series designed by Jonathan Ive and introduced in 1998 caused a sensation with its incorporation of transparent plastics, in what were often referred to as 'toothpaste colours', on casings and accessories. Ive's inno-

12. The language of simplicity: Braun travelling clock, Type AB 312,
by Dieter Rams and Dietrich Lubs

vative concept of what computer form could be cleverly signalled a new emphasis on accessibility and connectivity in the iMac series, targeting sections of the population who had not previously used computers. It certainly set a huge trend in motion, with the use of such colours so widespread that it became repetitive and meaningless, yet another trend ready to be superseded.

A striving to demonstrate individual personality through designs should not be surprising. Most designers are educated to work as individuals, and design literature contains innumerable references to 'the designer'. Personal flair is without doubt an absolute necessity in some product categories, particularly relatively small objects, with a low degree of technological complexity, such as furniture, lighting, small appliances, and housewares. In larger-scale projects, however, even where a strong personality exercises powerful influence, the fact that substantial numbers of designers are employed in implementing a concept can easily be overlooked. The emphasis on individuality is therefore problematic—rather than actually designing, many successful designer 'personalities' function more as creative managers. A distinction needs to be made between designers working truly alone and those working in a group. In the latter case, management organization and processes can be equally as relevant as designers' creativity.

When a design consultancy grows beyond a certain minimum

13. Style and connectivity: Apple iMac by Jonathan Ive,

size, the necessary time committed to managerial functions inevitably makes it difficult to maintain personal levels of creativity. Michele de Lucchi has a consultancy with some fifty employees in Milan and corporate customers around the world. Clearly, not all consultancy work can be executed by de Lucchi himself, although his personal control establishes direction and standards. However, to sustain his capacity as a designer, he has also established a small production company, enabling him to continue working at a level of personal exploration and self-expression not possible with the more strictly defined corporate emphasis of mainstream work.

In other areas of design work, however, a group ethos predominates. Many design consultancies are organized as businesses and lack any specific reference to an individual. They often have large numbers of employees located in offices around the world working on a huge range of projects. One of the best known, IDEO, was founded by combining British and American consultancies and by the late 1990s had offices in London, San Francisco, Palo Alto, Chicago, Boston, and Tokyo. Metadesign, after being founded in Berlin, similarly functions on an international level, with affiliates in San Francisco and Zurich. While some consultancies provide a general range of competencies, others can focus on a particular area of work. Design Continuum in Boston emphasizes close cooperation between designers and engineers with a specialist capability in designing medical equipment. Teamwork is frequently a characteristic of consultancy work and the specific contribution of individuals may be veiled.

Corporate design groups necessarily focus on specific products and processes manufactured by their company, which offers the possibility of going into depth on specific problems and working on several generations of products. Again, they take many forms. An ongoing problem in such groups is the need to maintain specific expertise without getting stale, which means injections of fresh stimuli. Some combine a small in-house group for continuity, with consultants occasionally brought in to add a broader perspective. In others, such as Siemens and Philips, the corporate group is expected to function as in-house consultants, having to bid for the company's work on a competitive basis against outside groups, and being free to do work outside the company. Some corporate giants, particularly Japanese companies, have very large in-house groups, 400 designers being not unusual, although many of these may work only on a detailed level, designing minor variations of existing products in an effort to satisfy a broad range of tastes.

If references to 'the designer' indicate a bias towards individuality in much design thinking and commentary, another widespread singular reference—the phrase 'the design process'

—suggests a unity that is non-existent in practice. There are, in fact, many design processes, adaptable to the immense variety of products and contexts in which designers work.

At one end of the spectrum are highly subjective processes based on individual insight and experience. These can be difficult to explain and quantify. Particularly in corporate contexts dominated by the numerical methodologies of finance and marketing, with their apparent ability to demonstrate 'facts', it is easy for such approaches to be underestimated. There is a welcome recognition in economic and business theory, however, that in many disciplines the kind of knowledge based on experience and insight—tacit knowledge—can be a vital repository of enormous potential. Much design knowledge is indeed of this kind, although this does not mean an ability to design should be limited to the tacit dimension. There is a vital need to extend alternative forms of knowledge in design that can be structured and communicated—in other words, coded knowledge.

Most practical disciplines, such as architecture and engineering, have a body of basic knowledge and theory about what the practice is and does that can serve as a platform, a starting point, for any student or interested layman. The absence of a similar basis in design is one of the greatest problems it faces. Emphasizing tacit knowledge means that many design students are expected to reinvent the wheel, acquiring knowledge in an unstructured manner through learning-by-doing. In effect, more rational methods of enquiry and working are considered irrelevant.

Tacit, subjective approaches may be appropriate for small-scale projects—for example, where the emphasis is on differentiating form. In contrast with large-scale projects involving complex questions of technology and the organization of interactions on many levels, personal intuition is unlikely to be capable of handling all necessary aspects. In such projects, rational, structured methodologies can ensure the full dimensions of projects are understood as a platform for creative solutions on the level of detailed execution. Where, for example, the fit between an object and user is of primary importance, ergonomic analysis based on data about human dimensions can ensure that a form will be appropriate for a desired portion of any given population. The Aeron chair, designed by Don Lawrence and Bill Stumpf for the Herman Miller corporation, is a finely detailed office chair creatively elaborated on the basis of minutely detailed ergonomic data.

Computer-based approaches have also been developed for application to the analysis of very large and complex problems. One such programme, known as Structured Planning, has been developed by Charles Owen at the Institute of Design at the Illinois Institute of Technology in Chicago. With the aid of computers, problems are decomposed into their constituent elements that can be analysed in detail and reconfigured in new creative

14. Form and ergonomics: Aeron chair, by Don Chadwick and Bill Stumpf
for Herman Miller

syntheses. In work for companies such as Steelcase, the world's largest manufacturer of contract office furniture, structured planning has been used to generate new insights and proposals for development in large, complex markets. For Kohler, producer of bathroom fittings, its application has generated a large number of product proposals, of which one to reach the market is a bathtub within a bathtub, enabling the bather to fill the inner bath to the brim for a deep soak.

Market analysis is also a long-established and powerful tool in generating ideas. In the early 1980s, the design group at Canon analysed patterns in copier sales and found the market was dominated by very large, highly expensive machines based on cutting-edge technology. Speculation about whether smaller machines, personal copiers, based on a miniaturization of existing well-proved technology at a relatively low cost, could be feasible led to a hugely successful extension of the market and a dominant position in it for Canon.

On another level, methodologies seeking to understand the problems of users have been adapted from disciplines such as anthropology and sociology. An example is using behavioural observation to gain insights into difficulties that people have in varying contexts, such as working environments, shopping, or learning. Detailed observation over time and space can reveal difficulties that can be addressed by new design solutions.

Although most objects are created with particular uses in mind, however, there are problems in basing interpretations on designers' original intentions. These can be undermined or even reversed in the processes of use by people's infinite capacity pragmatically to adapt objects to purposes other than those originally intended. (Consider for a moment the alternative uses to which a metal paperclip can be put.) A chair can be intended as a seat, but may also be used to stack papers or books, to hang clothes, to keep a door open, to stand on and change a light bulb. VCRs were originally intended by their manufacturers for playing prerecorded tapes, but were soon adapted by users for time-shifting television programmes, recording them on a blank tape so they could be watched at a time convenient to the viewer, rather than the broadcasting company. In general, the additional functions can either complement or enhance the original intention, although this is not always the case. Table knives or scissors can be readily used as injurious weapons, as innumerable police records attest.

Some manufacturers endeavour to use this talent for adaptation as a positive resource. If unsure of what to do with a new technology or product, they frequently launch it on the market in a form encouraging experimentation by users, hoping the huge talent for adaptability will discover feasible applications. After a 3M researcher discovered a new glue that would not stick permanently, the resulting range of Post-It products evolved very largely from observing how people adapted the original plain paper format to a wide range of uses, such as book-markers, fax labels, or shopping reminders. The spectacular evolution of sports shoes has followed a similar trajectory largely derived from observing new and unusual ways of how young people use them on the street.

Another way of involving customers is represented by IKEA, the furniture company founded in Sweden by Ingvar Kamprad in 1951. Now with stores all over the world and a thriving mail-order business, IKEA has redefined production processes by incorporating customers into them. In selling flat-pack components designed for easy transportation, it has to design each item so customers can assemble them easily at home, resulting in large cost savings, part of which are passed on to the customer as lower purchase cost. The success of IKEA has also been based on a consistent design approach, predominantly an updated Swedish Arts and Crafts style, which it projects in all its operations, giving it a local character in global markets. This has caused some problems in the context of use, however, as when it first marketed beds in the USA that were the wrong size for American sheets and covers.

In considering what level of innovation is appropriate and what design approach is best for particular products, the concept of life cycle is important. In the earliest stages after any new product appears, when uncertainty abounds, formal experiment will be a characteristic, with a variety of possibilities being probed. As the market grows and settles, products take on specific characteristics and become standardized, the emphasis swinging to production quality and cost. In the experimental stage of personal computers in the early 1980s, for example, a variety of possibilities existed. Then the IBM PC format became dominant, with Apple playing a subsidiary role for graphic applications. More recently, the emphasis has been on companies like Dell or Compaq delivering a product in which basic quality and performance are taken for granted, based on a highly efficient, cost-effective production system. In well-established, saturated markets, multiplying features and visual difference of any kind frequently becomes widespread. Conventional telephones, under the impact of increased competition from other systems such as mobile phones, have reached this advanced stage of 'feature creep'. It is supposedly possible to buy telephones with over eighty functions (most impossible to understand) in a superabundance of forms, including bananas, tomatoes, racing cars, sports shoes, and Mickey Mouse.

Sometimes basic product forms manage to resist this proliferation, however, becoming so well established in terms of functionality that it is extremely difficult to change them. An example is the electric iron, for which the basic sole-plate format is so appropriate for its task that minor variations of the existing form are the only design options.

A major constraint on design is presented by legislation on a variety of matters that might not specifically mention design, but sets tight parameters for performance. In the USA, this includes product liability laws, making manufacturers liable for injuries resulting from a product, and the Americans with Disabilities Act, which stipulates environmental and transportation requirements to provide access for people with disabilities. In Germany, a range of environmental legislation requires products or packaging to be made from materials which can be recycled, with manufacturers responsible for packaging disposal. Failure to incorporate such requirements into product specifications can be costly.

A further challenge for contemporary designers is the need to keep pace with evolving technologies. The replacement of mechanical sources of power and function by electricity during the twentieth century, and, towards its end, the widespread intro-duction of electronic technology, have fundamentally changed the nature of many objects. Theories about form being a reflection of function have been demolished by the dual effects of miniaturiza-tion in printed circuits and astonishing increases in processing power encapsulated in computer chips. Processes are no longer visible, tangible, or even understandable, and the containers for such technology have become either anonymous or subject to manipulations of form in attempts to create fashion or lifestyle trends.

An example of anonymity is the automated teller machines (ATMs) that have become such a common feature across much of the globe. They exist not as objects in their own right—indeed they are often incorporated into the wall of a building—but as a point of delivery for services that were once carried out by bank tellers. To do this they are a combination of hardware and software. The physical structure needs above all to protect the money contained inside. The key element for users, on the other hand, is the software, the interactive program enabling them to obtain cash. It is, therefore, not the ATM as an object in its own right that is important, but the interface with the computerized system. Their convenience is an enormous improvement on what previously existed, yet they are often cited as evidence of a widespread process of alienation. It is not the technology that is alienating, however, but inadequately thought-through design solutions to new problems.

There are predictions that in the future microchips will revolutionize an even-greater range of objects. It is feasible for a chair to have built-in sensors that respond to sitters, automatically adjusting to their dimensions and desired posture. Similarly, sports shoes that adjust to whether a wearer is standing, walking, or running, on tarmac, grass, sand, or rocks, are entirely con-

Objects

ceivable. The forms in which such conveniences are embodied will, however, raise more questions about the relationships between the designers of objects and their users. Are objects to be primarily the plaything of designers' egos, in a manipulative effort to create wants, or are they truly to answer needs in ways responsive to, even created by, users on the levels of both application and meaning?

5 Communications

'Communications' is here used as a shorthand term to cover the vast array of two-dimensional material that plays such an extensive role in modern life. Two-dimensional media forms have multiplied and expanded to a point where we are continuously bombarded with visual imagery. Their influence is pervasive, in both positive and negative senses: they can inform, direct, influence, arouse, confuse, and infuriate. Switch on the television, browse the Internet, walk down a street, read a magazine, or go into a store, and we are confronted with a huge array of signage, advertising, and social advocacy on a variety of scales. Some images will be permanent—a street sign, for example—but, in comparison to objects, a much greater proportion of communications is ephemeral, such as newspapers and advertising materials.

Another important difference between objects and communications should also be noted. Objects can exist as visual forms in their own right and can be used without any other reference. A vase or Lego building blocks for children, for example, do not necessarily require any accompanying text in order for them to be used or understood. They have visual or tactile qualities that communicate directly with great effect. Two-dimensional images, however, are different. As a means of personal expression they

15. Competition made visible: Hong Kong street signs

communicate with great immediacy. They can have a profound effect in stimulating a range of reactions, although this may not be exact or capable of calculation in advance. For practical purposes, however, in forms such as maps or diagrams, imagery in two dimensions generally requires being supplemented by text for it to establish any kind of precision. Attempts to use icons and pictograms effectively to convey meaning have had some success, especially in contexts where people from many countries and speaking many languages are expected to be users. The comprehensive signage system designed by Otl Aicher for the 1972 Munich Olympics is a classic example that has been widely imitated. Nevertheless, in general, an advertisement, or a brochure on how to use a product, or a chart or diagram without any text of any kind will probably be confusing and unclear. In general, therefore, a combination of print and imagery is fundamental in understanding communications.

As with the design of objects, numerous kinds of practice are involved in designing communications, covering an enormous range. Perhaps the most generally used is 'graphic designer', a term that emerged in the 1920s and that characterizes someone whose concern is with two-dimensional imagery. Like much terminology in design, however, it can be confusing, encompassing people who design letterheads for small businesses to those devising a visual identity programme for a major corporation.

16. Communication without boundaries: Munich Olympic pictogram system, by Otl Aicher 1972

Communications

Whatever the level of application, however, graphic designers employ a common vocabulary of signs, symbols, type, colour, and pattern to create messages and structure information.

Like designers of objects, graphic designers can also work as consultants or as in-house employees for organizations. Some consultants are able to work in a highly personal style, such as the American designer April Greiman, who, after initial training in the USA, studied in Switzerland, one of the fountainheads of modern typography. She is best known as a pioneer of the use of computers in design—'the leading lady of design with a mouse', as she has been termed. Greiman exploits the ability of computers to handle diverse materials, various kinds of images and text, and layers them in striking compositions of great depth and complexity. After many years of running her own business in Los Angeles, in 1999 she became a partner in the international consultancy Pentagram, but, as with all partners in this firm, continues to have total control over her own work.

Graphic consultancies can be giant organizations, perhaps the most notable being Landor Associates, founded in 1941 in San Francisco by the late Walter Landor, who was born in Germany and trained as a designer in England. He believed that understanding consumers' perception of companies and products was at least as important as understanding how products were manufactured, and on that basis, built his consultancy into one of the world's leading specialists in the design of branding strategies and corporate identity. Sixty years after its foundation, it has over 800 employees working in twenty-five offices spanning the Americas, Europe, and Asia. It has created innumerable brand images for companies that are known the world over. The range includes corporate identity programmes for numerous airlines, such as Alitalia, Delta, Cathay Pacific, Varig of Brazil, and Canadian Airlines. Other identity programmes from a very extensive list include France Telecom, FedEx, BP, Hewlett-Packard, Microsoft, Pepsi-Cola, Kentucky Fried Chicken, and Pizza Hut. Designs for a range of major events also feature in its portfolio, including the symbol for the 1996 Atlanta Olympics, and full identity programmes for the 1998 Olympic Winter Games in Nagano, Japan, and the 2002 Olympic Winter Games in Salt Lake City. The continuity of work and growth by the Landor organization over many years is impressive, especially compared to other large design consultancies that grew rapidly to considerable size, only to crash precipitously.

In-house graphic work for companies, compared to the design of objects, tends to be somewhat less specialized, since the range of materials is likely to be far broader, but a necessary focus will continue to be on what is relevant to the company in question. The spectrum of work and responsibilities is potentially huge. Businesses that routinely generate large quantities of brochures, instruction leaflets, packaging, and labels need a staff of graphic designers to maintain the flow of such materials. Some in large companies may work more on the level of creative interpretation rather than original concept, within the framework of a corporate identity programme devised by outside consultants. On the other hand, a corporate context does not necessarily restrict designers in this way—publishers of books, magazines, or record covers routinely require designers to create highly original, one-off material.

Government bodies of all kinds also produce huge amounts of forms and documentation. These often demand a major effort by citizens to decipher them and fill out the requisite information, with bureaucratic jargon, tiny print, and inadequate space to fill in answers. An example of how improvement in this field can be dramatic is the Passport Application form in the United Kingdom. Understanding the form's requirements was once a tortuous process, but effective graphic devices now enable it to be easily comprehended and rapidly completed, demonstrating there is no innate reason why designs for governments should be turgid. Indeed, it was the City of New York, in a period when the collapse of the city as a functioning entity was widely predicted, that commissioned Milton Glaser's use of a heart shape in his 'I love New York' device—one of the most imitated graphic forms ever created.

Public, non-commercial bodies of a wide variety also generate extensive design requirements. One of the most influential design programmes in broadcasting organizations is maintained by the Boston Public Television station, WGBH, with a staff of thirty designers. Establishing the station's visual identity requires a large spectrum of means, for both on-screen application and a variety of collateral materials. These include logos, programme introductions and titles, animated sequences, teaching materials, membership information, annual reports, books, and multimedia packages.

Many churches and charitable organizations also depend widely on published materials. The Church of Jesus Christ of the Latter Day Saints has a staff of sixty designers based in Utah, who design the very extensive range of print and electronic publications and packaging for goods that are a substantial feature of its missionary activities. A group such as Oxfam, dependent upon donations, also needs constantly to promote its cause to generate public support.

Large volumes of materials are also essential to museums, from floor plans of exhibits, to directional signage and the publication of major catalogues. A substantial area of expansion in recent years has been in online museum sites. Some of these simply duplicate information published in other forms, but others, such as the J. Paul Getty Museum in Los Angeles, have begun to exploit the educational potential of demonstrating the richness and variety of their collections to a much wider audience.

Neither can organizations focusing on political and social protest be ignored. The symbol of the Nuclear Disarmament movement is a classic example of the capacity of such groups to create powerful forms and is almost as widely copied as Milton Glaser's heart. A more recent example is the red ribbon-fold of Aids campaign groups.

On the level of techniques, a feature of communications is the extensive and expanding range involved. This can lead in the direction of both generalized integration and specialization. By the former is meant the way in which different visual elements can be combined in a particular communication. A piece of packaging, for example, might well combine material and structural criteria with illustrative and photographic imagery, a corporate logo, typeforms—combinations of typographic elements—used as expressive elements, brand names and symbols, instructions for use, and product information required by law. On the other hand, as the scale of projects increases, a specific element can frequently require specialist competencies, in a manner akin to the spectrum of abilities required to produce a motion picture. It might, for example, be necessary to combine typography, illustration, photography, information design, or interface design for computer programmes, each requiring specialists in the field.

Typefaces are one of the most basic building blocks in design, and typography—designing and composing letterforms—is a fundamental skill in creating printed imagery. The shape of a typeface can be designed for clarity, intended to communicate with maximum utility, or it can be powerfully expressive or evocative. With the introduction of computers, an astonishing range of typefaces has become available, enabling designers to explore examples from a wide historical and geographical range as well as more recently devised formats. Typefaces combined into words can be powerfully amplified or given a specific nuance by the choice of fount, or be shaped into expressive or decorative forms to serve as highly expressive elements in a design.

Publications come in a range of forms. Books are the archetypal vehicles for disseminating ideas and information. Although their demise has been widely predicted since the emergence of electronic media, they remain portable and convenient for flexible individual use and retain considerable advantages: there is no digital equivalent yet of the terms 'book collector' or 'book lover'. Newspapers and periodicals are more ephemeral and perhaps for this reason are somewhat more vulnerable to competition from electronic media. People often form communities of interest sharing a common sympathy for specific books, such as the Harry Potter series, or for particular editorial policies or standpoints. The visual identity of publications such as *The Times*, *Vogue*, *Rolling*

Stone, or *Wired* is an important element in creating such affinities. On a more intense level, many subcultures have also formed around publications, examples being the work by David Carson, a California designer for *Beach Culture* and *Ray Gun* magazines in the early 1990s. Computer manipulation enabled him to create kinetic images that struck a deep chord in the youth culture market targeted by these magazines.

Illustration, which lies at the artistic end of the communications spectrum, is a core skill distinguishing many practitioners. The distinctive style of Raymond Briggs or Quentin Blake, linked to a great talent for storytelling, has enabled them to carve out careers as author/illustrators. A younger generation of talent is exemplified by Sue Coe and Henrik Drescher. Coe, born in England and now based in New York, has produced print series using traditional techniques such as etching that raise social commentary to a level of burning intensity. Drescher, born in Denmark, educated in America, and now living in New Zealand, has work published in the *New York Times* and *Time* magazine, but his mordant, quirky style is at its best in the children's books he writes. His use of the computer is an outstanding example of the potential of digital technology as a creative tool.

Illustration, however, can also be a very specialized form of work, often requiring considerable technical expertise, as in technical or medical illustration. Some consultancies focus these skills on a particular outlet, such as educational and scientific publishing, or museum and exhibition display. Photography similarly covers a spectrum from work of the most personal nature to specialized forms for specific purposes, such as documentary photography, or photographing objects for sales or exhibition catalogues and other publications.

One of the most dramatic features of communications is the manner in which many aspects of design are being radically transformed by the growth in multimedia publishing, combining text, images, video, and animation in ways that open up immense new possibilities. The range and flexibility of this new medium are most easily experienced on the Internet. Its potential for direct experience and easy access is still in the early stages of development and there are huge questions of developing forms of typography and imagery specific to electronic publishing, as against simply replicating forms from other media. Above all, as business applications grow, some of the greatest questions requiring greater attention relate to the problems of navigating through complex sites and the vast amounts of information available. The more successful online sites, such as Amazon.com and Travelocity, show both the potential and the limitations of the new medium. They have pioneered the way in opening up possibilities for customers' choices through the design of sites that are very user-friendly. However, at the same time, it needs to be emphasized

Communications

17. Navigating the web made easy: Amazon.com page

that, although information processes are radically different, the product purchased through the process remains unaltered: the design of books and airline seats remains unaffected by such transformations.

The highest levels in sustainable growth arising from the revolution in electronic media have been in business-to-business applications, which have dramatically expanded. The capacity simultaneously to simplify procedures and give access to customers through their computers is opening up huge potential for improving efficiency. Suppliers can store vast quantities of information about products and services, enabling customers to order on a just-in-time basis, instead of tying up capital and facilities in large stocks. The main criterion in the efficiency of such systems, however, is information solutions that are clear, accurate, and comprehensible. If customers cannot speedily navigate through to what they need, a provider will be at a major disadvantage. An important emphasis in such online sites is that virtuoso visual effects are useless if the ability of users to take action is not taken into account.

The complexities of multimedia applications also exemplify a wider characteristic of communications, with innumerable further subdivisions and combinations of skills constantly being generated, such as photography combining with illustration in animated films, or with typography for film titles. The design practice of Saul Bass was built on the twin poles of film publicity and corporate logos. In the former, he was responsible for such classics as Otto Preminger's *The Man with the Golden Arm*, or Alfred Hitchcock's *Psycho*, in which he displayed an ability to combine various elements—visual imagery, type, and pictographs—with music into compelling sequences. These were the basis not just of titles, but of other publicity materials such as posters and advertising. In addition, he also devised corporate logos for firms such as United Airlines and AT&T. A graphic designer working on large projects might indeed need to know something of each speciality in order to function adequately as a manager of a range of such competencies. Once again, the stereotype of designers as artistic lone rangers can extend in reality into the combined talents of a group or team.

This same stereotype is also placed in question by the field of information design—a highly specialized branch of communications in which data on any subject are presented in ways enabling their use as a basis for decision making. Such information can be presented in many forms and media over a huge range. An everyday example is provided by weather forecasts. Data from numerous sources are rapidly translated into visual forms, enabling decisions to be taken about what clothing to take on a trip or what equipment is necessary for a job. This information is available from maps and text in daily newspapers, from television maps and animated sequences, or from online sites. The Weather Channel in the USA, broadcasting televised forecasts around the clock, and, in the United Kingdom, the BBC's regular forecasts on radio and television, are supplemented by web sites where detailed forecasts for the whole country, or specific regions or cities, can be obtained for a week hence. On another level, an American web site, World Pages. Com, provides directory information of telephone subscribers throughout North America, supplemented by detailed maps of locations and information on accommodation and facilities in the vicinity of each address. An innovative approach to providing market information is exemplified by Morningstar, a Chicago-based company, specializing in financial data services to facilitate decision-making by investors on sales or purchases of mutual funds. The core task is compressing very large amounts of information into a comprehensible format that, using numerous graphic devices, enables users to make informed and rapid investment decisions. Originally in printed form, information is now available online. The emphasis at Morningstar is on content as the primary need, not aesthetic expression, although the company's total image, by its consistency, does in fact generate a very distinctive aesthetic image.

In contrast, advertising is not primarily concerned with enabling users, but is one of the most specialized areas of persuasive communications, as well as one of the most pervasive, utilizing a blend of text and imagery to promote products and services. As such, of course, there is a considerable area of overlap between communications and objects, since the latter can be designed for maximum visual impact, with translation into advertising imagery in mind. In this sense, when consistently executed across all elements of a marketing campaign, the advertising image can condition perception of objects before they are actually seen. Most people, for example, will see an advertisement for a new automobile before they see an actual example on the street.

A particular feature of most advertising is that, while attempting to mould opinion, it cannot afford to offend anyone in a particular market, which accounts for much of the bland uniformity of the people and lifestyles it depicts. This had led some critics to depict a stereotypical image of advertisers as the puppet masters of modern society, manipulating everyone to do what is not in their best interest. Most advertisers, however, see themselves as mediating between trends in society and their clients' interests, both reflecting what is happening in society and feeding back a stylized version of it in advertising campaigns and imagery.

The influence of advertising, however, cannot be underestimated, particularly where it has been refined as an instrument of inducing mass consumption. In the USA, where such techniques were first evolved and penetrated deepest, its methods and imagery have become part of the cultural fabric. Even political campaigns for the presidency or other major offices are run as advertising campaigns, constantly adapting a candidate's image to changing circumstances. Such is the embedded influence of these techniques that the boundaries between image and reality frequently become blurred.

Another vague boundary is that between advertising and propaganda, the latter being a particular form of communication that attempts to shape opinions in support of political or ideological ends. Advertising cannot afford to stray too far from what its target audiences understand as reality, although it can warp perception by selectivity, through what it consistently chooses to emphasize or omit. Unlike advertising, however, propaganda frequently depends upon establishing an image by offending a particular group—depicting them in some stereotypical form as 'the enemy'. Although truth has sometimes been a stranger to advertising, lies and gross distortion are endemic to propaganda.

Clearly, the role of communications in modern society is huge, of deep significance on multiple levels, and in a considerable state of flux and change, with different cultures overlapping, combining, and borrowing from each other. On one level this can be seen as part of the process of globalization, with ideas flowing more freely across national or ethnic cultural boundaries. Even within cultures, however, there is a parallel process of exchange. Professional designers use forms, for example, graffiti, borrowed from urban street culture movements such as hip-hop or punk, while the public have access to computers or facilities in print shops that encapsulate professional skills in forms available to and affordable for everyone. A negative result has been a diminution of small graphic design businesses catering for local needs, but there are positive aspects from the overlap, as designers reach beyond a closely defined professional definition of their role and the public becomes more involved in communicative activities. If one of the purposes of communication design is to create a sense of identity in visual terms, the capacity of new technology to enhance mutual understanding between those who create images and those who receive them offers considerable potential for the future.

6 Environments

When considering environments, additional layers of complexity come into play. In common with objects and communications, form, colour, pattern, and texture are basic compositional elements, but the articulation of space and light is a specific characteristic of the design of environments. Moreover, in this context, objects and communications become closely interlocked with spatial elements, giving added emphasis to their functionality and significance.

A further important distinction is that environments are frameworks for activities, significantly affecting patterns of use, behaviour, and expectations in home life, work, leisure, and a range of commercial ventures.

In basic analytical terms there is an obvious distinction between internal and external environments. The latter may be considered the predominant domain of other disciplines such as architecture, urban and regional planning, and landscape architecture. In addition, the structures framing interiors are, of course, frequently determined by architects, engineers, and builders. There is, however, a range of environments primarily concerned with specific uses that come within the compass of design and largely distinguish its role from other forms of practice. The spectrum of functions and ideas about their design, however, is huge, and, in a brief compass, little more than scratching the surface of this huge diversity is feasible.

As with other areas of professional specialization, interior design spans a wide spectrum of approaches and professional functions. At one pole are those concerned with the decorative layout of specific spaces and their contents using available furnishings and materials in terms of their overall aesthetic effect, for such settings as private homes for wealthy people, restaurants, or hotels. These tend to be the outcome of stylistic trends and personal taste on the part of designers and clients, and can be considered more in terms of compositions of existing elements rather than design from first principles. At another pole, however, can be found the original creation of spatial concepts and layouts and the specification of equipment for specific purposes, such as offices, hospitals, or schools that have to meet a spectrum of often demanding criteria regarding health, safety, and efficiency.

In addition to this professional dimension, however, there is a feature of the creation of environments that is largely absent in other aspects of design. It is the one area of practice that on some level can involve very large numbers of people in design decisions: namely, in their home. The majority of any population are not involved in the design of the products or communications that surround them, but the domestic environment is still the prime sphere in which it is possible for people to take design decisions on their own terms. The research of Csikszentmihalyi and Rochberg-Halton, mentioned at the end of Chapter 3, concluded that people invest objects with personal meaning. With environments, this potential for creating personal meaning can not only be invested in existing forms, but can be actively involved in changing existing environments into preferred states. A significant manifestation of this trend is the availability of an expanding range of do-it-yourself products, publications, and television series, providing the means and information for anyone who wishes to transform a personal environment into a mirror of his or her needs and aspirations. The results may sometimes be bewildering. Excesses, such as plastic, imitation wooden beams stuck on to suburban living-room ceilings, or gold-coloured rococo decoration sold by the yard to be applied to the surfaces of plastic-covered synthetic-board furniture for bedrooms, can be comical, even grotesque. There is an important principle in this trend, however, which is often overlooked. The design of books, tools, and materials for such activities encourages people to take control over important decisions regarding their personal environments and, at some level, to be creatively involved in the realization of their ideas. The concepts and techniques involved are not particularly difficult and are within the competence of most people. Although self-appointed arbiters of taste might find the results of these activities easy targets for derision, they provide a significant example of how design can have an enabling function, facilitating participation by a broad population, in contrast to the more remote generation of professional solutions.

Interestingly, the situation is somewhat different in the USA, where the American Society of Interior Designers had over 30,000 members in 2001, with a substantial proportion specializing in residential design, and with close links to manufacturers of design-related products and services, such as textiles, wallpapers, furnishings, and fittings. In addition, most large furniture and department stores in the USA offer the services of professional designers in their employ to customers requiring assistance in purchasing. One Chicago furnishing retailer alone advertises the services of 200 designers available to customers. The proportion who pay to have their home planned is therefore much higher than in Europe, for example, where, in comparison, the Association of Dutch Designers has 180 members in the category 'environmental designers'. On a population basis, the Netherlands, a prosperous country and an example of design consciousness, has one interior designer per 89,000 people in comparison to one to 8,700 in the USA. One estimate is that a third of American homeowners turn to professional advice in some form in decorating their home. The possible reasons for this are many, among them, the influence of a mass culture that deskills the population by emphasizing comfort rather than activity, which furthers penetration of the culture by commercialized services, and, more recently, longer working hours by both married partners to maintain income levels, leaving little free time for home-making activities.

Within any society the spectrum of individual solutions in home environments makes it difficult to generalize about patterns. What is more clearly evident are sharp differences between various cultural and geographical circumstances. This can include such factors as whether homes are owned or rented, whether provision is predominantly in the form of houses or apartments, and the amount of space available or considered appropriate for domestic environments.

Again, the USA is an exception, the size of homes having doubled since the Second World War. To a considerable extent, this mirrors the extended range of possessions and facilities considered essential and needing to be accommodated. In terms of global comparisons, so much space is available that little thought needs to be devoted to the precise details of the functional hardware. American appliances such as washing machines, refrigerators, cookers, and bathroom fittings, for example, are large and generally old-fashioned in form and technology, yet inexpensive compared with those designed for European or Asian markets. In the average American home they can be absorbed into the spatial pattern without substantial thought about how they must be used in relation to competing needs. Multiple bathrooms are not unusual, separate laundry rooms are standard, and, if equipment lacks sophistication, there is the compensating factor of widespread access and affordability.

In comparison, the average Japanese home is tiny compared to those in America and requires detailed thought to accommodate a growing range of desired functions within very limited confines. Consequently, the design of both individual elements on the market and their internal arrangement in the domestic environment is subject to very different pressures. Bathtubs in Japanese homes are often small, for example, intended for a seated or crouched posture, rather than lying recumbent—communal bathhouses giving more space are not uncommon. Toilet and bidet functions are often incorporated into a single pedestal and controlled electronically. Similarly, instead of separate, large washers and dryers, the two functions are combined and miniaturized. Refrigerators are also small but technologically advanced, while cookers are broken down into small modular units to be fitted more easily into kitchen wall storage systems. The latter point also illustrates that spatial limitations force the axial emphasis in Japanese homes to a vertical rather than a horizontal plane—they have to stack instead of spread. In addition, it is still usually necessary for many

18. Expansion or concentration of the footprint?: American and
Japanese bathrooms

functions in Japanese homes to be organised on the basis of convertibility rather than in terms of dedicated space and equipment—for example, with living spaces switching to sleeping spaces and back again.

Within the framework of such general cultural differences, however, the home is still in most countries the one location where anyone can organize an environment to match his or her personal lifestyle and tastes, in a manner not available elsewhere. Although there are, of course, innumerable pressures to follow the fashions manifested in 'style' magazines, manufacturers' advertising and retailers' catalogues, the ability to personalize a space and inject it with meaning remains one of the major outlets for individual design decisions.

In contrast, an overwhelming majority of decisions on how workspaces are organized are made by managers and designers, and the people who work in them have to live with the consequences, with few possibilities for modification. As the twentieth century progressed, concepts of appropriate layouts for manufacturing plants and offices changed in response to changing perceptions of work and its management. With the rise of large corporations in the early part of the century, the ideas of Frederick W. Taylor and his successors in the Scientific Management movement were dominant. The ideas of Taylor and his followers were an effort to assert management control over work processes by imposing standardized procedures. He advocated finding 'the one best way' for any task and the main tools in organizing workers to fit this pattern were time-and-motion studies. Factory workers became subordinated to manufacturing sequences planned in every detail to maximize efficiency on the basis of mass production. Office workers sat at desks arrayed in uniform ranks, similarly organized and controlled in a strict hierarchy. In some bureaucratic systems, the position and size of desk and chair perceptibly changed with each increase in rank. In both factories and offices work processes were focused on the completion of highly organized functions for known problems and processes.

From the 1960s onwards, some companies began to experiment with looser systems of management, in which, within an overall emphasis on leadership rather than control, workers were encouraged to interact in teams and contribute more actively to processes. In some major Japanese companies, for example, worker contributions to manufacturing processes resulted in huge savings and improvements. The organization of factory spaces reflected this emphasis, with features such as areas of comfortable seating on the factory floor where workers could meet regularly and discuss their work. Such innovations made a substantial contribution to the competitive success of many Japanese companies. A parallel development in offices was in terms of a concept known as 'office-landscaping', in which layouts became more flexible, with widespread use of partitions to provide a blend of privacy and accessibility in the similar context of ideas about greater worker participation.

As with developments in all areas of design, this sequence in the evolution of ideas has been adopted erratically and all these stages of work organization can still be found, particularly when viewed on a global basis. Even with new technologies, old Taylorist concepts in their worst form can survive. Some companies providing services such as typing documentary information into computers are organized in spaces without windows, to avoid unnecessary distractions, with desks in rigid ranks. Video cameras behind the workers monitor every word and move and computer key-strikes are counted to ensure workers maintain a specified work rate. As in so many instances, the influence of technology does not lead in any specific direction, but is shaped and manifested on the basis of the values informing its application.

The potential for flexibility in many modern technological developments, however, also has many positive aspects that have been widely explored. In contrast to developments in manufacturing plants, Japanese offices can still be crowded, with ranks of steel desks reflecting hierarchical attitudes and the general shortage of space in the country. From the late 1980s onwards, however, construction of a spate of 'smart' buildings was completed, which sought to explore the potential of new electronic technology. The Tokyo City Hall, completed in 1991 to the designs of Kenzo Tange, for example, had twelve supercomputers, with others added later, incorporating sensors that could calculate human activity and automatically adjust lighting and heating levels. They also controlled security, telephone circuits, fire doors, and elevators. The offices typically had partitioned spaces and warm but muted colours. Smart cards gave the 13,000 employees access to offices and could be used for purchases in restaurants and shops in the complex. This was all a great improvement in terms of operating efficiency on previous environments, but did not represent a major advance in concepts of office work.

Some Japanese companies, however, were experimenting with new possibilities opened up by the concept of smart buildings. Research into working patterns showed office workers in Japan typically use their desks for only 40 per cent of the working day. Searching for greater efficiency, some companies introduced more flexible systems of working. Employees might sit at different desks according to the type of work being done to facilitate interchanges with colleagues. Using smart cards, their personal telephone could be routed to any desk.

All this was but a short step to transferring work out of the office. Companies like Shiseido Cosmetics devolved much of its sales activities in the early 1990s, enabling employees to work from home or regional offices, instead of spending up to four hours a day in long and exhausting commuter journeys at peak hours. Equipped with laptops capable of connection via mobile telephones to the company's main computer, salesmen could instantly access vital information for customers on such matters as availability, prices, and delivery.

While such developments brought many benefits, new problems also rapidly emerged. Devolving work undoubtedly created space savings and thus a reduction of high rents in city centres, but there was still a necessity for employees to work in central offices, even if on an occasional basis. This was particularly true of consulting firms, where many employees spent large amounts of time with clients and might only be in their home office for one day a week, or even one day a month. Many larger companies in the USA, such as Deloitte & Touche, Ernst & Young, and Andersen Consulting, began experimenting with a practical solution known as hotelling.

Basically, this is a space-sharing plan, by means of which workers can contact their home office electronically, reserve a space for a particular time span, and even order food and drink. At the office, personal telephone numbers and computer lines are routed to a reserved desk. A functionary known as a concierge is responsible for installing a wheeled cart containing personal files at the desk and ensuring that all necessary equipment, stationery, and materials are available. Even items such as family photographs are sometimes set up prior to arrival. On the worker's departure, files are packed in the cart for return to storage, supplies are replenished, the space is cleaned, and it is ready for the next user. The analogies with how a hotel functions are obvious.

Many workers initially had problems with this transient pattern of working, which required radical changes in behaviour and attitudes. It rapidly became clear that such solutions would overcome feelings of deprivation by workers only if levels of investment in technology, particularly software, and support activities were substantial.

The advertising company TBWA/Chiat/Day was an example of the dangers of wholesale change that was not completely thought through. In the early 1990s, it embarked on one of the most extensive experiments in hotelling, which resulted in highly publicized problems. In its Los Angeles and New York offices, the company pioneered large-scale experiments in what was know as 'the virtual office'. After a short time, however, employees rebelled against the pattern of constant circulation, which was increasingly regarded as an unnecessary disruption, and began to claim spaces of their own. In coping with the problems of continuous change in their business environment, it seemed that people needed a haven of stability and security.

Awareness of the imperatives of change in the business world is, of course, behind the search for new environmental patterns. Many managers, particularly in successful companies, are aware that, in an age of profound change, perhaps the greatest risk is complacency. In particular, with the explosion of information technology, it is clear that the amount of data and information available, which is increasingly exponentially, is of value only if interpreted and applied creatively. Such trends in management thinking are heavily reinforced by changes in manufacturing technology away from mass production towards flexible manufacture for niche markets combined with greater emphasis on attention to services. The result is a new emphasis on innovation as a primary necessity for competitive survival, which hinges, above all, on creativity. This in turn requires employees to be active participants in work processes, bringing their knowledge and experience to bear on problems in rapidly changing circumstances that have few precedents. The result is a move to replace organizational hierarchies and environments that inhibit interaction and communication, with new environments that encourage interchange in a flatter organizational structure, with a careful blend of private and common spaces. Ideas are generated and creativity stimulated, it is believed, through interaction and personal contacts, often on a casual, informal level.

If corporate strategy emphasizes such a culture of new ideas and products, the challenge now in designing work environments and their equipment and furnishings is how to provide a spatial organization that stimulates interaction and dynamic creativity. The outcome of this complex fusion of ideas emphasizing innovation is to create office environments that are small communities, with a very high degree of potential interaction between disparate elements of an organization.

Learning from its early experiences, in 1999 TBWA/Chiat/Day opened new offices in Los Angeles in a former warehouse with 120,000 square feet of space, designed by Clive Wilkinson. This reflected an interesting change of approach, from the concept of transience implicit in hotelling, to a concept of a community capable of flexibly encompassing different work patterns. The problems of the earlier virtual-office experiment were overcome by giving each employee a personal workstation, but employees also spend a substantial amount of time working in teams in spaces dedicated to major client accounts. The community concept is evident in elements such as neighbourhoods of workstations, a Main Street running through the centre of the space, and Central Park, an area dotted with ficus trees, as a place to relax. The idea is to provide a combination of private, team, and communal facilities on a highly adaptable basis, reflecting the changing nature of accounts held by the company, with the intention of encouraging informal contact and interchange.

A direct contrast to the idea of interior space as adaptive neigh-

19. Officescape as community: TBWA/Chiat/Day offices in
Los Angeles by Clive Wilkinson

bourhood is another characteristic development of modern life: the exponential growth in standardized environments. In archetypal form, these originated in the USA but have since extended to many other countries. Early examples could be found in upscale markets, such as the growth of the Hilton hotel chain to global prominence, based upon a concept that all their premises should be constructed to a standardized format, intended to enable travelling executives to feel immediately a sense of continuity and familiarity, whatever the location.

The greatest impact of this principle, however, has been through its subsequent spread downmarket on a huge scale. Among the most characteristic sights of innumerable small town and suburban areas of the USA are the 'strip malls' that fill roadsides for miles at a time. These are simply shops, restaurants, and services decanted from earlier concentrations and now spread in seemingly disorganized fashion along main roads, but with easy access for motor vehicles. Within the confusion, however, a high degree of recognition of particular companies exists, especially fast-food franchises. The buildings for, say, McDonald's, Pizza Hut, or Burger King follow a similar pattern across the country, indeed around the globe, which is instantly recognizable. Whatever the specific spatial dimensions of an individual site, the decoration, furnishings, and fittings also provide an immediately recognizable pattern for customers. Similarly, their menus offer

20. The landscape of assertion: US strip malls

highly standardized fare at accessible cost. The role of design, therefore, becomes that of providing a complete template across all activities and design elements, adaptable in detail to particular sites around the world, but always within the framework of over-all standards.

In the United Kingdom or Europe, where space is more limited and planning controls have largely restricted such sprawl, main shopping streets show a similar repetitive pattern, as the same combination of chain stores and food franchises takes over in city after city. The interiors of such diverse companies as Boots, MacFisheries, Mövenpick, or Wienerwald restaurants follow standard guidelines, and, again, embody a familiar pattern, and much the same products, whatever the location.

Another commercial trend influencing many aspects of design during the 1990s, and particularly influential in some categories of environments, was an emphasis on 'experience' or 'fun'—there were even job descriptions in design firms for 'experience architects'. This was part of a wider trend for more and more areas of life to be subordinated to the imperatives of mass entertainment, whether in television or news publishing, in sports such as football or wrestling, in shopping, or in eating out.

British pubs have long been subjected to development as 'theme pubs', as breweries have bought out independent owners and have sought to maximize trade by appealing to particular trends. Some, for example, try to recreate the feel of Victorian forerunners by such means as embossed wallpaper and cast-iron tables. The Irish brewing company Guinness provides a kit of reproduction items such as nineteenth-century packaging and posters to furnish the rash of 'authentic' Irish pubs that have emerged in major cities around the globe. Yet modern technology also offers the potential of micro-brewing, of beer brewed on the premises, with a highly individual character, in contrast to the standardized products of major brewers.

Similar dichotomies are observable in restaurants. It is still possible in many cities around the globe to find good food served in simple surroundings with unassertive service, as a setting for gastronomic pleasure and conversation. In the USA, however, a growing trend is for restaurants to be designed in terms of a particular theme, say, Italian or Vietnamese, with the service staff regarded as performers following a routine. Eating or drinking in such establishments is not allowed to be an improvisational social experience; instead diners are subordinated to routines under the rubric of entertainment. A synthetic nostalgia can often be a strong element in this emphasis, as in the extreme example of so-called medieval banquets, whose claims to historical veracity are as dubious as the 'authentic fayre' they serve, such as broiler chicken on wooden platters.

Neither is the function of shopping immune from such trends.

21. Shopping as theatre: Niketown, Chicago

A similar spectrum of provision exists, running from what are basically warehouses filled with goods sold on the basis of cost, such as the American retail chain Toys 'R Us, to highly designed environments invoking the mantra of entertainment, such as the Niketown concept, basically a theatre of consumer testing. The first of such premises was opened on Michigan Avenue, the major shopping street of Chicago, by the sports goods manufacturer Nike. It was intended, not as a place to sell products necessarily, since the company's products are still overwhelmingly sold through general trade outlets, but more as a promotional show-piece and test-bed, enabling potential customers to explore the company's range of sports shoes, clothing, and accessories and enjoy themselves while doing so, while their reactions to new introductions were gauged.

The emphasis on providing an 'experience' opens up the design of environments to a bewildering array of forms and themes that are sometimes whimsical and can arbitrarily change with great rapidity. In this process it is easy to overlook the more prosaic but equally vital needs of people in often unfamiliar and sometimes bewildering surroundings. As with all aspects of design, environments are becoming more complex—consider a modern airport such as London Heathrow or Tokyo Narita, which requires more systemic approaches to solutions.

7 Identities

Objects and environments can be used by people to construct a sense of who they are, to express their sense of identity. The construction of identity, however, goes much further than an expression of who someone is; it can be a deliberate attempt by individuals and organizations, even nations, to create a particular image and meaning intended to shape, even pre-empt, what others perceive and understand.

On a personal level, in the world of artifice we inhabit, one of the primary transformations available is of ourselves. For many people, personal identity is now as much a matter of choice as it is an expression of inherited or nurtured qualities, even to the extent of physical transformation—the number of people and amounts of money spent in the USA on cosmetic surgery of one kind or another are reaching staggering proportions. On a less drastic but no less powerful level, advertising continuously exhorts us to be the person we secretly want to be, with images of what we could or should be, a transformation ostensibly achieved simply by buying the proffered product.

The commercialization of personal imagery as a trigger for consumption has resulted in some curious effects as it has spread across the globe. It is possible, for example, for teenagers in Japan simultaneously to manifest characteristics imbued by an education in the national tradition, and to identify with other teenagers around the world in such matters as clothing, make-up, food, and music. In other words, it is possible to be at the same time a member of one culture and a member of one or more sub-cultures that might have little in common with the dominant form.

While such influences penetrate ever more widely around the world, another transformation is resulting from very large numbers of people migrating to more prosperous countries in search of a better way of life. Modern technology, such as satellite communications, small-scale printing technology, and the Internet, can enable people to be simultaneously functioning citizens of a host society and members, perhaps, of some professional subculture, such as medicine or architecture, while still maintaining intact in homes and localities what they consider to the essential culture of their origins.

Again, how this works for individual people is largely a matter of choice. While the reach and flexibility of modern communications makes it possible for migrants to stay easily in contact with a distant home culture and so sustain and reinforce their original sense of identity, they simultaneously slow any need to assimilate and come to terms with the very different conditions of the host culture. It can create a sense of richness and diversity in the host country, but obvious differences, visual differences in particular, can also become an easy target for resentment.

Another facet of the construction of identity stems from the large number of nations created by decolonization since the Second World War or freed by the collapse of the Soviet Empire in the late 1980s, resulting in a search for symbols to express the sense of new-found independence. Mythical and often aggressive creatures from heraldic sources—eagles, lions, and griffins—are frequently juxtaposed on coins and banknotes with images of bounty, such as smiling maidens in folk costume, bearing sheaves of grain. Here too, identity is seemingly a matter of choice from a range of possibilities.

Even in older established nations imagery can erupt as a matter of concern. Redesigns of the female figure of Marianne, the symbol of France, inevitably stimulate a barrage of passionate argument. Among the most bizarre features of the United Kingdom as the twentieth century faded were proposals to 'rebrand' the national image, of how the country was viewed by foreigners, in terms of a more up-to-date concept of 'Cool Brittania'. The resulting altercation—the term 'debate' would exaggerate the level of exchange—between dyed-in-the-wool conservatives defending the status quo, and those advocating a marketing-based model that everything should be changed to be 'cool', was inevitably inconclusive. Perhaps the fatal mistake of

22. Inventing tradition: the national identity of Slovenia

the advocates of rebranding was a failure to understand that commercial ideas cannot just be dropped into other contexts and expected to succeed. Arrogant assumptions that the world of business is the 'real world', as it is frequently termed, and its concepts thus a model for the whole of life, rest on gross oversimplifications. In practical terms, it is far harder for any government to control all the aspects of a society, even under a dictatorship, than it is for a commercial corporation to establish control over its product and services and so establish a brand.

Disputes about national identity may be bizarre, but there can be little doubt of its power to motivate, even in industrial countries when there seem few causes left to engage people. Another example from the United Kingdom in the 1980s was a profound reaction to the introduction of new telephone kiosks, following the state-owned telephone services being privatized as British Telecom. BT set out to define its independent status for the populace by replacing the long-established, bright-red telephone kiosks across the country. A new version, basically a glass box, was bought off-the-shelf at low cost from an American manufacturer. The new kiosks were claimed to be more efficient, which in many respects they indeed were. The models they replaced, however, had been used since 1936, becoming a distinctive icon of British identity, widely used on travel posters and tourist publicity, and the decision generated an astonishing outburst of public outrage.

British Telecom has since commissioned several redesigns of their kiosks, but without ever entirely mollifying resentment at the removal of a very familiar and unique element of the cultural landscape. Such reactions to change may be based on nostalgia, with, in this case, more than a leavening of irrationality, but the problems are real.

The influence of cultural differences on design practice is one of the most profound problems thrown up by the growth of globalization. Problems arising from cultural differences can be a minefield for companies with ambitions to extend markets. The American appliance company Whirlpool had to learn how to evolve a global/local approach to product development on the basis of product concepts adaptable to different countries. With a lightweight 'world washer' introduced in 1992, it was necessary to accommodate washing 18-foot-long saris without tangling in India, and to add a soak cycle for Brazil to cater for the local belief that only pre-soaking can yield a really clean wash.

In contrast, Gillette has been highly successful on the basis of a belief that cultural differences have little effect on shaving. Instead of spending millions to alter its products to suit the tastes of different countries, Gillette treats all marketplaces the same and tries to sell the same razor to everyone, a strategy that has been widely successful. The factor of culture is obviously linked to the

23. Defending tradition: old and new BT telephone kiosks

specific patterns of how particular products are used. General, global patterns may be applicable to some products, particularly the simpler functions, but others may require detailed adaptation. Demand for specifically different products may even be a factor in some markets.

A dilemma in designing across cultural boundaries, therefore, is the extent to which cultural identity is fixed or is capable of change. The problems of miscalculation can be severe, as is attested by widespread reactions in the name of protecting cultural identity against the patterns of cosmopolitanism, and particularly the freer flow of trade and communications characteristic of globalization.

Two points are worth emphasis in this context. First, there are enormous opportunities to affirm the particularities of any specific context and to design for them in ways not obvious to global organizations. In Korea, refrigerators are designed to accommodate fermenting kimchee, a traditional, spicy, pickled cabbage indispensable to Korean cuisine. In Turkey, the dolmus, a small minibus, is used for very flexible public transportation, even door-to-door. When expensive imported vehicles were found ill-suited to local needs, an industry emerged that developed models suitable for local conditions, to the extent of customizing a dolmus to the needs of any particular operator.

Secondly, while penetration of markets around the world

provokes a need to affirm local identity in terms of specific needs, there is a countervailing need for global businesses to adapt to the enhanced scale and diversity of markets involved. If new possibilities are feasible or desirable, a major question for designers is how to enable people from different cultures to navigate the problems of change. In other words, business should respond to different cultural needs in ways that improve lives: by designing products and services that are accessible, appropriate, understandable, and pleasurable, in ways they can absorb into their pattern of life. Cultural identity is not fixed, like a fly in amber, but is constantly evolving and mutating, and design is a primary element in stimulating the awareness of possibilities.

Above all, the agency that in design terms dominates discussion of identity is the modern business corporation, which spends huge sums of money on projecting a sense of what it is and what it represents. Corporate identity has its origins in military and religious organizations. The Roman legions, for example, had a very strong visual identity, with uniforms and eagle-standards bringing coherence to a body of men, as an expression of their common discipline and dependence. The first modern example was the Spanish army of the seventeenth century, which similarly introduced standardized dress and weaponry to enhance its feared reputation. On another level, the Catholic Church has probably the longest continuous organizational identity, based on the Imperial Roman hierarchy and clearly apparent through visual means, such as regalia and insignia.

Prior to industrialization, most business units were very small; even those with ten to fifteen people were considered to be of substantial size. Only a few businesses, such as shipyards, employed larger numbers. By the nineteenth century, with the evolution of large business enterprises, often spread over wide geographical areas, a need evolved for some common identification amongst employees that could also be projected to the public. The Midland Railway, a major company in Britain, for example, had 90,000 employees by the late nineteenth century and, through liveries for its rolling stock, typographic and architectural styles, and uniforms for employees, brought an overall coherence to its far-flung operations.

The emergence of mass manufacturing in the early twentieth century confirmed the dominance of big corporations. In 1907, the architect and designer Peter Behrens was appointed Artistic Director of the German electrical giant Allgemeine Elekrizitäts Gesellschaft (AEG), with total control over all visual manifestations of corporate activities. In this role, he was responsible for the design of buildings, industrial and consumer products, advertising and publicity, and exhibitions. A typeface he designed was used for the corporate logo of the company initials, brought unity to all printed matter, and is still the basic element of the company's visual identity.

More recently, Olivetti and IBM evolved as model examples in the period after the Second World War, although in very different ways. Olivetti, manufacturing a range of electrical and later electronic equipment in Italy, developed an approach in which consistency was not an essential ingredient. Instead, a number of distinguished designers were recruited, including Mario Zanussi, Mario Bellini, Ettore Sott sass Jr., and Michele de Lucchi. The company gave them substantial freedom and extensive support in their work, relying upon each particular item being an outstanding design in its own right, in the belief that the overall image of the company would thus be of continual creativity rather than conformity. Even the corporate logo changed with remarkable frequency. A remarkable feature of Olivetti policy was that the company did not employ designers on a full-time basis, but insisted they spend half their time working outside the company in order to stimulate creative vitality.

At IBM, designers of great ability were similarly used—Paul Rand, Charles and Ray Eames, Mies van der Rohe and Eliot Noyes, to name but a few. In contrast to Olivetti, however, the pattern was more tightly structured, with strict guidelines and standard specifications within which products and publications were designed. For a time, even employees were expected to conform to a dress code considered a desirable aspect of the overall corporate image.

By the early 1990s, Olivetti had serious problems in adapting to new technologies and products and the role of design in the company diminished. Ultimately, not even a stream of brilliantly designed products and communications could save the company from the consequences of inadequate responses to change—underlining the fact that design alone, no matter how outstanding, cannot guarantee business success. IBM was similarly hit by the emergence of highly competitive personal computer manufacturing companies, but maintained high standards in its design guidelines. In the 1990s, it began to regain ground and once again generated notable products, such as the Think Pad portable computer designed by Richard Sapper in 1993, and the Aptiva desk-top models. These were statements of intent that the company was still a major player, with design as an integral element of how it projected itself.

Although many identity programmes have evolved over a long period and have been incrementally updated while retaining an original flavour, such as the scripted Ford logo, it is sometimes surprising how rapidly other images can become established. One of the companies creating problems for IBM in the early 1980s was Apple, which under founder Steve Jobs evolved a striking corporate identity, with a rainbow-coloured apple logo and a commitment to design in all aspects of business. The Macintosh personal computer set the standard for ease-of-use in interface design, and even its packaging was exceptional. The box in which the Macintosh was delivered was so intelligently designed, with each item sequenced with clear instructions on where it went and how it connected, that unpacking was synonymous with successful rapid assembly and readiness for use. Subsequently, although the competitive position of Apple has fluctuated in what is the most volatile of industries, the commitment to design and innovation has remained substantial and integral to how it projects itself.

Identities have been even more rapidly established with the advent of electronic commerce using the Internet. It is often overlooked, however, that corporate identities, while profoundly important in creating a sense of instant recognition, and indeed trust, among prospective purchasers, can succeed on a sustained basis only if a distinctive visual image is underpinned by commitment to quality in products, operations, and services. This point is, if anything, even more true of service organizations. Federal Express, for example, founded in 1973, opened up a new market for the air freight of documents and packages. Twenty years later, with a fleet of over 450 aircraft and some 45,000 vehicles delivering around the world, the company realized its original logo did not reflect the reputation it had built for speedy and reliable service. Landor Associates was asked to suggest changes. A decisive point in the process was the realization that the company had universally become known as FedEx—indeed, the term was even used as a verb—and it was this that was chosen for the logo. It enabled a much bolder statement to be made on aircraft, vehicles, signs, and documents, and its simplicity not only communicated with greater clarity, but also cost significantly less to implement in terms of painting and printing costs than the earlier form.

The new identity, however, would have been ineffective had it not been backed up by efficient services, and, to emphasize this point, the roll-out of the new visual identity in 1994 was timed to coincide with another innovation. The introduction of bar-coding made possible a new proprietary software, FedEx Ship, to be made available to customers, with a simple interface enabling them to track or ship their packages. Previously, if customers wanted to know the whereabouts of a package, they would have to telephone FedEx (at the latter's expense) and employees would try to locate it while the phone bill mounted and customers became impatient. The new software gave better service by putting access and control in customers' hands, while saving FedEx substantial sums of money in operating costs.

A new visual identity can also be a signal of a major change of intent in corporate strategy. In the year 2000, British Petroleum (BP) unveiled a new identity programme that featured a dramat-

24. Clarity and cost-saving: FedEx redesigned corporate logo by
Landor Associates

ic image of a stylized sun-symbol in the long-standing corporate colour scheme of yellow and green, again by Landor. Accompanying advertising signalled a move to a wider pattern of activities, under the slogan Beyond Petroleum. This brought down on BP the wrath of environmentalists, who pointed out that the corporation's business remained overwhelmingly petroleum based. Whether the new image will be sustainable depends in great measure on the behaviour of BP in the future and the extent to which it can be judged against its claims for itself.

Changing a corporate identity can raise huge expectations but sometimes disastrously fail to deliver. The redesigned identity of British Airways (BA), by the London firm of Newell & Sorrell, launched in 1997, cost some £60 million. Its launch unfortunately coincided with a dispute with cabin staff, many of whom went on strike, resulting in cancelled flights, which was unfortunate, to say the least, for a organization projecting the quality of its service. A controversy also arose over a detail of the new identity, a decision to feature ethnic art from around the world on the tails of aircraft in an effort to reposition the carrier as an international, rather than a British, company. The tail art programme received some praise but also considerable ridicule and has since been quietly dropped, with a stylized version of the British flag replacing it. The problem of positioning is a real one, however, since 60 per cent of BA's passengers are non-British. Ironically, despite some farcical aspects of the new identity launch, such as the former Prime Minister, Lady Thatcher, attracting the attention of the press by ostentatiously draping a handkerchief over the ethnically decorated tail-fin of an aircraft model on exhibition, the design programme of BA is one of the most intensive of any of the world's airlines. It has delivered some genuinely successful innovations, such as seats in first and business class accommodation that convert into beds. In reality, the perception of BA in its target markets was in practice better than the unfortunate publicity surrounding the launch.

This illustrates what is probably the greatest problem in the field of corporate identity: a frequent confusion between image and identity. The former refers to the visual imagery enabling customers easily to recognize a particular company, obviously a desirable and necessary function; the latter, however, relates to how that image is understood by customers, or their expectations of the company. Image is a projection of how a company would like to be understood by customers; identity is the reality of what a company delivers as experienced by customers. When the two are consonant, it is possible to speak of corporate integrity. If a gulf opens up between the two, however, no amount of money flung at visual redesigns will rebuild customers' confidence. Put another way, image is credible only when supported by a good product or service. A good product or service, however, does not

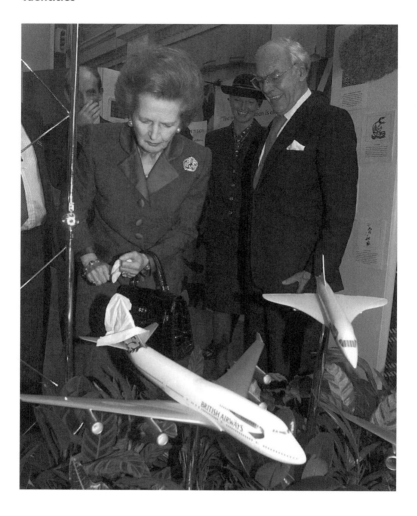

25. The risks of change: Lady Thatcher covering up the new
BA identity with a handkerchief

necessarily require an expensively contrived image. The optimal situation is when good products and services are complemented by consistent communications of high quality and reliability, when identity is the image.

8 Systems

The growing emphasis in design on systems of various kinds, in contrast to a focus on dedicated forms, stems in part from an awareness of the growing complexity of modern life, with multiple interconnections and overlaps between elements influencing overall performance. The spread of technical infrastructure systems is basic to modern life, as witness the failures of electricity supply in California that began in late 2000. The role of information technology in increasing awareness of connections between disparate functions (as well as increasing consumption of electricity) has also been profound. On another level, enhanced awareness of the environmental consequences of human intervention in natural systems and of the resultant concepts of ecological, organic relationships is also a contributing factor.

A system can be regarded as a group of interacting, interrelated, or interdependent elements that forms, or can be considered to form, a collective entity. The collective quality in its relationship to design can be manifested in various ways. Different elements can be combined in ways that are functionally related, as in transportation systems; by a common network of structures or channels, as in banking or telecommunications systems; or as a coherent structure of compatible elements capable of flexible organization, such as modular product systems. A further characteristic of systems is that the pattern of interrelated ideas and forms requires principles, rules, and procedures to ensure harmonious, orderly interaction. This requires qualities of systematic thinking, which infers methodical, logical, and purposeful procedures.

When designers have approached the problems of such systems in terms of formal, visual solutions, carrying over approaches to less complex tasks, these have often failed dismally to address the real problems of adapting to new requirements. As so often in history, new technologies tend to be defined initially in old forms and a transition period often seems to be necessary before new forms are evolved. Typical examples are the horseless carriage before it developed into the automobile, or desk-top computers, basically a television screen and a typewriter keyboard, which still await resolution. This is certainly the case with many systems which have tended to evolve in response to practical needs in the first instance, and only subsequently evolved to a level where they were considered systematically. Initially, cars existed in isolation, needing to carry fuel for long journeys and with personal owners responsible for repairs. Outside cities they ran largely on unmade roads. Only later did a systematic approach to road construction and maintenance, information systems, and support systems such as those providing repairs, fuel, and refreshment come into being.

100 min
300 max

80 min
240 max

2902.1
Direction to a motorway at the junction shown,
indicating route number

250 min
400 max

250 min
400 max

200 min
320 max

2903
Motorway junction ahead, identified by the number
shown on a black background, leading to the destination
and route shown. The number of lanes on the motorway
remains the same through the junction

26. Defining standards: British road sign system templates, UK Department
of Transport

Systems

It took half a century for coherently planned systems of high-speed roads, variously known as autobahns, motorways, or freeways, to become an accepted component of motorists' expectations.

In addition to the physical aspects of systems, information obviously plays an important part in communicating to users. One particular feature of road networks—road signage—illustrates some key features of design in a systems context. Each directional sign on a road network gives specific information in relation to the particular geographical point at which it is located and connections therefrom. They are not individually designed, however, but instead conform to a standard specification determining the size of each sign, the typeface and symbols used, and the colours in which they are displayed. In the United Kingdom, for example, motorway signs are blue with white letters; other major roads use dark green with yellow letters indicating road numbers and white letters for place names; for minor roads, signs are white with black letters. The format of signs is therefore strictly standardized to enable rapid recognition. Each sign gives highly specific information coded in a manner that can simultaneously be related to the system as a whole. The purpose of such a system is to give clear information about the consequences of taking a particular turning or direction, but leaving users to decide on exactly where they wish to go. It should be added that compatible, not necessarily identical, systematic approaches to other forms of information, such as maps or on-board directional computers, are also crucial to users' ability to navigate the system.

Directional signs are also supplemented with a system of road-side signs using symbols and pictographs covering a wide range of other purposes. International standards, as in Europe, have in some cases been established for this category. An important basic distinction is between communications requiring compliance and those facilitating decision making—between 'No Entry' or speed restriction signs, intended to prevent or control action, and those warning of potential hazards or problems, such as indicating school crossings or sharp curves in the road that require decision making by users.

Above all, the effectiveness of any system will depend upon its overall coherence, with clear standards enabling users rapidly to understand and navigate their way through without undue problems. This is particularly true of new systems based on innovative visual conventions requiring a degree of learning and adaptation by users. Computer programs are running into considerable problems in this respect, as designers attempt to create more and more icons intended to serve as a visual shorthand, with inevitable difficulties resulting from overload and lack of clarity.

Transportation provides other prime illustrations of the need for systemic approaches, as in, for example, the subways or mass

149

rapid transit systems typical of many major cities. As with the example of automobiles and road systems, understanding the systemic nature of urban transport systems initially evolved on a piecemeal basis before a detailed concept of it emerged after much trial and error. In this respect, the development of London Transport from the turn of the twentieth century to the Second World War is a key case study. Under the managerial leadership of Frank Pick, the organizational unification of disparate parts led to the establishment of systemic approaches on a number of levels, initially in terms of a common logo, typography, and signage, then to standard designs of trains, buses, and station fittings. Communicating an understanding of the system to users was significantly enhanced with the London Transport map designed by Harry Beck in 1931, a masterpiece of information design. Although not officially commissioned (Beck designed it in his spare time), it has been remarkably successful in enabling people to understand the system as a whole in a clear and unequivocal manner, subsequently imitated all over the world.

What any urban transport system illustrates is that the overall pattern can be broken down into subsystems in order to strike a balance between coordination and specific requirements. On one level are the problems of physically linking places and transporting people between them, which requires technical coordination of diverse elements for effective operation. Typically also, differ-

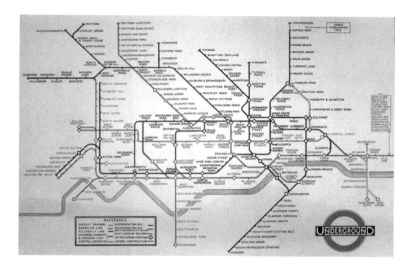

27. A pattern for the world: Harry Beck's London Transport map, 1933

ent kinds of vehicles, communications, and environments will be required, and standard approaches to each can provide considerable benefit in operation and maintenance. It is also possible to think of such systems not just in the sense of physical communication, but also as information systems. The latter concept focuses on the standpoint of users and their encounters with the range of functions and services. Observations of patterns of use can enable generic concepts to be established as a basis for common standards to be established across the system for the communication of information.

This can be illustrated by the diversity of forms encountered when taking a trip on a train or subway. Identifiers indicate the presence of a facility, for example, in the form of a sign over an entrance to a station, which the public can use if it so wishes. Information is provided about services in the form of maps, timetables, and fare tariffs. Instructions will be necessary to enable users to gain access, by buying tickets from automatic machines or from a kiosk. Further instructions will direct users into the facilities, to platforms for trains on various lines or directions. Restrictions will also be a part of the system, such as signs preventing users from entering operational sections, or those forbidding smoking. Further information on trains and identifiers on stations will be necessary to enable users to know when to leave trains. Stations can often be decorated with aesthetic imagery such as murals or mosaics intended to provide diversion and stimulus for travellers, while on the trains themselves, there may be other examples of expression, free-form individual communications, such as prints or poems, among the inevitable advertising. Even propaganda by organizations attempting to compel a shared belief is found. On leaving a train, instructions to make a connection or exit the facility in a particular direction, supplemented by maps of the vicinity, can enable users to become quickly oriented to the environment. The pattern of communications can be complicated in countries where one or more languages are in official use. In the Hong Kong Mass-Transit system, all signage uses English as well as Chinese ideograms.

In addition, of course, there is a similar pattern of environments and objects that interrelate with communication forms to constitute the system as experienced by users. Automatic ticket machines and the trains themselves are examples of the former, while booking halls, waiting rooms, corridors, and platforms are typical environments. The most effective systems in terms of ease of use are those that have patterns of consistency and standardization throughout the system, enabling users to know what to expect and sustaining a sense of security and familiarity. Designing to meet such needs requires the coordination of a broad spectrum of means—signs, spaces, vehicles, sound—that enable users easily to navigate any complexities. The Metro sys-

28. Coping with diversity: Hong Kong dual language road signage

tem in Lisbon, for example, has a repetitive pattern on station platforms of grouping together maps of the system set in the context of the city's geography; diagrams of Metro lines, clearly indicating the component elements of the system; and detailed maps of the immediate environment of each station. In the Tokyo Subway, maps of the system follow the London Transport pattern of abstraction and colour-coding for different lines, but take the logic one step further. Station signs and notices for each line are also in the colour of the line, and strips of colour are used along corridors and passages to give guidance to passengers seeking to connect to particular lines.

A particular advantage of such standardization is in the category of communications that embody specific provision for people with disabilities, which can be on the simple level of indicators, signs, and elevators available for people in wheelchairs. On a more complex level are the problems of people who are blind, for whom, of course, visual signage is redundant. The Tokyo Subway is typical of many systems that have adopted tactile means of communication, with stations featuring strips of tiles with raised dimples running along the centre of floor surfaces in corridors, enabling blind people using a stick to find their way. The pattern of tiling, and the feel of it, alter to signal junction points where more than one path is available. Special automatic machines with Braille instructions and buttons to summon help in case of difficulties are positioned at key points to assist in obtaining tickets and navigating the system. The tiles also lead to platforms, where their configuration orients blind users towards the doors of trains. The provision for the blind can indeed be considered as a subsystem within the greater whole.

Other levels of systems approaches in design that have grown rapidly recently are evident in the development and manufacture of products. New problems in this regard have emerged with the spread of globalization and regional economic unification, such as the European Union, which has amplified the need to bridge different markets and cultures.

Globalization, in particular, has placed greater emphasis on the seemingly conflicting demands of achieving economies of scale through greater commonality between products, while at the same time being able to adapt to the detailed requirements of tastes and compatibility in specific markets. This has taken several forms, but underlying them is a shift from standardized products to standardized components that can be flexibly configured to provide a variety of forms and satisfy a range of needs.

Early mass production was highly inflexible and worked most effectively when producing a standardized product in large quantities. Even variations on a relatively simple level could unduly complicate procedures, such as producing cars for different markets that required, for example, a switch between left- and right-hand drive. One solution was a principle known as centre-line design, which means configuring the design of a vehicle on either side of a central line, enabling it to be flipped to suit the driving practices of any particular market, but even this variance was costly and disruptive.

Design for mass production tends to be for discrete products, the performance of which is defined in a form that integrates specific assemblies for a particular purpose. It is a lengthy process, and this specificity, allied to individual styling, creates differentiation in the market. A new product requires an equally lengthy, and costly, process. Changes in manufacturing technology, however, particularly the trend for flexible production methods to supplant mass manufacturing, offer radically different approaches to design. These have in common a shift in emphasis from finished products to processes by which products can be generated and configured rapidly. A means of achieving this is the configuration of key elements of a product category into standardized components, with, equally importantly, standardized interfaces or connections. This enables systems to be developed that give users greater choice in adapting products to their own perceived needs, a process to which the label of mass customization, seemingly an oxymoron, has become attached.

An early example was the National Bicycle Industrial Company of Japan. It established a system whereby dealers could offer customers the opportunity to specify a bicycle model, for which customers' dimensions could be measured, and their colour preferences and additional components determined. When National received specifications, a computer capable of generating eleven million variants of models printed a blueprint for the customer's bicycle to be produced from a combination of standardized and cut-to-fit parts. The made-to-order model was delivered with the customer's name silk-screened on the frame.

Motorola's organization of pager production in its factory at Boca Raton, Florida, follows similar principles, being estimated to offer customers the capacity to produce some 29 million variants of pager. Production of a customer's model begins some fifteen minutes after an order has been placed at any point in the USA and is shipped the following day. An advantage for producers of such just-in-time manufacturing is the elimination of capital being tied up in inventories. For customers, the opportunity to specify the exact details of products they wish to purchase clearly delivers enhanced satisfaction.

In producing printers for widely different markets around the globe, Hewlett-Packard's approach to mass customization has been to focus on delaying any product differentiation until the last possible point in the supply chain, requiring the product design to be integrated with and adaptable to delivery processes. A basic product is delivered to a supply point nearest to customers, and is there configured to meet the specific requirements of the particular context, such as compatibility with the local electrical systems.

Flexible configurations are taken to a further level with the introduction of modular units. This means breaking down the overall structure of a product into essential functional components and interface elements, which are grouped in standard modular units, with further definition of add-on optional elements, enabling a large spectrum of products to emerge. Modularity enables each unit to be tested and produced to high standards of quality, and then be used in variable configurations to generate a flow of products adaptable to different markets or, again, to be customized to the particular specification of individual users. The establishment of modular systems switches attention from the finished product as the essential conceptual starting point to the design of processes within an overall systems concept.

On a fundamental level, a popular example of modularity remains the Lego plastic building blocks for children, developed in the late 1940s by Ole Kirk Christiansen of Billund in Denmark from earlier wooden blocks, which epitomize the astonishing variations possible from a rigidly standardized geometric format.

The origins of modular systems go further back, however, and appeared in designs for unit furniture as early as the first decade of the twentieth century on the basis of standardized dimensions of length, breadth, and height. They became common in the 1920s, enabling unit furniture to be adapted to any size of home or grouping desired by users. By the 1980s, kitchen systems by German companies such as Siematic and Poggenpohl were widely available in Europe. Customers could select a range of modular units to fit their particular space and needs, and a computer simulation could be created at the sales point, with a three-dimensional image showing the final effect and enabling choices on units or colour finishes to be adjusted. Once the choices had been finalized and the order completed, the specification was sent via computer to the factory, where the units would be made to order, again saving on the need for expensive stocks and warehousing.

Modular systems have been very widely used by electronic manufacturers to generate prolific variations of audio and visual products. One of the most spectacular applications of modular systems in this sense, however, has been by Dell Computers, which has harnessed modular designs to the potential of the Internet as a communications device, to define new dimensions of competitiveness. The company web site allows buyers to use the Internet or telephone to order a computer to their specification, which is then built to order from an array of modular components, allowing customers to follow its progress through to

29. Diversity from unity: Siematic modular kitchen system

delivery. The savings for the company from not having compo-nents locked up in large inventories have been huge, which makes it possible to establish substantial price advantage.

A further elaboration of such procedures is the concept of product platforms. These platforms group modules and compo-nents to serve a basic functional purpose, from which it becomes possible rapidly to develop and manufacture a variety of product configurations. This enables a basic idea to be modified rapidly in response to changing market or competitive conditions. A suc-cessful example was demonstrated by Sony after the initial favourable reception of its Walkman, launched in 1979, with the development of a basic functional module and an advanced fea-tures module. Each was the basis of warding off competition from followers, enabling a rapid succession of models to be launched to test a wide variety of applications and features at different lev-els of the market.

While Sony used platforms to stay ahead, Kodak used them to catch up in its response to the introduction in 1987 by the Japanese company Fuji of a single-use 35mm camera. It took Kodak a year to develop a competitive model, yet by 1994 it had captured 70 per cent of the American market. Although a follow-er in this particular category, Kodak launched more products, more cheaply, than Fuji. Again, a platform concept was the basis of this success, with economies yielded by common components and production processes, on the basis of which a series of such cameras could be launched rapidly onto the market.

In 1995, the Ford Motor Corporation embraced the platform philosophy when it embarked on a long-term programme of restructuring the company as a global organization. Product development was henceforth to be focused on vehicle types on a global basis, rather than specific vehicles for particular markets. This was intended to reduce product development costs, which in the auto industry have reached staggeringly high levels and can be justified only by markets of global dimensions. A platform product approach would enable Ford to manufacture components anywhere in the world wherever they could be most cheaply and efficiently produced, as the basis of a range of standard vehicle concepts. These in turn could be the basis of differentiated adaptations for particular markets, which could be rapidly developed as specific needs were identified.

These systems of development and design resolve the apparent contradiction between the need to manufacture products in high volumes economically and the desire to tailor them to meet the needs of individual customers. The aim is to exploit the juxtaposition of distinctiveness and commonality to deliver specific solutions through a cost-effective production system.

Other advantages of such approaches can be seen in the possibilities offered to provide greater value to users in terms of follow-up services. When Canon first produced its small personal copiers, it lacked a chain of service outlets. The problem was resolved by designing printing ink refills in combination with elements needing frequent servicing in a common module. Effectively, every time the ink was renewed, the machine got a new engine, so drastically reducing the need for repairs.

Perhaps the greatest challenge facing designers, however, is the need for greater compatibility between the artificial systems generated by human creativity and the systems of the biological world, the result of millennia of evolution. If we can understand the nature of systems in terms of how changes in one part have consequences throughout the whole, and how that whole can effect other overlapping systems, there is the possibility at least of reducing some of the more obvious harmful effects. Design could be part of a solution, if appropriate strategies and methodologies were mandated by clients, publics, and governments to address the problems in a fundamental manner. Sadly, one must doubt the ability of economic systems, based on a conviction that the common good is defined by an amalgam of decisions based on individual self-interest, to address these implications of the human capacity to transform our environment. Design, in this sense, is part of the problem. It is a subsystem within wider economic and social systems and does not function independently of these contexts.

9 Contexts

In broad terms, three areas of contextual influence are relevant to design practice: the professional organization of design, or how designers view themselves; the business context in which a majority of design practice is located; and, in addition, the level of government policy, which varies between countries, but in many can be a significant dimension.

Mention has already been made of the fact that design has never evolved on the level of a major profession such as architecture, law, or medicine, which have self-regulating rights that control entry and levels of practice. Indeed, such is the diversity of design practice and the variety of work involved that it is in fact doubtful if design should, or even could, be organized on this basis.

Nevertheless, professional societies have been formed in a great number of countries to serve a particular specialization or a general grouping of design capabilities, and these can represent the interests of designers to governments, industry, the press, and public, and provide a forum for discussion of issues relevant to practitioners. These may be skill specific, as with the Industrial Design Society of America, or the American Institute of Graphic Arts, or more general, as with the Chartered Society of Designers in the United Kingdom. There are also international organizations that hold world congresses where design issues across boundaries can be addressed.

Design organizations may make statements on how they view their work, and make recommendations about standards in practice, but the reality is that decisions about such matters are not taken by designers alone. Apart from private experiment and exploration for their own interest, a necessary function in sustaining creative motivation, most designers rarely work for or by themselves: they work for clients or employers, and the context of business and commerce must therefore be viewed as the primary arena of design activity. Ultimately, these clients or employers have the major voice in determining what is possible, feasible, or acceptable in design practice. Business policies and practices are therefore fundamental to understanding how design functions at the operational level and the roles and functions it is able to play.

There are problems in analysing business approaches to design, however, since specific statements on its role in the overall strategy of companies are comparatively rare. The positioning of design in corporate hierarchies is similarly inadequate as a guide, because of the immense variations found—design can, for example, be an independent function, subordinate to engineering or marketing management, or part of R & D.

How design actually functions is to a very large extent based on implicit approaches specific to each organization, based more on the inclinations of personalities and habitual behaviour. Out of all this diversity, however, some general patterns can be distinguished.

On an organizational level, design can be a central function or dispersed throughout an organization. A company such as IBM was long famous for tight central control over what products were generated and how they were marketed. In contrast, a conglomerate such as the Japanese electrical giant Matsushita devolves such control to divisions specializing in particular product groups, such as TV and video or household appliances.

In some companies there is a very clear distinction between the contributions of design based on long-term or short-term approaches. In the automobile industry, the German company Mercedes emphasizes long-term approaches, believing that its vehicles should still be recognizable whatever their age. This is ensured by centralized control of design and an insistence that each new model retain a continuity of characteristics that clearly identify it as a Mercedes. In contrast, General Motors has a policy of short-term change, with devolved design responsibility to divisions manufacturing under different brand names—such as Chevrolet, Buick, and Cadillac—and an emphasis on constant differentiation through the device of the annual model change. In the case of conglomerate organizations linking several companies, both product decisions and design implementation will usually be devolved to the constituent units. This is typified by Gillette, which, in addition to its major focus on toiletries, also owns companies such as Oral-B, specializing in dental products, Braun, manufacturing electrical products, and Parker Pens.

In the field of service organizations, airlines, banks, and franchise organizations such as fast-food and oil companies use design as one of the major instruments by which unity of identity and standards are maintained, even though sales outlets are in a number of different hands. A company such as McDonald's cannot exercise daily control over every aspect of every franchise around the globe, but uses design not just in products, but also in systematic approaches to preparation, delivery, and environments, as a key tool in establishing and maintaining general standards.

If the overall role of design in organizations is so varied that few general patterns are discernible, and then only dimly, there is if anything even less clarity on the level of the detailed operational management of design. Even in particular product sectors, where companies produce similar products for identical markets, wide variations occur.

The specific history of organizations and the personalities involved is obviously a vital consideration in understanding how design played a role in their activities. Some firms are initially based on an entrepreneurial insight about market opportunities;

others originate in a particular technological innovation. Less frequently, some have founders motivated by a sense of social responsibility, others are even established by designers wishing to retain control over essential aspects of their work. Some have had formalized procedures bringing consistency over long periods. Others, however, depend on the personal insights and inclinations of particular individuals in influential positions who believe design is crucial to their company's identity and reputation.

There is no clear pattern in how companies reach the point where design consciousness emerges and becomes incorporated into the battery of competencies considered vital for corporate survival. With some—Sony is a good example—that emphasis on high standards in product forms and communications has been present from its earliest years. In other instances it was generated as a response to crisis, demonstrating that design can play a role in changing the fortunes of companies. The smallest of the Big Three American automobile manufacturers, Chrysler, came back from a deep crisis with a range of vehicles in the early 1990s that were the most innovative to emerge from Detroit for some time. This was in substantial part due to the fact that its talented Vice-President for Design, Tom Gale, was able to function at the strategic level of corporate decision making and make new design concepts part of the overall corporate plan for reviving its fortunes. In many companies, in contrast, it seems that an understanding of design has yet to penetrate corporate decision making.

If patterns in the evolution of design in corporate consciousness are difficult to explain, how design loses its role in organizations is somewhat clearer. Even when a company can be considered exemplary in its design consciousness, there is no guarantee, as with Olivetti, that design will survive a major corporate crisis resulting from a failure to adapt to changing conditions of one kind or another. A change of management style and consciousness can also mean that carefully nurtured design competencies become dispersed and will no longer be considered as relevant; or there may be a clash of personalities, which seems to have happened at Chrysler after its merger with Daimler-Benz. Recently, some companies have exemplified a trend for design to be 'outsourced'—the jargon term describing a process of cost saving by relying on outside consultants instead of in-house design resources. Even companies that have a strong record of integrating design into their structures and procedures, such as Philips and Siemens, now require their design groups to function as internal consultants. This means they have to compete for corporate projects against external consultancies and are also expected to take on work outside the company in order to remain financially viable.

The trend for design groups to be divested may save money, but has the disadvantage that, if design is to be something that really distinguishes a company against its competitors, on something more a passing, superficial level, it requires consistent nurturing as something capable of delivering unique ideas. In this respect, the Finnish company Nokia, manufacturing telecommunications products, has consistently used design, often in subtle ways, to distinguish the usability of its products, and this has played an important role in enabling it in less than a decade to challenge established corporate giants in the field, such as Eriksson and Motorola.

Outside the world of large companies are the vast majority of businesses grouped under the general heading of small and medium enterprises (SMEs). These are rarely in a position to dominate markets as large corporations do, and must respond to markets either by moving very nimbly to follow trends, or by using design to create new markets. Italian lighting companies such as Flos and Arteluce, and Danish furniture companies such as Fredericia, have created and sustained niche market leadership, often at the profitable upper levels of markets, through high levels of design innovation in their products.

If formulaic recipes are difficult to discern, however, one decisive factor in smaller companies is clearly apparent: the role played by individual owners in setting standards for design practice. Three examples from different product sectors demonstrate

30. Usability and competitiveness: Nokia portable telephone

Contexts

31. Lighting, not lamps: ERCO architectural lighting systems

the potential of SMEs to grow if design is supported and integrated at the highest level. In England, Joe Bamford created JCB, a company manufacturing back-hoe loaders, used in earth-moving work, and set design standards that have contributed to his products sustaining their competitiveness over many years in world markets with giants such as Caterpillar and Komatsu. In Germany, ERCO, of Ludenscheid, has been transformed over a quarter of a century from an undistinguished manufacturer of domestic lighting fittings to a world leader in the niche market of architectural lighting. The vision of its Managing Director, Klaus-Jürgen Maack, brought a new focus on the quality of light as a deliverable, not the fitting. Any new product from his company should be a genuine innovation, he insists, with an emphasis on design in all aspects of his firm's operations. In the USA, a retired entrepreneur, Sam Farber, noticed older people with arthritic joints had difficulty in holding kitchen tools. He established a new company to manufacture a range of kitchen tools, with handles designed for easy grip and manipulation by a New York consultancy, Smart Design. These have proved to be a remarkable success, applicable to a much wider constituency than the elderly, and, over a decade, Oxo Goodgrips has reconstituted the market for these products.

Of particular interest are production companies established by designers to obtain greater control over their work, such as Ingo

Maurer in Germany, specializing in lighting, and David Mellor in England, designing and manufacturing his own cutlery designs in connection with a substantial retail operation. Perhaps the most outstanding example is James Dyson, whose dual-cyclone vacuum cleaners have toppled the products of major global companies, such as Hoover, Electrolux, and Hitachi, to become market leaders in the United Kingdom, with export markets being continually opened up. Dyson's stated intent to become the largest manufacturer of domestic appliances in the world neatly illustrates the point that big companies were once small companies with ambition.

If businesses are the vital arena of design decision making at the detailed, or micro-design level, many governments around the world have evolved what can be termed macro-design policies for the development and promotion of design as an important factor in national economic planning for industrial competitiveness. Similarly to businesses, governments also demonstrate considerable variations in the structures and practices shaping their policy aims for design. Some even become involved in design practice to promote specific ends, but, even when implementation is left to individual enterprises, the interaction between the two can be a vital element in determining the effectiveness of any national policy. This too, of course, can crucially influence the direction design takes in any particular society.

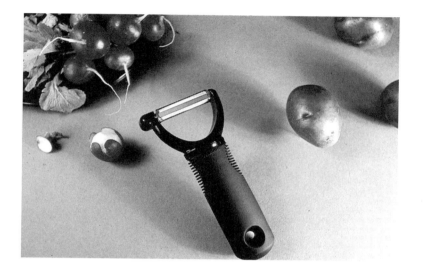

32. Needed by some, appeal for all: Oxo Goodgrips tools—'Y' peeler

Contexts

A government policy can be understood as a set of principles, purposes, and procedures about its intentions on a particular topic. In addition to explicit statements embedded in formal policy documents, however, implicit aspects of how policies are executed can also be highly relevant factors in understanding their effectiveness. In Japan, for example, there is a close informal network of contact and communication between government officials and business executives which is a powerful channel for exchange of ideas and cooperation.

Governments of many kinds have long included design as an element of their economic and trade objectives, though how this functions depends upon the nature of the government and its aims. Does it seek to exercise direct influence over industry, or even, as under Communist regimes, to own the means of production and distribution? Or, as in more democratic regimes, is there an effort to frame broad objectives and rely on cooperation with, or incentives for, industry to carry them out?

Intervention in economic affairs by governments was in the past most frequently directed to preventing innovation when it threatened government interests or was likely to cause social disruption. A significant change in the eighteenth century in Europe, however, saw the flowering of an economic policy known as mercantilism. Briefly, this was an effort to restrict imports and promote exports to enhance relative economic performance. First systematically formulated in France under Louis XIV, the means used to promote these ends included: incentives to stimulate the development of manufacturing at home; direct investment in production facilities; sheltering domestic producers from foreign competition by high protectionist tariffs; supporting merchant capitalists in competition overseas; investing in infrastructure and manufacturing capabilities; attracting talented craftsmen from other countries; and developing design education opportunities.

Underpinning mercantilism was a concept of an essentially static economy: since the volume of production and commerce possible at any time is considered to be limited in total amount, the commercial policy of a nation should target obtaining the biggest slice of the available pie at the expense of other nations. In this situation, design was considered a decisive factor in creating competitive advantage and by such policies France became a leader in the manufacture of luxury products, a position it holds to this day.

Fundamental to mercantilism, and any present-day government design policy, is the belief that states should act in economic matters in terms of their self-interest. This belief still endures and, despite the growth of regional groupings such as the European Union and the North American Free Trade Area, derivatives of mercantilism are still a powerful force in the policies of many governments, albeit in modified form. The emphasis is now on promoting technology and design as a means of gaining economic advantage by enhancing national competitiveness. The belief that these capabilities can be defined in national terms and promoted within the boundaries of a state as a national characteristic is increasingly a questionable assumption.

In European countries, design policy has generally been in the form of promotional bodies funded by governments but having considerable leeway in the details of how they function. This pattern first clearly evolved in the United Kingdom, which has one of the oldest legacies of design policy. When the UK opened up a substantial technological and economic lead as a consequence of the Industrial Revolution, French products still competed effectively based on superior pattern designs. As a result of recommendations by the Select Committee on Design and Manufacture established by Parliament in 1835 to address these problems, new design schools were established. A problem, however, was the belief that design in industry required an injection of art to effect improvement. Moreover, the only people capable of teaching in the new schools were artists. So the schools in fact evolved as art schools, and indeed the first of them, the Normal School of Design, was subsequently renamed the Royal College of Art. Continuing complaints by manufacturers of the resulting deficiencies of the system in supplying trained designers echoed across succeeding decades, resulting in other efforts to make design education better serve the needs of industry, which generally proved fruitless.

In the final stages of the Second World War, in 1944, the UK government established the Council of Industrial Design, later to be renamed the Design Council. Although financed by government, it functioned as a semi-independent organization, with the primary aim of promoting design in industry as a means of stimulating exports. In this original aim it must be judged a complete failure, since, forty years later, the UK balance of trade in manufactured goods went into deficit for the first time in two centuries. For much of its existence, the Design Council sought to function by persuasion and, as a result, had little power to alter anything significantly. Since 1995, it has been a slimmed-down body, showing great energy in promoting design as an element of government efforts to encourage innovation in industry. The United Kingdom still has a substantial trade deficit in manufactured goods, however, so much still remains to be done.

The German equivalent of the Design Council, the *Rat für Formgebung*, was founded in 1951 and similarly supported by government finance, in this case federal and state sources. For a time it played a substantial role in promoting design in industry and to the public at large, emphasizing not only an economic but also a cultural role for design in modern society. By the 1980s, however, funding had dwindled, and, although it continued its work in reduced circumstances, the main emphasis in promotional work switched to various design centres in the federal states, which emphasized regional developments.

An obvious problem with such bodies is that they are subject to sometimes fickle changes in the political climate. The Netherlands Design Institute, founded in 1993 and funded by the Dutch government, became, under the Directorship of John Thackara, one of the most dynamic focal points anywhere for debate and initiatives about the role of design in modern society. In December 2000, however, it closed, after funding was withdrawn on the recommendation of the Minister of Culture. Clearly, when a gulf of any kind opens up between how this kind of institution functions and politicians' perception of what it should be, the latter have decisive power.

In terms of such relationships, one of the most consistently successful European promotional bodies has been the Danish Design Council. Established after the end of the Second World War, it has been an integral element in establishing design, not just as a factor in Danish economic life, but as part of the dialogue about the nature of Danish society. This would have been impossible without the ongoing support of the government, which was evident in a new purpose-built Danish Design Centre that opened in the heart of Copenhagen in early 2000 and is a remarkable testament to a vision of design being seamlessly integrated into national life.

33. Design as state policy: the Danish Design Council

Contexts

In contrast, across the Atlantic, it is a curious fact that the USA does not have, and never has had, a design policy. Proposals aplenty have been generated by interested parties such as professional design organizations, but the Federal government remains impervious to such a project and only the states of Michigan and Minnesota have shown any interest in design as competence to enhance competitiveness. The reasons for this situation are complex, but in part lie in an economic mindset that regards design as something superficial, that can easily be copied by foreign competitors, and should not therefore be the recipient of government support.

Ironically, the development of design as a business tool in interwar America served as an example for Japan when embarking on a programme of economic reconstruction following the Second World War. The key government body responsible for Japan's industrial development policies is the Ministry of International Trade and Industry (MITI). Its policies set out to coordinate the activities of Japanese firms within specified sectors and so make them competitive in international markets. How Japan developed its design competencies as part of this effort is an archetypal model of how MITI functions. In fact, the Japanese approach is one of the clearest examples that modern variants of mercantilist principles are still thriving.

To the extent that design expertise in Japanese industry existed before the Second World War, it derived from European artistic or craft-based concepts. Japan was largely regarded as a country that turned out cheap imitations of foreign products. After defeat in the war left Japan's industrial capacity largely in ruins, MITI developed plans for reconstruction and economic expansion based on exports. Its early policies had two main planks: introducing the latest foreign technology; and protecting domestic industry while it rebuilt. The home market was viewed as a developmental springboard for exports.

As part of this policy, MITI began vigorously to promote design, inviting advisory groups of prominent designers from abroad, but, most significantly, sending groups of young, talented people to be trained in the USA and Europe, to create a cadre of qualified designers. Design promotion activities were stimulated by establishing the Japan Industrial Design Promotion Organization (JIDPO) as a branch of MITI and the 'The Good Design Products Selection System', better known as the 'G-Mark' competition, to promote the best Japanese designs.

On the basis of MITI's promotion of design, by the mid-1950s, many larger Japanese companies began to establish design sections and design began to be rapidly absorbed and integrated into development processes. Some new designers returning from overseas were employed in corporate design groups, but others set up independent consultancies, notably Kenji Ekuan's GK

Associates, and Takuo Hirano, who set up Hirano & Associates, which for almost half a century have been leading organizations in establishing the credentials of design in the business community. New educational courses and on-the-job learning led to a sustained expansion, so that, by the early 1990s, there were some 21,000 industrial designers employed in Japan. Despite the economic setbacks of the 1990s, MITI continues to view design as a strategic resource for the national economy, with ongoing policy reviews providing a framework of ideas and responses to new developments. Few people in the world remain unaffected by the shift in Japan from producing imitation goods to generating technically superior, well-designed products. In the process, Japan's economic standing in the world and its own standard of living have dramatically changed.

Other countries in East Asia have followed the Japanese model of design promotion with great success. In Taiwan, the Ministry of Economic Affairs has consistently promoted design, together with technological development, as a means of enhancing the intrinsic value of products in export markets. The body responsible for this policy, the China Export Trade Association, has played a large part in raising the profile of Taiwanese products from their earlier reputation as cheap copies. The twin aims of economic policy for the new century are summed up in a slogan linking technology and design as the basis for the future. So confident now are the Taiwanese in their products that they are aggressively carrying their message to their major competitors, having established Design Promotion Centers in cities such as Düsseldorf, Milan, and Osaka.

South Korea demonstrates a similar pattern. Devastated by war following the invasion of North Korea in 1950, the government set out in the 1960s to emulate the Japanese pattern of industrialization. Similarly, companies were encouraged to use designers to raise the standard and reputation of their products, with design education and promotion carefully fostered on a foundation of government funding and support. Like Japan and Taiwan, most early industrial products were imitations of foreign designs, but by the 1980s design education facilities in Korea were substantial and rapidly evolving, and on the level of both corporate and consultant design there was a rising level of achievement.

Other Asian countries such as Singapore, Malaysia, Thailand, and, more recently, China are similarly promoting design as a means of increasing their share of international trade. Throughout Asia this promotion of standards internally has been accompanied by efforts, both overt and covert, to restrict the penetration of domestic markets by overseas products.

Many governments evidently believe such policies to be valuable, since they continue to pursue them and often underline their commitment with substantial funding. Shoring up national competencies is often viewed as a buttress against the encroachment of globalization. It should be noted, however, that design consultancy, at its most effective, creative levels, is one of the most fluid capabilities in global patterns of trade irrespective of national boundaries. Encouraging the design sector as a service industry in its own right within a country to function regionally or globally, as in Singapore, could have powerful relevance when compared to narrowly conceived national policies.

In addition, in most countries, the provision of design education is also assumed to be the responsibility of government, though, again, there is no evidence of any proposals to shape design education in significantly new ways to gain a future advantage. On the other hand, serious research into design and its effectiveness is generally conspicuous by its absence, although governments widely sponsor research into many other aspects of business performance, such as technology and competitiveness.

Another striking fact is that design in the modern, professional sense seems to evolve at a particular point and level of affluence in countries' economic and technological development. Examples of design being used strategically at a national level to help build up an undeveloped economy are conspicuous by their absence yet could potentially be a constructive tool for benefit in emerging or Third World economies.

A fourth contextual level of particular relevance could be

cited: that of how design is understood by the broad public that its outcomes so widely and profoundly influence. How design is depicted in the media, the level of discussion of its relevance and contribution to economic and cultural life, how people think about their role in its use and application, are some aspects that serve as indicators in this context. The messages are either extremely confusing, however, or conspicuous by their absence. Since so much design in the twentieth century was determined by the perceptions of producers and what they decided users should have, it is hardly surprising that there are vast amounts of market data available, but little understanding of what people really think about design. In no other aspect is there a greater need for research to establish some clear indicators of how design is understood.

10 Futures

Two themes have recurred throughout this book: the extent of variations in design practice, and the manner in which it is being affected by far-reaching changes in technology, markets, and cultures. Design cannot remain isolated from these wider patterns, but the situation is confused. As in previous historical phases of change, a point arrives at which consciousness of the extent of change becomes a pressing issue, but uncertainty about what will eventuate means few definitive answers are available. Since the early 1980s, attempts to adapt old forms and processes to new purposes have been juxtaposed with wild experiments and many overconfident pronouncements of what the future will be. If the basic proposition in this book is that design has evolved historically in a layered pattern, rather than a linear evolution in which new developments eliminate previous manifestations, then we can expect new layers to be added that will alter the role and relationships of pre-existing modes.

Certainly, at one level, existing methods and concepts of design, especially those that emerged predominantly over the twentieth century, are continuing to evolve. Mass production is entering a new phase with its extension to global markets on the basis of sophisticated systemic concepts, as discussed in Chapter

8. It is already clear that computers have had a profound, transformative influence as a tool in design, extensively supplementing and enhancing, although not always replacing, existing means of conceptualization, representation, and specification. The use of giant computer screens enabling work to be processed in enormous detail, concurrently on several sites, together with virtual-reality representations, is widely replacing older methods of renderings and physical models as a means of developing concepts for production. Yet at the same time, in a typical pattern of juxtaposition, one of the most ancient means of exploring and representing visual ideas, drawing, remains an irreplaceable skill for any designer. Another procedure of enormous influence is the refinement of rapid prototyping machines, capable of generating from computer specifications three-dimensional forms of ever-increasing size and complexity in ever-shorter periods of time. Computers also provide the capability to combine and layer forms from multiple sources—text, photographs, sound, and video—to effect huge transformations in two-dimensional imagery. Design is simultaneously becoming more specialized in some respects, with more detailed skills in specific areas of application, and more generalist ones in others, with hybrid forms of practice emerging in parallel.

There are already sharp differences in the levels at which designers function within organizations, which can be expected to widen. Some are executants, carrying out ideas essentially determined by others, and even here, their work can be differentiated between routine variations in the features of products or the layouts of communications, on the one hand, and highly original redefinitions of function and form on the other. According to the type of business a company is in and the life-cycle phase of its products, designers may variously be involved in imitation, the adaptation of incremental features, major redefinitions of functions, or the origination of profoundly new concepts. They are also increasingly finding their way into executive functions of decision making at strategic levels that fundamentally affect not just the future shape of forms, but the future form of businesses in their entirety. Sony Corporation, for example, has a Strategic Design Group, reporting to its President, with a wide-ranging remit of charting possible futures for Sony. Behind such developments is the question of whether design is valued primarily in terms of a particular set of skills related to existing products or services, or is also considered as a distinct form of knowledge and insight capable of creating wholly new concepts of value.

On another plane is the difference between whether designers function as form-givers, determining form in a manner that allows no variation—it is either accepted or not—or as enablers, using the possibilities of information technology and powerful miniaturized systems to provide the means for users to adapt forms and systems to their own purposes. The growth of electronic technology, the manufacture of powerful microchips, and the generation of more sophisticated software at commodity prices mean that products and systems have the potential to be highly flexible in response to specific users' needs. Both roles, of form-giver and of enabler, will continue to be necessary, but the distinction between them is based on fundamentally different values and approaches, to a point where they constitute substantially different modes of practice.

More elaborate techniques and methodologies will undoubtedly emerge, particularly in larger, systemic approaches, but, as the tools become more powerful, it becomes necessary to raise the all-important question of the values informing design practice. Will the future pattern of what is produced, and why, continue to be primarily determined by commercial companies, with designers identifying with their values; or by users, with designers and corporations serving their needs? There is much free-market ideology claiming the latter to be the case, but the realities of economic practice make it plain that in many respects the former still dominates. Consider, for example, the number of telephone tree systems that begin by informing callers how important their call is, before leading into an infuriating electronic labyrinth of confusion and non-responsiveness, with no link to a human being. The gulf between image and reality in the commercial world is nowhere more evident than in how customers are treated. There is increasingly an inherent tension between, on the one hand, producers trying to control markets, and, on the other hand, the access to information and control potentially made available to users by new technologies. Any resolution will in most cases not be made by designers, but design will be a vital element in expressing the outcomes.

The question of which population designers address in their work is therefore fundamental. The basic needs of the small percentage of the world's population in industrialized countries have been largely met. Most people have adequate diet and living standards, and access to health and education in conditions of considerable freedom. The benefits in terms of openness of life choices, and access to education and information, are substantial. Freedom of access to information and increasing levels of customized products for a majority of the population, both using well-designed interactive sites, are among the benefits evident in the USA, which leads the world in levels of computer ownership and access. It is not certain, however, that the rest of the world will simply follow the US pattern. Already, China has a 'firewall' preventing its citizens from having access to web sites outside its borders. The design of systems can be used equally for purposes that can enhance or restrict freedom of information.

Poverty is a relative term, moreover, and there are still many problems in industrialized countries that increasingly require attention, to which design can potentially contribute, such as improving educational provision for the poor and unskilled (in the USA and the United Kingdom, around a quarter of the population is functionally illiterate); mitigating the problems of unemployment by creating opportunities to retrain frequently in a constantly changing economic climate; addressing the needs of ageing populations; creating more flexible welfare and medical provision; and addressing environmental questions, not just large ecological concerns, but more immediate problems such as noise pollution and stress in human environments.

Such problems can frequently be glossed over in markets dominated by excess wealth, with conspicuous consumption becoming endemic. In the context of the USA, where it was estimated in the year 2000 that 3 per cent of the world's population consumed 25 per cent of available world resources, there has been a growing emphasis on designing not just products and communications, but 'experiences'. This can in part be seen as an indicator that basic utility is something taken for granted. It also suggests that life is so meaningless for people incapable of experiencing anything for themselves that they have to be supplied with a constant flow of artificial, commercialized, and commodified experiences that take on their own reality. Design in this context becomes the

provider of bromides to block out anything demanding or uncomfortable.

The growth of globalization and industrial development and
urbanization in the so-called 'Third World', in 'Developing' or
'Peripheral' countries— accounting for some 90 per cent of the
world's population—also raises pressing questions regarding the
economic and cultural role of design. Some global corporations
have 'hollowed out' their workforce in their home country, maintaining only core management and design functions, while transferring production to wherever a source of cheap labour exists,
showing little sensitivity to the diversity of local cultures they
affect in the process. Sweeping assertions in corporate circles that
with globalization the role of national governments is increasingly irrelevant sounds suspiciously like wishful thinking. Outside the
small number of industrially advanced countries, government
may be the one institution capable of resisting the more predato-
ry aspects of commercial expansion and cultural encroachment,
which can in any case originate equally from within their borders
as from outside. Unfortunately, in practice, there are too many
governments, themselves based on corrupt instincts, that are will-
ing allies in such exploitation.

The processes of globalization, however, should not simply be
depicted as a juggernaut of large corporations taking over the
world, as seems to be the case in the wave of protests against such

bodies as the World Bank and the World Trade Organization. Innumerable small and medium companies are increasingly involved in global trade, representing a very broad spectrum of products and services that cannot be depicted in terms of crude stereotypes of capitalism.

Many examples can indeed be found of smaller commercial companies with a sense of responsibility to their users. The Finnish company Fiskars transformed the design and manufacture of an existing product, scissors, by basing its whole approach on careful ergonomic studies of use in practice, with the aim of making each product safe and efficient for its specific task. So successful was this approach that the company subsequently extended it to other product categories, such as garden tools and axes. Such developments do demonstrate, however, that commercial success can be based on design being used in a manner compatible with social values.

Idealistic claims by designers, however, that in some innate manner they represent the standpoint of users is clearly unsustainable, especially given the number of designers servicing the needs of conspicuous consumption in wealthy societies, while basic needs around the globe remain unsatisfied or not even addressed. Yet there are indicators, small but hopeful, of what is capable of being achieved when the problems of developing areas are understood and addressed. One such is the clockwork radio concept of Trevor Bayliss, intended to give rural communities in southern Africa who lack electricity supply access to government information on how to combat AIDs. In Chile, two young designers, Angelo Garay and Andrea Humeres, conceived of packaging for light bulbs, which is normally discarded, to be adaptable for use as a light shade in poor homes where bare bulbs are the norm. More such small-scale tangible design solutions could have an enormous cumulative impact if more companies understood that their own self-interest, in terms of the necessary profitability for survival, could be better advanced by close attention to customers' and potential customers' need. A creative solution for a specific problem, based on particular local needs, can frequently have innumerable applications in other locales and for other purposes. Bayliss's clockwork device to power a small radio, for example, has been adapted for use in electric torches.

Although huge commercial potential exists in meeting user needs, a nagging question recurs: if basic requirements become more completely satisfied, will the whole world turn to conspicuous consumption, and with what consequences? In this sense, design is not simply an activity whose course will be charted by practitioners, but an expression of what societies believe to be quality of life on a sustainable basis. Designers cannot provide the whole solution, but should be part of the debate.

In considering the role of design in the future, therefore, a major question requiring an answer is whether designers will be merely technocrats, devoting their skills to the highest commercial bidder without consideration of the ends they serve. Or is there instead a dimension of social and environmental purpose requiring acknowledgement in their work? How much remains ignored, even in the most basic aspects of advanced societies, was dramatically evident in the US presidential election of November 2000, when the design of electoral forms and the devices processing them were clearly inadequate in communicating to all citizens what their choices in voting were, revealing a lack of feedback to confirm voting choices, and giving no opportunity to change a mistake. Discussion of solutions has predominantly rested on consideration of hardware and its cost. If bank ATMs were equally as inadequate in their procedures, there would be a huge outcry, but it seems that acknowledging democratic rights does not carry the same weight as commercial functions.

If technology is indeed to be humanized, and its benefits brought to increasing numbers of people around the planet, it is necessary to recognize that it is designers who determine the detailed interfaces in all their forms that implement technology in everyday life. To what extent the values their designs embody will be primarily intended to generate profits, serve people, or harmonize with ecological concerns, and whether all can be combined in some kind of viable commercial balance, are matters of no small importance.

To answer such questions, and many others of significance, requires as a precondition that design be understood as a decisive factor shaping all our lives, all the time. There are few corners of our environment, or aspects of the objects and communications enveloping us, that could not be significantly improved on some level in greater or lesser degree. Only when we understand that all these manifestations of design are the outcome of choices, ostensibly made on our behalf, but in most cases without our involvement, can the meaning of design in the contemporary world change. Only when it is adequately understood, debated, and determined as something vital to everyone will the full potential of this human capacity begin to be realized.

Further Reading

The problems discussed in the opening chapter of this book regarding the meaning of the word 'design' are amply evident in available works published under this rubric. There is a dearth of general introductions to design that give any kind of overview of the spectrum of activity it covers; instead, there is an abundance of works on the style of places, usually emphasizing interior furnishings and fittings for those with surplus income, with books on historical period styles following the pattern of art historical categories also providing rich fare. Such books have value in developing a visual vocabulary, but only rarely explore the nature of processes or design thinking.

Perhaps the area with the greatest number of publications is design history, although here there tends to be a dominant focus on the nineteenth century onwards. However, Philip B. Meggs, *A History of Graphic Design* (New York: John Wiley & Sons, revised 3rd edition, 1998), is a useful reference text and an exception in tracing the origins of his subject from early societies. A good collection of essays exploring the social significance of graphic design is Steven Heller and Georgette Ballance (eds.), *Graphic Design History* (New York: Allworth Press, 2001). On environments, John Pile, *A History of Interior Design* (New York: John Wiley & Sons, 2000), is a sound introductory history, while Witold Rybczynski, *Home: A Short History of an Idea* (New York: Viking, 1986), is a very approachable and fascinating discussion of many aspects of home design and furnishing. For products, my own *Industrial Design*

Further Reading

(London: Thames & Hudson, 1980) surveys the evolution of this form of practice since the Industrial Revolution, although the later chapters are somewhat dated. There are several general historical texts. One of the best is Adrian Forty, *Objects of Desire: Design and Society Since 1750* (London: Thames & Hudson, revised edition, 1992), with an emphasis on the emergence of modern consumer culture. Penny Sparke, *A Century of Design: Design Pioneers of the 20th Century* (London: Mitchell Beazley, 1998), is strong on furniture design; Jonathan M. Woodham, *Twentieth Century Design* (Oxford: Oxford University Press, 1997), treats design as an expression of social structures; Peter Dormer, *Design since 1945* (London: Thames & Hudson, 1993), is a general overview of post-war developments with an emphasis on craft design; and Catherine McDermott, *Design Museum: 20th Century Design* (London: Carlton Books, 1998), is based on the collection of the museum.

Design practice is also not well served. Quite a few books on this aspect can be described as design hagiology, essentially uncritical forms of promotion for designers and design groups to establish their position in a pantheon of classic work. An account of work at one of the world's leading consultancies, which generally avoids such pitfalls, is Tom Kelley, *The Art of Innovation: Lessons in Creativity from Ideo, America's Leading Design Firm* (New York: Doubleday, 2001). The work of a design group in a global manufacturing company is presented in Paul Kunkel, *Digital Dreams: The Work of the Sony Design Center* (New York: Universe Publishers, 1999), a profusely illustrated examination of projects by Sony design groups from around the world. A volume published by the Industrial Designers Society of America, *Design Secrets: Products: 50 Real-Life Projects Uncovered* (Gloucester, Mass.: Rockport Publishers, 2001), stresses the processes of design, rather than the end products, and discusses and illustrates fifty examples of projects from start to finish.

Peter Wildbur and Michael Burke, *Information Graphics: Innovative Solutions in Contemporary Design* (London: Thames & Hudson, 1999), uses numerous well-illustrated cases to make a good introduction to this specialist form of communication. Some interesting new ideas on design for working environments are explored in Paola Antonelli (ed.), *Workspheres: Design and Contemporary Work Styles* (New York: Harry N. Abrams, 2001), a catalogue of an exhibition on this theme at the Museum of Modern Art in New York. A partner in a London consultancy, Wally Olins, presents his arguments that corporate identity is as much about creating a sense of unity within companies as affecting prospective purchasers in *Corporate Identity: Making Business Strategy Visible through Design* (Boston: Harvard Business School Press, 1992). As a sourcebook, some 200 examples of recent identity design at a range of levels and complexity are presented in David E. Carter (ed.), *Big Book of Corporate Identity Design* (New York: Hearst Book International, 2001). An interesting comparison with similar German practice can be made by reference to a series of yearbooks, Alex Buck and Frank G. Kurzhals (eds.), *Brand Aesthetics* (Frankfurt-am-Main: Verlag form), the first of which appeared in 1999.

The roles objects play in people's lives have not been explored in any great depth from a design standpoint, but there are useful texts treating this aspect from a variety of other disciplinary perspectives. Mary Douglas, a noted anthropologist, and an economist, Baron Isherwood, emphasized goods as instruments of contemporary culture in *The World of Goods: Towards an Anthropology of Consumption* (London: Routledge, revised edition, 1996). Sociological research was the basis of *The Meaning of Things: Domestic Symbols and the Self* by Mihaly Csikszentmihalyi and Eugene Rochberg-Halton (Cambridge: Cambridge University Press, 1981), which demonstrated how people construct personal patterns of meaning from the objects surrounding them. Donald A. Norman, *The Design of Everyday Things* (New York: Currency/Doubleday, revised edition, 1990), written from a psychological standpoint, is still an excellent introduction to basic issues of user-centred design in everyday objects, although some of the cases are dated. Some interesting ideas on the dependence of technological innovation to social context are found in Wiebe Bijker, Thomas P. Hughes, and Trevor Pinch, *The Social Construction of Technological Systems* (Cambridge, Mass.: MIT Press, 1987).

Jeremy Aynsley, *Nationalism and Internationalism: Design in the 20th Century* (London: Victoria and Albert Museum, 1993), is a short introduction to the broader interplay between the global and the local. In general, however, the role of government in promoting design is a theme awaiting substantial research and publication. My own essay on the development of Japanese government policy as part of its economic strategy to rebuild its economy after the Second World War can be found in John Zukowsky (ed.) with Naomi R. Pollock and Tetsuyuki Hirano, *Japan 2000: Architecture and Design for the Japanese Public* (New York: Prestel, 1998). A good example of how themes in design can be publicized by a national design promotion organization is the series of small books published by the Danish Design Council in Copenhagen. Its web site (www.design.dk/org/ddc/index_en.htm) is also worth a visit, while that of the Design Council of the United Kingdom (www.design-council.org.uk/) contains much interesting material, including publications and reports that in some cases can be downloaded.

The principles of business aspects of design were well described in Christopher Lorenz, *The Design Dimension: The New Competitive Weapon for Product Strategy and Global Marketing* (Oxford: Blackwell, 1990), although the case studies used are now dated. One of the best collections of examples of the role of design in corporate strategy can be found in John Thackara, *Winners!: How Today's Successful Companies Innovate by Design* (Aldershot: Gower Press, 1997). Approaches to the management of design are well covered in Rachel Cooper and Mike Press, *Design Management: Managing Design* (Chichester: Wiley, 1995). Insights into the practical problems of managing design in large corporations, based on his experience at Hermann Miller & Philips, are provided by Robert Blaich with Janet Blaich, *Product Design and Corporate Strategy: Managing the Connection for Competitive Advantage* (New York: McGraw-Hill, 1993). A heart-warming account of the struggles of designer-entrepreneur James Dyson to bring his new concept of a vacuum cleaner to market can be found in his *Against the Odds: An Autobiography* (London: Trafalgar Square, 1998).

On the subject of how design needs to adapt in the future, and the purposes it should serve, there are some interesting views in a volume of short texts by Gui Bonsiepe, one of the most profound thinkers about the role of design in the changing circumstances of our age, collected under the title *Interface: An Approach to Design* (Maastricht: Jan van Eyck Akademie, 1999). One of the best books on the dilemmas presented by the profound changes in technology taking place is *The Social Life of Information* by John Seely Brown and Paul Duguid (Boston: Harvard Business School Press, 2000). Technological solutions alone are inadequate, the authors argue, and, if designers are to make them comprehensible and useful, the human and social consequences need to be understood and incorporated into their work.

Index

Index

Index